Love Lesson

a novel

Edith Chevat

Published by Biblio Press

for

Valon Books
New York

Library of Congress Cataloging-in-Publication

Chevat, Edith,
    Love Lesson   :   a novel / Edith Chevat
        p.   cm.
    ISBN: 0-930395-27-1
    I. Title.
    PS3553.H43L68   1998
    813'   .54--dc21   98-20798
                                                          CIP

Valon Books
POB 209, Bowling Green Station, New York, NY 10274-0209

Cover by Doris B. Gold and Rivanne, Brooklyn, NY
Author photo: Rena Cohen

Printed in the United States of America

Acknowledgments

Grateful acknowledgment is made to these periodicals and anthologies in which excerpts from this novel have appeared, at times in different form: *Bridges, Sojourner, Other Voices, Prometheus, Broomstick, Women, The One you Call Sister.*

The epigraph by T.S. Eliot is from *Four Quartets.*

Special thanks to: Suzanne Pred Bass, Joan Larkin, Ruth Mandel, and Nettie Tamler.

What we call the beginning is often the end
And to make an end is to make a beginning.
The end is where we start from....
We die with the dying:
See, they depart, and we go with them.
We are born with the dead:
See, they return, and bring us with them.

T. S. Eliot

For Izzy

1

"Three days are enough," my brother said. "My business can't wait."

"You know it's too much for me," my sister agreed as she prepared to leave.

Husband, children, friends, have all returned to life. I alone remain to mourn the seven days decreed by Jewish law. I, Millie Kaits, wife, mother, teacher, an orphan now in fact as once I wished to be, I give full measure, not one day less.

Here in the apartment where my mother lived, I sit alone. The place seems smaller now, different yet the same, as if the space she used to take has vanished with her death. Yet every room is a monument to how it used to be, packed with relics of her life: a pin cushion in the shape of a woman's high heeled shoes, my grandmother's fish kettle, a bag of rags saved from sewing chores, a samovar, plastic covers on the furniture, pictures of Bubbe, pictures of Aunt Bertha and Uncle Arthur, pictures of me in my carriage...

Light cuts the air, the white light of summer noon, clear, still, filling the empty street. In the distance a black shape appears. It grows larger and larger. There are legs beneath it. The clop, clop of footsteps punctuates the waddling walk. A pocketbook swings from one side. A shopping bag hangs from the other. Only when she is upon me do I see the face. My mother bends to look at me as I sit strapped in my carriage. Her big black umbrella closes us in, hiding the sun.

Sunlight streams through the windows and falls across the table, chairs, stove, knick-knacks from the five and ten: a bust of a Grecian woman carefully glued together, a miniature kerosene lamp, a woman lighting Sabbath candles. Motes whirl slowly in the slanting rays, dancing souls I think, bits of those who lived here once. Outside through the kitchen window, I imagine clothes hanging on the line, the way they used to, the towels and union-suits from the laundry, my mother's rayon bloomers and my cotton underpants done by hand. I see us as we used to be. She, the mother, I, the child...

It is dark. I scream. I kick. I say the worst thing I can think of. "I hope you die. I hope you die." I am three or four.

It is quiet. I have been locked in the closet. I was bad. I have to wait until she lets me out. I do not understand what was bad.

I was born bad, my mother says. She could tell even before I was born. She needs to teach me before it is too late. She needs to get the badness out of me before I end up in the Crazy House.

She took me to Kings County once. She pointed to the barred windows, to the people behind the bars, the crazy people. "You'll end up there," she said. "I can tell. We need to watch out."

I sit in the dark. The smell of camphor is familiar. I have been here before. It is the storage closet. A row of clothes hangs in the front. The vacuum cleaner stands in one corner. I can feel the rubber boots. All in a row. They smell. In the back there is a recess where my mother puts the out of season clothes, where she stores things too good to throw away, things too new to give away. She wraps them in tissue paper and old sheets, she puts them in moth balls and camphor. She hides them from the world. I, too, have been hidden away in the dark.

I make up a world full of sun. I make believe I'm an orphan waiting to be found. I imagine how things will be when I grow up, how everyone will love me, how important I will be, how I won't even look at her, how I will discover a cure for dying and give it out to everyone but her.

The door opens. I promise to be good. I promise never to do it again. I do not know what *it* is.

"Take me to your house," my mother had begged. "It won't be long now; I'll be dead soon."

I did not take her home to die. I could not take her back across the years. I'd come too far. I'd made my life, I did not want the past revived.

The dead are in the past, I tell myself. But here in the apartment where I never lived, it all comes back, swimming round inside my head, bits and pieces bobbing up like orange peel and coffee grounds in dish water. It is all here, all in the same breath, like a set of nesting dolls, each within the other, old and young, girl, woman, mother, daughter.

I see her as she used to be: hair jet black, an apron over her house dress, her stockings rolled below the knees, her slippers worn at the heels. She is cooking, cleaning, baking...

"Ma!" I call inside my head. "Ma." A word to break the wall between us. She doesn't hear. I didn't speak. Something always held me back. Even now when she is dead, something holds me back.

I break something.

I do not come when my mother calls.

I make a face.

I am not polite.

In a way I do not understand, I am bad.

My mother has to punish me. She gets the cat o'nine tails.

I have done something very bad.

I run to my father. I stand behind him. I hold on to his leg.

"Get out of the way," my mother yells. "She'll get it now. I'll show her who's boss in this house."

She pulls me away from my father. I look at him. He turns his head.

My mother hits me and hits me.

I sit in a corner behind a chair and I cry.

My father comes. There are tears in his eyes. He gives me a lollipop. He gives me a penny, "Don't cry," he says. "Crying doesn't help."

"Stay out of her way," he says.

From room to room I go. Closets, drawers, papers. Sifting, sorting, probing. Searching. I seek the truth. But what is that? I cannot tell the difference between what happened and what I think occurred.

"Children are their mother's future," my mother always said. I was not what she bargained for.

Mothers are their daughters' past, I always thought. She was not the past I wanted.

Everyone is in the living room, Uncle Arthur smoking a cigar, Aunt Bertha holding my baby sister, Uncle Arthur swinging my brother 'up to the sky', his golden curls bouncing. My brother laughs. "He's a good boy," says my mother.

"Shush" says my aunt looking at me. "She'll hear you."

"Let her hear," says my mother. "It's time she knew what good is."

I stand in the doorway to the living room, watching the happy, laughing people. My father sits in a corner, out of the way. My mother serves tea and passes cookies. She ignores me. My aunt beckons with her finger and a smile.

"No," says my mother. "Sweets to the sweet. Not for her, the evil one."

Deliberately she passes the cookies to my brother. He takes two. My mother turns away. My brother sticks his tongue out at me.

I stand in the doorway and watch. I go to the drawer where the sewing things are kept. I wait for the right moment.

My mother, carrying the empty cookie plate, brushes past me. She doesn't see me or so she pretends. I jab her with the open safety pin. In the buttock. It is as high as I can reach.

"I'll kill her," she screams. "Crazy. She's crazy."

My uncle restrains her. "It's nothing," he says. "She didn't mean it. She doesn't even understand. Take hold of yourself. She's only a child."

"A child! She's not a child. She's a *momser*. You know what you have to do with a *momser*? You have to kill it. It's a sin to let a *momser* live."

I stand there. I am not afraid. I have done a bad thing, but I am not afraid.

Love compels, but hate binds. Hate ties the hater to the hated like a shadow which sometimes runs ahead and sometimes lags behind. I did not know that all the time love lies watching, waiting, waiting for the light to shift so it can stretch and grow.

I want to set the record straight:
Did she love me?
Was she glad I was born?

2

The first time my mother told me she was dying, I didn't believe her.

She had called at midnight, that dark, blurred time when every sound becomes a fear and every fear a deed, the time when conscience comes to call.

"I'm bad," she said. "Very bad. I have to go to the hospital. The pain. It's bad. Malke, help me."

My mother never called me Malke. She always called me Millie, not the Mildred that was written on my birth certificate, not Mollie, a loving transliteration of Malke, but Millie. Like a horse. Malke meant she wanted something. Malke meant she was afraid.

My mother was always calling. During the day. At dawn. In the middle of the night. My mother was getting old and something was always the matter. Her feet hurt and her hands. She had pains in her stomach and in her head. She was afraid of falling, afraid she'd lie alone in the dark and no one would come.

We had prepared for emergencies. We had practiced phoning in the dark. I had strung a buzzer to the neighbor next door. I had driven alone to my mother's apartment clocking the time. We had rehearsed and drilled even though I knew the drills, like shelter drills in schools, were meaningless. Still one had to pretend, one had to believe there was something to be done—something *I* could do—even in the face of the ultimate emergency, the face of death.

We had prepared for emergencies and here one was. Or was it? What if it weren't? What if this were just another of the games my mother played with life? I was suspicious; I didn't want to get sucked in by one of her tricks.

I had left home as soon as I could, working my way through the University of Michigan where I met Sam. We moved to Chicago. I had a job, a husband, children, a life different from the one my mother had, different from the one I thought she wanted for me. But the future crept up behind my back. Sam, an hydraulic engineer, was transferred to Long Island. So we had come back, and before I knew it, I was bound up with my mother again.

I told Sam he didn't have to come with me to my mother. I said I'd call if there was anything I needed, if there really was an emergency. But he wanted to come. He wanted to know what was happening. He was the one who did most of the caretaking. He drove her to the fish store and to the butcher, listened to her endless complaints, to her clever and complicated plots to get even with relatives and friends. It was not as if he didn't have a mother of his own. But his mother was his sister's responsibilty, *she* took care of her. It was my mother to whom he related, my mother to whom he was drawn.

We made the trip to Brooklyn in half an hour. We parked at the entrance to her building in a no-parking zone. My mother had moved twice in the three years since she'd sold the house she finally owned. At first she had refused to move. "Where would I go?" she asked. I argued, threatened, tried intimidation: the neighborhood had changed; there were no meat stores or fish stores, no place to buy rolls or a Jewish paper; the other houses had been abandoned or vandalized, the copper tubing sold for money or drugs; the streets weren't safe; she'd be robbed or worse; there was no one to call for help; she didn't need to worry about a house at her age, she ought to be taking it easy and enjoying life. Then one day, almost out of the blue, she had decided, hired movers, packed, and in a matter of weeks, had moved. Within a year, she moved again, to the housing project she had always disdained.

The buzzers weren't working, the door to the lobby was unlocked. So was the door to her apartment. Still in her house dress, my mother was sitting in the kitchen near the phone. She should have kept the door locked. She could have been robbed; she could have been killed.

"You'll need a sweater," I said. It was August but I did not want her to catch cold.

"Take the blue one," my mother said. "It matches my dress."

I was suspicious. Everything was evidence, proof she was up to her old tricks. How sick can she be? I asked myself. I wouldn't care about the color of a sweater if I were sick.

Sam dropped us at the emergency entrance and went to park the car. The waiting room was crowded. People were holding their heads or their stomachs. A man groaned. A child cried. They came hoping to ward off pain, drive back death, the ones with gunshot wounds or heart attacks, those with heat strokes and broken legs, the baby with bleeding feet. Nobody wanted to suffer; nobody wanted to die.

I found an empty wheel chair, seated my mother in it and headed for the triage nurse. What if she were sick? What if she were dying?

"She's in great pain," I told the nurse. As if on cue, my mother moaned. "Can you see if it's a heart attack? She's old," I said. "At least eighty, maybe eighty-five." My mother's age was one of the secrets of my mother's life. Even now when it no longer mattered, she held on to the myths she had made.

"She has high blood pressure," I said. "She never complains." The lies. The truth. I was a good actress, the role familiar. I, the devoted daughter, she, the loving mother.

In the examining room, I became the nurse, the caring mother. In silence, I helped my mother onto the examining table. I rolled the stockings down, removed the housedress, adjusted the wig to cover the bald spot, pulled off the bloomers.

"Lie down," I said as I draped a green sheet over her legs. I did not want her to catch cold, I did not want her exposed to prying eyes.

The nurse came with a diuretic. My mother's blood pressure was up. Something was wrong; she was not pretending in order to get attention. Not this time.

I stood at my mother's side—there was no place to sit—and waited for the doctor. I stood looking at the walls, the cabinets, the curtain that closed us off, thinking. Was this the beginning? Was she going to die? She didn't look like a woman whose life was running out. She moaned, she cried, "It hurts." Still *her* mother had lived until ninety, *her* grandmother had lived to ninety-eight. *She* could live to a hundred. There could be years of phone calls, years of emergencies. Years. As much as I thought I wanted to be free of her, I could not imagine life without my mother. I could not imagine my mother dead.

"Malke, I have to pee."

The diuretic was working.

"I'll call the nurse."

"No. I can't wait."

I got the bed pan. I drew back the sheet. My mother's legs were still shapely, there was no swelling, no varicosity. She was always vain about her legs. They showed breeding, she said, like hands. She always had her nails done, not like me, whose nails were chipped, the cuticles raw. Even now, her nails gleamed, blood red. Hands and legs, they showed who you were.

I pushed the bed pan under the sagging buttocks, lifted the hips, pushed and lifted. What if she missed?

No sooner did I get the bed pan out and place it covered with a paper towel on the cabinet, then my mother asked for a drink of water. Then we waited, my mother on the examining table moaning, I, standing nearby watching. An hour later the doctor came and made the diagnosis: bursitis, indigestion, hypertension. The pharmacy would fill the prescription. Take two as needed. Rest.

I dressed my mother: I sat her up, rolled the stockings up to her knees, slipped the housedress over the undershirt, pulled the bloomers up and drew the dress down. I draped the sweater over her shoulders, adjusted her wig. "Lift your arm," I said. "Move your foot." I did not touch with tenderness. We did not talk.

We walked through the waiting room, my mother's arm hooked through mine. I had forgotten her cane. Was that why she seemed so short, her head coming just to my shoulder? Or had her spine twisted even more, dwarfing her even to my five foot two?

We walked past other women with their mothers, women with their fathers. It's always the daughters, I thought, discounting Sam. Always the daughters who grow up to be the mothers of the parents.

We drove back to my mother's apartment, my mother sitting in the front seat with Sam, I in the back as if I were a passenger in my own car.

I have scarlet fever. I sit in bed, my mother's sweater over my pajamas. Towels are stuffed around the sealed windows to prevent a draft, the covers piled around me. My father and brother and baby sister have gone to stay downstairs with my grandmother; my mother and I are quarantined together.

Paper dolls lie on the pillow, their clothes neatly stacked in a cigar box. A rubber band ball, four inches in diameter, lies between my legs. I finish the last page in the coloring book, and put the crayons back in another cigar box. The worst is over, the fever gone. I feel healthy enough, ready to go outside, ready to go back to school, but my mother says I am quarantined for three weeks. I sit and peel the skin from my feet. I have nothing to do.

I hear my mother in the kitchen. She has picked up the groceries left at the door and is making lunch. She comes into the bedroom, carrying a big bowl of chicken soup from which mashed potatoes rise like a mountain. "Here," she says, "It's good for you."

I don't want to listen to my mother. I don't want to be good. I won't eat. I am ready for drama.

"Come," says my mother. "I'll feed you."

I watch as she pulls a chair over to the bed, balancing the soup and a towel in her hand. Almost six years old and being fed? Fed by my mother? I am sicker than I thought. Or is it a trick? Is there bad tasting medicine in the food, stuck deep in the mashed potatoes, bitter medicine like the powder that comes in little paper packets like gum wrappings, powder mixed with orange juice I drink down in one gulp, not like my brother who has to be held by my grandmother while my mother holds his nose with one hand and forces the spoon down his throat with the other.

I clench my teeth. I shake my head.

"Oh," says my mother. "What will I do with you?"

There is anger in her voice and resignation. She is caught in this sick room as much as I.

"Tell me a story," I demand. "Show me the pictures." I am aware of the power my sickness brings. The demand is not unusual. When my mother is in a good mood, she does not mind looking at the picture album she brought from Europe. The pictures remind her of her life before she came to America, before I was born.

"All right," she says. "First eat."

"No," I say. I have learned not to trust my mother's words. She says one thing and does another; she promises and then changes her mind. "Let me hold the album."

She puts the towel on the dresser and the plate of soup on the towel, then bends to the bottom drawer where the sheets lie, white, starched stiff, ironed in the laundry. The album is there between the sheets, wrapped in an old pillowcase stuffed with camphor balls.

My mother unwraps the album. The smell of camphor fills the room. She puts the album in my hands, golden yellow, smooth and shining like satin. In the center there is a picture of a girl wrapped in a shawl standing among her sheep. My finger traces the blue and silver flowers that surround the picture. My hand steals to the lock that holds the album closed.

"Eat first," says my mother.

I open my mouth, turning my head only as far as necessary for the spoon to reach. I do not take my eyes from the album.

"Tell me," I say as the soft potatoes slide down my throat.

My mother sighs and settles back in her chair. I know she is pretending to be angry. She does not do what she doesn't want to. She enjoys telling these stories, when she's in the mood.

"My friend Olga gave me this album. That's her Russian name. In Yiddish it's Goldie. That's her picture on the first page. She gave me the album when I graduated from Gymnasium. So I'll remember, she said."

I look at the picture. Olga's face is round, her hair, parted in the middle, covers the ears before it is pulled back. A wide belt pulls in her waist. My mother's friend. I take another spoonful of food. I turn the page. Here is a picture of Olga and my mother, their arms entwined. They stare straight ahead. Friends. It's hard to imagine my mother with a friend, a girl with other girls.

There is a picture of my mother playing a violin and Olga playing a flute, a picture of Olga and my mother playing chess. They wear white shirts with high collars and dark skirts. In the middle of the collar is a pin. A cameo, my mother says.

"Where is she now?" I ask, as I have before.

"Who knows?" says my mother. "In Europe still. Or in Palestine. She did not stay at home. She became a Bundist, then a Zionist. Her father threw her out. He said she was no good, she didn't listen."

I turn a page. And another. I look at the half familiar faces, too many for me to remember, the names strange, the stories confusing. I touch the pictures of those I know—Uncle Arthur, Aunt Bertha, then a little girl not much older than I, my mother already grown up, Bubbe, Zayde in a chair separate from the others. I point. I want the story of the picture.

"When things got bad, we decided to come to America. First came the Zayde. He came to a cousin in Washington. Bubbe and me and Aunt Bertha and Uncle Zelig—he was a baby then—and Uncle Kalman, he had consumption and they wouldn't let him in, and Uncle Arthur, we stayed in Europe. So Bubbe made a picture of the whole family and left a space for the Zayde. Then we sent the picture to America and Zayde took a picture sitting on a chair and they put the two pictures together to make one picture"

I look carefully. I think I see where Zayde's chair sticks out from the other chairs. I think my mother's family is very smart.

I hold out an old newspaper clipping from a Yiddish paper.

"That's Malke," my mother says. "The Zayde's bubbe, the one you're named after. She lived with us, let her be in peace, she lived to 104." I look at the picture in my mother's hand, a dark haired woman, staring straight ahead, looking younger than my grandmother does now. "All the women in our family live long," my mother says in the voice that wants me to remember. She expects me to live long, she expects me to be like the women in her family, to be like her.

"I remember her," she says still holding the picture of Malke, the Zayde's grandmother, the one I'm named after. "She lived with us. When the Zayde got married, he took her with him to the Bubbe's house. Bubbe's family was rich, they were merchants. It was the custom for the bride's family to support the new couple. The Zayde's family was very refined, a family of scholars and rabbis, with a tradition of learning and study. His mother died when he was a baby and Malke raised him. She lived a long time. She was still living when I was almost grown up. She promised me her bedding when she died." My mother stops. She looks sad, as if she is going to cry.

"What happened to the bedding?" I ask. I think she is sad because the Germans took the bedding.

"Nothing," says my mother and turns her head away. She does not want to tell me what happened to the bedding.

I come to a picture of a man and a woman standing in front of a sleigh. He has a high collar on his shirt and holds a cigarette in his hand. He looks like a movie star. "Max," my mother says. Her voice changes when she says his name and her face lights up. "A cousin. On my mother's side. Very refined, from a very refined family." The woman, dressed in a fur hat and boots and holding a fur muff is my mother.

"In winter we rode in a sleigh. A big horse pulled us. We had a blanket over our feet. All the young people rode in sleighs. Some would race. Sometimes we'd sing."

She reaches for the album. "He married a cow," she says, her voice hard.

I hold tight with both hands. "No," I say.

"No more," she says. She takes the album, shuts it, puts it back in the pillowcase.

I want to see more. I want to learn what happened before I was born. I am beginning to understand that my mother was once a girl, she rode in a sleigh, she did things her mother did not like. I hold these ideas in my head but they slip and slide this way and that. It is hard to think of my mother before she was my mother.

Back in her apartment, I prepared my mother for the night. I helped her into her nightgown. I put Sam's old athletic socks on her feet. Her feet were cold.

She sat at the edge of the bed, the pink scalp clearly visible through the growth of thinning white hair that lay like a skullcap on the jet black ends. She had stopped dyeing her hair. Then she took her teeth out and put them in a glass. Back and forth she began to rock, moaning as she did, "What will become of me?"

Pictures fill my head: my grandmother in my uncle's arms, my father in his high topped shoes, my mother arguing with a neighbor, my mother hanging out the clothes, my mother baking challah, my mother picking flower seeds, my mother...

I wake one morning to a quiet room. I can take my time getting up. My mother has taken my brother and my baby sister downstairs to my grandmother's house. She has gone to help someone die.

I lie in bed, stretching, turning this way and that way, imagining the time when I will have a bed all to myself, thinking about the time when I, too, will sit with the dying.

I share the twin bed with my mother, sleeping head to foot. My sister sleeps in a crib near the door. My father and brother sleep in the other room. "Oh, a girls' room and a boys' room," people say. They laugh as if there is something dirty I don't know.

We live in my grandmother's house. She and my grandfather, the Zayde, and Uncle Arthur and Aunt Bertha live downstairs. We have a four room apartment upstairs in the front. Tenants live in the apartment in back. We are tenants too, but not like the others. My grandmother is the landlady.

My mother wants to be a landlady. "What kind of life is this?" she says. "A landlady—that's something. Then I'd have an income, I'd have a place. I could be somebody. I could be my own boss. Oh, how I've fallen—a tenant in my mother's house!"

She blames my father. It's his fault they've lost their money, his fault my mother is not a landlady.

"Your fault, your fault," she says as if she's spitting.

My father unwinds the *tefillin* from his arm. He has finished the morning prayer; he has thanked God for restoring his soul.

"How do you know you have your own soul back?" I ask. I imagine the soul a tenant, able to choose its own house. He laughs and pats my shoulder. "Don't bother your head with such things. God knows what He's doing."

I go into the living room and watch my father put the *tefillin* away. He smiles and tells me he's going out. I go into the kitchen and drink the half-glass of fresh squeezed orange juice my mother has left for me.

I go back to bed. I worry. I want to make sure it is me who gets up in the morning, that there hasn't been a mix-up in the night. I make my own ritual. My father binds his head and arm, I smell under my arm and my hands after they have been between my legs. He rocks back and forth and says a prayer, I blow a long breath out. Then I settle down into bed—the feather quilt puffed all around like a nest, sure now it is really me.

I think about souls riding up to the sky, hovering in the air, round and full, long and thin,weaving and dancing, held to earth by strings of breath.

My chest tightens. I am afraid. I don't want to be alone. I want my mother. I leave my bed, hurry with my dressing. Suddenly, for no reason I can explain to myself, I think that someday my heart will stop, the steady beat flutter, gallop, flutter and stop like the wings of a butterfly held by a pin. There'll be a final beat, a last breath, and I'll be dead.

Everybody dies, my mother says. Everybody.

My mother sits with the dying. The rabbi comes and says a prayer. Then the Burial Committee comes. My mother is not yet a member of the Committee. She is an apprentice, called to witness the start of the soul's journey back to God.

"What do you do there?" I ask. I want to be initiated into the grown-up world whose business is death.

"What should I do?" she answers. "I sit and I watch."

"What do you see?" I persist.

"There's nothing to see," she says. "Only God sees. I sit and watch; I sit and I listen. You're not supposed to leave the dying alone. I told you before, someone is always supposed to be with the soul until it goes back to God." And she goes on with whatever it is she is doing—washing dishes, peeling vegetables, shoveling coal—me, trailing behind her like a tail on a kite.

"Will you die?" I ask. "Will I?"

"Poo, poo," She spits to ward off the evil eye.

"Everybody dies," she says. "The lucky ones have a long life. The others..." She shakes her head. "It's in God's hands." She stands quietly for a minute. Then, "Go, go! Go outside and play."

The girls play jacks, the boys roller skate. I think about God.

My mother says she can look into the secret places in the middle of my head. She can tell when I am lying or when I am bad.

"I can see," she says. "It won't help if you cover your head. I'll find out. And," she pauses for emphasis, "if I don't see, God will. God sees everything. He does not need to look; He sees and knows without looking."

I stand at the edge of the enamel topped kitchen table while my mother chops onions and raw fish in the big wooden bowl. I watch and I listen.

"You can fool people," she says as she chops, "you can even fool a mother sometimes, but you can't fool God."

The chopping stops, her hand in the air. My heart thumps. My mother's silences are more frightening than her words.

"God will see you, no matter what you do or where you are," she says again. "And then you'll..." Her voice trails off, as her chopping resumes.

I cannot imagine how God punishes. My mother slaps and shakes, she calls me names, she withholds treats. God's punishments are left unsaid, too terrible for words.

I think about God as I sit at the window looking out at the rain. I think about Him as I sit on the stoop in the sunshine. He is an old man with a long beard. His eyes are blue like my grandfather's, the blue of the sky early in the morning on a cold winter's day. He sits on a throne, roaring like a lion, His magic sword twisting every which way, lightning spurting from the end. The Zayde, my grandfather, sits on a special chair in the dining room. No one else is allowed to sit there, not even Uncle Arthur, not even when there is no more room at the table.

My grandfather is tall like God but he does not have a beard. He has a long curly mustache and thick eyebrows. He wears a tall yarmulke on his head and he has a gold watch with a long chain. His eyes are blue like my mother's. My eyes are brown like my father's.

"Get out of the way," says my mother. "Zayde is coming." I run to the side so as not to be in his path.

"Shush," says Aunt Bertha. "Don't make any noise. Zayde is praying." I stop singing a lullaby to my doll.

Even Uncle Arthur steps aside when Zayde comes to the table. Uncle Arthur lives here, and Aunt Bertha and Bubbe. Bubbe is the landlady but it is Zayde's house.

God's house is in the ark in the Shul. He is everywhere but that is His special place. I am not allowed there. My father and Zayde go there and Uncle Arthur. They bow and chant and pray. I sit upstairs with my mother and Bubbe.

I decide to see God's house. I walk down the street to the Shul, and up the long row of stairs.

The door is unlocked. I walk down the aisle, past the wooden benches to the East Wall and the bimah where the ark rests. The *bimah* is like a big open porch. Chairs like thrones line the railing. Sun streams through the colored windows making rainbow patterns on the polished floor. It is very quiet. There is not even a clock ticking away the time.

I look up to the balcony where I usually sit. It is a long way off. I stand before the ark, staring at the golden lions embroidered on the wine colored velvet cloth, the Lions of Judah. My fingers trace the line of flowers and touch the red and blue stars. I begin to pull the curtains aside. Suddenly a door bangs. Footsteps. My heart begins to pound. Is it God? I turn. It is the *Shamus* who watches God's house.

"Hooligan!" he shouts.

I begin to run.

"Hooligan!" he shouts again running toward me with raised fist. "God will punish you for this. God will punish you."

I run home, up to the bedroom and into the bed. I pull the covers tight around me, the pillow over my head. I hide from God. I do not want Him to see my sin. I do not want Him to take my soul. I do not want to die.

3

When the phone rang. I did not want to answer. I thought it was my mother.

This time it was Julie. My daughter did not call as often as I would have liked. I was the one who did the calling, who tried to maintain contact.

I had tried to be a modern mother. I had said, "I want you to call if you need anything. Anything. That's what families are for."

And Julie did call, whenever there was a problem: "We were arrested... We need bail. I was mugged... I'm in the emergency room. I'm joining a commune... I'll send you the address. I'm moving in with Doug... We're thinking of splitting up. I'm joining the Revolutionary Brigade." Even, "I'm going to China. What can I bring you?"

"How are you?" I asked. "What's new?"

It was Sam's birthday, his fifty-sixth. Julie wanted to know what to get him. She thought she might come to New York to celebrate. A birthday was a birthday even if it wasn't one of the big ones.

Sam would be pleased. He always wanted to see the children. He loved it when they remembered him. He kept every one of the presents they had made: handprints in clay, a juice can covered in glitter, a mug that said "World's Greatest Father". They were there on his bureau. Oh, they had made things for me, too. I had kept them for a year or so and then put them away in a box in the attic. I couldn't bear to throw them out, but I did not want them collecting dust.

I must admit I was somewhat jealous of the children's relationship with Sam. I didn't remember Julie wanting to come to New York to celebrate my birthday. I had been the disciplinarian, the one who saw that the homework got done, the piano practiced, the science project in on time. Sam had taken them to ball games and museums, taught them to swim and play tennis. He'd had it easy, I thought, all of the fun and none of the work.

Still it was something to look foward to, something to take my mind off my mother. Her calls had continued, the complaints incessant, my mother insistent: She couldn't walk, she couldn't sit, she couldn't eat, she couldn't sleep. She felt bad. I didn't know what to do.

My mother was fighting for her life and she wanted things the way they used to be. She fought the way she knew, as if death were a neighbor she could snub, a trespasser she could vanquish with a lawsuit. She fought as if she were a general and I was her army.

"Maybe she's afraid," Sam suggested. "Maybe she doesn't want to be alone."

After a week of phone calls and complaints, I was ready to listen. There was plenty of room in our house. Even if Sam and I each took a room of our own in addition to the one we shared, there was still the den downstairs. A change might do my mother good. And it would be better for me than going back and forth to Brooklyn every day, better than the endless phone calls. We'd manage, Sam and I. So I reasoned, determined to be careful. I would not get sucked in by her need. I would not let my guard down.

"It's too cold here," my mother said as soon as she stepped through the front door.

"I'm afraid I'll fall," she said clutching the end table as if she were blind or crippled, or a baby learning how to walk.

"What good are the dishes if the rest of the house is *traif*?" she complained as I unpacked the pots and pans, and set out the paper plates and plastic forks and made room in the cabinets for her things so she could keep kosher.

Sam had carried the bed down from Julie's room. A box spring and mattress, it was the easiest to move. I'd kept a room for Julie even though she had never really lived here with us. She chose to stay in Chicago when we moved back to New York. Matthew came with us. He had no choice, being sixteen. Still I always felt he wanted to come to New York, wanted to live with us. He was interested in family and family origins. A traditionalist, he even liked our furniture, a sideboard in the dining room, beds with headboards, footboards, and slats. Julie always preferred simplification. Even as a child, less was better. Not like me. I wanted pieces with intricate parts, things hard to move, things to tie me down: a house, silver, drapes, rugs.

We put the bed in the dining room near a sunny window so my mother could look out, so she wouldn't have to climb stairs. She'd be only a few steps from the kitchen, a short walk from the bathroom.

"You're trying to kill me," she said when I showed her the bed. "There's a draft here. I'll catch cold and die."

I made tea. I served it in a glass the way she liked. I offered her lump sugar she could put between her teeth. It takes time, I told myself. She needs time to adjust. She misses her things, the place she called home.

"It's time for my medicine," she said, "Get me the pills."

I had arranged the jars of pills on the kitchen counter. They were within arm's reach of where she sat, easy enough to get them herself. I thought it would be good for her to be as independent as possible.

She stared at me with the same look she had when I was a child. It still worked. I handed her the jar. I did not unscrew the cap.

"Do you want some water?" I asked.

"Yes," she answered. "But take it from the kettle, not from the sink. Last time you gave me water that was too cold."

No matter what I did it wasn't right. No matter how much I did, it wasn't enough. She always accused me of failing her. She'd call my brother in Charleston and tell him I was neglecting her. She'd grumble about what a misfortune it was that my sister Tibby was so sickly. If Tibby were only well, she'd say, Tibby would know how to take care of her.

She'll never change, I told myself, as I went about my household chores. I was surprised how angry I felt.

She woke up from her nap with a cry. "I wish I could die already. God, let me die! God, why are you torturing me? Save me, God! Let me die!"

My mother had never wished for death. She used to say it was a sin not to live every minute of life. She said once you start thinking of death, you were no longer sure of life. My mother had never been afraid of dying. She had been a member of the burial committee; she helped people die. She always said, "Death comes when it pleases."

I called Sam at work. He agreed I should call my brother.

My mother sat in the kitchen waiting while I dialed.

My sister-in-law, Gail, answered the phone. I felt awkward. We had never been friends, just relatives by marriage. We chatted for a while about the children, about how my mother was doing. I tried not to complain or make things seem worse than they were. I was careful with my words, as if what I said about my mother would reflect on me. I needed Gail to understand and approve. Alvin would never do anything without Gail's okay.

When Alvin got on the phone, I explained the problem, choosing my words carefully. I did not want to upset my mother who sat there listening, waiting. I did not want to antagonize my brother whose help I wanted.

Alvin couldn't see why my mother couldn't continue to stay with me. "What's the big deal?" he asked. "So she complains. That's the way she is. You're not going to change her now. What else do you have to do?"

My brother had never accepted the fact that my job was important to me. He still thought women worked only because they had to. I had majored in math in college and while I enjoyed solving problems—in math there was always an answer—I found I did not want to work with numbers. I was drawn to the new immigrants or their children, those trying to find a place in the world. I thought I was drawn to what I myself needed. Maybe I just wanted to do good. Whatever it was, I began to teach English as a second language even before there was such a specialty.

My brother saw no reason why I couldn't take care of our mother at her house if she did not want to stay at mine. "You've only got one mother," he said.

"What does he say? Tell me what does he say?" my mother asked. "Nu! Nu!" She banged her cane on the floor impatiently.

"A change would do her good," I said. "Just a week. How hard can it be for a week?"

"No way," said Alvin. He reminded me of the visit my mother had made in the spring. "Do you know what she told the neighbors?" my brother asked. "She said we didn't take care of her. She said we didn't feed her; she said we were no good. Do you know what she told Gail? She said Gail could kiss her ass because she was a Fineman and Gail was nothing. How do you like that?"

There was admiration in my brother's voice, pride in my mother's fighting spirit. He'd never been embarrassed by my mother's coarseness. "She acts like a poor soul," he continued, "but Gail says she's just like the cow that gives milk and then kicks you in the teeth. There's no way you can please her. She even said we brought her here against her will. There's no way I can let her visit. At least not now. I've got to give it time. Maybe later when Gail calms down."

He was sure I could handle any problem that came up.

I gave the phone to my mother. I did not say goodbye. It was still possible my mother could convince him, maybe she could change my brother's mind.

"Well," my mother said. "How are you, my son?"

I walked into the living room. As much as I wanted my mother away in Charleston, I did not want to hear the way she manuevered my brother into doing what she wanted.

No sooner had I turned on the TV and settled myself in a chair when she called.

"Malke," she said. "Hang it up." She never said please or thank you. Not to me. She was always polite to strangers. Loving words spilled from her lips when she talked to my sister. Honeyed words rolled from her tongue when she talked to my brother. But for me, the firstborn, there were only orders, commands barked as if I were a stone, as if I were nothing.

"Well?" I asked after I put the phone back in its cradle.

"He said I should go to a hotel. He said he'd pay. He said things will be better when I get my strength back."

"That's nice," I said. He's just like Uncle Arthur, I thought. He thinks money can buy anything.

"He thinks he can buy me with money," my mother said echoing my thoughts. "I was going to a hotel anyway, for the holidays. Let him pay. That's all he is good for."

I called my sister. She ought to know what was happening. She ought to know how her mother was.

"I wish I could help," Tibby said. "I wish I were stronger."

I reassured her the way I always did. She couldn't help it if she was sickly. She couldn't help being the baby and needing to be spared.

"I'll call often," Tibby said. "We'll talk."

I'd have to do it by myself: find the hotel, pack my mother's things, look after the house, drive her.

"It's all right, Ma," I said. "We'll find a place. A nice place." I felt sorry for her. She *was* old. She was my mother.

"It's no good," she said. "It's no good to get old. Who cares what happens to an old mother? The world goes its own way. Who listens to an old woman? Who hears her cries? Oh! That it has come to this! What good is a life that it should have such an end?"

I did not try to comfort her.

. . .

The heart is the seat of the soul.

What happens when the heart is cold?

Every morning my father thanked God for restoring his soul. He thanked God for giving the cock intelligence to distinguish between day and night. He thanked God for not making him a heathen. He thanked God for not making him a slave. He thanked God for not making him a woman.

My grandfather said, "Many and wondrous are the cycles of the soul." He said if we suffer it's because we have received the soul of someone who did evil. He said good deeds create good souls.

I do not understand the will of God.

I do not understand the six million.

I did not understand my mother.

I cannot explain what made me so cold and unfeeling when she was dying.

One morning when I am almost six, my mother wakes me up.

"Hurry up," she says. "Go stay with Mrs. Klein. Today is Uncle Kalman's funeral."

Uncle Kalman is Bea's father, my mother's brother. Last week my mother told me not to go to Bea's house; she told me to be nice to Bea because her father was sick. My mother said Uncle Kalman could die, Bea might become an orphan.

I dress hurriedly not bothering with the belt of my brown dress. I braid my hair, drink the orange juice and run down the stairs to the porch. Mrs. Klein stands across the street, my sister in her arms, cheek pressed to cheek. My brother, holding his toy truck, stands next to her.

"Come here," she orders me.

I pretend not to hear.

I walk down the steps and stand near the gate.

People cluster in threes and fours, whispering. It is early in the morning but the heat spreads like a fire. It is early in the morning but the street is quiet. Death covers the street like a quilt.

"Such a young man," says Mrs. Greenberg, the pickle lady.

"Not so young, I heard," says Mrs. Berger. "They made him younger than he was."

"Such a shame," says Mrs. Pincus, the butcher's wife, as she clucks her tongue and puts the edge of her apron up to her eye.

"They say he suffered so. Better to die young than to live like that," says Mrs. Schecter, putting her hands on her hips as if defying anyone to disagree. "That's not a life."

"It's worse for the living than for the dead," whispers Miss Mintz, the one who never married and lives with her mother.

"She's afraid of life," my mother said of her. "She'll live and die in the shade."

I smile when Miss Mintz's eyes catch mine. I like her. She always says hello and asks how I am.

"You're right, you're so right," Mrs. Pincus says to Miss Mintz. "We should cry for the living not for the dead. Can the dead hear? Can they see? What's there to cry for? It's Bea we should cry for, Bea and the baby. Orphans. They've become orphans."

There is a murmur, as if from a breeze, but it is only sounds of agreement. I know what they mean. Cousin Bea is an orphan now, she has a mother but her father is dead, and orphans are everyone's responsibility.

"I heard," says Mrs. Schecter, "she won't be alone too long." She pokes an elbow into Mrs. Pincus' side. "If she plays her cards right, she could end up with the brother, a single boy."

They are talking about Bea's mother and Uncle Arthur. They think Uncle Arthur will marry Aunt Gussie.

"Shush," Mrs. Pincus says and points at me. "The walls are listening."

A hush falls on the street. The neighbors move toward Bea's house. I go with them.

From the next block, I can hear the sound of the elevated trains. Cousin Bea has come out of her house. She is six months older than I am. She wears her navy blue sailor dress. She has a navy blue bow in her hair. Her black patent shoes shine, and her socks are neat and even.

"Poor Bea," says Miss Mintz again, as she stretches out her arm and pulls Bea up against her, one hand around her head. All eyes turn toward the stoop. A path opens. I lean against the flower pots that separate one house from the other, trailing one hand in the dirt. We wait for the men to carry the box out of the house. There is a rustling sound as the watchers move closer together. Bea stands there with her head pressed against Miss Mintz; she does not look at the men carrying the box down the steps. For a moment, I imagine the box slipping, the body moving through the air. The eyes fall out, and the arms and legs come loose like those of a broken doll. When the soul is gone, there is nothing to hold the body together.

The men place the box in the hearse. Bea's mother walks behind it, arm in arm with Uncle Arthur. Aunt Yittel is there, and Aunt Bertha, and my mother, and Bubbe and the Zayde. The procession forms behind the hearse. Bubbe is crying, "That I should live to see this day!"

Bea is too young to go to the cemetery. She will stay with Miss Mintz. I'm supposed to stay with Mrs. Klein

The funeral procession stops at the shul down the street. After the Rabbi says the prayer, the neighbors go back to their houses. The funeral is over. I start to walk after the cars.

"Where are you going?" Mrs. Klein yells.

I ignore her.

"Come back. Come back. Wait until your mother finds out."

I walk to the corner, as far as I am allowed to go. The hearse and cars are going to the cemetery. All the grown ups are going to the cemetery. Children are not allowed.

Everyone goes to my grandmother's house. It is the house of mourning.

"Be good," my mother warns. "Be nice to Bea. She's an orphan now."

Everyone sits in the dining room drinking tea, eating cake and talking. The mourners sit on wooden boxes, the visitors sit on chairs.

"Such a tragedy," says Mrs. Klein.

"He suffered so, until the very end," says a second cousin from the Bronx.

"Consumption," I hear a woman whisper as if the word brings the disease.

"It was *bashert*, pre-ordained," my mother says. "A gypsy knew. She told him he would die if he came to America."

My grandmother wails and moans and beats her chest. *"Veh iz mir!* Woe is me!" she cries. "What have I done that I should be punished like this? Better not to have children than to have them die. Better not to be born than to come to this." She rocks back and forth on her wooden box. She rocks in her stocking feet.

Aunt Bertha is feeding Bea tea with milk from a spoon. My mother holds my baby sister. My brother Alvin sits on Uncle Arthur's lap.

Upstairs the mirrors are covered with sheets. I want to play the piano. It's not allowed. I walk from room to room looking. I go into the toilet. Clothes soak in the tub, towels and sheets, ready to be scrubbed on the washboard. I sit on the edge of the tub, legs dangling, My hand swishes the water around, making waves and patterns. I think about my uncle lying in his grave.

Suddenly I slip. Water splashes on the floor; someone's underwear sticks to my leg. I am soaked through and through.

People come running. My mother picks me up and sets me down on the tile floor. She shakes me.

"You rotten kid," she says. "Look what you have done. Don't you have any respect for the dead?" She slaps my face, she grabs my arm and pulls me along. "Such a curse," she says. "Forgive me," she says to the world at large. I am her sin.

My mother takes me upstairs to our apartment. Even though it is still daylight, she puts on my pajamas. "Stay here," she says. "Don't leave."

She locks the door and goes downstairs.

I lie face down in the bed, the covers pulled tight around me, the feather pillow over my head. It is so dark even my fingers pushed up near my face are hidden from my eyes. It is very quiet, like an empty room where a clock ticks. My heart beats in my ears, like the roar of the ocean trapped in a sea shell. I try not to move. I am hiding. I am not hiding from my mother, although I hide from her often, I am hiding from God.

I fall asleep.

"Come," says a voice. "Come up to me." As far as I can see in all directions there are graves and tombstones. Some are shaped like people, no taller than I, and some are almost as big as a house. The stones sway back and forth like men praying in the shul. Puffs of spirit, like smoke from a cigar, begin to rise from each stone. They turn into rays of light that reach straight to Heaven. "Come," says the voice again, and the souls begin to go up to God. "Everybody dies. Everybody comes to me."

My mother's head appears. "I can see you," she says. "You can't hide from me."

There is a pushing and moving in my chest. It is my soul trying to get out, going up to God, leaving me to die, my body cold and green like the earth in springtime.

I scream. My heart is pounding. There is a thumping in my ears, sweat tracks down my chest, my legs are tangled in the bed clothes.

"Ma," I call. "Ma." Then I remember. Uncle Kalman died. My mother is downstairs. So is my father and my uncles and my aunts. I am here alone.

The thumping of my heart is softer now. It's only a dream, I tell myself. Make believe. No one dies from a dream. I comfort myself with words I've heard my mother say. Still I am afraid.

It is afternoon but I recite the morning prayer. I thank God for restoring my soul. I ask Him to forgive my sins. I pray there is plenty of time before I die.

Then I sit at the edge of my bed and wait for my mother.

4

My mother always visited the cemetery during the High Holy Days.

She used to go with my father. He would drive her and sit in the car while she visited with her mother. My father could pray as well as anybody but my mother always hired a *Yiddle* to say the prayers. It was an act of charity, she said. There were all these devout men trying to make a living from God, and who would pay them here in Godless America?

After my father died, when I was living in New York again, my mother began to insist that I go with her.

"How does it look?" she'd say, "that I should go to the cemetery by myself? What kind of daughter would let her mother go there alone?"

It didn't matter that I worked, that it was an hour's drive to her house and then another half hour to the cemetery, or that there were only so many days between Rosh Hashonah and Yom Kippur—she couldn't go on Friday, and Thursday was no good so it would have to be Wednesday unless I wanted to go on Sunday the way the refined people did—all that mattered was that she wanted to go and I was to go with her.

I didn't have time, I'd say. Where was it written that she had to go during the Days of Awe? Why must it be in the morning? Why couldn't she take a taxi? I'd be glad to pay.

Every year I protested and every year I found myself back in the cemetery. This year she was willing to go before the holidays. We had found a hotel and she would stay for a month, a month without complaints, nights without phone calls. This year I did not protest. This year she said soon I wouldn't have to take her, soon she'd be in the cemetery forever.

My mother dressed for the occasion. She wore her second best dress, not the one she wore on holidays or for visits to relatives, but the one she wore on the Sabbath. It was a rayon print with a collar edged in lace. She always wore her wig when she went out, but for shul and the cemetery she added a hat, brimmed but without a veil. Veils were for weddings and Bar Mitzvahs, veils were for uptown. My mother had a rule for everything, and every rule was kept.

Usually when she went out, she carried only a small change purse which she clutched in her hand, a foil, she said, for would be robbers. Since she was with me that day, she carried a big pocketbook, double handled, black like her shoes. She carried her cane even though one arm was linked through mine. She was afraid of falling. Her spine was twisted, crippled by arthritis. Another fall, she said, and she'd die.

I dressed in casual defiance: slacks, a sweater, sneakers, no hat. I wanted no part of the superstitious nonsense that made up my mother's life. As far as I was concerned, religion was not only the opiate of the people but one that enslaved women in particular.

The cemetery was in an old part of Brooklyn bounded by an elevated train and a street littered with junkyards. It extended for several streets, the stones white and straight, the rows neat and orderly, manicured, suburban, except for one corner, the corner we came to visit. Here the family rested as they had lived, crowded together. There was barely enough space between the stones for someone to walk, and I had to be careful where I put my feet. Some stones had yellow stickers indicating perpetual care. Some graves were covered in boxwood, clipped and trim like the hedge that used to grow near the iron railing of our house. There were stones made of elaborately carved granite and some of white marble, clearly expensive. One or two looked old and worn, about to fall over. Almost all of them held pebbles and small rocks, each left by a visitor as if it were a calling card.

It was all so familiar. I had come here often, for holidays and funerals, so my mother could visit her relatives. Our family plot. I called it ours though I'd never be buried there. I called it ours because three generations of Finemans lay in the ground there. Fineman was my mother's maiden name, and although it was close to fifty years since she bore that name, a Fineman was how she saw herself.

"A good location," my mother said as we walked toward the short partition that separated our section from the rest of the cemetery. "A corner. You don't have to creep and crawl over strangers to come here."

"It's not really a corner," I said taking the word literally.

"Better that way," said my mother. "So people can't throw their garbage. And the wind doesn't howl so much when it's not on a corner." My mother could always turn things around to suit her purpose.

When we came to the other side of the partition, my mother stopped, her eyes darting here and there, up and down. She was looking for the man who said the prayers. "Where is he? That no goodnick. He's always here, always waiting to make a few dollars. Except when you need him." She shifted the straps of her pocketbook higher up on her arm, a nervous habit.

"He'll come," I said. "If not, you'll find someone else."

She ignored me, looking around as if she were a prospective buyer for a new house.

"A good view," she said. She poked the earth with her cane. "The ground is firm. It won't flood when it rains." She pointed toward the graves. "The Finemans. Such fine people. God knew what he was doing when he gave us the name. The best family. Even in Europe. Everyone knew the Fineman family. They came from miles around to ask my grandfather questions from the Talmud. And my grandmother," she clutched my arm. "My real grandmother," she leaned toward my face. "You know my grandfather had three wives, but the second, my real grandmother, was a real *balabuste.* She cooked, cleaned, and made a little money baking cakes. Such fine people. And look what has become of them."

"Everybody has to die," I said.

"You don't understand," she shook her head. "You don't understand."

I knew what she meant, but I felt perverse and disagreeable. Such a fuss about a family. Such a fuss about a name. My mother always talked about the Finemans, how respected they were in the old country, how much better that made us, how much was expected of me as a result, how I was supposed to behave and dress. All my life I'd heard the stories. All my life I could not resist provoking my mother.

"Fine people," I said. "What about Uncle Arthur? Didn't he go to jail for black market activities during the war?"

"Pfu." She made a spitting motion with her lips. "That was a mistake. He didn't do anything. It was his bookkeeper. Besides, times were different then. Everybody did it. Just he got caught."

"Well, what about Cousin Mary? Didn't she have to get married? Wasn't Lillian born six months after the wedding?"

"So it happens sometimes. But they got married and they lived together until he died. It happens. It doesn't mean anything."

There was no point in arguing, but I couldn't control my need to needle, my need to prove my mother wrong. She thought the Finemans were fine people, better than everyone else, and nothing would change her mind.

I was getting impatient. I could still get back to work in time for the department meeting on how to mainstream non-English speaking students. I did not want to spend the day in the cemetery. I couldn't see the difference it would make if my mother chose one of the other men. They all had that same look. Unwashed, seedy, eager.

"Take somebody else," I told my mother, as I motioned to one of the men standing near the entrance. Short, thin, beardless, he looked like all the other men who worked the cemetery on important occasions.

"It's no good. It won't come out right," my mother said. She was superstitious. She thought it would be bad luck if she didn't have the same man she always had to read the prayers for the dead. Bad luck. It might even mean someone would die.

"It'll be good. It'll be good," the man said. "God hears the prayers if they're said from the heart."

"No good. No good," my mother muttered.

"Shall we start?" the man asked.

"Start. Start. You think I'm standing here because I'm a tree?" She led the way, the man close behind, I bringing up the rear.

My mother stopped in front of a grave with a picture on the tombstone. Uncle Kalman. His wife, Aunt Gussie, had wanted his children to know what he looked like when they came to pay their respects. I didn't remember him, though I remembered his death. How I had envied Cousin Bea. The orphan. How I had wished I, too, could be an orphan, with attention paid, presents given, transgressions overlooked. Bea had lived down the block then, and every Friday, as busy as my mother was, she'd put Bea's hair up in rags so she could have Shirley Temple curls for the Sabbath. My hair was naturally curly, my mother used to say, it didn't need any help. My hair, she said, was all right the way it was.

"Kalman," said my mother looking at the stone. "He was the oldest. He died of consumption."

Every year my mother stopped first at her brother's grave. Every year she said the same thing. Every year the *Yiddle* asked if he should say a prayer. Every year my mother said no. "He has children, a son, an accountant. Let them come and pray for him." Every year the prayers started at her sister's grave, the sister who never married and so had no children to honor her memory. I watched my mother while the *Yiddle* prayed. I wondered what she was thinking. Once when my father was sick, he had confessed that Aunt Bertha was the one he had loved. My mother, he claimed, had seduced him. My mother, he said, had told her father she was pregnant. I had never told my mother, never dared asked for confirmation. I did not want to find out that I, the first born, was the reason for the marriage, that I, unwanted and unplanned, was the cause of my mother's downfall.

My mother pointed to a grave. Cousin Rachel's son. "A boy yet."

"A boy," I protested. "It says he was forty."

"He was a boy," my mother said. "He never married."

Like Uncle Arthur, I thought. A boy until sixty. That's when he married. After his sister Bertha died.

"Well, Missus," the *Yiddle* said. "Shall we continue?"

"All right," said my mother. "Say a little blessing for my brother Arthur. He was no good. I told him he would end up in the cemetery with his head in the ground but he didn't listen. He was no good. He thought money could buy everything. But it can't buy respect. It can't buy happiness. Better he should have remained a boy than to marry that *kurve*. A grandmother she was, but a whore."

"So why are you saying a prayer for him?" I asked even though I knew the answer I'd get.

"What can I do?" my mother asked. "He has no children."

My father was buried next to Uncle Arthur. How ironic, I thought, as I always did, that the two important men in my mother's life should be next to each other. My father, the failure; my uncle the success. My father the butt of my mother's wrath; my uncle, the object of her envy. My father, Hymie Abramowitz, who made her give up the Fineman name; my uncle, Arthur Fineman, who kept it but did not hand it down. Both buried side by side. It was the way people died, unplanned, out of order. My grandfather had wanted a place for everyone, a place befitting the family, where a husband could be with his wife, a mother with her daughter. It had not worked out the way he had planned. Uncle Kalman had died too soon, his wife lived a long time; cousins separated them from each other. A sister-in-law rested near Aunt Bertha, a cousin took an uncle's place. But there next to my father, was the space reserved for my mother. She had seen to that.

"Here's where you'll put me," she said when the prayer for my father was done. "Here I'll lie." She stopped and looked at me. "For you, there's no place here, Millie. But," she said reassuringly, "they're still selling plots on the other side of the cemetery. There's still time. Otherwise, you'll have to be in Long Island, all by yourself, far away."

What difference will it make? I wondered, surprised at the bitterness I felt. Would she treat me better in death than she had in life?

"Say *El Molay Rachamin* for my husband," my mother told the Yiddle. "Chaim ben Hillel. And say it for his father, too. Hillel ben Chaim. And for his mother, Teibel bas Nachum."

The prayer done, my mother moved down the rows, pausing at the grave of a cousin, at the graves of two more brothers, the graves of sisters-in-law and finally, almost in the center of the plot, stopped at a stone larger than the others, my grandparents' grave.

I remembered how my grandfather was laid out on the dining room table, his chin tied with a rag, pennies on his eyes, how Uncle Arthur stood there, looking at his dead father. I did not remember anything special about my grandmother's funeral. She had died in a nursing home and her funeral was modern, in a funeral parlor where everything was clean and antiseptic.

My mother told the *Yiddle* to pray for her father and his mother and father and for his grandmother, Malke bas Sorke. "That's where your name comes from," she said to me. "From her, my father's Bubbe."

Yes, I repeated silently; I am named after Malke, Malke, the Queen, Malke, the daughter of Sarah.

After the *Yiddle* said the prayer for my grandmother and her mother and father, my mother maneuvered herself between the stones, careful not to step on the grave. She grasped the monument over her mother's grave with two hands and pressed her body against it. Holding on to the stone, she began to rock back and forth. She was ready for her visit.

"Mama," she began. "Mama. I miss you." My grandmother had been dead for thirty-five years but my mother spoke as if my grandmother were alive. "Mama," she said, "I've come to talk my heart out. I've come to tell you how I suffer." She sounded like a little girl, as if she had never grown up, as if she still needed a mother.

I moved away, embarrassed at this recital to the dead.

I walked among the stones, examining epitaphs.

Devoted husband.

Beloved mother.

Rest in Peace.

Forever in our hearts.

How ironic, I told myself, "Forever in our hearts" for a brother cursed every day. "Beloved Father" from a son who hadn't seen his father for twenty years. "Devoted Husband" for a man who never earned a living.

I stopped at my father's grave. He lay in the midst of my mother's family as if he belonged there, as if he had been one of them. I remembered how we used to walk to the water on Rosh Hashonah, my hand in his, how he'd empty out his pockets and throw away his sins. I remembered how my mother hit me, how my father turned away.

My father. Rest in Peace.

I imagined myself in a grave. I imagined myself dead. What would be said of me? And by whom? Who would come to place a stone and say a prayer? And where? I was to be cremated in the modern way, my ashes scattered to the winds, finally the *luftmensch* my mother always said I was. "A girl gets married," she used to say. "She makes a home, has children, her children have children, and there is always someone to say *Yahrzeit*, always someone to say the prayers for the dead. What else is there in life if not death? What else is there if not continuity?"

My mother was still crying and talking to her mother. I motioned to the *Yiddle* who stood waiting. "Say something for my children," I whispered. "Let them be happy."

I did not tell him how I worried about my daughter Julie, twenty nine years old and not yet settled down. I did not tell him that Matthew lived in California and hardly ever called or wrote. I did not tell him how hard I'd tried to be a good mother. I didn't believe in the power of the dead, in superstitious nonsense. Still, "Pray to my father," I said. I told the *Yiddle* Julie's Jewish name, Judith bas Malke. I told him Matthew's name, Moishe ben Samuel. "Tell my father to use his influence," I said.

I pressed a bill into the *Yiddle's* hand. My mother had given him five dollars. She thought that was enough for all those prayers. I gave him ten. I wanted the full prayer. It couldn't hurt.

Lies.

Twisted truths or worn beliefs, still lies.

They sound like truth; they make the same waves in the air. They hurt like truth. Said by teachers, rabbis, mothers, they sit like stones upon my chest:

"A girl grows up to be a wife."

"A girl grows up to be a mother."

"Without children there is no past."

My mother said she could see inside my head.

Lies.

"God knows. God remembers."

Lies.

Told out of love and the desire to please, said out of fear and the wish to protect.

Still lies.

I seek the truth.

"Be careful what you wish," my mother said. "It may come true."

She's too young," says Aunt Bertha. "She's only six. It'll weaken her brains."

"A girl in *cheder!* What does she need it for?" says my Aunt Gussie, the Widow. "Piano. That's for a girl." Aunt Gussie pays fifty cents a week for Bea's piano lessons.

"I didn't know you had so much money you could throw it away," says Uncle Arthur.

"Am I asking you?" says my mother. "Fifty cents a week I can afford. And if I can't, don't worry, I won't come to you."

"Stop the foolishness," says my grandmother with a sidelong glance at my grandfather who rocks back and forth intoning the blessing after the meal.

My father says nothing. He is a guest in the house of his in-laws.

Zayde says it can't hurt me, He says I have a good head on my shoulders, better for a boy, but what can you do? "You have to take what God gives you." Then he tells my mother, "Just watch she doesn't learn what she shouldn't know."

He tells Uncle Arthur to give me a quarter. "To smooth the path of learning," he says. He tells my mother to give me a cookie. "To sweeten the path."

So it is decided.

The Rebbe leans over me, pointing with his yellow stained finger to a place on the page, his thumbnail thick and curved, hard like a piece of wood. It is my first day. I am learning the alphabet and the three diacritical marks that go with it.

For my benefit the class recites the letters and their sounds.

"Aleph aw - Aw."

"Bais aw - Baw."

I sit in the first row, the newest student, the youngest, the only girl. The other students have been sent here to prepare for their Bar Mitzvahs. I am here because my mother says girls should learn the way boys do. I am here because she wants to keep me busy so I can stay out of trouble.

I open my notebook and begin to copy the Hebrew letters. We study Hebrew so we can read God's words as He wrote them. We translate the Hebrew words into Yiddish, the language of Jews.

"In the beginning, *Elohim*, the Lord God, created the heaven and earth."

"Rebbe, who made *Elohim?*" I ask.

"Nobody made *Elohim.* He was always there."

"Rebbe, did He speak Hebrew or Yiddish?"

The Rebbe puts his lips together, shakes his head. "He spoke! He spoke! His language. It didn't matter which one. No one could hear Him."

I listen as the Rebbe explains each of the words. "Some people," he says, "translate the first word to mean 'in the beginning,' other people translate it to mean 'when'."

I want to ask how there can be two ways to understand God's words. But I don't. I sit and listen. I sit and learn.

A boy reads the next passage. "God saw how good the light was, and God separated the light from the darkness. God called the light Day, and the darkness He called Night"

The Rebbe explains that a day then was not like a day now. Maybe it was longer, maybe it was shorter. "What is important," he says tapping his pointer on the wall, "is first there was light, but even before light, there was the word. It was with the word that God made the light. Without words we are nothing and there is nothing."

I believe what the Rebbe says.

I learn how God separated the sky and the earth. I learn how He made the sun, the moon and the stars, how He made people in His image, male and female He created them.

First one student reads, then another. I learn that when the Lord God made the earth and the heavens, there was no person to till the soil, so God formed man out of the earth.

"Rebbe," I ask. "At the beginning it says God made people. On the sixth day, after He made the animals, He made people, male and female. Then later it says He made Adam and Eve. Where did the first people go?"

I have heard the words of God and take them to mean what they say.

The Rebbe considers my question. He shakes his head, nods, mumbles. He is thinking. The boys snicker. They do not ask questions of the Rebbe.

"That was a different man and woman," he says to me. "An experiment. Adam is the true man."

Each student recites a verse and translates it into Yiddish. "And the Lord God fashioned into a woman the rib He had taken from the man. This one He called woman, from man was she taken. Hence a man leaves his father and mother and clings to his wife, so that they become one flesh."

I understand what he means. That is why my father lives with my mother in my grandmother's house. I do not understand about Uncle Arthur and Aunt Bertha. They are brother and sister and they live in my grandmother's house. I do not understand why Uncle Arthur doesn't have a wife, why Aunt Bertha is an old maid.

We read and we learn. We learn about Cain and Abel, and how Cain killed his brother and was barred from the land and how he knew his wife and she had a son.

"Rebbe," I ask. "Where did Cain's wife come from?" The Rebbe frowns. He curls his lips and shakes his head. "Stop with the questions," he shouts.

"But Rebbe," I continue. I am not afraid of his anger. He is a Rebbe; he cannot hit like a mother. "First there is Adam and Eve, then Cain and Abel, where did the wife come from?"

There is a quiet in the room. Everyone pays attention now. Is there a mistake in God's book? Has the Rebbe told a lie? You can marry a cousin sometimes, but not a brother or a sister. Was Cain's sin more terrible than killing a brother, a sin so terrible it could not be told?

"No more questions, " says the Rebbe, his face so close to mine, I can see his yellow teeth, feel the moisture of his spittle on my face. "No more questions. You must show respect for the word of God."

Months before school began my mother took me to register. She brought proof of my birth date. She brought proof of my vaccination, as if proof was needed. My scar was fresh and clear, the vaccination after the fact, a requirement of law. I had diptheria when I was a year and a half old. I don't remember, but I recall hearing about it, how I almost died, how hard it was for my mother who had a new baby, how she had to give the baby to Aunt Bertha to care for.

"She was always sick," my mother says about me. "Name it and she had it," she tells the neighbors. "Croup, diptheria, whooping cough, chicken pox, and measles. Sick but healthy," she says. "Knock on wood."

School begins. There is only one street to cross. I can go by myself.

Miss Robinson is not at all like my mother. She looks like a lady in the movies. She is skinny and she wears silk dresses and necklaces. Her cheeks are red and her lips; she smells of flowers. She wears rayon stockings and high heels. Her handkerchief has lace around it. She plays the piano and sings to us. She is Irish.

I wear a cotton dress and new high topped green shoes. My mother says high shoes prevent weak ankles. One of my father's clean handkerchiefs is safety-pinned to my dress. I am always first on line, ready for school.

In school we color in leaves and count to ten. We learn Columbus discovered America and we sing the alphabet song. We draw black cats and Jack O'Lanterns. We write our names. We talk about the Pilgrims and the first Thanksgiving. We prepare for Christmas: paper chains, colored candy canes, colored Santa Clauses, a big star for the top of the tree.

Miss Robinson plays the piano. We sing Jingle Bells. Every time we sing, someone is chosen to shake the bells. Once it is my turn. I jingle them hard. I imagine an open sleigh just like the one my mother used to ride. I imagine Santa Claus coming from Europe in his sleigh.

The kindergarten children are to perform "The Night Before Christmas" in the auditorium. I have a good memory. I will say the words and the class will act out what I say. Miss Robinson practices with me. She teaches me how to say the words right, not to sing-song like a foreigner.

"Santa Claus comes every year," says Miss Robinson. "He flies through the air and leaves a present for all good children. If you've been a good boy or girl, you will get a present."

I believe what Miss Robinson says. A teacher knows. Like a Rebbe. "Respect!" That's the word my mother uses. Respect means to listen and obey.

I run home from school, rush up the stairs. I do not unbutton my coat or take off my hat or unwind the scarf wrapped around my neck. I take the time only to step out of my galoshes and leave them in the hall. "Santa Claus is coming," I say. "He'll come on the roof when we're sleeping. You have to leave the roof door open so he can leave me a present."

"What Santa Claus? What nonsense is this?" says my mother as she sits at the kitchen table sorting buttons.

"Santa Claus is coming," I repeat.

"Santa Claus is *goyish*, a *goyish* belief. Jews don't believe in Santa Claus."

I stand defiant in the kitchen doorway. I don't know what to say.

"There is no Santa Claus," says my mother looking at me over her shoulder. She laughs. "Foolishness. Only an ignoramus believes in Santa Claus."

"The teacher said. The teacher said," I yell. For once, I do not want my mother to be right. I want to believe the teacher's words. I want Santa Claus. I want things the way people say they are.

"The teacher said, the teacher said," I repeat.

My mother turns back to the buttons.

Every day I remind my mother that Christmas is coming. Every day I tell my mother how good I've been. I do whatever she tells me to. I don't make noise. I help. I know Santa Claus will bring me a present. Every day I tell myself, "The teacher said." How can I face the other children if Santa Claus doesn't come? What shall I tell the teacher?

On Christmas Eve I remind my mother to leave the roof door open. I lie in bed listening for Santa Claus, imagining the sleigh. I strain to hear the sound of reindeer, a clip clop like a horse but softer. I remember how my mother looked at me just before I went to bed.

On Christmas morning I wake up early. Still in my pajamas I rush to the hall. There on the stairs near the seltzer bottles and the sack of potatoes is a small paper bag. I take out the red satin ribbon; it's long enough to go around my head and tie in a bow. I remember seeing a ribbon just like this in Woolworth's. Shirley Temple ribbon. I remember I asked my mother to buy it for me. I remember she said, "No."

"What is it?" asks my mother. She has followed me out to the hall.

I hold the ribbon out to her.

"Oh!" she says, a smile on her face as if she knows a secret. "Look what Santa Claus brought for you."

I look at my mother, standing there smiling, pleased with herself. I wrap the ribbon around my finger. "Yes," I say looking down at the floor. "Santa Claus brought the ribbon."

My mother has told a lie. I don't know why, but she has tried to fool me. I must be careful.

5

Even before the holidays were over, my mother announced she was going to stay at the adult hotel in Long Beach for the rest of the month. She would not have to cook or clean or shop; she'd have company, and she could rest and get better.

At first things were fine—no complaints, no phone calls. Then, at the end of the first week, things began to change, the calls coming closer together, more frantic. The nights were the worst, as if she were a child afraid of the dark. Diet didn't help, or pills. It was not something that could be fixed.

One morning, at the end of the third week, right after Sam had left for work, a call came. Not from my mother this time, but from the hotel manager. My mother had not come down to dinner the night before. She had not touched the tray they had sent up. She had not come down for breakfast.

At first I thought she might really be sick. Then I thought she might be getting back at me, angry because I hadn't come to visit her the day before. I remembered the stories she used to tell to get her way, the lies, the plotting and planning, trying to even the score. "Nobody plays me for a fool," she used to say when she had an argument with a neighbor.

The trip to Long Beach did not take more than half an hour, but it was a convoluted drive through winding side streets, over a toll bridge and down a depressing boulevard lined with welfare hotels and old age homes. I had made that drive so often in the time she was there, I could drive without thinking. But I was never prepared for the toll. I always found myself on the bridge groping in my purse for the fifty cents I needed as if I had never done this before.

Parking was not a problem. There was always a space near the entrance, even in the afternoon. Residents in adult hotels do not need parking spaces. Single room occupants and welfare clients who inhabited the seedy hotels fronting the boardwalk, did not own cars. Only visitors had cars, and the staff.

My mother had not even asked my advice. She had asked her friends from Hadassah, and they had warned her about the hotel where the dining room was too far from the elevator and the one where the elevators were so small there was no room for more than three people and you had to wait an hour to go to the lobby. One hotel had crazy people and another had old furniture that smelled. Finally she had consulted her Rabbi and he had recommended Seaview by The Sea, a hotel owned by his son-in-law.

I walked up the steps to the lobby.

"That's the daughter, Millie Kaits," I heard someone say as I crossed the lobby.

"I'm here to see Mrs. Abramowitz," I told the woman at the switchboard.

"She didn't come down for breakfast," the woman said.

Outside my mother's room, I stood and listened. Like a spy. I wanted to catch her in the act, I wanted to see if the radio was on. How sick could she be if she could listen to the radio? Ear to the door, I stood listening. Nothing. Not even breathing.

I opened the door. My mother lay stretched out on the bed wearing her blue flannel robe, the one with orange and red flowers. She always liked color. Even now, as old as she was, given a choice, she would head for the reds, the fuschias, the royal blues. She had her stockings rolled below the knee and she clutched a handkerchief in her hand. Her eyes were closed, her breathing irregular, a great raspy intake and a moaning exhale. Her skin had a yellowish cast.

"Ma," I said. "Ma, I'm here."

She opened her eyes. For a moment, her face looked broken, as if the parts had been put back together and did not quite match. "Aah," she said lifting a hand to her face. She began to move her feet over the edge of the bed, tried to sit up by grasping the edge of the bed with her hands, tried, failed, tried again, succeeded.

"I didn't eat for two days," she said.

I closed the door behind me but remained standing in the doorway. I would have to be careful; she was getting right to the point without even a hello.

"I vomited whatever I put in my mouth. I couldn't even drink the tea."

I did not remove my jacket.

"Oh, what will become of me?" my mother said as she rocked back and forth. "Someone have pity on me."

She did not look particularly sick. Maybe she wanted some attention.

I moved over to the only chair in the room, near the window on the other side of the bed, facing my mother's back. How typical, I thought, I always end up with her back to me.

I remembered a visit to New York when Julie was ten and Matthew was seven. We had come in for Mother's Day. My brother had sent flowers, my sister had made a phone call, but we had come all the way from Chicago. Sam wanted to honor our mothers. I had protested. I was a mother too, I'd said. I had not wanted to go back.

My mother did not invite us to stay over. She said the children could stay with her but there wasn't room for us. Sam and I stayed in a motel, but we visited with her that night. She had prepared franks and beans, bought cokes for the children.

Mother's Day dinner was going to be at Sam's mother's house. My mother had been invited.

"What's the matter?" my mother asked when I gave her the invitation. "She never heard of restaurants?"

I didn't answer.

"What will she give us to eat? She never puts in salt."

I tried to change the subject. It was a day for celebration, I said. Mother's Day.

"Also a mother. If she was such a good mother her children wouldn't have died."

I told her she was speaking nonsense, there was no penicillin then so people died of pneumonia, of appendicitis. I could feel the anger rising, but I held my peace. I didn't want a scene in front of the children. I didn't want them to see how a mother and daughter fought.

Sam's mother was pleased and excited at the idea of our company. "All the way from Chicago," she said. She made it sound as if we had come from Europe. Sam's sister was there with her family, and my mother-in-law had put up a bridge table for the children. She had made flanken and mashed potatoes and had opened a can of peas. She spoke about how happy she was to have us all there. She said, "Thank God for my children." She said, "I love my children"

"Love!" said my mother. "What do you know from love? I loved my children, I sacrificed for them. I gave up my life for them."

I don't know why I did it, the shock on my mother-in-law's face, the anger that had built up from the evening before. "You never loved me," I said. "You don't know what love is."

A hush fell on the table. Even the children were quiet.

"Every mother loves her children," my sister-in-law said.

"Let's have some wine," said Sam .

"I could use a drink," said my sister-in-law's husband. We went on with our dinner as if nothing had happened. But I saw the look on my mother's face, the way she turned around in her chair and gave me her back.

"It can't be two days since you ate," I said now. "I was here the day before yesterday after you came from the dining room."

"You don't believe me," my mother accused. She did not turn around. She talked to me as if I weren't there, as if there were a telephone wire connecting us. "I went to the dining room but I didn't eat. I didn't eat for two days. And I didn't take the medicine."

Aha! There was the clincher, the rubbing in of the guilt. "What do you want me to do? Tell me what you want and I'll do it," I said, surprised that I meant it.

"I don't know myself," she said quietly. "I don't know what to do." She sighed, a low, mournful sound, feeble yet filling the room. Then she lay back on the bed on her side, her back still to me. We didn't speak. She could have been asleep. Except for the breathing. Except for her words hanging in the air.

"Should we call a doctor?" I asked knowing no doctor would come here. She'd have to go to a hospital. I would have to get an ambulance. And then... I could not look ahead.

It's her own fault, I thought. She wanted to come to this hotel. She picked this run-down building in a seedy part of town.

"Should I call a doctor?" I asked again. I wanted her to be the mother I remembered, the mother who always knew what to do. I wanted to tell her everything would be all right, but I couldn't. I wanted to tell her I loved her, but I thought it wasn't true, and I didn't want to lie.

"I don't know," she said. "I don't know what to do."

I got up from the chair and began pulling the blanket up around her legs, her hips.

She turned onto her back, her eyes closed. Her hand found mine and held. "What should I do?" she whispered, the sound no more than a breath, the words no more than a sigh.

Life isn't fair. Things don't work out the way we need.

Distrust between us hardened, a concrete span I could not cross.

I did not understand that life is a series of accidents from which we choose, no rhyme or reason. I did not know life refines, how we take shape in yielding, how there is something to be said for holding on, something splendid in letting go. I was afraid. To change is to eliminate. I thought growing up is to turn away. I turned away. From her. From all that used to be.

I did not know how alike we were.

New tenants move into the back apartment. They have a boy older than I, a girl younger. They pay a month's security but they do not pay for painting. "Living in other people's dirt," says my mother. "Low class."

"Sherman." My mother says their name as if it were bitter food. "Did you ever hear of a Jew named Sherman?"

The Shermans come highly recommended. Mrs. Sherman is the niece of Mrs. Pincus, the dry goods lady. Still there is something funny there, the neighbors say. The Shermans have a boarder. They have rented out their living room.

"Who lives without a living room?" asks my mother, making a spitting sound. "Do they think this is the East Side?"

"There are boarders and there are boarders," Mrs. Schechter says, her voice rising at the end. She winks one eye and thrusts out her hip. The women laugh and turn back to the fruit and vegetable wagon. They squeeze the grapefruits, heft the carrots tied into little bunches, pick out the grapes. I admire the horse. He paws the ground and shakes the oat bag tied to his head. I want to pet him but I'm afraid. I imagine he is Black Beauty sold away to work out his days.

"If they're so well off, how come they have a boarder?" my mother asks Uncle Arthur. She always asks but she doesn't expect an answer. It's her way of saying what she wants without coming right out and saying it.

"So what's wrong with a boarder?" asks my Uncle Arthur. He's always ready to bait my mother. "Some people try to help themselves. They change with the times. They don't keep digging up what used to be."

My mother puts her lips together. She is holding back her words.

My mother and my uncle are always arguing. They yell, they curse. Sometimes my mother starts, sometimes my uncle. But no matter who starts, my mother wants to finish.

In the evening, Uncle Arthur counts his money. He owns a live chicken market. Everybody works there: Aunt Bertha, the Zayde, Uncle Zelig, everyone except my father. My father works in a shop. He stands at a machine and presses pants. My mother wants him to go into business for himself. My mother wants my father to be like Uncle Arthur. After supper, after my grandfather has gone to sleep, Uncle Arthur takes out the money sacks my grandmother sewed on the sewing machine, and spills the money out on the table. On Thursdays, if business is good, if everybody came to buy chickens for the Sabbath, Uncle Arthur points to the money and says, "Here, take a nickel off the top."

I take my nickel and watch while Aunt Bertha counts the dollar bills. She smooths them, puts them in piles, crossing one pile over the other. Uncle Arthur sorts the change: quarters, dimes, nickels and pennies. Sometimes I am allowed to count the pennies. I make careful piles, ten to a pile so that Uncle Arthur can put them in paper packets. Sometimes I'm allowed to keep the left-over pennies. I never keep the left over-nickels or dimes.

"Here," says my uncle this evening. "Take a dime to go with your nickel."

"So, Big Shot," says my mother, "and who made you such a *gansa macha?* You think you were born that way?"

Quiet falls across the table. I wait for the words to strike, like slaps across the face.

My mother is always trying to get back at her brother. She says it's her money that made him what he is. She says he borrowed the money from her when my father was rich. She wants him to pay it back. Then she can buy her own house, she won't have to be a tenant.

"You're living on my money," she always tells Uncle Arthur. "My money. You're eating and drinking my blood and sweat, taking the bread from my children's mouths."

My mother has tried different ways to get her money back. She wrote a letter to the *Bintele Brief* in the Yiddish paper, and even though she disguised her name, Aunt Bertha said everybody knew.

"A *shande*," said my grandmother, "A shame to put such things in the paper."

My mother wrote to the Yiddishe Court on the radio. She wrote about her brother and the loan she gave him, she wrote that she had notes to prove it.

"A *shande*, said the rabbi who judged according to the laws of Moses and the spirit of the Talmud. "A brother ought to pay his sister what he owes."

"*Dreck*," said Uncle Arthur. "What does he know?"

For a week after the radio program, my mother did not go downstairs to visit my grandmother when Uncle Arthur was home. She did not allow me to go either. She said we should not speak to a man whose heart was made of stone.

One evening my mother looks up from the paper she is reading and announces she will sue. "Justice," she says. "In America there's justice. There are courts. Laws. In America a person can get justice." My mother goes to see the lawyer. She goes by herself. She does not tell anyone what the lawyer says.

Robert and Irma Sherman teach me and Alvin how to play Monopoly. It is their game. They always buy Boardwalk. They always have hotels. They always have money to get out of jail. Money is the key to winning. There is no justice when it comes to money.

We play in the hall on the landing. My mother says the living room is for company, and she doesn't want her kitchen messed up. The Sherman's living room is rented to the Boarder so we play in the hall near the mop and pail. We play quietly so not to bother Jack the Boarder.

Jack works at night. He is short and dark. His hair is parted on the side and smoothed back with Brilliantine. He has a thin mustache. He wears his snap brim hat pulled over his eyes. The suit he wears to work is nipped in at the waist. He is a bachelor. My mother says he is a big spender.

He always tips a nickel when he gets a message that there's a phone call at the candy store. My grandmother has a telephone but she doesn't allow the neighbors to use it. She's afraid they'll take advantage, they'll come in the middle of the night and she won't be able to sleep. My mother uses my grandmother's telephone only when necessary. She doesn't like people doing her favors, even if it's her own mother.

"Good morning," says Jack, tipping his hat when he comes home.

"A bum," says my mother.

"A fine man," says my father.

"What does he do for a living?" asks my grandmother.

"He's no good," says my mother.

"Ask," says my grandmother. "It can't hurt to ask."

"Jack is a bookkeeper," says Mrs. Pincus. "He works downtown."

My grandmother invites Jack for a glass of tea.

My mother is angry. I can tell the way she puts her mouth together. Still on Sunday, she gets dressed up. She wears her blue dress with the red and white flowers. It is soft and smooth, like silk. I do not have to dress up, but I do have to wash my hands and face and stay out of trouble.

My mother is going to my grandmother's house for tea. She is going to see if Jack is a good match for my Aunt Bertha.

"So," asks my mother, "where did you live before?"

"I roomed in Brownsville," says Jack sipping his tea. My grandmother has put the glasses in the silver holders. There is a tablecloth over the oilcloth. Paper napkins sit folded in the crocheted napkin holder.

"I hear you're a bookkeeper," says my mother. Jack nods.

"A good line of work," says my mother. "You've worked for a while?"

"A few years."

"Your parents, your mother and father, where are they?" my grandmother asks in Yiddish.

"Dead," says Jack in English. "I'm an orphan."

"Oh. A shame. Let them be at peace." My grandmother pauses, then, "Your father, what did he do?"

"I don't remember."

"So, how were you brought up?" Uncle Arthur's voice is sharp.

"An uncle, my mother's brother. They knew Mrs. Pincus' mother. Through them I came to the Pincuses and to the Shermans."

My mother nods and my uncle takes a bite of his cake. Jack gave the right answers.

"Tell me," says my mother, "you make a good living in your line of work?"

"It's all right," says Jack. "But I want to go into business for myself."

I see the looks that pass from one to the other like a ball in the game we play in school. Aunt Bertha sits with her head bent, her eyes watching her hands fold and refold the paper napkin. She is wearing her black dress with the white lace collar, the one my mother said was slenderizing.

My mother leans back in her chair. She does not ask how come Jack works at night. Neither does Uncle Arthur. "Another glass of tea, here," he says to Bubbe. "Do we have to wait until the Messiah comes ?"

They sit, drinking tea and eating cake.

One day it is raining. I watch the drops fall. I sit at the window counting my money. I make piles of the pennies and nickels, I stack the four dimes and the two quarters separately. My grandfather gave me the second quarter when I could read my first passage from the Torah. I count the money. I am saving to buy Skating Sally.

Skating Sally is a doll in a trunk. She stands in the window of Dave's candy store. There is a sign right in the middle, "Skating Sally, $4.95".

Every day on my way home from school I stop to see Skating Sally. I press close to the window, my breath making a cloud I have to rub away. I imagine holding Sally in my hands, changing her clothes. She has four different outfits. I imagine taking her skates off when I put her to sleep. I imagine me wearing a dress just like hers and skating while everyone watches. I want skates even more than I want Skating Sally but my mother says I'll break a leg and be a cripple. Then no one will marry me.

I count my money. One dollar and eleven cents. I don't have enough. I remember what my mother said, "You can't get what you want just because you want it." I remember how my father smiled and looked sad. He touched my arm and whispered, "I'm sorry. If I had the money, I'd buy it for you." He used to be a waiter in a hotel downtown. "A saloon," my mother says. He used to be rich but he lost all his money in the Crash. "A fool," my mother says. Now he works in a pants shop. "Struggling to make a living," my mother says.

I pick up the Indian Head penny Jack gave me. "For good luck," he said. "Keep at it, kid."

"You're too old for dolls. You're in the first grade already," I remember Cousin Bea said sticking her nose up in the air.

My mother comes to tell me she's going to the butcher. She tells me not to leave the house.

I sit at the window and draw skating outfits on old paper bags. The rain falls drop by drop. I see my mother, holding my father's big umbrella, walk down the empty street. I put my money in my cigar box and put the cigar box in the drawer under my nightowns. Alvin is playing with Robert, and Tibby is downstairs with my grandmother. There is nothing to do. I go into the kitchen.

From the kitchen window, I see Mrs. Ffeiffer's wash hanging across the alley. "What's the point of taking it in," she said when my mother called across the alley to tell her it was raining. "It's wet now, so it'll get wetter."

"A lazy housekeeper," my mother said.

I pull a chair over to the refrigerator. I climb up to turn the radio on. The chair tips over and I fall. My arm hurts. I look at the floor to see if I damaged the linoleum. I push the chair back to the table. I don't want my mother to find out.

The next day the sun shines. Rhoda, Blanche, Ethel and I play jump rope in the alley. We play Double Dutch. I trip on a crack in the cement. Rhoda calls my mother. She comes running. She picks me up and looks me over. I hold my arm against my waist.

"What is it?" she asks.

"Nothing," I say.

"Let me see your arm."

"No."

"Let me see your arm."

I use my left hand to try to move my right arm. It hurts.

"Oh what has befallen me! She broke her arm." My mother's screams bring my grandmother and the neighbors.

"Put ice," says one.

"No, not ice. Heat," says another.

"Nonsense. Wrap it tight," says still another.

"It's nothing," says a fourth. "What are they making such a fuss about?"

"Where did you fall?" asks my mother.

I point to the crack in the cement.

"Aha!" says my mother. "She'll pay. I told her to fix the cement. I told her someone would fall. She has cracks all over, even on the sidewalk. I told her she's responsible. Mrs. Ffeiffer the bastard, Mrs. Ffeiffer the witch. Come see what you did. See what happened. My daughter is crippled from your sidewalk."

She pushes me ahead of her like a prize, yelling loud enough for everyone to hear. "Come! See what happened. See how my dear daughter is hurt. Don't worry, she'll pay. She'll pay. I'll sue her for all she's worth."

.　　.　　.

I sit in bed, my right arm in my lap, my hand limp like the head of my stuffed doll when it was caught in the drawer and I pulled and pulled and pulled.

My mother is looking at my hand, my grandmother stands on one side and Aunt Bertha and Uncle Arthur stand on the other. My father stands by himself at the foot of the bed. He looks scared. I see my brother in the doorway. He begins to stick his tongue out, then quickly puts it back.

"Should I call a doctor?" asks my mother. She and my grandmother exchange looks, then both look to my uncle. A doctor is serious.

"You don't need a doctor," says Uncle Arthur.

"Maybe we should call the cupping lady." My mother's voice rises.

"What will she do? It's nothing. Give her an aspirin. It will heal itself."

They stand around the bed waiting for my hand to heal. It lies there, limp and still, a stranger.

Jack the Boarder comes to say hello. "Here kid," he says and tosses a bubble gum card onto the bed. I use my teeth and left hand to unwrap the gum. Pee Wee Reese. A triple card for trading.

A day passes. Still my arm hangs limp.

My mother tries her tricks. She hands me her change purse from her apron pocket. "Here," she says. "Take a dime."

I have my own tricks. I open the purse with my teeth and take the dime with my left hand.

She bakes cookies and allows me out of bed to press down with the cookie cutter. I use my left hand. She shows me how to do cross stitch embroidery and offers to let me work a corner of the tablecloth she is making as a present for Cousin Tzirel's wedding. I tell her I'll do it when my hand is better. She offers to teach me how to knit, getting some of her green wool and two extra needles. I tell her it's too hard to follow.

My grandmother comes back. "Be careful," I hear her whisper. "You may end up with a cripple."

The cupping lady comes. She looks at my arm, touches my shoulder, shakes her head. "Maybe she hurt a nerve," she says.

My bed is moved closer to the window so I can sit in the sun. In the street, children play, children with two good legs and two good arms. I sit and watch; I sit quietly while relatives whisper in the living room and neighbors come to stand and stare.

Uncle Arthur brings the doctor.

The doctor moves my arm back and forth. He pulls and twists. I feel pain like lightening burning up my arm. The room moves round and round. I scream. I put my arm against my chest and bend my head over it. My mother gasps. My father says, "Enough."

My uncle moves over to my side. "Let's make a bargain," he says. "Be good and let the doctor examine you and I'll get you a surprise."

I close my eyes. My arm hurts. I think about Uncle Arthur's words. I sit up straight. I nod. I clench my teeth.

The doctor puts two sticks against my arm. He wraps the sticks with gauze. Then he puts my arm in a sling. "Give it time, " he says. "It will heal."

Uncle Arthur comes back. He puts Skating Sally in my lap. I forget about the doctor. I forget about my arm.

Soon I am well enough to sit downstairs on the porch. "Watch your hand," says my mother. "Don't move."

She carries a can of paint and a paint brush. She goes down the stairs and into the alley, too far back for me to see.

Soon I hear Mrs. Ffeiffer's voice. *"Meshuga!* She's crazy. Crazy. What are you doing?"

I run to the side of the porch. Heads pop out of the windows. My mother is painting a line down the middle of the alley.

"Stay on your side," my mother yells at Mrs. Ffeiffer. "Stay off our property."

My grandmother comes out of the basement door. "What are you doing?" she asks my mother. "Are you crazy?"

"Now everyone can see which side of the alley is broken. They can see it's her side, not ours."

"Enough," says my grandmother. "Come in the house. A shame people should see this."

My mother goes into the house with my grandmother, but the line remains.

We are forbidden to cross the line, me, my brother, my sister, my father. My mother cannot forbid the Shermans from crossing the line but everyone knows if they want to be my mother's friends, they cannot cross the line.

Even though the line does not go all the way to the sidewalk, my mother knows exactly where the end of it should be. When she needs to go to the grocery or the fruit store or the laundry, she crosses the street, walks on the other side to the corner, then crosses back. She will not walk on Mrs. Ffeiffer's property. She will not take a chance on getting crippled.

Days pass. My arm begins to heal. The painted line begins to fade. Still my mother crosses to the other side. Still I am forbidden to go into Mrs. Ffeiffer's house even though my friend Blanche lives there, in the apartment that faces the Shermans. From her living room window you can see into the window of Jack the Boarder's room.

The girls from school come to Blanche's house to see Jack as he stands in his BVD's. They giggle because he doesn't wear a union suit. They oh and ah as he combs his hair and smooths his mustache. They think he looks like a movie star.

"He lives in my house," I say defiantly. "I can see him whenever I want." What I say is a lie. I can't let them know how much I want to visit Blanche, how much I want to go into Mrs. Ffeiffer's house and look through the window at Jack the Boarder.

One day our garbage cans are found lying on their sides, the garbage spilled.

"You *machashaffa*, witch," yells my mother out the window toward Mrs. Ffeiffer's window. "I know you did it."

She runs out of the kitchen, down the stairs, out on the porch, down the steps, into the alley and across the faded painted line. She flings Mrs. Ffeiffer's garbage cans on their sides.

"You'll find out who you're dealing with," yells my mother.

"I'm not afraid of you and your whole Coxey army," yells Mrs. Ffeiffer.

That night Uncle Arthur calls up from the hall. "Sorke, Sorke, come downstairs."

My mother sticks her head over the hall railing.

"You want to talk, you come upstairs," she says.

"Are you crazy! Why did you knock her garbage cans down? Why are you making a *gansa tzimmes* out of nothing? It's not even your garbage cans."

"A foot taken to the dog is a kick to the owner," says my mother.

"What are you talking about? We don't need a feud. This isn't Europe. It's America. We can straighten things out. We can talk."

"Talk? Talk to a witch!" My mother leans way over the railing. I wonder if she will tip over and fall. "Do you know what she said? She said we're *schnorrers*, we sit with the dead to get a free meal. She said the Bubbe was older than the Zayde, that he married her for her dowry."

"So. So she has a big mouth. What harm can words do?"

"Yeah. Words don't hurt? You know what she said about you, big shot? She said you weren't really a man. She said you were a man only for your sister."

Quiet falls on the hall as if it were a thunderclap. I try not to move. I don't want my mother to see me. For once, Uncle Arthur doesn't answer. My mother straightens up. She looks sad. Is she sorry she told? What does it mean—a man for your sister?

Then I hear the door slam. My uncle has gone into the house.

My mother goes to a lawyer. She sues Mrs. Ffeiffer for money for the doctor's bill, she sues for the sleep she lost worrying about my arm, she sues for my arm still stiff and sore. "Who knows how the arm will grow?" she says to all the neighbors. "She could be a cripple yet." My mother sues for damages done her good name. "A person can have money and cars," she says, "but without a good name, what are you?"

I am busy. I am back in school trying to make up the work I missed. I go to *cheder*. But I am still not allowed to play. It takes a long time for an arm to heal. I sit on the porch and listen to the women talk.

"Such a nice Jewish boy," says Mrs. Schecter.

"Tut, tut," says my mother.

"His poor mother," says Mrs. Pincus.

"Full of holes," says Mrs. Greenberg. "What will happen when the Messiah comes?"

Two bodies have been found outside the pool room door. Dead. One is a stranger. The other is Limpy Lefke, a boy from the next block. A Jewish boy. Dead now. Dead with holes in his body, fated to live with holes in eternity. I touch my belly, imagining a hole.

"Don't go near the pool room," my mother warns. "The pool room is for bums. From there it's one step to Murder, Inc. and the electric chair."

The pool room is on the corner under the elevated trains. It has big windows and sprawls over the whole corner on two streets, over the haunted house, over the Chinese laundry, over the dry goods store and over the fish store. It is up a long flight of stairs. Every day when I go to *cheder*, I stare up at the pool room. I try to see inside the windows. I want to see dead bodies with bullet holes.

On Monday, dish night, we go to the movies. My mother missed a night when I hurt my arm. She is short a soup dish. She is willing to pay full price for me so I can also get a dish.

We walk past the pool room. I look up the stairs, hoping to see something, hoping for a glimpse of what is forbidden. Jack the Boarder steps back into the shadows. He puts his fingers to his lips. He pulls someone behind him. It is my cousin Jerry. Jerry is sixteen years old and goes to high school. I open my mouth. Then I close it. Jerry is doing something bad. So is Jack. I will not tell.

We watch Clark Gable take off his shirt. He is not wearing an undershirt. "Don't look," says my mother and covers my eyes with her hand.

Two days later while Alvin and I eat breakfast, my mother starts getting dressed as if it were a holiday. I go into the bedroom and watch while she laces up her corset and hooks her brassiere to it. She has a smooth line, straight up and down. She puts her stockings on, pulls her bloomers up and steps into her patent leather shoes. She wears a black and white dress. After she sprays on perfume with the atomizer, she puts on a hat with a little veil that covers her eyes. She carries white gloves. "I still have a good figure," she says.

"I'm going to court," she tells me. "The case is today. Eat lunch at Bubbe's"

My mother is home when I come from school. She is wearing her house dress and and apron. Her stockings are rolled below her knees and her house shoes flap when she walks.

She has her angry look, her eyes squeezed small, her mouth scrunched together.

"That crook," she says when I come into the kitchen. "If he thinks I'll pay him, he's got another guess coming."

I go into the bedroom to change my clothes. I hear a pot bang on the sink, a cabinet door slam; I hear her talking to herself. "He tells me I have a good case. 'Perfect,' he says. 'A sure thing.' I promise him fifty-fifty. 'Fifty-fifty,' he says and we shake. So why should I pay him? I got nothing. Fifty-fifty from nothing is nothing."

I do not understand what happened. I decide to be good all day.

I am already in bed when I hear my mother come upstairs from talking to Uncle Arthur.

"I'll fix him," I hear her say. "He won't get off so easy."

On Friday, my mother is waiting for me when I come home from school. "Don't change your clothes," she says. "I want you to come with me." She takes her apron off, rolls her stockings up above her knees and puts on her regular shoes with laces. She puts powder on her face from a box marked Rachel and puts on lipstick. She hooks her arm through her pocketbook and then lifts two money sacks from the table, one only half full. "Can you carry it?" she asks.

I nod. They look like the money sacks my uncle has. There is money inside; I can feel it.

"Where are we going?" I ask.

"Sh," she says. "You'll see."

We walk down the stairs, cross the street to the other side and we walk to the corner and around the next street until we come to a house with a sign that says Irving Greenspan, Attorney-at-Law. We walk up the stairs to the porch. My mother goes first. She rings the bell. A man opens the door.

"You want your money?" she asks. "Here's your money." She empties the sack on the floor. Pennies roll out, hundreds of pennies. Some fall in the hall, some fall on the porch, some roll off the steps into the street.

She takes the sack from my arm. "Here," she says. "Here's your money." More pennies roll out. Some roll in the cracks of the floor, some fall in a pile near Mr. Greenspan's feet.

"It's all here," says my mother. "Every penny. Count it."

Mr. Greenspan stands there, his mouth open.

My mother grabs my hand and pulls me back to the street.

"That will show him," she says as we walk home. "He can't play me for a fool." Then she smiles; she smiles all the way home.

6

"**D**id you try the chopped mushrooms? It's something new," Bea said looking at my plate already half filled with eggplant lasagne and salmon mousse. "I have a fantastic caterer. She comes all the way from Philadelphia."

It had taken us three hours to drive to Lakewood, New Jersey, the roads already slippery, even though the first blizzard of the season was not due until the next day. I had come to Cousin Bea's son's Bar Mitzvah even though I did not believe in these rites of passage, rites my own son had not performed. I was nostalgic for the past. I wanted to see if there was a pattern to life and how mine fell into it.

Suddenly Bea grabbed my arm.

"What's the matter," I asked, alarmed.

"My feet hurt. I can't stand up. I'd better change my shoes."

I couldn't tell if her feet were swollen or not. They were always large, the ankles as thick as the calves. Bea was never stout. None of the lumps and rolls that plagued her brother Sidney. Not that she was thin, just solid, "fully packed," we used to say.

"Why don't you sit down for a while?" I suggested.

"I can't now. There's too much to do. I'll just change into sandals." She turned away from the table. "Don't forget to try the chopped mushrooms," she reminded me as she hobbled off.

She's over-tired, I told myself. It must be hard planning and executing a son's Bar Mitzvah. I could imagine the strain of seeing relatives and friends one hadn't seen for years. I myself had been anxious. I had thought of all the reasons I shouldn't come. A cousin's son's Bar Mitzvah was not an obligation. We had lost touch over the years. I wouldn't know her son even if we met face to face. It was far. A storm was predicted. As much as I was pulled to my past and the people in it, I dreaded it. It was easier to live with what I remembered than to discover what I might have forgotten.

Bea was back.

She had removed her shoes and replaced them with sandals. Even so her feet seemed to billow over the side like bread dough left to rise too long. "It's from standing all day," she explained. "You know people will come to the house later. I made two turkeys and cole slaw and polished the silver."

She wore a navy dress with white polka dots, rayon, the kind of dress my mother used to wear when we were children. Bea was only six months older than I, but she looked like an old lady. She still wore braids. They were done in a coronet around her head, but they were still braids. She had never cut her hair short.

I wore a green dress with faggotted inserts and a string belt—it was an afternoon Bar Mitzvah, no frills, not even music in the rec room of the Temple where we ate. I'd bought the dress in the junior department of a specialty store, bought it because I thought the V neck was flattering to my figure, bought it because it was size 11 and I could still get into it. I wore sling back high heeled sandals. My legs were one of my good features and I did not mind showing them off.

"You've changed so," said Bea. "I would hardly recognize you."

Was she referring to the way I dressed or to me? I had tried to change, tried to be different from the people I grew up with, who had seemed limited, settled. I didn't think it showed, that it was something Bea could see. Her words made me feel I had done something wrong.

"Excuse me," she said and was gone again.

"Boy! What a spread!" said my brother Alvin. I hadn't seen him for months, not since the end of the holidays when he and Gail had visited my mother before she left for the hotel. We talked on the phone. I wanted him to know what was happening. He had a right to know—she was his mother, too!

"They really did it up! And all dairy. Must have cost a pretty penny." Alvin whispered loud enough to be heard within a five foot radius.

Ssh!" said Gail. "Don't talk about money now." She sounded like his mother, not his wife. She was squinting at the food at the end of the table. She was near-sighted but too vain to wear glasses. "Once you put them on," she always said when she saw me wearing mine, "you never take them off. Your eyes get used to them and you're stuck."

"What are these?" she asked pointing to a pyramid of perfect white spheres. "Oh, I see," she said before I could answer. "*Gefilte* fish. I can get those anytime."

"You should see the dessert table," said Sidney. "I never saw so much food. My sister sure knows how to do things right."

Sidney had never been part of my life. He was an infant when his father had died, too young to make an impression on me. We had seen each other at family events. He attended them all—Bar Mitzvahs, weddings, funerals.

"Be careful you don't get it all over you. We didn't bring a change," Gail said as Alvin reached for the macaroni salad, his sleeve dangerously close to the beet colored horse radish. Although he was dressed formally—a navy blue pin striped suit, white shirt, regimental striped tie—he wore crepe soled brown bucks. He'd always had trouble with his feet, always worrying about fallen arches. Now Bea and her feet. Was it a family trait? Would my feet give out too?

"Well, Millie! How are things?" Sidney asked heartily as if he were about to slap me on the back. He was so typically my idea of a C.P.A. We had sat through the two hour service only three rows apart, and we had been in the dining room for some time through greetings and introductions and drinks, but it was the first time he'd spoken directly to me. He had ignored me even at Uncle Arthur's funeral. Now he sounded as if we were buddies.

"I'm surprised you made the trip," he said reaching for a piece of lox, the bottom of his tie brushing the potato salad.

"What a thing to say!" Gail came to my defense. "Did you taste the kugel?" she asked almost in the same breath.

"I didn't mean anything by it," Sidney said as he wiped his tie with a napkin. "It's such a long trip just for a day. How come you didn't come last night and stay over?"

I explained how there were special problems in school in December because of the holidays. I told him I needed to visit my mother. I listed the chores around the house. I couldn't believe my behavior—apologetic and defensive—I, who couldn't care less what Sidney thought.

I edged over to Sam. "Let's sit down," I urged.

"And Tibby. How come your sister didn't come?" Sidney, still dabbing at his tie, had pursued me round the table.

Tibby wasn't well, I explained. Sciatica. "You know how sickly she's always been. Weak." There I was again, making excuses, protecting my sister the way my mother always told me to.

"Did you try the chopped mushrooms yet?" Bea was back, blocking our way to the tables. "A real delicacy." She went on and on about the caterer and the help, taking deep breaths, as if she were swimming, her face still familiar, still the girl with whom I had shared my childhood. I remembered how upset I was when suddenly she grew taller than I, a sure sign we weren't the twins I pretended we were, a sure sign we were growing up. And now, she was a stranger, recognizable, but still a stranger.

"Everything is wonderful," I said, telling her what I thought she wanted to hear. "The food is delicious. A great variety! You did a good job." After all these years, after all we had shared, that was all I could think to say.

"You'll come to the house later, won't you?" Bea asked almost wistfully. "Maybe we can get a chance to talk. It's all right, isn't it, that it's all dairy?"

"Of course," I said. "Dairy is a refreshing change." I made excuses about the evening, the weather, the long drive, the need to visit my mother. Who could argue with that? A devoted daughter, as if I had a loving mother.

She asked me about the children. I told her about Matthew's job in computers, that Julie was in graduate school studying to be an art therapist.

"The girls today, what do they want?" said Bea.

I bristled even though I knew she was talking about her own daughter more than mine.

"It's nothing personal," she said, "I have a daughter, too. She's studying sociology."

"I hear you're still teaching," she continued.

I nodded.

"You always were ambitious, even when you were a little girl," she said. "Do you still draw?"

I shook my head. I used to draw. But no one had liked my drawings. The teacher said they weren't ladylike. The teacher had said I should draw like my cousin Bea and held up a drawing of a vase of flowers, delicate, lace-like. I had drawn a tree, leafless, struck by lightning.

"Do you?" I asked.

"Oh, no," she said, sounding surprised I would even ask. "There's no time, what with the house and the children and the Temple Sisterhood." She turned away, surveying the room, checking I supposed, to see that everything was going smoothly.

"Try to come tonight," Bea said as if she had not heard my excuses. "Come over and eat something before you go," she urged as if we would starve between three and six, as if we were in the desert instead of Lakewood, New Jersey.

Excuses came easily. Bea was the hostess, she had to think about food. I was trying to understand her behavior, the distance between us. I remembered how we used to be, Bea and I.

She had been the cousin of promise, always doing well in school. But she had married soon after high school. I had been invited but I didn't go. It was only a year after I had left home and I was not yet ready to face my mother. Bea had had a baby almost immediately, waited ten years for the second, and eight more for the third, whose Bar Mitzvah this was. I had always thought she spaced her children so she would not have to make decisions about herself, so that she could remain a mother, safely at home.

I used to feel superior to Bea. I had not hidden out in the old roles, caught in old traps. I thought I'd given up the past, let it go like the clothes I gave to Goodwill. But it was still there, inside, in the way I felt—about Bea, about my mother, about me. I felt sad. We were all trapped, one way or another. I was spending so much time with my mother, I was beginning to think like her.

We had been assigned tables. Sam and I were seated with my brother and sister-in-law, cousins and a man who looked vaguely familiar.

"Buffets seem to be in," said Gail as she seated herself on my right. "I prefer to be served." She leaned forward to whisper in my ear, "What's the matter with Bea? There is no reason to be out of shape today. There are so many options for body management." Her lips tightened as if she could not bear to let the words through. It was her special look of disgust, just like my mother's.

I turned my attention to the others, glad that Sidney and his wife Florence were seated at the head table. I was finding it harder than I'd thought seeing my cousins, reminded of how we had been, seeing what they had become. We had been eight cousins, four aunts, three uncles, second cousins, *landsleit* from Europe, my grandmother's house always full of people, preparations for people. Eight cousins, not one I'd choose for a friend now, only one or two I'd even recognize if our paths chanced to cross. Three of them were seated at our table, Aunt Yittle's children: Jerry who once told me he'd dance with me when I grew up and now walked with a cane, Leo who had not bothered to introduce his new wife, and Toby who was given the same name as my sister but changed it. They were all who were left, eight cousins and my mother.

"Nice to see you, Millie," said Jerry. "How are things?"

We exchanged biographical information. Jerry had never married. Was he gay? I wondered. I imagined my mother asking, "Are you a *faigele*?" She never hesitated to let her tongue carry what was in her head.

The man next to Jerry smiled at me. "Do I know you?" I asked, thinking he might be a relative on Bea's husband's side. Or a friend.

"Don't you remember me? Sheldon. Sheldon Shapiro. Shecky."

Shecky! Of course I remembered Shecky! My friend Marilyn's boyfriend who lived on the next street. The medium build, the medium height, the sandy hair, the face still blurred, like a poorly focused photo. Nothing memorable, except our having been young together. He smiled and I thought I saw a glimpse of the boy I once knew. "How are you?" I asked. "How are things going?" I was afraid to be specific, afraid of hearing something I didn't want to know.

Shecky still lived in Brooklyn, not far from the old neighborhood, in Starrett City. He'd been married, divorced, had a son he didn't see. I was flooded with sadness. He looked older but he was still the boy he used to be, still after all these years, a boy.

He asked about my mother. He always meant to stop by and say hello but something always interfered.

"How old is she now? " he asked.

"In her eighties," I said proudly. "Her mind still clear."

"Oh, she's more than eighty," said Toby. "She's at least ninety. Probably more."

"How can you say that?" I asked annoyed at her tone, bothered by something behind her certainty. Was she saying my mother was too old, that she had lived too long? "That would make her forty when I was born."

"So. It's possible," said Toby. "How old are you now?"

"You know how old I am. I'm seven years older than you are."

"Well your mother is ninety, if she's a day. I remember my mother telling me how the family lied about her age because she was an old maid when she got married."

"What difference does it make?" I asked. I did not bother to keep the annoyance out of my voice. Why did she care? What difference could it make if my mother was 80 or 90?

I felt a hand on my shoulder. "Everything all right?" Bea asked.

We nodded, murmured words of approval. What else could we do? It is not polite to make a scene at a celebration.

"How is your mother?" Bea asked, her hand pressing into my neck.

"Fine."

"You know she should have come. The least she could have done was come. She knows I have no one else on my side of the family. I offered to put her up in a motel. She could have walked from there. She's not so weak she can't walk."

"She's over eighty," I said. "Things are hard for her."

"Your mother doesn't have it hard. My mother had it hard. Your mother just doesn't care about me. She never cared about me."

"How can you say that?" I asked, remembering the doll carriage, the Heidi dress, the countless admonitions to be nice to Bea, Bea the orphan.

"Maybe she cares, maybe she doesn't. But she always does what she wants. She could have come to my son's Bar Mitzvah. My only living aunt."

"It's hard," I said, looking toward my brother for help. Alvin was pretending he hadn't heard.

"It's not hard if she wanted to," said Bea.

I clenched my teeth holding back the words. I felt caught between what Bea was saying and an unexplained need to defend my mother. I could not understand why Bea was hurt. She knew my mother had trouble standing, let alone walking. She knew my mother had pride: she did not want others to see what she had become. Why was it so important for my mother to be here? Did Bea want to show off, flaunt all she had? Did she want my mother's praise? Yet there was something in what Bea said. My mother could have come. She always did the right thing, tried to make the right impression. She was always proper, she knew how to dress, she gave to charity, she took care of orphans. I had always considered my mother a good person. I thought she just wasn't good to me.

I tried to find something else to talk about, something else to say. There was nothing. How I had envied Bea. My mother had worried about her; my mother had cared about her. How I had wished I were an orphan like Bea, so I could have my mother's love.

I thought I'd put it all behind me, broken the old ties, put my childhood away in a box in much the way my mother used to store old clothes on a shelf in the closet. But there it was again, the same old feelings. Nothing had changed. We grew older, made new friends, established new families, but we were still the children we used to be, still needing what we needed then.

We arrived at my mother's apartment in Brooklyn at seven. We would spend the night, do her shopping in the morning, get her ready for the week, and leave.

My mother had come home. We had not needed to call a doctor at the hotel. She had fallen asleep and awoke from her nap feeling better. But she began missing meals. She sat down in the elevator and could not reach the button to open the door. She complained about the service—there were roaches in the bathroom, the sheets weren't changed. The man next door filled the halls with cigar smoke. There were calls from the management, calls from my mother.

Sam and I had brought her home two weeks early. We thought it would do her good to be in her own place among her own things. I thought we could manage with housekeepers and cleaning help. But there was always some complaint about the women I hired and she fired: one stole a bottle of aspirins; another did not give her fifteen cents change from shopping; one mixed the dairy and meat dishes; another looked at her funny. I couldn't say anything. Our relationship had become a cold war, a wrong word could create an incident.

I kissed her cheek. Sam did the same.

"So you finally came back from the affair."

"Ma, we left as soon as we could."

"And tomorrow. What's the matter, the world will come to an end if you stay with me for a whole day?"

"Would you like some tea?" I asked, ignoring the complaint. "Did you eat yet?"

"Eat. Eat. I ate. How much does an old woman eat?"

"The kitchen looks different," I said," trying to change the subject, Are the curtains new?"

My mother told me where she bought the curtains and how much they cost. She told me her neighbor across the hall had the same curtains she threw out three years ago. She said her neighbor was out of style, her neighbor was cheap.

"So how was the food?" my mother asked.

In great detail, I described the table setting, the food.

"So she served dairy! What does she think, you came for breakfast?" I started to protest. Dairy was in style; it was healthier.

"Cheap. That's what she is. Cheap like her mother."

I shook my head. There was no point in arguing. I envied Sam who had gone into the living room to watch TV.

"And Bea. How is she? Still the same?" I nodded. "So, life is not treating her bad. And her husband, still skinny?" My mother spat out the word as if it were a disease. I nodded again. "So he doesn't eat and she's always on a diet. No wonder they have money."

"Everyone asked for you," I said hoping, for once, to avoid the argument that came on every visit.

"Ask. Ask. What good is ask? Do they call? Do they come to see me? For them, I'm dead already," she whined. Did she miss her relatives? Or were there old scores she wanted to settle?

We sipped our tea in silence. I wondered if Sam was asleep. I wondered if he was leaving us alone for a mother-daughter talk.

"So where did she seat you?"

I explained the seating arrangement. "She had a place for you at the head table," I said still hoping to please.

"So what good is that? My children at one table and me at another."

"She would have called you up to light the first candle." I didn't know why I was doing this. Nothing I could say would please her.

"You think that would give me pleasure when my own daughter did not give me such pleasure."

"But we did not have a Bar Mitzvah for Matthew."

"So, so how could I go to her son's affair?"

She was doing it again, needling, provoking, drawing me into arguments. She was angry because she had missed the Bar Mitzvah. She was angry so she let it out. She didn't miss Bea or the event itself, she missed the status it conferred, being the center of attention. Had she ever loved Bea? Had she ever really loved anyone? Were they all only acts of charity, the expected behavior of an exemplary Jewish woman? Was it all for show—showing the neighbors, showing the family, showing God?

Sam and I slept in the living room, I on the fold out bed, Sam on the sofa. It was little enough we could do. One night out of thousands.

I could not fall asleep. I always found it hard to sleep in unfamiliar places, in strange beds. I found it hard to sleep in my mother's house. I tried to find something to think about, something that had nothing to do with my mother or Bea or my children. But I couldn't. I was like a dog with a bone. I couldn't let it alone.

I kept remembering: my mother and father sharing a bed, Bea and I standing back to back trying to see who was taller, my grandmother preparing for Passover, my father in the hospital, My mother arguing with Uncle Arthur. My mother shopping in the downtown Brooklyn department stores. My mother sewing quilt covers. My mother feeding my sister Tibby. My mother.

. . .

Did she come when I cried and hold me in the dark? I don't remember.

Did she do to me what was done to her?

Did she try to save me from the she she saw in me? I don't know.

She pushed me away when I came too close, and she pulled me back when I went too far.

She did not draw me near enough to lean against her side.

Did she want me taller, shorter, thinner, fatter, smarter, duller?

I tried to please.

Did she want me different, better, worse?

I tried to be like her.

I waited for a sign, a word.

"I almost died when you were born."

"You're too smart for a girl."

"You think you're different? Wait and see."

I wanted her to love me.

On Saturday night we go to Bubbe's house to wish Zayde "a good week." Cousin Bea comes with Sidney and Aunt Gussie.

We are eight cousins on my mother's side, four girls. Tibby is my sister and Aunt Yittel's Tibby is only a baby. So it is just Bea and me. She is six months older so sometimes we're the same age and sometimes we're not. Now she's ten and I'm nine and a half. Bea lives around the corner now, near enough to come to Bubbe's house every Saturday but far enough so I do not see her evey day. We go to the same school. It is Bea's father who died when she was a little girl. That's why she's an orphan.

"Bad girl," my mother used to say when she slapped my hands because I wrested my doll carriage from Bea's grasp. "Remember she's an orphan."

"Here," Aunt Bertha used to say, handing Bea a ribbon or a box of crayons. "If your father were here, he'd buy it for you." I used to wait for her to give me something, but she didn't, not even a smile.

"Sweet child," my grandmother used to say in Yiddish. "If only your father were here to see you."

That's how it used to be. We weren't friends then, only cousins. Now it's one for all and all for one. Now we walk down the street elbows locked, and no one can break the hold. Now she parts her hair on the right, I on the left, and when we put our heads together our parts touch. She has braids and I have braids. We measure ourselves one against the other to show we are the same size. We even have the same shoes: brown Buster Browns for school, black patent Mary Janes for holidays. We are more than friends, more than sisters—twins.

One Saturday night Bea and I go upstairs to my grandmother's parlor to play. We pretend to play the piano. We begin to play doctor. We decide to play love.

"You be the man," she says.

"I don't want to," I say. "I was the man last time."

"Okay," she says. "You can be the lady but this time only."

"First you have to call me up on the telephone," I say. "You have to ask me for a date."

We put one hand to our ears, the other to our mouths—our telephones.

"Hello," Bea begins, then stops. "What's your name?" she asks.

"Claudette," I say, "What's yours?"

"Clark," she answers.

"Hello, Claudette? This is Clark."

"Hello, Clark," I say pitching my voice higher the way I think Claudette Colbert does. I take a deep draught on the imaginary cigarette I hold, a cigarette in a long holder.

"Listen Claudette, I want to see you tonight."

"Tonight? I'm busy."

"How about tomorrow night?"

"I'm busy tomorrow night. Do you think I'm just sitting around waiting for you to call?" I ask the way I imagine Claudette would.

"What do I do now?" Bea whispers.

"You have to send me flowers—and a box of candy. Whitman Sampler. You have to come to my house with the candy and you have to say, 'I can't live without you.'"

"I don't want to say that."

"All right. Let's pretend you did. Now you have to love me."

"Come on," I coach. "You're the man. You're supposed to kiss me. On the lips."

Bea touches her lips to mine. It will have to do. I make believe I push her away; then I let out a big sigh the way they do in the movies.

"Now you're supposed to hug me hard, so hard I can't breathe. But we can skip that. Then I'm supposed to lie down on the sofa and you kneel at my side."

Bea sits down on the floor.

"Bea, you're supposed to be on your knees. You're supposed to feel me up. You're supposed to touch my bust."

"Do I have to?"

"Yes. And kiss my arms and my neck. I read it in Aunt Bertha's magazine."

Bea puts her mouth on my arm. She leaves a wet spot.

"Not like that. Do it nice, say something nice."

Bea makes a face and wrinkles her nose as if she's holding a damp dish rag. I close my eyes and imagine Bea a man feeling me up. I know I'm supposed to act hard to get; I don't know why exactly, except a man will not want a cow if he can get the milk for free.

Bea picks her head up. "Let's stop," she says. "I don't like this."

I sigh. I think she doesn't want to be the man. We both know it's better to be the woman in the game of love.

"Millie. Bea," my mother calls. "What are you doing upstairs? Come down now."

On Wednesday when I come from school my mother is waiting. "We're going downtown," she says. "We need to buy you a dress for Cousin Bluma's wedding."

"Everyone knows, " my mother says, "things from the store are better." She sighs and narrows her eyes and sucks her cheeks in. I know she is thinking how much it costs.

We take the elevated train. I count the stations until we get off at Nevins Street. We walk past Martin's and A&S to May's Department Store. My mother says she knows the owner. "You can get the best buys here," she says, the emphasis on the "you", in the teacher voice she uses when she wants me to remember.

My mother marches straight ahead through pocketbooks and bathrobes. She tucks her gloves inside her pocketbook. She wears her spiked heel shoes. She has good legs. She says legs are a sign of breeding. She marches straight ahead and up the escalator to Children's Clothes.

Up and down the aisles she goes, pushing dresses from one side to the other. She holds one up, then another. "A rag," she says. Then, "Here. This is it. Taffeta." She holds the rust colored dress up for me to see: short, puffed sleeves, lace around the neck, a black vest with velvet laces. My dream dress, just like one Heidi wears in the movies.

"Oh Ma!" I say.

She holds the dress against me. "Yes," she says. "That looks good. We have to make a good impression. No one should know how low I have fallen." She means she has to put on a show even though my father lost his money.

"A perfect fit," says my mother. "The right dress shows who you are." She stands behind me as I look in the dressing room mirror.

A downtown dress is special. My dresses come from Mrs. Yellin's store or from my mother's sewing machine, from the remnants she buys or has left over from making quilt covers. She goes downtown, buys a dress, copies it for half the price, then she returns the dress before the seven day money back guarantee is over. But this time, she will not return the dress.

I do not watch while my mother pays. I am busy imagining myself at the wedding. I wear a velvet ribbon in my hair. People point. They say, "Oh," and, "Ah," when they see my dress. I imagine Cousin Bea's surprise. How happy she will be for me. I have a special dress; now I am a special girl.

Uncle Arthur has a Ford, but there isn't room for us, so Jack the Boarder gets a car from a friend to drive us to the wedding. "You're looking good," Jack says to me. "A few more years and you can start dating," he winks.

We drive to Eastern Parkway. We go in the doorway and up a long flight of stairs. My mouth waters. I smell the food waiting behind the screen that hides the tables—*kishka*, chopped liver, roast chicken. I smell powder and perfume, cigars and whiskey, smells of a wedding.

I smooth my dress, puff out my chest. I think I'm getting a bust. I want to grow up. I want to be a lady.

I listen to the music of the three piece band. I imagine the day I'm a bride, and everyone is waiting for me to be led to the canopy.

"Millie," says a cousin who lives in Queens, "how nice you look."

"You're getting big," says her husband. "Before you know it, we'll dance at your wedding."

"She has plenty of time," says my grandmother's cousin's daughter whose husband left her. "Marry in haste, repent in leisure." She pats my shoulder as she walks away.

"Such a big girl," says a woman from a group surrounding my mother. "To think Sorke has such a big girl." I look at my mother; she is pleased with what the woman says.

"That's a beautiful dress," says Cousin Dora, a little woman who has come all the way from Chattanooga, Tennessee. "Did your mother make it?"

"Can't you tell it's from a store?" asks the woman on her right. "Sorke sews well but not as good as this."

"It's too old for her," my Aunt Yittel says.

"Hey Millie," says my cousin Jerry. He is six feet tall and eighteen years old. "Still a boy," my mother says. Marriage makes you a man but a bust makes you a lady. "Keep growing like that and next year we'll dance close," he says. I pretend not to hear.

Cousin Leo races past, he's chasing Alvin. I don't run after them. I'm too old to act like a kid.

I walk back and forth on the landing hoping to see Bea the minute she comes in. I check the coat room, look in the powder room, straighten the laces on my vest as I pass the mirror. I smile at myself as I smooth my hair and pat my curls. I am impatient for Bea to see me.

Then there she is. Bea!

Everything stops. The sound goes off while the picture keeps going. All I see is Bea. She is wearing my dress: velvet vest, ruffled hem, puffed sleeves—the very dress. Exactly. Except hers is blue.

I close my eyes and count to three. Maybe it's a mistake, a trick played on me by my own eyes, something I can erase, like a movie where they fool you with things that aren't there. I open my eyes. This is no movie.

"Look," says Channa Raisel, Bubbe's cousin who has come all the way from Boston. "They have the same dress. Isn't that adorable?"

"Oh," says my great Aunt Ethel, the one who lives in the Bronx, "just like twins."

"It must be Sorke's doing," says a man I don't know. "She would do something like this."

I see my mother, her black hair marcelled, her blue eyes pale like water. She is smiling. "It's nothing," I hear her say. "My brother's daughter. Could I do less for her than for my own daughter? How else should a sister be?"

Things click into place. She's always nice to Bea; she's nicer to Bea than to me. My mother.

Everywhere people look. They smile, they nod and poke. We are a novelty, the twin cousins.

I look at Bea. She doesn't smile. Is she angry about the dress? It's not my fault we have the same dress.

"Let's go to the powder room," I say, "and look in the mirror."

"No," she says. "Go away. My mother says you're bad."

Aunt Gussie takes Bea's hand. "Come," she says. "Let's find our table." Aunt Gussie doesn't look at me.

I stand near the doorway. I watch my mother talk to this one and that one. I watch how people smile at her. She looks happy. She worries about how things look. She cares what people say and think. She doesn't care about me, I tell myself. I feel a stiffness deep inside, hard and cold like stone.

Bea sits down near her mother. She spreads her Heidi dress across her knees. Aunt Gussie is talking to my mother. I see them look at me.

As soon as we get home, my mother tells me to wait until she puts Tibby to sleep. She has her mean face. Something bad has happened.

"What have you done?" she asks when she comes back into the kitchen.

I stand in the doorway. I say nothing. I have done so many things, I don't know which one she means.

"You played dirty with Cousin Bea. You dirty girl. It's a sin the things you did."

"I didn't do anything," I say trying to remember just what it was we did, what part was the sin.

"She did it," I say. I don't mean to blame Bea, only to tell what happened. It takes two to play love.

"And you? What did you do? Did she force you? Did she tie you up?"

I stand in the doorway and say nothing. The doorway is safe. If I see my mother go for the strap, I can run away. If my mother just sits and yells, I can stand and wait.

"Sin lover! Sin lover!" my brother hisses from the living room where he has been listening.

"No more love. No more dirty games. Hear? And no more playing with Bea. She's just like her mother. No good. My brother's daughter, but she talks like her mother. The whole family she told! Everyone she told!"

"No more." My mother stands up. It is decided. "You don't play with her or with Sidney. And don't go there."

I don't understand what is wrong. I don't understand why my mother is angry. I read about love in a magazine. I read about love in *The Good Earth.* I read how O Lan squatted in the fields and her baby came out. Like a bowel. I don't understand, but I'm happy there's no strap.

On Monday I go to Hebrew School early. Abie and Philip and Shecky and I go to the haunted house next to the *cheder.*

The boys have cocoons in a shoe box. They are waiting for the butterflies to hatch. I want to see. We climb through the boarded up door and walk through the part where the store used to be. Two boys from the 8th grade are there. One has a cigarette in his lips. The other boy is named Butch. He has blonde hair and his own two wheel bicycle.

"You have to pay," the boy with the cigarette says.

"I don't have any money," I say.

"You can pay with other things," the boy says and laughs. I move closer to Abie.

"Here. You want to feel the stick?" says the boy. I move closer to the shoe box.

"Not that stick, this one," says the boy. I look. His thing is sticking out of his pants. I look at Butch. He turns away.

"Dirty bastard," I say and run out.

When I get to Hebrew School, I go to the back to the toilet. Abie Perlmutter is standing there. "Do you want to see my thing?" he asks.

"It's no thing," I say and push him away. When I come out, we read about Joshua and how Rahab the harlot hid his spies and how she put a red ribbon in the window to keep her house safe from the vengeance of Joshua.

On Tuesday when I come home from school, the Rebbe is in the kitchen with my mother. I go to change my clothes.

The Rebbe leaves.

"What will I do with you?" my mother asks when I go to the Frigidaire for a glass of milk.

I wait to hear the new complaint.

She tells me the Rebbe said I am to old to go to *cheder* with all boys. "You're smart, he says," my mother explains, "but since you're not going to be Bar Mitzvahed, there's no use your staying in *cheder.* If you want to learn, he said, you should go to Talmud Torah."

I stand near the kitchen sink, drinking my milk and watching my mother. Is she angry? Will I be punished? I think of the Rebbe. What did I do that he wants to send me away? I remember Abie near the toilet. Did Abie tell what I said? Did Abie tell what I said in the haunted house?

My mother sits sewing a hem on my sister's dress. She does not look angry. Will she send me to Talmud Torah? I want to go. I want to learn. I want to go where my brother can't. He is going to be Bar Mitzvahed but I am smarter than he is. I can read the commentaries in the Torah and he is still trying to learn his *aleph beis.*

I finish my milk. I do not go to Hebrew School that day.

On Saturday night, eight people sit around Bubbe's dining room table, six grownups and Cousin Bea and me. I have gone by myself to the corner store to buy the lox and bagels. Bea didn't even ask to go. She didn't argue about being older, or about being an orphan. She just sat near her mother, her head down. I think she is still mad at me for playing love. When I went to play the Victrola, she didn't ask to hear Barney Google. Something is wrong.

I sit next to my mother eating my bagel, spread with cream cheese and dotted with lox. I try to get a piece of lox in each bite.

"So quiet," says Uncle Arthur, looking at Bea. "What's the matter with her?" he asks Aunt Gussie.

Everyone looks at Bea. She hides her face against her mother's arm. I stop eating.

"She's having a little trouble with her bowel," says Aunt Gussie.

"What kind of trouble?" asks my mother.

"She can't go," says Aunt Gussie.

"What is she saying?" my grandmother asks. They have been talking in English.

"It's Bea," says Aunt Bertha. "She's constipated."

"Constipated? Does she eat prunes in the morning?

"Prunes!" says my mother disdainfully. "That's for prevention. Prunes won't help when you're already constipated. Milk of magnesia. That'll fix her." My mother nods her head.

"She won't take it," says Aunt Gussie. "I tried and she started to choke and spit up. What could I do? I couldn't hurt her."

"Better to choke a little than to be stopped up," says my mother. "She'll poison herself."

"What kind of talk is this at the table?" asks my grandfather. Uncle Arthur laughs. "It's women's talk," he says.

"So," says my grandmother. "You're finished. You don't have to stay and listen."

My grandfather says his prayer and leaves the table. Everyone sits and looks at Bea, her face and head hidden now in her mother's lap.

"How many days has it been?" Aunt Bertha asks.

"Three," says Aunt Gussie.

A hush falls on the table. Three days. I look at Bea. Did God stuff her up because she played love? Will God punish me? I decide to take milk of magnesia before I go to sleep, even though I had a bowel movement this morning.

Every morning, my mother asks if I moved my bowel. She asks if it was the same as yesterday. She asks if it is hard or soft. Sometimes she comes to look before I flush the toilet. She says, "A healthy bowel means a healthy person." Sometimes she gives me mineral oil to take. I like it. I lick the spoon.

"Three days," Uncle Arthur repeats. He looks serious. Does he remember Uncle Kalman, Bea's father? Did Uncle Kalman's stomach get sick too? Uncle Kalman died from consumption. I think consumption has something to do with eating and eating has to do with the stomach. The stomach is a serious matter. I put my half eaten piece of bagel down. I do not want any more.

"So why don't you make an enema?" Uncle Arthur asks. "In a few minutes everything will be over."

"She says she doesn't want it. She doesn't let me," says Aunt Gussie.

"Nonsense," says Uncle Arthur, his face a sneer. "A girl eleven years old, a *pisherke*, to tell you what she wants. I'll give her a say. Right across the mouth." He slams his hand down on the table so hard his tea glass jumps and shakes.

I stare at Bea. She looks back at me. I look away. I'm glad Bea is constipated. She told and now she's being punished. I believe in justice. I'm happy when justice triumphs. I am also relieved. For once I am not the criminal standing before the court. That's how I think of Saturday night at Bubbe's house. It's like a court where everything we did during the week is reported and weighed, reviewed and discussed. Then there's the judgment. Usually the judgment is in words, words that cut deep like a knife, leaving a scab waiting to be picked. Tonight it is Bea who is the criminal.

"Three days, you say?" Uncle Arthur asks. "Why wait? Make the enema now."

No one disagrees. It is decided. Bea will have an enema.

My mother gets up first. Then Aunt Bertha. Then Aunt Gussie who pushes Bea up. I hang back, hoping no one will notice me; I do not want to be sent outside.

We walk up the stairs in a long line. My grandmother walks slowly. "Why are you creeping?" asks my mother. Uncle Arthur stays downstairs. This is women's work.

Aunt Gussie takes Bea into Aunt Bertha's room.

Then my mother and Aunt Bertha go into the bathroom. I scoot across the hall to my grandmother's room. It is dark. Two beds line the wall on either side of a window that opens into Uncle Arthur's room. His room is the sun porch at the back of the house. Zayde is sleeping in one of the beds. I am afraid to stay in the room. I am afraid my grandfather will wake up and then he'll be angry.

Aunt Bertha's room is next to my grandmother's room, a doorway opens to Uncle Arthur's room. Quickly I run through it into Uncle Arthur's room. I want to see them give an enema. I've never had to have one. I look through the doorway. I see Cousin Bea lying on Aunt Bertha's bed.

"We need someone tall," says Aunt Bertha. "Jerry would be good. He's the tallest."

"He's not here. We need someone," my mother says again. She is holding the enema bag.

"Arthur, Arthur," Aunt Bertha calls. "We need you."

Uncle Arthur stands on a chair. "The higher the better," my mother says.

I look at Bea. Her mother is stroking her hair. "Nice girl. Pretty girl," Aunt Gussie says in Yiddish.

"Well? Is she ready?" Uncle Arthur yells. "I can't stand here all night."

Aunt Gussie rolls up Bea's dress and takes off her bloomers. She turns Bea on her stomach. Bea begins to cry and scream. She kicks her feet.

"Hold her feet, Sorke. Hold her feet," Uncle Arthur says to my mother.

"Wait," my mother says. "Did you use vaseline?"

Aunt Bertha shows my mother the nozzle of the enema bag. It is longer than I imagined.

"So what are you waiting for?" asks Uncle Arthur.

Aunt Bertha goes over to the bed. Bea screams and screams. I feel scared. I hold my ears and close my eyes. I open my eyes but I keep my ears closed. I want to see what happens.

I can't see too much. Aunt Bertha bends over. Uncle Arthur holds his arm up high. My mother holds Bea's feet. Bubbe holds her arms. "Now," says Aunt Bertha.

Uncle Arthur pulls the catch on the hose. I can see Bea screaming.

"Enough already," I hear my grandmother say. I have uncovered my ears.

"Hold it in," says my mother. "It's no good if she doesn't hold it in for a minute."

The minute is over. Aunt Gussie walks Bea to the bathroom. Aunt Bertha helps.

"Such a *tzimmes* over an enema," says my mother. I don't know who she's talking to. "If she were my child, it would never come to this."

Everyone is waiting to see what happens. "Well?" asks Uncle Arthur.

"Finished," says Aunt Bertha.

"*Mazel tov*," says Uncle Arthur and goes downstairs.

I make myself small and sneak out of the room. My mother looks the way she does when she wins a game of chess from Mr. Greenberg, the insurance man, as if she knows a secret, as if she's someone special.

Uncle Arthur and I sit at the dining room table.

"Well," he asks, "do you need an enema, too?" I shake my head.

On Sunday I go into my mother's bedroom. Now that we're older, Alvin sleeps in the living room, Tibby and I sleep together, and my mother and father share a bed. Usually they sleep head to foot the way my mother and I did when we shared that narrow bed. Today my mother and father are lying side be side.

I stand in the doorway looking at my mother and father. My father is smiling. My mother looks funny. I have come to ask my mother how many rolls I should buy for breakfast.

Every Sunday my mother gets rolls for breakfast. Every Sunday she buys three rolls, an eighth of a pound of lox which she fries with onions and eggs, and the Yiddish newspapers. In the summer she likes to go early. She looks in people's gardens and sees what flowers they have. Sometimes she asks for the seeds.

Now that I'm almost eleven I am the one who goes to the store. Still every Sunday I ask how many rolls and how much lox.

"How many rolls?" I ask.

"Three," says my mother. "You know it's three. Why do you ask?"

She is angry at something.

My father smiles. One hand is under the covers. I see it move. I see him pinch my mother.

"Stop it," says my mother. She pushes at his arm.

My father laughs.

His hand moves again.

My mother slaps the cover where his hand is. She does not slap hard.

"Stop," she says.

My father laughs.

"Stop," I say. "You're hurting her."

I don't know why but suddenly I'm angry at my father; I'm angry at my mother.

"Go," my mother says to me. "Go get the rolls."

7

"**O**pen it for me." My mother pointed to the container set on the tray. She waited, unfolding the paper napkin, spreading it out in a diamond shape with one point stuck inside her nightgown where years before the cleavage of her breasts had been. We were in her hospital room.

I had decided to come after UPS delivered a package for Sam from Julie. "Open it," he had said on the phone from his office. "You don't need my permission to open a package from Julie." It was a brightly striped pair of walking shorts and an orange shirt to match. "For Dad on his birthday," the card read. "Have a perfect birthday for a perfect Dad. Sorry I can't be with you. Love always, Julie."

I was happy for Sam. And for Julie. I felt sorry for myself. I thought I had been a good mother, but I couldn't say I had been perfect.

I had come early, at dinner time, so there would be something for my mother and me to do, something to focus on, and thus avoid the anger that lay between us like a third rail. I had come on Friday night so we could welcome the Sabbath together.

When her stay at the hotel hadn't worked out, I thought we could manage with housekeepers, cleaning help, home attendants. I had even hired a Soviet emigre so they would have something in common. I thought it would be easier for all of us if my mother were in her own home, among her own things. I was willing to come twice a week, three times if I had to. But the calls started again. She couldn't sleep. She couldn't eat. She couldn't breathe. Then came the alarming call: Her feet were swollen, she was weak, she could not get out of bed.

I watched while they wrapped her in blankets and put her in an ambulance. I watched as they wheeled her into Receiving. She was quiet then, still. She did not complain.

"Don't worry," I said. "Everything will be all right. They'll take care of you." She had turned her head away. She looked so small, frail, like a baby.

My mother always believed you could wish things on yourself. She had wished to outlive all those she thought had done her harm. And she had. "Be careful what you wish," she used to say. "You could be sorry." I believed her belief. Now I wondered if it were my fault she was here, my fault, because I had not been a good daughter, because I had wished her dead.

She sat in a chair, a sheet tied around her middle to keep her from falling. The nurses did not want to be held responsible if she fell, so they put her in a makeshift high chair, a high chair for grownups, for old mothers.

"What is it?" she asked pointing to the food. "Where is the fork? Give me the fork," she demanded.

I gave her the fork and answered her question. "It's chicken," I said. I cut the flesh into bite size pieces. "It looks good."

She moved her head down, her eyes close to the tray. "Is there juice? I want juice." Her tone was petulant, demanding. She reminded me of Tibby when she was sick and feverish; she reminded me of a child, helpless, afraid.

"I'm going blind," she said. "I tell you I can't see. You don't believe me, I can tell."

I handed her her reading glasses so she could see the food. She had two pair of glasses, one for reading and one for seeing. She was too vain for bifocals. "I don't need them," she had said, "not like you."

"Oh," she said, seeing the food. The horned rimmed tinted lenses magnified her eyes. They were blue, the color of sky, the color of water. Blue.

"What should I eat first?" she asked. I moved the fruit cup toward her. She always liked the sweet first.

"What's this?" she asked ignoring the fruit, and plunging the plastic fork into the compartment tray, then thrust it eagerly into her mouth.

"Potatoes," I said.

"Good." She ate some of the potato and began on the chicken. There were string beans as well. I remembered she didn't like string beans.

"Do you need help?" I asked.

"No. I can do it myself." She took another bite of chicken. She liked to eat one food at a time.

"I dropped a piece. I dropped it." She sounded upset, as if she expected to be punished.

I knelt on the floor and looked for the piece of chicken near the feet clad in Sam's cast off athletic socks. She would not wear the slippers provided by the hospital or those I'd bought. She wanted her own slippers, the ones worn down at the heel, the ones with a place for her bunions. She wanted her own slippers but not here in the hospital—they'd be stolen here. She wanted her own slippers in her own home.

I put the piece of chicken in the trash can. I remembered how she always made chicken and soup on Friday night. Boiled chicken, never roasted. She always liked chicken. Even at weddings where my father always asked for sirloin tips, she had chicken. Even at my sister Tibby's son's wedding in the Temple in Newton where they had fetticini Alfredo and sherbert between courses, my mother had chicken, complaining that the roasted chicken was too tough, boiled chicken would have been softer.

My daughter Julie had come to the wedding. She looked lovely in a violet dress that darkened the color of her eyes. "A beauty," my mother had said. "But what good is looks? She'll never get married." I was stunned.

"How can you say that?" I asked. Julie was only twenty six then.

"I can tell," my mother said. "You'll never have *naches* from her. You'll never have that kind of *naches* from either of your children."

I had gone to stand by Julie; I wanted to protect her. I believed what my mother said. I believed my mother had the power to see the future. I was afraid her words could come true.

She finished the chicken and belched.

"Try the string beans," I urged. "They're good for you."

"No," she said firmly. Explanations were not necessary.

"Drink some tea," I suggested. I watched while her trembling fingers slowly lifted the paper cup.

"No sugar," she said.

"They forgot." I apologized for the nurses and the hospital. I went to the room next door. "Any spare sugar?" I asked. Both women shook their heads. I went to the room on the other side where the patient was known for hiding sugar packets in her dresser drawer. I went to the dresser and took out two packets.

When I came back, my mother had finished the tea.

"How about the bread?" I asked.

"I ate bread for lunch," she said. "It's enough."

I bit my tongue. I had been about to ask if she was still worried about her weight. I had been about to complicate the visit.

"I'll get you some jelly," I said as I walked toward the other bed. My mother's roommate lay staring at the ceiling. Her son was a cancer specialist and so was her grandson. She was dying of cancer.

I took the strawberry jam. I told the woman she had orange and grape left. I told her she had jelly packets from breakfast and lunch on her dresser. She had never spoken. I didn't know if she could hear, but I thanked her anyway.

I spread the jam on the white bread and handed it to my mother. "I want a roll," she said.

"They serve rolls on Sunday," I said.

She folded the bread in half and ate it like a sandwich. I noticed that two of her teeth were chipped. They were false teeth but the chips made them seem real. I wondered if they could be fixed.

She stuffed the remains of the bread in her mouth and sucked the jam from her fingers. She lifted her cup to drink some tea but it was empty. She held it out to show me she had finished. She removed the napkin and looked down at her nightgown. "Millie," she asked me, "is it clean?"

"Yes," I said. "Clean."

The nurse came for the tray.

"You didn't make a mess," she said to my mother. "You did a good job. You were a good girl."

My mother beamed.

How it could have been!
How it should have been!
I did not take her home to die;
I did not sit and hold her hand;
I was not the daughter she wanted.

Anger fills the space once held by pain.
She followed the rules: She fed me, clothed me, gave me a place to sleep. But she was not the mother I needed.
People remember the best things. I forget.
People forget the worst things. I remember.

As the mother so the daughter.

When we were in kindergarten, Marilyn sat all the way in front. Now she sits in the row next to me. Seats are assigned according to our place in line, how tall we are, and we are the same size. Whenever "Take Partners" is announced, we reach for each other's hands. Usually we're the first ones ready.

We don't have much to say to each other: I read a lot; she is popular. I have a paper doll family and Skating Sally; she has real roller skates, and a wardrobe of clothes she keeps in her own closet. She has been to Washington to visit an aunt who works for the government, and to Vermont for a vacation, Vermont, the Green Mountain State. Her mother was born in America, my mother is an immigrant. Her mother shops in New York, my mother buys in Brooklyn. On her birthday she ate in a restaurant, on my birthday, my mother said, "This is your birthday in the English calendar." "This is not your real birthday." Our lives are not at all the same.

We don't even look alike. She has long, light brown hair that her mother puts up in rags every night. Every day she comes to school with long fat curls. My hair, which I braid myself, is dark and wiry, the ends held in place by rubber bands.

Everyone knows Marilyn should not be in the smart class. But no one cares. Marilyn is good, quiet and neat. The teacher says Marilyn is polite. Her dress is always starched, her stockings don't sag, her handkerchief is in her pocket, not safety pinned to her dress.

Marilyn is a Peppette pledge. The Peppettes are a social club. They wear purple jackets with "Peppettes" written in gold letters on the back, their names embroidered over the right breast pocket: Gloria, Vivian, Anita and Rachel. I imagine my name written in gold: Millie.

You can't be a Peppette until you are in the sixth grade, although you can be a pledge at the end of fifth grade. Marilyn's jacket does not say "Peppettes" or her name, but everyone knows Marilyn is a pledge. It is through Marilyn I hope to become a pledge. It is only through Marilyn that any of us, Doris or Blanche or I, can become pledges.

Whenever it is my turn to choose up sides for punch ball, I choose Marilyn first. When we have to exchange test papers, I exchange with Marilyn. I always believe her when she says it's an eight, not a three, a one not a seven. I always agree when she says it's an i, not an e. When I'm chosen to be Head Monitor, I pick Marilyn to be my aide.

One day Marilyn invites me home for lunch.

"Go," says my mother. "But don't let it go to your head. An Auerbach pees like everyone else." She means I shouldn't be afraid. She means I'm just as good. "Money goes. Here today, gone tomorrow," says my mother. She makes a fuss, but I can tell she's pleased. She's letting me go even though it means she will have to take Tibby and walk my brother home for lunch.

Marilyn lives in a private house, the bedrooms upstairs. The houses are tight against each other, no alleys in between. There are porches with wooden railings painted green and white. Just like the houses in the movies.

Marilyn has her own key. "My mother plays mah jong in the afternoon," she says. Through the foyer we come into a long, dark room, the curtains drawn. There are rugs, draperies, polished wood, a baby grand piano. I want to touch the keys, to hear the sound it makes. Instead, I follow Marilyn through the dining room into an up-to-date kitchen with gray and pink flowered paper on the walls, grey and pink linoleum on the floor, the glass doors of the cabinets painted over, the table covered with pink oil cloth. I try to remember everything so I can tell my mother.

"It'll only take a minute," she says. We have to be back in school early since we're monitors.

"Sit over there," she says, pointing to the far end of the table. I do as I am told.

She puts some water up to boil, opens a can of baked beans and puts them in a saucepan. She spreads two napkins out on the table. "To catch the crumbs," she says as she lays a plate on each napkin. She folds another napkin, sets it with a knife and fork near the plate. "It's the fork on the left, the knife on the right," she says. Then she puts the specials in the boiling water. Specials and beans, a treat reserved for special occasions. For lunch!

We eat in silence. I am careful not to spill anything and make a mess. I drink seltzer, Marilyn has milk. Her mother thinks kosher is not necessary in modern countries with good hygiene.

When we finish, Marilyn washes the dishes and the pots, crumples up the napkins. "You have to push your chair in when you're done," she says.

We're back in school just in time. On Fridays, after we get our homework for Monday and after we clean the room, we have story hour. I have been chosen to read to the class. I sit in Miss Davis' big chair and I read from *Robin Hood and His Merry Men* while Miss Davis does her roll book. Friday is my favorite day.

On Monday we have our arithmetic test. I am the first one finished. Arithmetic is easy. I bring my paper up to Miss Davis. She puts 100 across the top. I go back to my seat, to wait for the class to finish. First one, then another of my classmates bring their papers up to be marked. There is the sound of someone crying. I turn around. It is Marilyn. She failed the test.

"Don't cry, Marilyn," I whisper.

"Who's talking?" Miss Davis' voice is angry. "Who's talking during a test?"

Everyone looks at me. I raise my hand.

"Bring your paper here at once," Miss Davis says.

I carry my paper up to her desk.

She has her red pencil in her hand. Swoosh. She makes a big zero on the paper.

"That's what you get for talking during a test," she says.

I am turned to stone. I cannot find the words to say; I cannot sort the things I feel.

I go back to my seat, my face hot.

Someone snickers. I look at Marilyn, she looks away.

I look down at my paper. A big red zero.

"That's not fair," I call out. "I got 100 for the work. If you want to punish me, give me a D in conduct. You can't make 100 into a zero."

No one moves. The class stares first at me, then at the teacher.

"You've got a fresh mouth," says Miss Davis. "You need to learn a lesson. Apologize."

I don't know what to do, what I'm supposed to apologize for. I don't understand how my talking in class can change my right answers into wrong ones.

I am sent to the assistant principal.

My heart pounds; my hands feel cold; there's sweat on my forehead. I'm afraid.

Miss Calahan wears a suit. Her hair is bobbed; her eyeglasses hang from a chain around her neck.

"Well, what have you done?" she asks. I explain about the 100 and the zero. I say it isn't fair.

"You can't talk back to a teacher," says Miss Calahan. "You have to apologize for being fresh." I put my lips together like my mother does. I was not fresh; I will not apologize.

I am banished from school until my mother comes.

"Apologize," my mother orders. "Tell her you're sorry." She doesn't want the neighbors to know I am bad. She does not want to go up to school and argue with the teachers. "I have more important things to do." I think about Mrs. Feiffer, I think about the lawyer. I, too, believe in justice. I put my lips together. I will not apologize.

The next morning I get dressed for school, but I stay home. My mother walks my brother.

"Apologize," she orders when she comes home. "They said they won't let you go to school until you apologize."

I stand and wait. I cannot apologize for something I didn't do.

"Stubborn," says my mother. "She's so stubborn." She talks about me as if I weren't there. She's talking to the world. She's telling the world what a problem I am. "If she's not careful," my mother continues, "she'll end up in real trouble. If she's not careful, she'll end up in the electric chair."

I spend the day alone. I play with the dolls I put away for Tibby, the stuffed doll I made myself and Skating Sally. I make new outfits for my paper dolls. I read *What Katy Did at School*. I sit in the closet and pretend I'm grown up and can do as I please. I think about school. I look at the clock and think: 9 o'clock—milk money collection, 10 o'clock—recess, 11 o'clock—current events; 12 o'clock—lunch.

My mother goes about her chores. She shops, scrubs potatoes, gets the laundry back, hangs it out, the pulley squeals when she moves the line, like chalk on the blackboard. We do not speak. She is punishing me for being home.

Then she yells, *"Machashaffa!* Witch! Bastard! Deformed monster! You should walk in the street and the earth should open up and swallow you."

I run into the kitchen.

My mother is standing at the open window, the wet wash on a chair, the clothespin bag open. She stares across the alley at Mrs. Feiffer's laundry.

"That *machashaffa,"* she says again, her eyes squinting the way they do when she threads a needle, her jaw sticking out. "Shit. Shit. She's nothing but shit. Does she think she can insult me like that? My father was a merchant. My grandfather was a scholar. People came from all over to talk to him. We come from genteel people. Refined. Very refined."

I still don't see what has upset her. She always has a reason for her anger even if I don't understand it.

"Look!" My mother points. "Look how she insults us!" I look. All I see is Mrs. Feiffer's wash. "Look!" says my mother again. "Look where she hung the underwear."

I look. I see union suits hanging right in front of Mrs. Feiffer's window, across from our kitchen window.

"She did it on purpose," says my mother. "She's telling me to kiss her ass. She's still making fun of me because I lost the case."

Then I remember. There is a sequence to the hanging of the wash. The underwear goes first, right after the knot on the clothesline, so the underwear will end up all the way in back, over the yard, where no one can see. After the underwear go the nightgowns, then the towels, then the handkerchiefs. The ladies' underwear goes in the house over the bathtub.

"I'll fix her!" says my mother.

I go back to the hallway to draw a house with a chimney on the roof. I make a picket fence around it and draw a girl inside the fence. It is almost three o'clock; soon I can go to Talmud Torah.

When I come home, the women are outside talking. They whisper and laugh. Mrs. Schecter nudges Miss Mintz. She points. "Here comes the genteel child of the genteel mother."

I walk up the stairs to the hallway. My grandmother is standing at the bottom of the stairs. She is yelling at my mother.

"Meshugene! Crazy one! What have you done? The whole street is talking about you."

"Go in your house," my mother says. "You have nothing to worry about. They're not talking about you."

I walk up the stairs. I try to make myself small, to stay out of the way. I do not know what has happened. My mother looks pleased. Her eyes are big and bright, her face is red.

"I fixed her," she says. "She can kiss my ass and rub her nose in it."

The kitchen window is open. I see the wash hanging on the line. I see my father's union suit hanging in front of our window. My mother has broken the rule: she has done what Mrs. Feiffer did, she put the underwear in front of the window.

That evening we go downstairs to my grandmother's house for tea.

"Well, Sorke," says Uncle Arthur. "You made a *tzimmes* today." He smiles as if he heard a joke.

My mother begins to smile, then she stops. Her face is still smiling even though her lips are not. "A *tzimmes*? No, not a *tzimmes.* Just settling a score."

"But shit!" says my uncle. "Where did you get it?"

My mother shakes her head. "Some things better should remain a secret," she giggles.

"A *shanda*, shame!" says my grandmother. "What will people think?"

"What kind of *shanda?*" asks my mother. "When you're dealing with lower class people, you have to act so they'll understand."

"But shit," says my uncle. "Who would have thought to put shit on the underwear?"

I look at my mother. I feel my mouth open. How did she do it? Did she take it out of the toilet? Did she touch it? I feel my mouth open wider. I close it. I think my mother is not like other mothers.

"Come on, Sorke! Tell the truth! You can tell your own brother. What did you put on the underwear?"

"Enough, already," says Aunt Bertha. "It's disgusting."

"What's disgusting? A little dirt from the backyard? Let her think it's shit. I wouldn't dirty my hands for her."

"Dirt from the yard? Who would have thought it?" says Uncle Arthur. "Dirt from the yard. So, Millie," he turns to me, "what do you think of your mother now?"

I look down at the table. I don't know what to say.

By Thursday, I'm anxious to go back to school. I have already missed assembly and library. Thursday is bank money and nature. My mother is teaching me to play chess. She does not say anything about apologizing. She doesn't care if I stay home. She doesn't care what happens to me. I want to go back to school. I have nothing to do. At three o'clock I walk to the corner to watch while my brother crosses the street

I see Marilyn on the other side of the street. She is walking with Doris and Blanche. Their arms are linked. Marilyn wears her purple jacket. "Marilyn, Marilyn," I call. She pretends she doesn't hear me.

On Friday, I dress for school. I wait for my mother to go to the bakery for challah. Then I go to school. I go to see Miss Callahan.

I tell her I am sorry I was fresh, I'm sorry I spoke during a test. I will apologize to Miss Davis. I don't say anything about the zero. I don't say I think Miss Davis was wrong.

I wait for Miss Davis outside the teachers' room.

"Here's your problem student," I hear a teacher say.

"Yes, Millie," says Miss Davis. "Are you here to see me?"

"I'm sorry I was fresh," I say. All the teachers stand and listen.

"Anything else?"

I hesitate. "I'm sorry I spoke during a test."

"Anything else?"

I shake my head. I'm not sorry for anything else.

"All right," she says. "Let's go back to class."

As soon as we take our seats, Miss Davis announces a special treat. She will let us hear a story while she finishes her clerical work. The class is pleased. Some children applaud. She picks me to sit in the big chair and read to the class. "You can start now," she says as if nothing happened, as if this was a regular week.

Right and wrong don't matter, I tell myself. All that matters is following the rules, doing what teachers want. Except in books. Except when you're grown up, then you can do what you want.

I open *Robin Hood and His Merry Men*. I begin to read.

My mother always said, "Trouble follows trouble." God must have been listening. I came home from the hospital to a call from Julie in Chicago.

"Ma," she said. "I'm pregnant."

Julie's voice was strong, even, the same kind of voice that had once announced an A in art. "Now don't say anything. Just listen. I'm going to have an abortion. My mind's made up. I thought you'd want to know."

That's when the feeling started, as if I'd been shot in the heart, when I began to think that maybe my mother was right. The apple does not fall far from the tree. Julie was giving me the same kind of pain my mother said I gave her.

What could I say? What *should* I say?

Hesitantly I began. "Are you all right?"

"Fine. It's nothing. It's all arranged."

"I'll be there. Tell me where."

"You don't have to. But if you want to..."

Then the address, the time, the particulars. Like a visit to the dentist, an appointment for a manicure.

"It happens all the time now, Ma. It's not like it was in your day."

I held back my words.

"It's nothing. Takes an hour."

I bit my tongue.

"Some of my friends have had two and three."

I choked on my disappointment.

An abortion. For a moment it seemed worse than a miscarriage, worse than a dead baby. Then I would be able to cry, grieve, mourn. It's no one's fault, I could say. Next time it will be different. Next time...

I was surprised at my reaction. A woman had the right to decide, I believed. I could not have made such a decision, but that did not mean it wasn't right for others. For others, not for Julie, not for my daughter.

I knew even then this wasn't a phase, a decision prompted by special circumstances. An abortion had to do with family, with continuity. "Children's children are the crown of the elders," my mother used to say. An abortion had to do with me. My grandchild.

"Don't worry," Sam said when I told him why I was packing. "Julie will be fine. It happens all the time now."

He didn't understand and I couldn't explain. I knew Julie would come through this all right. I could not get rid of the feeling that it had all been thought out beforehand, before the need even arose. I could not get rid of the feeling that it had something to do with me, with the kind of mother I had been.

"Would you want her to go through with the pregnancy and have the baby?" Sam asked as we lay in bed holding each other. "Twenty-nine, unmarried, no steady income. You know what that would mean. You know who'd end up with the problem. Do you really want Julie to come live here, with a baby?"

What could I say? What could anyone say? I felt sad, as if someone had died. I buried my head in Sam's shoulder and closed my eyes. I pretended this was my world; the other, the one out there, the one in which Julie lived, where abortions were routine procedures, that world did not exist.

I told no one. Certainly not my mother. Not my sister or brother, not Matthew. He and Julie had been close as children, but now she lived in Chicago and he lived in California, and they each had their own lives. I didn't even tell my friend Laura, my best friend, someone I could always count on. I told myself there wasn't time, they wouldn't understand. I told myself I was blowing things out of proportion.

There was no problem at work. I told everyone I had to spend time with my mother. They understood.

I went to Chicago alone. Sam wanted to come, he wanted to be there for Julie and for me. He could take some of his sick days. It wasn't necessary, I told him. It might exaggerate the significance of the event. It was something a mother did, it was something between mothers and daughters.

Coming back to Chicago should have been exciting. I had lived there for twenty years. Julie and Matthew were born there, they had grown up there. Those were happy years, filled with friends, a big house near the lake; I worked as an adjunct at the university, went to meetings of SANE; I thought I'd get a doctorate some day. I thought Julie and Matthew would live happily ever after, if only we could keep the world from blowing up.

I had not wanted to go back East; I had not wanted to go back to my childhood, to my mother. A promotion for Sam, an hydraulic engineer in a new firm. How could I stand in his way? Julie had stayed. She was a freshman that year. Our moving meant that now she would be away at school. There would be no more talks, no news about the latest movie or dance company, no seeing her face shine when she was excited and happy. Julie was so much a part of me, it felt strange for us to be living in different cities, as if a piece of me were missing.

I still had friends in Chicago, neighbors. I had not called. I did not take advantage of their offers to put me up 'any time'. I checked into a motel, rented a car. I wanted to be alone. I wanted this to be between Julie and me.

"I don't want children," Julie announced as we drove to the clinic.

"You don't mean it," I said trying to sound casual. "You're upset. You'll feel differently later."

Julie shook her head. "I've thought about it for a long time. I don't want to be a mother." She said it as if it were a matter of fact.

A horn honked behind us as the car veered out of the lane. I did not know what to say.

"Times have changed," Julie said. "It was different in your day."

She was trying to explain, but she sounded patronizing. What was so different? Did she think I didn't have choices to make, that it had been easy for me? I knew about independence and making my own way. I had left home after my high school graduation. I saw myself as a freethinker, and my mother was chaining me to tradition. But never, not even for a minute, had there been a question about children. I always knew I would have my own family. The future meant children..

"What about Doug?" I asked. They had gone together for two years, before moving in together. But Doug still held the lease to his old apartment, subletting it to some students, just in case. That was the problem these days, young people not willing to make a commitment. For a moment, I wondered if it was something we had done, I and the women of my generation.

"Doug?" She looked startled, as if I were asking about a stranger. "Oh, he'd marry me if I wanted. And we'll probably still stay together. But I don't want to have children." She turned her head to stare out the window as if she were a tourist seeing these streets for the first time, Julie who had lived here all her life.

She's upset, I told myself. She is trying to justify the abortion.

I pulled into the first garage I saw. This was no time to worry about finding a parking space.

"I like kids," Julie said. She made no move to get out of the car but sat up against the door looking straight ahead. "I might even go into some sort of art therapy with children. But I don't want to be a mother." She looked at me then, for the first time. "You were a pretty good mother, Ma," she said. "You were always there, always ready to drop everything when I needed you. Like now. But I don't want to do that. I don't want to choose between me and someone else."

"But Doug would help," I said. I liked Doug, the little I knew of him. He worked in legal aid and did volunteer work for a self-help group working out of a store front. He played the clarinet, did his share of the housework. He seemed kind, considerate, gentle. Like Sam. "Doug would help," I said again.

"I know," Julie said. "He's a good guy. A lot like Dad. But when you come down to it, it's my decision. It all ends up with me and how I want to live my life. If I was going to be a mother, I'd want to do it right, go all out. And I don't. I just don't."

She got out of the car and stood waitng while I locked up. She had that look on her face, the same look my mother used to have when she'd made up her mind about something, the look that said I'd better keep out of her way, I'd better keep quiet.

Our talk was over. We walked into the clinic side by side, as if we were really in step.

The waiting room was just that, a waiting room. Nondescript furniture, nature photographs on the yellow walls, artificial plants, a room for waiting.

I was not new to waiting rooms. I had sat and waited in more than one, but this was the first time I sat waiting knowing full well the outcome beforehand.

I remembered another waiting room not very different from this one, except there were prints on the wall, prints of children, of mothers and children. There had been another phone call, six months after we had moved back to New York. Julie. Excessive bleeding. For weeks now. She hadn't wanted to scare us. The college doctor. Only a cyst. What should she do?

I took the next plane to Chicago. I took her to Dr. Topkins, the doctor who delivered her. Together we sat holding hands, waiting. Was it...? Would it...? No. The ovary was intact.

How happy we had been, Julie and I. We had celebrated, gone to Marshall Field's to try on silly hats, drench ourselves in sample perfume. I insisted Julie buy something, a hand printed scarf from India, earrings, a new book bag. Insisting even though I knew that whatever we bought would be worn once or used twice and then, like other gifts and bindings, discarded, lost or given away. I was the one who wanted the moment remembered, something tangible to record the unspoken but definite assumption about the future, about the babies to come.

"We buy our children with things. We bribe them with gifts," my friend Laura once said in bitterness. Laura's daughter had left school, left home, gone off alone. How superior I had felt. I had been so sure of Julie.

"I won't give them anything," Laura had gone on in defiance. "They want to be grown up, let them take responsibility for their behavior. They can't come running back to Momma whenever they get in trouble."

I wanted to say something wise, for my own sake if not for Laura's. But what could I say? "A mother's a mother forever." It sounded like something my own mother would say.

When I repeated the story to Sam, he was reassuring. "It's not the same," he had said. "You and Julie talk. She still comes to us for help." He had even found comfort in the arguments, the accusations she'd begun to make that we'd become complacent. We had not sold out exactly, but we had been seduced by our times. We had a big house, two cars when there was perfectly good public transportation available. "At least she cares enough to tell us how she feels," Sam said. "At least there's contact."

Maybe there was something about fathers and daughters, mothers and sons. Sam always seemed to understand Julie. I had an easier time with Matthew. It had nothing to do with Freud—it was just the complement of opposites. Julie and I were too much alike. We acted on each other like mirrors in the fun house, exaggerating and distorting our most typical qualities. We turn away, I thought, from those we see ourselves becoming.

Even as a child she had been defiant, refusing to sit in the seat the teacher assigned. She had not wanted to sit according to alphabetical order, her place in life determined by an accident of name. She had wanted to choose.

Alphabetical order was not the issue, I told her. There wasn't enough of a principle here worth risking suspension. But to Julie a principle was a principle, no matter how small.

I wanted to shake some sense into her. "You can't go through life fighting every set of rules," I said.

I wanted to praise and protect her. She was so brave, How wonderful to care, how extraordinary to stand up and fight for something so small.

But anger and fear won out. I told myself she had chosen her own path, she'd have to face the consequences. If she made her bed, she'd have to lie in it. She had not asked for my advice beforehand. I would not offer it now.

I kept my hands at my side. I did not reach out. I did not even smile.

If only I had hugged her, stroked her hair. If only I had not been so unbending.

I looked at the clock again. Should I go out for coffee? A walk? Idle questions. I knew I couldn't leave; I knew I'd sit glued until it was over. I wanted to be there for Julie, see her as soon as I could. I pretended it was all for her, but I knew some of it was for me.

I was filled with the past. It overflowed the boundaries of time and space, and spilled into the waiting room. I remembered the day Julie was born. My mother had called me long distance.

"A girl first," she said. "It's better that way." I didn't know what she meant, but I knew I had pleased her.

I remembered the day I brought Julie home. That was the day she came into the world, not the day of her birth—not the days in the hospital where I could have her only for limited intervals, but the day she came home to the room that had been ready for months.

There at home, I held my jewel—Julie—named for the Rosenbergs, Julius and Ethel, put to death for spying, killed, I was convinced, because they were Jews. A mother dead, her own children still babies. Boy or girl, I had decided it would be Julie. I could never have named her Ethel, a name from my childhood, a name my mother would have chosen. Everyone thought I was naming her for my grandfather, the J for Jacob. Sam knew. The name would be more than a memoriam, more than a promise. Julie would be an achievement.

I held her and touched her, urged her to eat and grow. "Eat, eat," I whispered to the infant at my breast. "Take. Take more. I have enough for you, for everything you need."

And the wishes. "Grow beautiful and strong. Grow up free to shine in the dark. A jewel who lights up the world." I had visions of Julie grown, like the figureheads of ships of old— hair flowing, face to the future, undaunted and unafraid. I kissed the creases in her neck and changed her diapers. I woke at night to see if she was breathing. I wrapped her in blankets and carried her from room to room; I sang "Hush Little Baby" and *"Afen Pripetchik,"* songs whose words I had half forgotten, whose meaning I never knew. A continuation, I thought. Someday you'll sing to your daughter.

Now I sat and waited

I remembered how I once played Hannah in a Chanukah play. I had wanted to be Judith who cut off the general's head and saved the city, but "You will be a good Hannah" the teacher had said. "You will know how to cry for your children."

I had practiced being Hannah, trying to imagine myself dead, my children dead. I remembered how I walked up to the platform in a long dress my mother had made out of a sheet, the lights turned down; everyone quiet. I talked about my first born and how he had died for God; I talked about my second son and how he had died for God; I talked about my seven sons. My voice shook as I watched myself become Hannah. "Kill me!" I pleaded. "Kill me!"

I screamed and wailed for my children. I was a good actress. I knew how to pretend.

But this wasn't a play, and I couldn't cry.

. . .

"How do you feel?" I asked when it was over and at last, I was allowed to see her.

"Fine," she said. "I'm really fine."

Fine, I thought. She just had an abortion and she says she's fine. I didn't believe it.

I looked at her lying back against the pillow, her eyes half closed, her hands fingering the edge of the blanket the way she used to when she was a child except here there was no satin binding to stroke and smooth. Her hands hadn't changed, long fingers, smooth cuticles, the nails unpolished but trimmed. Artist's hands. She had started out as an art major and then switched to psychology. She wanted to help people. "People are more important than paint," she'd said. Still she had always managed to take good care of her hands. She looked thin, pale. There were dark patches under her eyes, blue eyes like my mother's, like Sam's. She looked tired, fragile, injured. I found myself shaking. I did not want my daughter to hurt.

"It's because of me," I said. "You don't want to have children because of me."

"Not exactly," she said with that uncompromising honesty that was so much a part of her. "You were a good mother, but I saw what went into being a mother, the care, the time. I don't want that for me." She put her hand on mine as if she were the mother, I the daughter.

I wanted to reach out, take her in my arms and hold her, break the wall I felt between us. I wanted to... I didn't know what I wanted, just not this.

"I..." I began, stopped. Better to keep quiet. Better to act casual, pretend. I was good at that. I had been so afraid of making the same mistakes my mother did, I had pretended I was different. I didn't need, I didn't want, and all the while I chipped away, a knife against stone. I wanted her different, but not too much so. I wanted her to be what I thought I could have been.

"Are you angry?" she asked.

"I'm not angry," I said lying. "I don't want you to live according to my needs." I was only half lying. "I always thought we wanted the same things." I was telling the truth.

"We do," she said. "We have different ways of getting them." She withdrew her hand, lay back against the pillow and closed her eyes.

"Take your time," I said. "I can wait. You can spend the night if you want. I'll be here."

"No. I'll be ready to leave soon. I'll just rest for a while."

"Yes," I said. "Rest. I'll wait."

I sat in the chair near the window. I was surprised it was sunny, surprised it was so clear and bright.

I did not understand her, my daughter. I did not understand any of them, the new generation. They never looked back. An abortion and not a twinge of remorse, a decision about the future and not a hint of hesitation.

She'll pay, I thought. Everyone pays, one way or the other. In cash or in kind, as my mother used to say. I was shocked. My mother's words, her way of looking at the world, as if life were a scoreboard, as if life was fair. I did not want to be the kind of mother I'd had.

"I love you, Julie," I said. "It will be all right."

We make the same mistakes over and over again. We repeat our sins, slipping back deeper and deeper into that we wish to avoid. The past binds us like a gene inherited. If only we could wipe it clean, rub it out like a stain.

I did not understand my daughter.

My mother did not understand me.

I feared for my daughter.

Did my mother fear for me?

Forgive me mother—I cannot cry.

Strong, unbending, disappointed, I am the living testimony to who you were.

I would like to weep for you, Mother. I would like my tears to overflow and spill from my eyes. I tore my dress on the left side, I poured ashes on my head, but I could not cry.

I slept through your dying... I did not wash you... I did not bind you or comb your hair... I did not clean your nails... I did not look upon your face... I kept the coffin closed.

I rummage through your things. A Yiddish dictionary, a collage of photographs, a lampshade fringed by your own hands, a glass ribbed washboard. I did not know you.

I am so lonely.

To sin against a parent is to sin against the past. Honor links the generations.

To sin against a daughter is to sin against the future. Love connects us to our seed.

I try to understand how it came about.

Zayde dies.

"I told you he didn't need an operation," my mother says to Uncle Arthur. "Prostate. Prostate. A man of eighty. What did he need it for? He could have lived to a hundred."

"You're always complaining," says Uncle Arthur. "You always think you know better."

"Well, he wouldn't have died if he stayed home," says my mother. "No one has died in this house."

"Sh," says Aunt Bertha. "Mamme will hear you."

The burial committee comes to do its work. My mother stays downstairs with Bubbe and my aunts. Uncle Arthur is alone in the upstairs sitting room next to the dining room where the men are washing the body on the table used for important company. When they finish, Uncle Arthur motions to me. "Come," he says. "Come say goodbye to the Zayde."

I shake my head; I'm afraid of what I will see.

"Don't be afraid," says Uncle Arthur as he takes my hand and pulls my along. "It's only Zayde."

The dining room is dark, the shades pulled down, a sheet hung over the mirror on the sideboard. The coffin is on the table, Zayde inside. Pennies cover his eyes. He has a rag tied under his chin, his body wrapped in a cloth like a mummy. There is a funny smell in the room. Ice makes puddles in the trays around the body.

Uncle Arthur stands and looks at Zayde. His face is white and pinched as if something hurts.

The men from the Shul carry the coffin out to the porch and lay it to rest on wooden milk boxes. People stand on the steps and in the street. The family stands on the porch, my mother on one side of Bubbe, Aunt Bertha on the other. All my aunts are here. They stand behind Bubbe, and their daughters stand behind them. I stand next to my mother. Daughters are supposed to help their mothers.

My father and my uncles stand with the other men near the Rabbi. The Rabbi makes a speech. He tells how Zayde came to America, how the first thing he did, the very first thing was to look for a Shul. The Rabbi tells how hard life was, how Zayde lived in other people's houses, how wherever he went, he put God first.

"He never forgot," says the Rabbi, "that he was a Yiddisher *mensch.*"

The Rabbi continues the story of Zayde's life, how the war came, how he had to wait ten years to bring his wife and children here, how he bought a house, how he became the first president of the East New York Avenue Shul. "Even in bad times," says the Rabbi, "in the worst of times, he never forgot God's words. He never forgot the ways of our fathers."

Zayde is buried near cousin Bea's father in the family plot. There is room here for Bubbe and for my mother and father, for all my aunts and uncles. Everyone has a place. But there is no place for the children. There is no place for me.

At night when we go back to our own house, I ask my mother about her life. "Where did you live?... What kind of food did you eat? ... Who took care of you?"

My mother goes to the linen drawer and takes out the photo album wrapped in a towel. When she opens it up, pictures and post cards fall out. I hold up a picture of three women wearing aprons with white cloths covering their heads. "That's me," she says pointing to the one in the middle. "That's when I worked in the soup kitchen. During the war, the big war. The Germans came to Poland. They opened the kitchen for the poor people. It was an honor to work for them. An honor."

My mother looks at the picture for a long time. I cannot imagine my mother working. I can't imagine my mother working for the Germans.

"Everybody thinks the Germans are bad because of what they do now. But they weren't bad then. They brought electricity. They treated us fair. Genteel." She rummages among the pictures until she finds one of a group of soldiers standing in front of a little house. "We had five rooms in the house. They paid us five marks a day for the dining room. Not eveyone had a dining room. They took our dining room for an office. They gave us a cow and a horse. They gave us seed to grow potatoes and corn. They were good, the Germans. They didn't rape, or loot, like the Cossacks, or the Polacks. The Polacks were the worst. They would take a horse and open the belly and put a Jew in and then they bury the horse and the Jew together. Sometimes they just picked out ten Jews and shot them." She spits. "Let them rot in the earth, the Polacks."

She slips the picture into the pocket in the back of the album. "The Germans were good to us. Not like now," she says again. "They gave the people guns before they left, before the Polacks came back. Kalman, Bea's father didn't want to take it. He was afraid. But I took a gun. I wasn't afraid. I hid it in the barn in the earth, under the cow's feet." She smiles remembering.

My mother tells me how babies used to die. She says Bubbe did not take good care of her children, she had too many. She had eleven but only five lived. My mother tells me how she washed her dead baby sister and cleaned her nails. It took an hour to comb the baby's hair. It was so long and curly. They put candles around the body and said a prayer.

She tells how Aunt Bertha was saved from the evil eye. They gave her to another woman to raise, a woman whose children didn't die. They made believe they sold her. They changed her name.

"Tell me more," I plead, my hand on the picture album my mother brought from Europe. "Tell me about when you were a girl. Tell me why Zayde came to America. Tell me about the baby." I want to know everything. I want to hear about my mother's family. I am surprised and pleased. I have ancestors just like the people in the books I read. There are stories in my family just like the stories in books.

She tells me how Zayde came to America, how Bubbe's father was rich, how he bought a pass for 700 rubles so Zayde could go to the city to buy kerosene and salt to sell in the town, how something bad happened and Zayde had to go away. Bubbe took care of everything. She opened a store and sold retail. She had a good head.

I listen to my mother's stories. I try to imagine Bubbe in a store. I try to imagine Bubbe in business. It is too hard.

"A good head," my mother says. "The women in the Fineman family have good heads for business."

"How did you come here? Where did you go?" I ask, aware suddenly how accidental life is. What if my mother had not come to America? I might have been born in Europe. I might not have been born at all!

"We came. We came," my mother says. "We had to leave in a hurry. We paid an agent who took two hundred people to Warsaw. From there we went to Antwerp. Then we came on a ship to Ellis Island. We had plenty of money. A good thing too. Bubbe was afraid they would not let Uncle Kalman in. He had consumption. But money is honey, it makes everything go." She gets up to put the album away. A postcard falls out. It looks like a picture of a vase. I look, it becomes a face. I keep looking and it becomes a vase again. My mother laughs. "They were the latest fad," she says, "when I was a girl." She takes the postcard out of my hand and puts it away in the back of the album. "That's how life is. What you think you see is not what there really is."

I want to ask more questions. I want to ask how it felt to come to America. I want to ask how old she was. I want to ask about the gun in the barn under the cows, but something has changed. She looks like she does before she gets angry. It is better not to ask.

On Sundays if the weather is nice, Jack and I sit on the bench in front of the house and read the jokes. We read to each other. He reads Gasoline Alley and Dick Tracy. I read Winnie Winkle. "A girl should read about her," says Jack.

We sit close together. I pretend I'm grown up and Jack is my husband. I pretend we're in love. I like the way Jack smells. "He uses cologne," my mother says in a disapproving voice. "A sissy," she says.

Sometimes Rifka, the Rebbe's daughter, walks past.

"Good morning, Miss Cohen," Jack says. Rifka nods and smiles. Her eyes look down but I see her look at Jack.

Sometimes Jack is home when I come from school. "How's tricks?" he always asks.

"A bum," says my mother, "A man home in the daytime—a bum."

Jack doesn't say much. He sits on the porch or on the bench, and whistles. When he sees my mother carrying the garbage down, he takes it from her. When he sees a woman carrying bundles, he asks if he can help. He always wears a suit and a hat, felt in winter, straw in summer.

Jack asks my mother if she wants fresh eggs from the farm, or cream, so she can make butter. "It's cheap," he says, "and fresh."

"Come on, Millie," he says with a smile. "Let's go get eggs for your mother."

The farm is on the other side of the school, past the trolley line where there are no more houses, near the water where my father goes to throw his sins away.

As we wait to cross the trolley tracks, Rifka comes by. "Good morning, Miss Cohen," says Jack tipping his hat.

"Good morning, Mr. Bernstein," says Rifka.

"Out for a walk?" says Jack.

"On an errand for my mother," says Rifka. "I'm going to the farm for eggs."

"What a coincidence," says Jack. "We're going to get eggs for Millie's mother. Shall we go together?"

Rifka nods and smiles. I have a bad feeling in my chest. Another bad feeling in my stomach.

I don't watch stepping from the curb. Jack puts out his hand. "Here, hold on," he says.

"Here is my arm for you," he says to Rifka offering her his elbow.

We cross the street, Rifka holds Jack's arm and I hold his hand. We get to the other side. Jack drops my hand, but Rifka still holds his arm.

Jack and I go for other walks. "The slow season," he says. "A good chance to see the neighborhood."

On every walk we meet Rifka. She and Jack talk and whisper. Sometimes they forget about me. Sometimes Jack buys me an ice cream cone. Sometimes we walk in a row holding hands.

Rifka never walks home with us. "I'll take the short cut," she says when we get to Livonia Avenue. Then she goes one way, and Jack and I walk another way.

Mrs. Sherman comes to visit my mother. I hear them whisper in the kitchen. Mrs. Sherman is afraid they'll blame her. She swears she knew nothing about Jack and Rifka. She swears she has her own worries, what with her husband on the road for months at a time, a husband who doesn't always send her money. How could she manage without a boarder? He left his clothes, but he paid for the month. What should she do?

I feel sad, the way I did when my mother gave my doll and carriage to my sister, as if I've lost something that belonged to me. I thought Jack belonged to me. Now he has run away. Now Rifka is going to have a baby.

"A bum. I knew he was a bum," my mother says. "And they wanted him for Bertha." She spits three times to ward off the evil eye. "Better an old maid than a bastard's mother."

Still she goes from house to house asking for donations for Rifka, Rifka who is pregnant but has no husband.

The baby dies. It was a blue baby. It had holes in its heart.

"God's punishment," says Mrs.Schecter.

"A Mitzvah," says my mother. "What kind of life is it for a bastard?"

"A pity," says Aunt Bertha and a tear rolls down her cheek. Aunt Bertha wants a baby. She would not mind being a bastard's mother.

They bury Rifka's baby.

The women stand in the street and talk about Rifka, how she does't eat, how she doesn't sleep. How she sits on the floor in the corner, with wide open eyes that don't see, how she rocks back and forth, how she bangs her head against the wall, how she screams and cries, "I want my baby. I want my baby."

"She lost her mind," says Mrs. Pincus.

"They should not have taken in a boarder," says Mrs. Schecter.

"Such a shame," says Mrs. Greenberg, the pickle lady.

"Poor Rifka," says Miss Mintz.

"You always have to pay for what you get," says my mother. "Nothing in life is free."

Inside the house, we can hear the Rebbe praying, his words rising up to God. "Oh, Lord of the Universe, compassionate and powerful. Take pity on my daughter." We can hear the Rebbitzen crying, "Oh my daughter! Oh my daughter!"

"We should do something," says my mother. "It's a sin. Life is for the living. She should not give in."

"What can we do?" asks Mrs. Klein. "It's in God's hands."

"If God wanted you only to use His hands, He wouldn't have given you a head," my mother says.

"Millie," she says. "Go get the doll, the doll that sits in the chair. Hurry. Go! Now!"

Is my mother losing her mind? She's sending me to get a doll!

"Hurry! Hurry! Go, I tell you," she says, giving me a push.

I run down the block and across the street. In our apartment, I run straight to the living room.

There she sits, a doll as big as a baby, the doll Uncle Kalman gave me before he died. I am not allowed to play with this doll. I pick her up carefully. I lay her down over my arm and her eyes shut. I smooth the silk dress, I fix the pink bow. I hold the doll up against my shoulder the way you hold a baby. I have to hurry.

"What took you so long?" asks my mother giving me a pinch. "I could have gone to the Bronx and back." She takes the doll from me. The women move aside, making room around my mother. "Give me a blanket. Where is a blanket? What's the matter? Are you all turned to stone?"

Someone hands her a crocheted shawl. She wraps the doll in the shawl as if it were a baby. She carries the bundle in her arms the way you carry a baby. She marches up the stairs to the Rebbe's house right into the kitchen. The women crowd in behind her. I go, too. We stop in the doorway.

My mother whispers to the Rebbetzin and then walks to the wall where Rifka is sitting on the floor. "Rifkele," she says. " I found your baby. Come. Come sit in the rocker. Come rock your baby."

The room grows still, as if the world stopped turning. I hold my breath.

My mother rocks her arms the way you rock a baby. "Come," she says, "here is your baby." Then she takes Rifke's arm and gently, slowly, so slowly, she helps Rifke stand up. She leads her to the rocking chair. "Sit, Rifke. Sit and rock your baby," she says.

Rifka is quiet now. Her mouth hangs down as if it is broken. My mother puts the wrapped doll against Rifka's chest. Rifka's arms curl around the doll. "Rock your baby," says my mother and she gives the rocker a little push.

Rifka begins to rock. Back and forth, back and forth, her bare feet pushing on the floor, her knees apart. She rocks and rocks. Tears fall down her cheeks, one after another, long big tears. Rifka rocks and rocks. She does not scream anymore.

9

The reports weren't good. My mother was retaining water, her circulation was poor, her legs were weak. She couldn't walk.

The nurses in the hospital had tried to teach her to use a walker.

"I can't stand up," she said.

"Try," I urged, as she stood there leaning on the wall.

"You're not trying," I said ready to catch her if she fell.

"I can't," she said.

Still she did manage to get to the bathroom by herself. From chair to dresser to door, she managed to pull herself along. She needed help in getting up from the seat; she couldn't reach to wipe herself. I couldn't bring myself to wipe her.

The doctor said she couldn't live alone.

She could have stayed home with an attendant and had a normal life, visiting me, seeing her friends. But she had decided she didn't want strangers in her house, poking around in her things. If she couldn't stay with me, she wanted to be someplace where people would not see what had become of her, where she would be among strangers whose job it was to take care of her. She wanted to go to a home.

The search began.

The Bronx was out. She had never lived there and was not about to start now. It had to be kosher. It had to be clean. Queens was too far, though Rockaway was a possibility. We rented a wheel chair, developed a routine. In the morning the attendant looked after her. At night she made phone calls. In the afternoon, when I got out of school, we looked for a home.

There were questions, tests, the questions directed at me as if she wasn't there, the tests aimed at her as if she were a child. Could she get out of a chair unaided? Was she incontinent?

"What is your name, dear?"

Could she feed herself? How long would it take her to wheel herself to the dining room?

"What is today's date?"

What about her reflexes? Her interactive social skills?

"Who is the president of the United States?"

"Do you like to play Bingo?"

There were waiting lists. Some could be set aside with the right donations. Some could be bridged with the right connections. I became adept at folding and unfolding a wheel chair, skilled at finding parking spaces close to entrance ways. I learned to ignore the residents lined up in front of their rooms waiting to be taken to lunch. I smiled at the women shuffling along the corridors pushing their walkers before them. I said hello to everyone whose eye caught mine.

We exhausted the Rockaways. We scoured Brooklyn. Only Staten Island was left. Staten Island, the burgeoning borough.

I called my sister in Newton. "I can't do it," she said. "It makes me sick just to think of my mother in a home."

I called my brother in South Carolina. "Why do I have to come look at it? A home's a home. You're old enough to choose."

It was my mother who chose. Manor Haven in Staten Island. Brand new. The latest in facilities. A home away from home. Five minutes from South Side Hospital. You never have to worry how your parents are. I signed my mother in, left a deposit, arranged to bring her on Monday.

.   .   .

I called my brother. "Why do I have to be there just to take her to a nursing home? You know how to drive."

I put my foot down. I told him he had to come. I told him I would not do this alone. I told him I would move back to Chicago and not leave a forwarding address. I told him she was his mother, too.

He and Gail flew up from Charleston. It was only a two hour flight. They did not plan to spend the night. Gail kissed me. "You were always strong," she said.

My mother supervised the packing. Some dresses were too good to take. Some not good enough. Some she consigned to Jewish emigres. "Let them get pleasure from my misfortune," she said. She took stockings and nightgowns, housecoats and necklaces. She did not take her corset or her shoes. "If you can't walk, you don't need shoes," she said.

She's taking the move well, I marvelled.

She handed me an envelope with the names and phone numbers of three rabbis. "For my funeral," she said. "Give them $100 each. Show them I'm not cheap."

I protested. "You have a long time yet to live," I said. "You're not even a great-grandmother yet. Don't you want to be around to see your first great-grandchild?"

"I want a plain pine box," she said.

"You'll be back soon," I said. "All you need is rest. You just have to get your strength back. When you can walk a little, you'll come home." I believed what I said.

We were ready. She sat in the wheel chair. She wore her beaver coat even though it was April, even though the for-sythia was in bloom. She wore the blue hat and scarf she had crocheted herself. Her gloves were blue to match. She carried her black bag, the one with the secret pockets. She wore her slippers.

Gail pushed her out into the hallway while I locked the door. I used my old set of keys. My mother had her keys in her pocketbook. I wanted her to have them, to feel independent. I wanted to believe she was coming back.

She did not take a second look.

"Don't forget to take the candlesticks," she said as we helped her into the car. "Two for you and two for Gail. The ones from the Bubbe for Tibby. She's the youngest."

"Don't talk like that," I said harshly. "You have plenty of time left." I always thought my grandmother's candlesticks would go to me. I always thought they went to the oldest daughter.

My brother did the driving. It was my car, but I sat in the back so my mother could sit up front. Sam and Gail followed in Sam's car. They thought putting a mother in a home was something a brother and sister should do alone. They thought it was something that would bring us closer together.

Tibby didn't come. "I couldn't bear it," she said. "You know how sensitive I am. I'll visit when she's settled."

We had planned our arrival for lunch time. "She'll get to know the other residents," the social worker had said. "It'll help her make the change, and she'll adjust more quickly."

Gail and I unpacked. We put her radio on the table near her bed. We set out her favorite pictures: her grandchildren, Bubba and Zayde, Uncle Arthur and Aunt Bertha. We put out her comb and brush, the lipstick in the little case with the mirror attached. I put the azalea plant on the window sill. "A gift from Julie," I said.

Julie had called. "I know it's hard," she told me. "I know there's no other way right now." I wanted to believe she meant what she said, that she didn't blame me. I wondered what she was learning from this; I wondered if she was thinking that some day she'd have to put me into a home.

My mother sat in the wheelchair watching.

"They have a manicurist here. Every Thursday," I told her. "My treat."

I put the new pink mohair shawl I'd brought her around her shoulders. She brushed it aside. "There's no telephone," she said.

"I took care of it," said Alvin. "They'll install it tomorrow."

"You told me a private room," she said.

"There aren't any private rooms now," I said. "You're first on the list."

"List. List. You think I'll be here forever?"

"They said in a week."

"You didn't bring the address book. What good is a telephone if I have no telephone numbers?"

I promised her I'd bring it tomorrow. I'd make a special trip so she could have her address book.

The social worker came to take my mother to lunch. "You don't have to stay," she told us.

"We'll wait until she comes back," I said. I could not leave yet. I could not go and leave my mother here alone.

We waited in the day room at the end of the floor. Aside from the yellow paint on the walls, there had not been much attempt at decoration. There wasn't much furniture—a large TV set, a few bridge tables, a few easy chairs. They're just getting started, I told myself, they'll make it look homey.

Sam and I sat at one of the tables. Gail stood in the doorway, a sweater pulled tight around her, the sleeves pushed up to show her gold braclets. My brother sat slumped in an easy chair, his sneakered feet stretched out in front of him, his Burberry raincoat bunched around him. I still saw him as a skinny little boy clinging to our mother, telling tales about how I hung around the candy store with the tough kids, how I cut Hebrew school. I still remembered how he broke the blue wine glass I always used for Passover, how my mother blamed me.

"Couldn't you have found something better, something more established?" he asked, a twist of his hand taking in the entire room.

"It's the best there is," I said feeling defensive, as if this were all my doing.

"It's a little barren for a day room," Gail said. Her ungloved hand clutched an unlit cigarette. I remembered she was trying to cut down.

"You have to give them a chance," said Sam. "They're supposed to have an excellent program."

We had been pleased with the social worker's description—a full arts and crafts program, Bingo twice a week. My mother could enjoy herself, flourish if she wanted to.

"Well there doesn't seem to be much equipment," said Gail shaking her head, her jet black hair pulled back in a pony tail.

I had never noticed before how much she looked like my mother, how much she sounded like her. It was the personality more than the looks, the attitude more than the appearance, the way they had of meeting the world, always ready to attack. Did men really marry their mothers? If so, what about daughters? Did they marry their fathers? I looked at Sam, in his tweed jacket with the leather elbow patches over a crew neck sweater. I had married him because he was not like my father. He would not let me become like my mother.

My mother. What was she doing here? My grandmother had died in a nursing home. But that was a long time ago when things were different. This was not the way it was supposed to be.

"Take it easy," Sam said putting his hand on my arm. He could always tell when I was upset. "She'll come back soon. Everything will work out. There's no other way." He turned to Alvin. "Knowing Sorke," he said, "she'll be running the place in a week. We don't have to worry about her."

Easy for him to say, I thought, moving my arm away from his hand. She's not his mother.

"You could have found some place closer," said Alvin. "Staten Island. Out in the boondocks. You need a map to find your way."

"It's not too late," I said almost believing my words. "You can always find another place. You can take her to Charleston, to your house." I wanted to show him up. He was always criticizing me, he never thought I did anything right.

"You didn't have to be in such a hurry," he said. "You could have waited a while."

"Come on, Alvin," said Sam. "You know we couldn't wait."

"I know her better than you," Alvin waved his hand in my drection. "You're only married to her but I know her. She doesn't care about what's good for her mother. She doesn't want to make the effort, she'd have to give up her time." He smirked, self- satisfied.

Stinking pig. Lousy bastard. Words from my childhood. They sat on the tip of my tongue. I could not get them out.

There we sat, all of us together, pretending, acting the parts: son, daughter, sister, brother.

I remembered a weak little boy always cowering in a corner, always needing protection and defending, inept, incompetent at most activities of childhood. Except Monopoly, he had always been good at that, buying property, putting up hotels, aiming at Boardwalk. I had felt sorry for him, superior. Now he owned a textile mill in South Carolina. Non-union. He sold to Burlington and Arrow shirts. He had acquired the establishment aura: a Lincoln Continental, an American Express Gold Card, shirts with alligators, a change of name from Abramowitz to Abrams.

He had made it. A success. King of the Hill. He owned the most expensive property on the board. But who was he? He was not at all like our father, Hymie Abramowitz, a little man, who never owned more than two good suits at a time, happy on Shabbos when we all sat down to eat together. A man trapped by his own good nature, by a wife who was my mother. "The Deddy" we called him. Not Dad or Pop or Der Tatte. "The Deddy." Not Yiddish, not English, distant somehow. My mother was always called Ma. Ma.

Sam was standing up. He was going for coffee. Gail wanted some too. "Why don't you come?" he suggested. "The social worker said it would take a while for lunch what with the ones who have to be fed and the ones who take their time."

I shook my head. I did not want coffee. I did not want tea. I did not want to be here.

I watched as they walked away, Gail looking good in that suave sophisticated way of beauty parlors and exercise class and money. She always knew how to take care of herself. She'd told me once how much she envied our relationship, Sam's and mine. She thought it was more equal than hers and Alvin's, Sam and I talked, shared things. She thought I was lucky to have found Sam.

I could never tell her I had married Sam to make sure I would never have to go home again, that I wanted someone to give me a life different from my mother's. I let her think what she would. We kept our conversations light, chit chat, as if we did not have an intertwined relationship. I let her envy me for having something she couldn't get.

Yet there had been one time, after her surgery for a pinched nerve, when Gail had cried and expressed regret for marrying Alvin. Alvin was damaged, she said, a mama's boy in the mold of Uncle Arthur. She praised me for having had the guts to get out. I tried to comfort her; it was the operation, I said, she'd feel better in the morning.

Later, when I tried to talk to her, she denied everything: I was making it up; it was the anesthesia or the pain killers. She was a happily married woman, and this was just another sign of how I made trouble.

I stood up. I should have gone with them. I could not bear sitting here with my brother, waiting. But I could not leave and allow him to remain, to appear as usual, the good one, the one who sent flowers on Mother's Day, who came up twice a year and took her to the Lower East Side to shop and then to Ratner's to eat mushroom barley soup and cheese pirogen.

I was the bad daughter. I did not call often enough, stay long enough, do enough, do it right. Even as a baby, my mother said I had been difficult, willful, crying. I did not listen; I went my own way.

I thought of all those times I was awakened in the middle of the night. My mother's voice, "I have pain. I can't sleep." Where was he when she had to go to the hospital, when she needed a bed pan, when she needed someone to talk to? Where was he when we prepared for emergencies, when we practiced phoning in the dark, when we drove through the streets of Brooklyn in the middle of the night?

Now he was here. Now, when it was too late.

I walked to the doorway and looked down the hall. No sign of her yet. She was still at lunch. She. I still found it difficult to call her Mother. I called her Ma when I had to address her. Sam called her Sorke. Sorke, Sarah, Abraham's wife, not a mother until she was ninety, then a mother with a vengeance, forcing Abraham to get rid of Hagar and Ishmael, so she, Sarah, could protect her son's interest. Her son. Would she have done as much for a daughter?

Remembering made old wounds bleed. I needed to talk to someone or I'd explode. Something was ending, leaking away, bit by bit. I needed to talk to someone even if it was Alvin.

"What do you think?" I ventured.

"What do you mean, what do I think? You heard the social worker. She'll be all right. The only thing to do is to wait and see what has to be done. Then make sure she gets the right care. You know how these places are. You have to shmear a little here, a little there. You have to let them know who you are, that you're not going to take any crap." He waved his hand, his diamond pinky ring flashing, his nails manicured, a perfect picture of the self-made entrepreneur. Soon he'd say, "Money is no object. I want the best." Then he'd go back to Charleston and I'd be left holding the bag. As usual. The good son and the bad daughter. How come the bad daughter always gets stuck?

"But what do you think?" I asked again, not sure that I really wanted to know. What I wanted, I realized later, was to make believe that he and I, brother and sister, were friends. But Alvin had been lost to me since childhood, and there was no way to get him back.

"I told you what I think. It's a shame. It's not right. Something could have been worked out, if you'd put your mind to it, if you cared." He turned to me, shrugged as if he were about to declare something obvious, something everyone knew, "You never got along. You never loved her."

I felt myself go stiff.

Then I saw the look, arrogant, sneering, my mother's look. "You don't care," she used to say. "All you think about is yourself."

"You don't know what you're talking about," I said. "You never did."

"And you know? All you know is from books. From life you know nothing."

There it was again, the old war, the same battles. The fists and knives and plates still flying. Old scores? They never die.

My mother was back.

"How was the food?" Alvin asked heartily.

"How were the other people?" Gail asked.

Sam reached for the pink shawl which was trailing behind the wheel chair, and adjusted it around my mother's shoulders. She did not push his hand away.

I noticed a stain on the front of her dress, a piece of noodle curled in the middle. "You don't have to stay here. "I said, surprised I meant it. "If you don't like it, you can go home."

She looked at me then, eyes staring, frightened, angry. She wanted to be saved and she wanted me to do it.

I felt trapped, an animal in a snare. I wanted to be free, of the past, of her. Let it be over, I prayed.

I did not mean for her to die.

There is a natural order to things, day and night, birth and death. There are rules, tradition, the past, the future, right and wrong. Guilt matters.

I pretended I didn't care.

Words fill my head, thunder in my ears, the rhythm of my mother's voice, the pulsing of her breath.

A taker is not a giver.

A half truth is also a lie.

A good friend is better than a brother.

Even the best swimmer can drown.

How come a mother can take care of all her children, but all her children can't take of her?

. . .

Passover is almost here. My mother has a new dress, red, white and blue. She has a navy blue straw hat with red cherries on the side. My mother let the hem out from my dress from last year so I can still wear it.

Alvin and I help carry the boxes of dishes and pots from the bin behind the furnace. Then I stand at the sink, a towel around my waist, and wash the dishes while Tibby dries. Bubbe peels beets for borscht. Aunt Bertha chops the fish that swam in the bathtub. My father sits in the doorway and grates horseradish. Tears run down his face even though he's sitting in the cold air. My mother polishes the candlesticks and the silver wine cups, one for Elijah and one for Uncle Arthur. Uncle Arthur sets up an extra table. There is a right way to do things and a wrong way. I watch what my mother does so I will know what is right.

My mother puts the candlesticks next to Bubbe's place, five candlesticks, one for each of Bubbe's children. Bubbe had eleven children. They died in Europe when they were babies. There are no pictures of the babies who died.

My mother takes two of the candlesticks and holds them to her bust. These are the two that came from Europe; they belonged to Bubbe's mother; these are the candlesticks my mother wants. Every year my mother asks Bubbe for the candlesticks. Every year Bubbe says, "It's not time yet. I'm still here. When I'm gone, they'll go to you." This year my mother does not ask. This year my mother says, "A taker is not a giver."

Bea comes to help. She wears a green dress and rayon stockings. She thinks she's grown up. We cover the tables with damask tablecloths, napkins, silverware, plates one on top of another: for fish, for hard boiled eggs, for potatoes we dip in salt water. My mother watches to see if we do it right. We put the wine glasses in saucers to protect the tablecloth. Some of the glasses have gold rims, some are green, one is pink, one is blue. Almost all the glasses have long stems. The blue one is my favorite.

"That one's for me," I say.

"It's mine," says my brother who has come to watch us work. He moves the glass to another place.

"I used it last year," I say and put the glass back where it was.

"So what," says my brother as he moves it back. "It's a new year and a new ball game."

I reach for the glass. My brother pushes my arm. Pieces of blue glass lie on the tablecloth and on the floor.

"Hoodlums," Uncle Arthur shouts. "Look what you've done." His hand is raised to hit.

"No." My mother puts her hand on my shoulder. I belong to her; only she can hit me.

"It's only a glass," Aunt Bertha says. She picks up the pieces one by one.

"If she were mine, I'd give her a *zetz* she'd never forget," says Uncle Arthur.

"But she's not yours," says my mother, pushing me away, her fingers digging into my bones.

"Are you going to get it!" my brother whispers.

"You're so free with advice, why don't you give some to yourself," says my mother to Uncle Arthur.

"If I wanted to hear your voice, I'd call you on the telephone," says Uncle Arthur.

I move away from the table; I don't want to be in the middle when my mother and Uncle Arthur fight.

"Stinkerke," my uncle yells at my mother.

"Bastard," my mother calls her brother.

"You'll end up like an onion with your head in the ground."

"You don't have to become an onion, you stink like one now."

"You know why you talk shit, because that's what you are—shit."

"You're a crook, Arthur, a gangster. They'll put you away in the electric chair yet."

They are always fighting, as if they are two live wires taped together, the exposed ends ready to spark. They fight about money, about respect, about the past and the future. Tonight they fight about the relatives from Washington Heights, the ones who are coming to the Seder.

Raisel is the widow of Zayde's brother. She and her two daughters have been brought to America by Uncle Arthur. My mother wants Uncle Arthur to bring the other two children to America. My mother says family is important. My mother says Raisel is good for the money. She says Zayde would help them. She says it's the right thing to do.

Uncle Arthur laughs. "You want to be a benefactor, you do it," he says. "Or let Hymie. Let your husband stand for them." He looks defiant as if he's daring my mother to say something, as if he's daring her to cross the invisible line between them. Uncle Arthur has come to the line's edge. He knows my mother will not cross it.

The seder begins. My wine glass is a green juice glass. Bubbe lights the candles. We drink the first cup of wine. We dip potatoes in salt water; we eat matzoh and bitter herbs. Cousin Sidney, the youngest boy, asks the Four Questions.

After supper, Alvin and Sidney and Tibby plan how to steal the Afikomen. Bea and I are too old for such nonsense. We are old enough for woman's work; we help clean the table.

"We have no one here," says Raisel. "Only my brother Morris, and he's no citizen yet. He's only here two years and he has no income."

"What will it cost you?" my mother asks. "They only want a loan. You can't take it with you. A shroud has no pockets."

"When I want your advice, I'll ask for it," says Uncle Arthur. He's about to say something else when Bubbe says it's time to finish. Bubbe has taken Zayde's place. Now Bubbe makes the rules and when she talks, everybody listens. I hurry back to my seat.

The seder cannot finish without the Afikomen. Alvin asks for a dollar for each cousin. Everybody knows that's too much.

"How about two cents?" asks Uncle Arthur. He is making fun of Alvin, offering less than what is fair.

"Nu," says Bubbe. "Will we sit here all night?"

"All right," says Aunt Bertha. "A nickel. A nickel to each one." She gets up as if she's going to get a roll of nickels.

"A quarter, a quarter!" I yell. I'm surprised at myself. I thought I was too old to care about getting money from Uncle Arthur.

"A quarter!" says Uncle Arthur. "Just like your mother. What do you think—I'm made of money?"

"A quarter won't kill you," says my mother. "It's only once a year."

"If it's only once a year, then you give the quarter." says Uncle Arthur.

"Nu," says Bubbe again. " We have to finish."

"A quarter," says Alvin. " A quarter, a quarter," say all the cousins, even Jerry who is almost grown up.

It's agreed, a quarter for each of us. We have won against Uncle Arthur. Even my mother smiles.

Now we come to the end. Tibby opens the door and everybody stands up for Elijah.

"It will be a good year," Bubbe says.

Mamma has gone downstairs to talk to Uncle Arthur and Aunt Bertha. She goes every day and every evening. Bubbe is sick: She pees in the bed; she doesn't move her bowels; she cries; she has to be fed; she is like a baby. Uncle Arthur and Aunt Bertha want to put Bubbe in a home. It is too much, they say; Bubbe is too old.

"Enough already." Uncle Arthur tells my mother. "She has to go to a home. They'll take care of her there. This isn't the old country. This is America. Who keeps someone like this in the house in America?"

"It's a shame," my mother says. "Who heard of such a thing, putting a mother away? I remember how Der Tatte's bubbe lived with us for years and years. No one put her in a home."

"Shame! Shame! All you care about is how it looks, what people will say. She can live to be a hundred. She's making us crazy. In the home, they'll take care of her. She won't be able to get away with things, twist them around her little finger. 'This is too hot, this is too cold. I want this, I want that,'" Uncle Arthur mimics Bubbe's Yiddish. "She doesn't eat, she doesn't drink. We'll get sick from her. This is the way it has to be."

"It's not right. It's not right," my mother says. "I won't let you put her in a home."

"You won't let? What will you do, shoot me? Will you shoot me like you shot the Polack?"

I gasp. I move back from the railing in the hall where I have been listening. I can't believe what I heard. Is this another one of the insults they sling at each other, or is this something real, hidden like the diamonds in the vault?

"Sha! Sha!" says my mother. "You're talking foolishness. And where would we be if I didn't shoot? What would have happened to Bertha? What would have happened to all of us?"

The hall is quiet now. Maybe they've stopped fighting. I'm ready to go into the house when I hear my mother begin to cry. "It's not right," she says again "It's not right."

"Right! What's right? You come downstairs for an hour or two, and you think you know everything. You don't have to get up in the middle of the night a hundred times. You don't have to worry when you're in business that maybe she set the house on fire or she fell down the steps. You're such a good daughter, take her to your house. Take her upstairs. Here, I'll carry her for you. You take care of her."

I stand in the doorway listening, imagining how my uncle looks when he is ready to get his own way, standing feet apart, his blue eyes narrowed, sure of himself, I imagine my mother the way I've seen her when she's angry, eyes burning, her chin stuck out, the look that makes me afraid, the look that says she's ready to explode, her anger falling on us, burying us like the people in *The Last Days of Pompeii.*

"If she dies, it's on your head," my mother says. "Der Tatte would still be alive if you didn't force him to go to a hospital."

Uncle Arthur does not allow her to finish. "The same old stories. He had an operation. On his prostate. What should we have done, let him suffer? The doctor said it was nothing. And it was nothing. So he died. Everyone dies. No one can live forever. He was eighty years old. God should only let me live to be eighty."

"We could have had nurses," my mother answers. "He could have come home sooner. You could afford it. You're just stingy. The same thing now with Mamma. You can hire nurses, day and night. You're cheap, that's all. Cheap. You won't spend a penny. You think you'll take it with you to the grave? You think you'll get a better place in the ground with your money? In the cemetery you'll have the same income like everybody else."

Uncle Arthur laughs. "Good. Maybe then, you'll stop bothering me about money." Uncle Arthur is not afraid of my mother. He is a man of the world, a man of money. He has taken us, his nieces and nephews, to Coney Island and bought us hot dogs at Nathan's. He let us ride the roller coaster and the Loop the Loop. Even my mother has gone to Chinatown with us where she made a show of not eating, not even rice, but she drank a little tea. After all, she said, the tea in her own house comes from China, so what could be so bad?

Uncle Arthur is a big spender. My mother calls him cheap because he owes her money. Uncle Arthur borrowed money from my mother when my father was rich, money he used to buy Bubbe's house, money he used to buy the business. When my father lost his money, my mother had to come live in Bubbe's house. She had to be a tenant.

"I wash my hands," my mother says. "It's on your head."

My mother comes upstairs. "He's no good, no good," she says. She picks up a frying pan and slams it down on the gas range. "He knows the Bubbe doesn't want to go; she doesn't want to leave this house. Nobody died here."

My grandmother thinks she'll die if they take her from her bed. She needs her own bed and her own pillow, the one she brought from Europe.

My mother thinks Bubbe is right. "It's on his head," she says.

I want to say something to my mother, something that will make her feel better, something to show I'm on her side. "I can take care of Bubbe after school," I say. A home is for the poor, the low class, those without family. I don't want to be shamed.

"What are you talking about?" my mother yells. " You want to be a servant for Arthur! You want me to be a servant for my brother? He can afford it; he can hire somebody. Let him use the money he owes me. Let him use the money he stole."

I am thirteen years old, but I am still a child in my mother's house.

Today they take Bubbe to the home.

"We kept Zayde's bubbe in the house," my mother tells me again as she sits in the kitchen, her arms on the table. She looks tired. "Malke, the one you're named after. I had to change her bed, but we didn't put her away like a dog."

It is so quiet I can hear the water drip in the sink.

"She promised me her bedding. Malke said I took care of her so well, she wanted me to have her bedding. She had good bedding, very fine bedding."

My mother stops talking. I want to ask what happened to the bedding, I want to know why she's telling me the story.

"How could a mother hurt her own child?" My mother is talking out loud but she is not talking to me. She is talking to the world. "She promised me the bedding, Chaia Malke promised. But the Bubbe took it, my own mother. She took it and brought it to America. She took it for herself."

The story lodges in my brain. My mother wanted something that my grandmother took away. It's like the pickle dish in *Ethan Frome.* It's wanting something you can't have. I like fitting people to things I've read, but I can't now. I want to go downstairs, to see what will happen. I am afraid of what I'll see, but I don't want to miss it.

I edge toward the door.

"See how it is," my mother says. "See how it is in America." She slams her hand on the table, so hard the glass shakes in the saucer. "No one will do that to me. No one."

Uncle Arthur did not get dressed up to take Bubbe to the home. He is dressed for work, his shirt unbuttoned at the neck, his pants stained with blood and dirt that can't wash out. Aunt Bertha is wearing a cotton house dress, her face puffy, her big nose red, a long hair growing out of a wart on her cheek. She is no raving beauty, my mother says. Still that isn't a reason for not being married.

Arthur and Bertha are brother and sister. I still don't know who is older; I still don't understand why they go everywhere together, even on vacations.

Uncle Arthur goes into Bubbe's room. I hear talking. Bubbe screams, "No! No! I won't go. Help! Please! Save me!"

Uncle Arthur comes into the living room. He is smiling as if he is pleased. "She's strong," he says to Aunt Bertha. "I didn't know she was so strong."

Aunt Bertha looks upset. She puffs on her cigarette and walks back and forth. "Arthur," she says pleading. "Arthur."

Uncle Arthur sighs. He goes back to the bedroom. When he comes out he is carrying Bubbe. She cries and moans. "No. No."

Her head is thrown back, her face and neck all wrinkled like a dead chicken's skin. Her legs are bunched up like a baby's, one arm hangs on the side. Suddenly she screams, long and high, the scream of someone who hurts.

"Save me," she says in Yiddish. "God! Help me! People! Save me!"

I'm afraid. I don't want to see. I want to cry but I don't know why. I don't want to get old; I want to grow up but I don't want to get old. I don't want to go to a nursing home. I want to comfort Bubbe. Bubbe Faigel, a little bird. She looks different now. Like an animal whose name I don't know. It's hard to think of her as Bubbe, Mamma's mother. This is not the Bubbe I know.

Uncle Arthur carries Bubbe past me. Drops of water fall on the floor. Bubbe has peed.

The next morning my mother announces she is going to the home. I am to go with her, the way a daughter should.

My mother is always telling me what to do: "Go to the bakery and buy rolls... Come downtown with me, you'll carry the packages... Come right home after school and watch Tibby, she doesn't go in the street... Stay in the house and help Alvin with his homework."

Even though I'm in the eighth grade, my mother is still the boss. "You're smart enough already," she says.

"Just do it for me," she says. "What does it take? A few minutes. You're young. You have lots of minutes."

"Just do it for your brother. You only have one brother. You'll never have another. Some day you'll know what that means."

Sometimes I complain. Then my mother says I am smarter than my brother, so what can he do? She says I am stronger than my sister, so is it Tibby's fault? It's God's will, she says, so what's the use of complaining?

Then, just to make sure, I understand, she says, "One of these days, I'll be dead, then you'll have nothing to complain about."

We take the train to the Bronx. My mother is silent until the train reaches 149th Street and comes out of the tunnel. "I remember how we kept Zayde's Bubbe in the house. Malke, the one who lived to be a hundred and four. I had to give her tea," she sighs. "She promised me her bedding. Malke said I took care of her so well, she wanted me to have her bedding. She had good bedding, very fine bedding."

She stops talking until we get to the home.

"A real fighter, that woman," the caretaker says. "We had to tie her down. It's nothing. It happens that way sometimes but she'll come around. You have to give it time. Her heart is strong. Like a woman of sixty. I can't believe she's eighty three. Stubborn, these old ones."

The caretaker talks on and on. My mother walks with her; I walk behind. I remember Bubbe from before, from when I was a little girl. She was always old, but then she looked like other people. Now she looks different. I remember how she looked yesterday when Uncle Arthur carried her out of the house. Like a baby, a big ugly baby, or an animal whose name I don't know. Bubbe.

I try to remember everythimg my mother told me about her. She has ten grandchildren and five children. She had eleven children, but they died in Europe, when they were babies. My mother told me how they put straw on the floor and lit candles and washed the dead baby and how it took an hour to comb the curly hair. That is all I can remember.

We come to Bubbe's ward. I remember how she used to give me a dime or a quarter. "Here," she would say, "buy some candy. Go to the movies. Don't tell your mother." She came from a rich family, an important family, my mother said. A strong woman, my mother said, who stayed in Europe alone with four children while Zayde and Uncle Arthur went to America.

The beds are lined up along two walls. They have bars on them like cribs. Next to each bed is a little dresser and a metal screen with cloth sides. Someone is coughing. Someone is singing. Someone is crying. Someone is screaming.

I follow my mother to the row of beds near the windows. In the middle of the bed, there is a lump. The lump moves. It is Bubbe. Her wrists are tied to the bars with strips of rags. Her face looks straight up, the eyes staring at the ceiling. Her cheeks are sunken in; her mouth hangs open; she has no teeth. "Ahh! Ahh!" she sighs.

I want to cry but I don't know why. I want to make nice, to reach out and make it better. But this is not Bubbe. I don't want to touch what's in the bed. I want to run away, escape what I see before me.

I turn away from the bed and begin to walk toward the door.

"Where are you going?" my mother asks. "There's nothing to be afraid of"

I wait in the hall. When my mother comes back, her face is red; she looks as if she has been crying. I have never seen my mother cry.

We walk toward the train station. "See how it is," my mother says. "See how it is in America." She clasps my upper arm, her nails digging into my skin. "No one will do that to me. No one," she says. "I will die first."

10

Tibby was coming to see Mama. She had called every day, first my mother, then me, to make sure I knew everything my mother said or did not say, but this was her first visit since Alvin and I had put Mama in the nursing home.

I went to the bank, to my mother's vault. I wanted to be ready for Tibby's visit.

Someday, I had thought, I would come into what was rightly mine. Not money, there wasn't much of that, and what there was would have to be divided three ways, but jewels. Jewels would be my legacy. "Someday," my mother said, "the diamonds will be yours. Yours and Tibby's. Jewels go to the daughter." Not that I would wear diamonds; I wasn't the kind, and I didn't go places where diamonds were necessary, but jewels would make amends. They were a covenant between us, security, like money in the bank.

I had never come to the vault alone, even though for twelve years, ever since my father died, I had been the co-signer. It was a precaution against the day when I would have to disperse my mother's legacy. I was the oldest, the only one who lived in New York, so I was in charge. But even on that first day when I came to sign the signature card, I had not seen the treasures my name guarded.

"It's none of your business," my mother said, "what I have and what I don't have. Someday but not now." So I had waited while she walked through the iron gates into the vault itself and carried the little box to the examining room. In all the years since, I had heeded my mother's words; I had never come to see what would be mine.

In the tiny examining room, I took inventory: Two diamond cocktail rings; five U.S. savings bonds, one in each of the grandson's names; an Israeli bond for Julie, the only granddaughter; a rhinestone bracelet watch; a cancelled check for $10,000 dated October 1929; three Kennedy silver dollars; a diamond and sapphire pendant on a silver chain; my father's citizenship papers; a pair of what looked like diamond shirt studs my father might have worn when he was rich, but after seeing the screw backs, I decided were earrings; my mother's passport, the one she used for her trip to Israel; a pocket watch; a mother of pearl pin watch the case broken; wrist watches; a Waterman pen and pencil set still in its case, the pen the kind you filled.

Here it was—the treasure, the diamonds of my mother's stories. Here were the stones my mother used to pave her way, the rocks that held her place. Pawned, reclaimed, borrowed against, repossessed: they had paid for my brother's Bar Mitzvah, a catered affair before such affairs were commonplace. They had provided the down payment for the house my mother bought from Uncle Arthur, the house my grandmother owned that went to Arthur, sold when he and Aunt Bertha moved to Florida. They had paid for the car, the furs, the carpeting, the things that showed the world who my mother was, how refined she was.

I held the earrings in my hands. They did not look real. There was none of the sparkle, the fire and ice, characteristic of diamonds, the setting more bronze than gold, old fashioned rather than old looking.

My mother always wanted diamonds, something she could count on. She wore her gold wedding ring and her gold watch. She kept the cameo at home, with her pearls, hidden in her underwear. Her jewels, the diamonds, she kept in the vault, arriving like royalty when the occasion demanded, a queen visiting her treasure house.

I never wanted diamonds. I craved my grandmother's candlesticks. I longed for the teapot shaped like an elephant that sat on top of my mother's refrigerator. I yearned for my father's teffillim, the black leather boxes she gave away with his clothes and shoes on the day she burned his papers in the week after his death. Sam had bought me a watch when we got married. A watch edged in diamond chips. Something valuable I could use. I never wore it.

"Someday," my mother always said, "the diamonds will be yours. Yours and Tibby's. Jewels go to the daughter."

"There's plenty of time," I said. I had smiled and tried to look pleased. It was not jewels I wanted.

I never liked diamonds. I always thought they were cold like ice or glass. I did not want to wear a piece of rock around my neck. I did not want a chunk of glass sitting on my finger. Jade was something else. Jade has a way of connecting to its wearer, subtly changing with the change in blood and gland, a personal barometer. Rubies, too, have a special way. Or so I'd been told. I'd never had rubies. I'd never even seen them up close. I imagined they were like garnets, but deeper, brighter, more like blood. I would not have minded rubies. Or opals, creamy smooth. Amber is what I had, glowing, warm, like the sun. And turquoise, the gem the Hopis think is sky. Lapis intrigued me, and jasper, carnelian, malachite—Bible stones whose names still held the power and glory of what once was. But diamonds! They left me cold.

Gail had diamonds. My mother had given her a diamond ring for her twenty-fifth wedding anniversary. My mother had taken the ring off her own finger and handed it to Gail. Just like that, right in the middle of a family dinner. My mother always had a sense of timing, she knew just how to get center stage.

"You'll get the cocktail rings," she'd said to me. "The necklace goes to Tibby. The cameo to Julie. It's not worth much. It's not good gold. Julie, my only granddaughter, should have it. For a remembrance. You'll get the cocktail rings. You'll get the cocktail rings and my Persian lamb coat."

She had not said anything about the earrings I held in my hand.

"I can't believe you don't want diamonds," Tibby used to say, fingers flashing, ears sparkling, her wrists ablaze, her diamonds a price tag that showed her worth. She was like my mother, always on show, trying to impress the neighbors, putting a value on how things looked as if there were an outward sign that showed just who we were.

I remembered how I used to take lunch to school on Thursdays when my mother went to help my father in his chicken store. It was too much for my grandmother to give me lunch and watch Tibby and Alvin. Few children ate lunch in school, only the poor who had free lunch or those whose mothers worked.

On Thursdays, I help make my lunch. Sometimes it is a fried egg sandwich. Sometimes it is salami on roll. We do not have a thermos so I carry tea in a jar. "A jar is fine," my mother says. "It can double as a glass."

One day my mother does not have a jar so she gives me tea in a bottle, a clean scrubbed bottle that still says "Slivovitz, 100 Proof." I do not pay attention. A bottle is a bottle and meant to be used.

I sit in the lunchroom eating my sandwich. I hurry to finish so I can go out and play. I take a swallow of tea. I need to quench the thirst that salami brings.

I hear laughter. I see Mr. Pincus whisper to Mrs. Finnerty and point in my direction. I turn around to see what it is that can make teachers laugh. There are only children sitting at another table, eating. I take another bite and lift the bottle to wash it down. "Having a little drink, huh?" Mr. Pincus' voice falls on me like a slap.

Mrs. Finnerty shushes him even as she smiles. I feel ashamed. Guilty. Of what I do not know. Teachers do not laugh without a reason.

.   .   .

"I'm too old to eat in school," I tell my mother at three o'clock. "They don't let you go to the toilet." That's when I begin to eat lunch at home and wear a key around my neck.

On Thursdays when my mother goes to help my father and Alvin goes to Hebrew School, I take care of Tibby. I watch she doesn't fall and hurt herself. I watch she doesn't run into the street and get killed. I take her to the bathroom. I tell her to pull her underpants all the way down so they don't get wet.

Tibby needs to be taken care of. She has weak blood. She goes to first grade now and I have to wait for her at three o'clock. She walks so slow. My friends call. "Hurry up Millie," they say. I stand and wait for Tibby. Tibby—Toible—a little dove. My sister is chubby and pink and cute. Everyone pinches her cheek. They pat her head and give her a squeeze.

On Thursdays Alvin eats in school and I have to give Tibby her lunch.

"I don't want bananas and cream," she says pushing her bowl away. I catch the bowl before it drops off the table.

"I don't want bread and butter," she says, throwing her bread on the table so it lands butter side down, and I have to clean it up.

"I'm not going to school," she says, folding her arms across her chest when it's time to leave.

I grab her arm, pull her off the chair. "Oh," she screams. "Ow," she yells.

"Crybaby," I say. "I didn't hurt you."

"I want Ma," she says. "I want Bubbe. I don't want you."

"Let's go now," I say, afraid we'll be late.

"Crooked eyes!" she calls. "Crooked eyes and crooked back, with a body like a sack."

I know she is trying to provoke me. She wants a scene, she wants Bubbe to come and punish me. She wants us to be late; she doesn't want us to go to school.

"Stop it," I say. I shake her hard.

"Crooked eyes. Crooked eyes," she yells. She looks like she is laughing. Slap. I hit her across the face. I wait.

She kicks my shin. It hurts.

"Brat. Lousy brat," I yell. I want to stop her words. I don't want a sister.

She grabs my school books and throws them on the floor. "Book worm," she yells.

I hit her. I hit her again. She kicks and screams. She reaches for the container of cream. She throws it on the floor where it makes a mess. She knocks down a chair and runs to the other side of the table. I go after her. She grabs a fork. I pick up a knife.

"What's happening here?" Mrs. Sherman stands in the doorway. She takes the knife from me and the fork from my sister. "Wait until your mother finds out what happened here," she says.

I pick my books up from the floor. I want to go to school. I don't want to stay in this house. I take my sister's hand and pull her into the hall. I don't ask what Mrs. Sherman will tell my mother. I'm glad she came. I'm glad she came before I killed my sister.

I picked Tibby up at the airport. She wore her hair in the bouffant style of her youth, sunny yellow now, the color changing with the changing years. She wore Eigner shoes, a linen suit—she was allergic to wool. Her allergies protected her. Alvin had moved far away but he'd never left home; he was still a little boy. Tibby had left later than I and had tried to grow up. She gave up her health so she could keep herself. How could anyone make demands of a sick woman?

There were gold chains around her neck, rings on her fingers. She had not agreed to marry Charlie until she had the ring on her finger. Two carats, square cut. "If you don't start out right," she told me, "there's no telling how you'll end up." Her bag looked like a Gucci. Was it real or imitation? I could never tell. Once I admired a ring she wore. Gold with a little garnet in its rose shaped center. "Here," she said laughing,

"It's yours." I protested, I couldn't take something valuable like that, I said. She laughed again. "Take it," she said. "You think it's real. Everybody does. It's not. People expect me to have the real thing because I look like I have the money, so I fool them. I mix the real with the fake and no one knows."

Tibby was not going to stay the night. She would not stay in our mother's apartment—she did not feel comfortable there without my mother—and I lived too far out on the Island. She'd come to see our mother and the house of our childhood. "For old times sake," she said.

At the nursing home, I said hello to my mother, checked with the attendant and went to sit in the lobby. I wanted Tibby and my mother to have this time alone.

Tibby did not stay long. "It's too sad," she said as she took a tissue out of her purse and blew her nose.

We drove to our old neighborhood, burnt out now, but the house still stood. My mother would have been proud. Two black women were sitting on the porch where I used to sit.

"Let's go," Tibby said after a brief look. "It's not the same. I don't feel comfortable."

My mother's kitchen was color coordinated: the wrought iron chairs white, the upholstery orange; the fiberglass curtains orange with a white and green design; the light fixture, Tiffany imitation, orange with varicolored fruits along the rim. The white walls held copper plaques, mementos from Israel. A picture of Golda Meir cut from a newspaper and carefully framed, hung in the center of the dining area wall.

Tibby laid her bag on the orange and white checked tablecloth, settled back in her chair, careful not to disturb her hair.

"Have you seen them?" she asked about the diamonds as if she was talking about old friends. "Does she still have them?" She was putting paper towels over the table cloth as if the plastic tablecloth needed place mats, her blood red nails gleaming. When it came to hands Tibby was like my mother, her nails always polished. Tibby used to be a secretary, a receptionist really, until she married. I never understood how she could do typing and filing and still keep those nails. Her nails were even longer now, a sign she didn't use her hands; she was rich enough to have a maid. She still lived by the values she learned in childhood. "You can always tell a woman by her hands," she used to say. I used to hide mine, the cuticles ragged, the nails chipped. I used to be ashamed of my hands, hands that washed dishes and scrubbed floors, hands that refinished furniture and worked in the garden, hands that now filled the tea kettle and set it on the stove.

"They're magnificent," Tibby said. I knew she meant the diamonds.

"I guess," I said my back still turned. "I haven't been to the vault yet." It was easier to lie with my back turned.

"I don't understand you," Tibby said. "Why don't you go and look? The vault's in your name too." She sounded disappointed as if I'd failed her, as if she'd expected something else.

"Why should I?" I asked holding my hands above the kettle as if to hurry up the boiling. "She's not dead yet." I hoped I did not sound as touchy as I felt.

"That's not the point," said Tibby. "You have a responsibility. Besides, aren't you curious? Don't you want to see what you'll get?"

There was no point explaining that I knew what I'd get, that it was not what I wanted: My grandmother's candlesticks, already promised to Tibby, my mother's cameo, pledged to Julie.

"I'd really like the earrings," Tibby said. "Don't get me wrong. I don't mean anything by it. Mama should live to be a hundred and twenty! But I've always wanted those earrings. I remember how fantastic they are. Long. Were they two strands or only one? I can't remember."

Startled, I turned to look at my sister. Was this a trap? Was she trying to find me in a lie? There were no such earrings in the vault. Had there ever been? Had my mother sold them to pay for some emergency? Had she given them to Gail? Or were they but another of the myths that fed our fantasies, twisted into fact by time and repetition and Tibby's own desire?

I couldn't tell Tibby the earrings she described did not exist. She'd know I'd been to the vault. Even later, when the legacy could be claimed, she would not believe me. She'd always think I'd taken the earrings for myself. I had trapped myself. That's what came of trying to play my mother's game, of trying to behave the way my sister would.

We can always share the studs, I thought, one for each of us. I imagined Tibby with one earring; I imagined how she would feel not to get what she wanted. I smiled as I served the tea in the glass cups and saucers my mother had gotten at the movies when we were children.

"What are you smiling at?" she asked as I handed her a paper napkin and a spoon.

"Nothing really. Just remembering," I said. I was not really lying. I did remember.

"Oh me too. I was remembering how Mama got the dishes. She used to take you with her to dish night so she could get an extra dish. She never took me."

I started to protest, but caught myself in time. You were a baby, I wanted to say, she couldn't take you. I watched as Tibby picked up her cup, put a napkin in the saucer to catch the drips. She was compulsively neat. Once when Matthew was in college, and Sam and I were at loose ends, we had decided to see Boston, and, of course, we stayed with Tibby. She had a flannel backed tablecloth on the formica kitchen table, but she had put place mats on top of that. How careful I had been not to get crumbs on the floor or even on the table! I was afraid she'd start vacuuming while I sat there. It had not been a comfortable weekend. I was smoking then and no sooner did I put out my cigarette, then she'd grab the ash tray, dump the contents down the garbage disposal, wash and rinse the ash tray and return it to the exact spot from which it had been taken. After that I always made some excuse why we couldn't stay over.

"Do you remember all those dinners, the holidays and all the relatives?" she asked. I sat in the chair near the window, the one my mother always sat in. "Then things began to change." Tibby said. "After Bubbe died. That was the first funeral I remember. Mama began to fight with Uncle Arthur. I remember they had a fight about the candlesticks and about the money he owed her. It was after Bubbe died. Then there was no one to hold the family together." She looked at me as if expecting confirmation.

"Do you remember when Mama finally bought the house? How angry you were! Even though you didn't live there any more, you wrote a letter. You wanted us to move downstairs so it would really be a house. But Mama wouldn't move. All she did was take an extra room out of the back apartment so Alvin could have his own room, so he wouldn't have to sleep in the living room."

I remembered. I remembered that I never had my own room. I had to share with Tibby. Alvin got his own room, Alvin who didn't care where he slept.

I remembered the fights, how Aunt Bertha said my mother had the cameo so she should have the candlesticks. I remembered how my mother got the candlesticks, how Uncle Arthur made her buy them from Aunt Bertha's estate after Aunt Bertha died. My mother never spoke to him after that. He died alone in a hospital in Florida. "He lived like a dog, and he died like a dog," my mother whispered at his funeral. I remembered how my mother rented Bubbe's apartment to a family with five children, refugees, and how my mother complained about them, the noise they made and the dirt. Then years later, when the neighborhood changed and my father died, my mother lived there alone. She would not move. She had lived here and she would die here, she said. "Nobody died in this house," she said.

"Do you remember Alvin's Bar Mitzvah?" Tibby asked swirling the tea in the cup as if she were getting ready to read the leaves. "You wore a gown. I was so jealous."

A gown! The graduation dress I made myself in sewing class, refurbished with pink ribbons, my mother's idea, to make it look different from what it was.

"And Mama with her diamonds and Bubbe with her pearls."

I did not remember that.

"She was a tough old lady, Bubbe. I was always a little bit afraid of her. She really kept the family together though. You've got to give her credit."

"I thought it was anger that kept the family together. Anger and arguments," I said surprised at how strongly I felt, surprised I'd said as much as I had. It wasn't Bubbe's dying that broke things up, or Uncle Arthur's moving to Florida. It was not having the house to go to. There has to be a center, a place for people to congregate. It was the place that pulled us in, the people part of it, like furniture in a room. It was the place we had to leave before we could be free of the people.

"Family was not so important to you," Tibby said, dismissing my words. "You were always with your friends, trying out new things. Some of them were a little weird, or maybe it was because you took everything so seriously. Like the time you got religious! How I envied you! You were so independent." She stood up, went to the sink and got the sponge.

I didn't know what to say. I had envied Tibby. I thought things came easily to her, able to get what she wanted without even asking. I had always considered myself bound by convention, unable to break the constrictions imposed by birth and class and time. I thought Tibby was my mother's daughter, concerned with things and their market value. I was like my father, who had no place in the family, who lost his money and pulled my mother down. My father who wanted to study Torah and do good works.

My mother is ashamed of my father. She says she married the wrong man. "He fooled me," she says. "I thought he was a rich man. He gave me diamond earrings and a diamond necklace. He bought me a fur coat and a fox stole. But I was taken for a fool." She means he lost his money; she is not a landlady.

It is her idea for my father to get a store. She thinks he can make a better living selling chickens than he can working in a shop where all they talked about is strikes and unions.

She has a head for business. She is always thinking of ways to make money on the side where all it costs is time and work.

"It's my right," she tells Uncle Arthur. "You owe me."

We are in my grandmother's house. My mother, my father, my uncle, and my aunt sit around the table. I am young then, young enough to sit on the floor under the table playing with Whitey's tail, watching my grandmother's shuffling feet come nearer as she brings the hot water for tea. My mother's foot, in her street shoe, is tapping. My father wears high shoes like a baby's. He has weak feet, my mother says. Even Tibby now wears Oxfords, Buster Browns. My sister is sitting on Aunt Bertha's lap. Five years old and still a baby. I imagine my Aunt Bertha blowing on some tea and feeding my baby sister. My hand tightens on Whitey's ear. He begins to growl. I make nice.

"What would it cost you?" My mother says.

"Cost? It will cost." Uncle Arthur says, "Do you think I'm a *graff pataff* that I can support the whole world?"

"Why not? Do you have a family of your own? Who is closer than a sister? Especially when it's her money that made you what you are."

My uncle's feet move apart. Is he getting up? I see Aunt Bertha's hand touch his knee. His feet go back the way they were, one in front of the other.

My mother wants my uncle to give my father chickens at cost. Uncle Arthur says there is a good market with the colored people so my mother finds an empty store in a good neighborhood. My mother says they'd be fools not to take an extra store in a black neighborhood.

"If we can't have our own house," my mother tells my father, "at least we can have our own business."

"What good is a life like this? " she says. "Never to know if you still have a job. One week bringing in a few pennies and the next week nothing. Always afraid of the boss."

My father says nothing.

But that night he comes with my mother downstairs to my grandmother's house.

"Is it a deal?" my mother asks.

No one talks. Aunt Bertha's knee pushes Uncle Arthur's knee.

"It's a deal," Uncle Arthur says.

My father will have a shop and sell chickens and eggs on one side of the store while the butcher sells meat on the other side. On Thursdays when it will be busy—"Please God"—my mother will go to help him.

It is my mother's idea to save the down of the goose and duck and sell it to the pillow man. It is her idea that my father should not give credit to his customers. "Better to throw the chicken in the garbage than give it away for nothing," my mother says. "Respect. You need to earn respect."

"You can pick up quite a bundle of change," she tells my father. "You have to go with the times."

The people in the new neighborhood shop on Saturday, payday. They want cheaper cuts of meat, fryers and fowl instead of capons and pullets, lungs and soup bones instead of flanken. They don't need the meat kosher-killed.

"Someone has to sell to them," my mother says.

"But Shabbos," my father protests.

I listen from my bed, envisioning my father dressed for the Sabbath, my mother lighting the candles to welcome the Sabbath Queen while we wait for my father to come home from shul so we can eat the Shabbos meal.

"Someone has to do it, " says my mother. "It might as well be us. God will forgive us. He knows we can't help it. He'll understand."

My mother knows about God. She knows He knows we come from a refined family. He understands why my father has to break the Sabbath.

So, on Saturdays, my father gets up early and dresses in his Shabbos suit, but instead of shul, he goes to his new store. In the afternoon, my mother dresses in her Shabbos dress and high heeled shoes. She is vain about her legs. "Your legs show breeding," she tells me. She dresses for Shabbos, but she goes to help my father close up the store. "Otherwise they'll rob him blind," she says.

I try to make up for my father. I want to be a good Jew the way he used to be, the way my grandfather was. I join Young Israel. Zelda, who comes from an observant family, is assigned to be my guide. I have a lot to learn. I am almost thirteen years old but my religious training is just beginning. My brother will be Bar Mitzvahed, then he'll be a man. But I am learning how to be a Jew.

We celebrate the Jewish holidays: we sing songs, study the traditions, learn what it is to be Jewish. There are six hundred thirteen required good deeds in the world. They are called *mitzvahs*. A girl grows up to be a woman and light the candles on Friday nights... Keeping kosher is an obligation... Of all the mitzvot, keeping the Sabbath is the most important and the hardest. "For it is written," the teacher says, "God blessed the seventh day and hallowed it. The Sabbath," the teacher explains, "is God's gift to the Jews."

I go to services on Friday night and Saturday morning. I bless the food before I eat and after I finish. I observe the dietary kosher laws and help others to do the same. When my mother urges Tibby to drink her milk, I remind her that it is not yet six hours since she ate meat. When Alvin gets up late and has to rush to school, I remind him that soon he'll have to get up early and lay phylacteries. When I see my father dress as if for shul on the Sabbath and then go to the store, I say nothing. I pray that soon he can return to the ways of our fathers, that my mother will stop pushing him to make more money. I pray that God sees how I obey His rules.

Zelda and I become friends. We agree to pray every morning at 7:30 and every evening at 10. We think of each other as we send our spirits up to God.

She instructs me in the ways of Jewishness: A girl must keep her arms and chest covered. When a girl gets married, she shaves her head and gets a wig. A girl has to be pure for her husband. Never eat Chinks. Most important: Keep the Sabbath. No work must be done on the Sabbath. I cannot turn on the lights, or play the radio, or light the stove.

"What if someone falls and you need light to see?" I ask.

"Turn the light on the night before," she answers.

"Isn't the light working then?" I ask.

"A light can work, but you can't," she answers.

I think of my father but I say nothing to Zelda.

Zelda instructs me in the specific ways of a pious Jew. I have to be careful I do not break the rules even accidentally. My shoes must be polished on Friday. Zelda does not comb her hair on Saturdays because she might break some of the hairs. Breaking the hair is like writing a letter. Forbidden. She advises me to braid my hair on Friday as she does. I touch my braids, not as long as hers, and wonder how it feels to wear a wig. My mother doesn't wear a wig, neither does my grandmother. "It's not necessary in America," my mother says when I ask her.

"Are you going to be bald?" Tibby wants to know. I don't even bother to answer her.

Zelda says I cannot carry anything on the Sabbath, not even a handkerchief. I must put it in my dress pocket on Friday, or if my dress has no pocket, I must tuck it into the sleeve so when I put on my dress on Saturday it will be part of my dress.

"What about my prayer book? Can I carry that?"

"No. Nothing." She puts her lips together the way my mother does when something is settled. "Some day, when there is an *eruv* here, then you can carry a prayer book." An *eruv* is an imaginary fence around the streets where we live. Inside the *eruv* it will be as if we live in one house. Then we can carry books and handkerchiefs. But we can never work. And we can never break our hair. Or tear toilet paper.

"You have to tear the toilet paper on Friday," Zelda says. "Tear as much as you think you'll need. Better to have more than not enough."

She gives me a list of rules: I can't play the radio. I can't do homework. I can't read school books because then I'd be doing homework. I can read library books, if they're for pleasure not for school. But I can't go to the library because I will be making someone else work. I argue that the library is open whether I go or not. But the rules are clear. I can not go to the library.

Now I go to the library on Monday. I try to get enough books to last the whole week. When Uncle Arthur takes all my cousins to the Chinese restaurant, I stay home. I pray for them.

I make neat piles of toilet paper. I tear paper for everyone in the family. I put stacks of paper on the sink and the window sill and on the little footstool where my mother keeps the shoe cleaning material. I wash myself on Friday and braid my hair. Before I go to evening prayers, I make sure the Sabbath flame is on the stove. If it is not, I will have to eat cold food and drink cold water instead of hot tea. I can hardly wait for the new year and the high holidays. I can hardly wait for Yom Kippur when I can fast and pray all day, when I can show God just how good a Jew I am.

There is one problem I cannot overcome. The movies. I love the movies. I go whenever I have 25 cents. I used to go every Saturday. Sometimes my mother made me take my sister. Sometimes I went by myself and sat in the kiddie section. On Saturday, I could see five cartoons, a Zorro and two movies. I would buy a box of Goobers and eat one nut at a time. Now that I am *frum*, I can't go to the movies on Saturday. Now on Saturday, Alvin takes Tibby. I stay home. They have seen *The Old Maid* and *Dark Victory* and *Four Feathers* and *Young Mr. Lincoln.* I have seen *Wuthering Heights* and *Goodbye Mr. Chips* and *Mr. Smith Goes to Washington.* I have gone with my mother on dish night.

I miss the movies. I yearn for things the way they used to be. But it is all part of what it means to be a good Jew, part of the temptations I have to resist, temptations that pull me away from the world of my fathers.

The Wizard of Oz is playing at the Supreme. I ask Zelda if she wants to come with my mother and me on dish night. She tells me she saw it on Saturday at the Premier. I am shocked.

"How can you go on Saturday?" I ask. I wonder if there is a rule I don't know, an exception for the "Wizard of Oz.".

"My father pays the man on Friday," she says.

I say nothing.

"It's all right. I"m not carrying any money. It's not work. I even buy the candy on Friday and put it in my pocket ahead of time. So when I put my dress on, it's already there."

I have a bad taste in my mouth like after eating a cold soft boiled egg.

On Saturday, I go to morning prayers. I watch Zelda pray, her handkerchief in her sleeve, pieces of toilet paper in her pocket just in case.

When I come home, I tell my mother I am going to the movies. "I have my own money," I say. "I will take Tibby if you want,"

My mother opens her mouth, closes it, then she says, "So, it's not so easy to be a *frume Yid.*"

She does not ask me any questions. She gives me six cents for candy. Tibby eats all the Raisinettes and sugar buttons.

I watched as Tibby sponged the table clean. We had never understood each other. I used to think it was our place in the family, the years between us—she the youngest, I, the oldest; she the baby, I, the big sister—the resentment that came from that, feelings we'd never lost. I had moved away; we had never had the chance to change things.

"Maybe if I had some of your strength, I wouldn't have been so sick all these years. Maybe being sick is the only way I could get what I wanted." She reached for her purse, picked it up, put it down again.

"Oh, Tibby," I said.

For a moment quiet filled the room as if even the air hung in balance. My sister, willing to share herself.

I reached out to take her hand.

Tibby's fingers touched my palm, pressed down. She smiled, and gently moved her hand away. "It's too late now," she said looking into her cup as if she could read the leaves. "We are what we are." She did not pretend to drink her tea. "To think you were once religious, you who wouldn't even Bar Mitzvah your son."

I got up to put my cup and saucer in the sink. I remembered how I used to take care of her, how she ate all the Raisinettes and sugar buttons when we went to the movies, how I always looked out for her. I remembered how she used to say, "You have to take advantage of opportunities."

"I just remembered." she said. "The bracelet watch. Do you remember it? My God! It would be worth a fortune if it was real."

"And the cocktail rings. She used to wear them all the time. They were her favorites." Tibby stacked my cup and saucer with hers. "You really ought to look," she said. "The vault's in your name too."

She's not dead yet, I wanted to say. It's too soon to divide the loot. I felt cold. The air was more February than May, I thought as I stood at the sink side by side with my sister. A shiver passed through my bones. Inside nothing moved. I was frozen, a solid block if ice. My mother and my sister, my father and I. Nothing changes, I thought. We are what we were. Just more so.

My grandfather's words came back to me, what he used to say every time my mother and Uncle Arthur argued about money: "In the hour of man's departure, neither silver nor gold nor precious stones nor pearls shall accompany him, but only Torah and good works." I thought about my father who never had time to study Torah.

One Saturday when I am almost fourteen, I am sent to help my father. It is my mother's job and she fills it every week. She is never sick. But Tibby has chicken pox, and my mother has to stay and see she doesn't scratch and end up with pock marked skin.

It is a long walk but straight, down Livonia Avenue under the el to Stone Avenue and then a few more blocks to Thatford. My mother thinks the train is only for those who can't walk. "If your feet can't get you there," she says, "it's clear you don't need to go."

I like the walk. It is an adventure, passing the pool room, bridal stores, a movie theater, across a bridge over the railroad tracks. I like Brownsville with its tenements, children playing in the streets, women sitting on the stoops, the big library.

My father's store is small, stuck between a dry cleaner on one side and a corner drug store on the other.

"A good location," said my mother when she picked it. Everyone needed a drug store, if not to buy aspirins then to use the public phone. Coming to or from the drug store a person could be tempted to buy a chicken or eggs. That's what my mother said. "Location is important," she said. "It's not everything, but it's important."

My father is alone in the store when I get there. He smiles as if he is happy to see me. "You didn't have to come," he says. " I could have managed." He makes it sound as if I have more important things to do. He makes it sound as if I can leave, while all the time he strokes my arm or fingers the ribbon at the end of my braids.

He is always touching my hair or my arm, as if to prove I am real. It bothers me, these pokes. There is something crude about them. He never hugs me or holds me in his lap the way fathers in books do. He never kisses me, or tells me how to act or offers me advice. It is clear he doesn't know the finer ways.

My father's store is like my father, small and messy. He sells chickens, some cold cuts, and eggs when he can get them. He sells the chickens whole, the feathers still on. Only when somebody buys them does he clean and dress them. His fingers are nimble but rough. He often tears the skin when he plucks the feathers.

I take a seat on an upended crate near the cash register ready to see that no one robs my father blind.

I sit and stare out through the plate glass windows at the people passing by. My father sweeps the sidewalk near the doorway, bits of feathers stick to his shoes, the edge of his bloodied apron swinging with the rhythm of his sweeps.

A customer comes in, her shopping bag already bulging.

"How are you, Missus?" asks my father leaning the broom against the wall. Quickly, without much thought, she picks a chicken from the few remaining.

"I'll have it ready in a minute," he says and takes the chicken to the back to pluck the feathers. The woman waits near the doorway. She doesn't look at me, nor I at her.

My mother is right, I think. Anyone can come in, walk over to the register and take the money out. Then what can my father do? I am glad I'm here to see that no one robs him blind. It is clear my mother knows just how things are.

There are a few customers, not many. My father sells three chickens and some eggs. He sells half of a long fat bologna to a man who takes it out unwrapped. My father cuts the other half in two and places them on the counter top as if inviting purchase. There are only two chickens left.

My father starts getting ready to close up shop. He straightens the paper bags and begins to sweep, sending feathers flying. Soon it will be time to leave.

"Do you want something before we go?" he calls to me. "A soda maybe?"

I would like a soda. I would like to sit at the drugstore counter sipping a cherry coke. I know I shouldn't leave. I have been sent to stay and watch. I cannot leave my father here alone.

A boy comes in, about Alvin's age but shorter and thinner. He looks older though, more than ten. He doesn't walk but swaggers as if he is someone important. His shirt is held together by a safety pin, the bottoms of his pants are rolled. He doesn't look at me, but I know he sees me plain.

My father stops his sweeping, his hands upon the broom.

"Got any work today?" the boy demands. He sounds as if he's asked the question before. "Sweeping? Cleaning up?" His voice is tough, disdainful, as if he's too good to sweep dirt.

"Nothing for you," says my father. I sense a tension I don't understand. I put my hand upon the cash register, then move it quickly back onto my lap, afraid I've called attention to where the money is.

"Nothing now," repeats my father. "You're late," he adds, as if explaining.

"Okay, okay," says the boy, dismissing what he doesn't care to hear. "Gimme a chicken, a good one. Get the feathers off good. And don'tcha tear the skin, hear?"

"Let's see your money," says my father, standing easy and relaxed, his hands still upon the broom. Even I can see this scene's been played before.

"It's here. It's here." The boy holds out a fist closed tight around some coins and bills crushed together. "Don'tcha trust me?" he laughs.

My father leans the broom against the wall, takes a chicken from the counter, making a show of it as if for some important customer. They don't say a word, my father with his dirty hands, the boy in shabby clothes. They look the chicken over head to feet. Then, as if some unseen signal passes between them, my father carries the bird to the back, as if it is a trophy in some contest I do not understand.

I sit and do the job I have been sent to do. I sit and think how careful one must be of how one lives, whom you choose for friends, who your parents are. I don't pay attention to the boy who stand and waits.

Something breaks into my thoughts, a move no bigger than a blink. The boy still stands, his back relaxed against the counter, except that now he stares at me. There is something there within his look. Defiance, anger, hate or fear. I can't tell what it is. I sit up straight and look again. Where once two pieces of bologna lay, only one now fills the empty space. My eyes go to the floor behind the counter. Perhaps it fell—that might be what I thought I saw. I slip down from the crate ready to track the missing piece.

My father is there beside me, one hand upon my arm, his other hand clutching the neck of the freshly plucked chicken. "Okay," the boy says, as if indeed, he has been asked.

My father wraps the chicken as it is, head and legs still attached. "Let's have the money," he says to the boy. He does not count the coins and bill thrust into his palm but hands it all to me, his eyes upon the boy. It seems the price has been agreed upon before; it seems this has happened more than once.

As the boy begins to leave, the paper bag beneath his arm, his eyes flicker past my face, the fragments of a smile move across his lips.

"But Pa," I begin, concerned about the missing piece of wurst.

He doesn't allow me to continue. "It's time to go," he says. "We did enough already. We'll leave a little early and take our time."

"But Pa," I try again. "I think that boy took something. I think that boy's a thief." I am angry now, as if, somehow, I have failed to do my job.

"It's all right," my father says. "Don't worry. I know his mother. They're very poor." I don't see his face. He is busy emptying the cash register, stuffing bills and coins into the little sack my mother made. He draws the strings together, twisting the whole upon itself, then stuffs his day's income into his pocket. Only then does he turn to me. "It's just a game," he says. "It happens every week."

He goes to the back to change his clothes. It will not do to let people know he works on the Sabbath. He wears his Sabbath suit but he doesn't change his shoes.

We do not talk as we walk home, hand in hand, with swinging arms and matching steps.

We come into the kitchen and there is Tibby, sitting on my mother's lap.

"You're home early," is all my mother says as if this were an ordinary day.

I never tell what happened. My mother doesn't ask and so I don't have to lie.

Diamonds, rubies, sapphires, jade—treasures from the earth.
The harder the stone, the greater the value.
The more the weight, the more the worth.
The rarer the piece, the bigger the price.

How do I decide the value of a tea pot shaped like an elephant, never used? The price of my grandmother's candlesticks? The worth of the pictures in my mother's album?

Words weigh me down. Logic is no rock on which to stand. I want something simple, plain, an explanation I can use, a definition, a measure, like pound, gram, grain. Thus and so, so much of a life. Thus and so and thus and so, so much more of a life. Born, lived, died.

My sister says, "Appearances count."
My brother says, "Money makes the world go round."
My grandfather said, "We can store treasures in this world or in the world to come."
My father lost his money. He worked on the Sabbath. What is his measure?

11

Julie called. She wanted to come to New York to see her grandmother.

"There's plenty of time," I found myself saying. "You don't have to rush things. She's not dying yet."

But Julie knew what I would not let myself see.

She arrived that evening. Sam met her at LaGuardia on his way home from work. They were laughing when they came into the house, like old friends who had found each other after a long separation.

Julie kissed me on the cheek and told me I looked well. Tired but well. It was late and we sat right down to dinner. I had made her favorite foods: veal parmesan and spaghetti, steamed zucchini, garlic bread. She did not touch the veal. I had forgotten she was not eating red meat.

We did not talk much. She wanted to know when Sam was going to wear the shorts she'd bought him, when I was going to take a vacation and take it easy. She thought Sam and I ought to plan something nice for the summer, for our anniversary, a trip, a resort, some-place where there were people, where there was life. She did not mention Doug, and I did not say anything about the abortion.

It was late and Julie went up to bed early, to sleep in her room. In the morning we drove to the nursing home. We did not touch or talk. I respected her silence.

I went in first. I did not want to frighten my mother.

"Ma," I said. "I have a surprise for you." My mother was sitting in her wheel chair, staring out the window.

"Grandma." said Julie coming in behind me before I had finished. "Grandma, it's me, Julie."

My mother's face lit up. I was pleased my daughter could bring my mother pleasure.

"So," said my mother. "You came to tell me something?"

"No, Grandma." said Julie. "I came to see you."

"I thought you came to tell me you're getting married."

"Grandma. I came to tell you I love you."

"You love me? Well, why not? A granddaughter is supposed to love her grandmother."

My mother's words sounded harsh and unaccepting, but I knew she was pleased. I could tell from the way she smiled, the way she reached out to hold Julie's hand. Julie knew it too. She smiled and hugged her grandmother.

"I brought you some things," Julie said as she reached into her back pack. She pulled out a bottle of Aura lotion, almond scented, the kind she had given me for Mother's Day the year before. She began rubbing the lotion into my mother's hands, finger by finger, then up her arms. She tried to put some on my mother's face, but my mother pulled her head away. Then Julie took out a bottle of toilet water and put some behind my mother's ears, and on her wrists, and around her neck. My mother smiled and held the bottle while Julie rummaged in her bag for two gaily wrapped packages. "It's a present," she said.

My mother unwrapped the paper eagerly, like a child on her birthday. One of the packages held a necklace made of seashells which Julie draped around my mother's neck. I would never have bought my mother such a necklace. I was sure she'd throw it down in disdain and say it was cheap. The other package had a comb and brush set. The back of the brush had a picture of an old fashioned woman on it, a shepherdess perhaps.

"I'll brush your hair," said Julie. "I remember when we visited how I used to watch you brush your hair, how beautiful it was."

I sat on a chair in the corner of the room and watched while my daughter brushed my mother's hair. I remembered brushing Julie's hair when she was a baby. How soft and fine it was! I did not remember ever seeing my mother brush her hair.

"Tell me a story, Grandma," said Julie as she brushed. "Tell me a story the way you used to."

"Stories! Who remembers stories?"

"Tell me about when you were a girl. Tell about when you were in Europe," said Julie.

"In Europe? In Europe I cooked for the Germans. I graduated from the Gymnasium. I was very smart. I had a good head. In the album there is a picture with me in an apron when I was a cook. The Germans didn't take just anybody. They rented a room in our house. We were a fine family. We had a dining room. Not everybody had a dining room."

My mother's voice drifted off as if she were seeing herself as she used to be.

"Tell about your friend. Tell about Olga."

I was surprised to hear a name I had not heard since I was a child. I did not know my mother had told Julie about Olga.

"What should I tell you? Olga was my friend. We went to Bund meetings together. I was a Bundist. You didn't know that? My mother forbid it. Uncle Arthur told her and my mother said that in her house we have to do what she says. She said they would arrest me. She said if I wanted to be arrested it was my business, but they would come to the shtetl and they would make a pogrom and it would be on my head. She said Olga was no good, she was leading me into trouble. She forbid me to see her. Olga. My friend, Olga."

My mother went on with her stories. She told about the Polacks who put a Jew in a horse's belly. And she told about Aunt Bertha hiding in the barn. She did not tell about the gun. She told about her youth and her childhood, the images clear as if they had happened yesterday, clearer than what did happen yesterday. She spoke, her voice strong and vibrant. Even when she told about the hardships, about not having enough to eat, about trying to make ends meet when my Grandfather was in America, she sounded happy, as if she were telling a story that had happened to someone else, or one that she had read in a book. Was that how it was going to be? Would I, too, sit in a wheel chair and tell stories to my grand-daughter, stories without bitterness and anger? If I did, it would have to be to Matthew's daughter. Julie was not going to change her mind about having children.

"I have more presents," said Julie. She took out a pair of slip-pers lined in terry cloth. "To keep your feet warm," she said, "and something special. I looked all over for it." She handed my mother a small package. My mother took it eagerly as if she were a child getting a sweet to eat. I could not imagine what there was in such a little package. My mother had trouble opening it. Julie did not offer to help. She knew part of the fun of a present was opening it. Finally it lay there, in my mother's hand, a lipstick, my mother's favorite color, ruby red. I knew it would be just the size to fit into her little lipstick holder, the holder with a tiny mirror attached to it.

"Oh Julie," said my mother. "Just what I wanted."

I stood up. It was time to go.

We drove home along the Belt Parkway, Julie sitting in her corner of the front seat, seat belt safely secured, staring out at the ocean. She'd always loved the water and could sit for hours watching the waves. We did not talk.

She was quiet even after we got home. She went and sat in the living room staring out the window at the yard. I thought she might be looking at the irises or the lillies. I thought she might be looking at the signs of spring.

I busied myself in the kitchen. I remembered how Julie had kissed my mother goodbye, how she had fluffed the pil-lows on my mother's bed, how she had turned to take one last look.

"What time is your plane?" I asked from the doorway.

"Did you have to do it?" She wasn't looking at me so I couldn't see her face, but I thought I heard accusation in her voice.

"I know you tried—you hired housekeepers. There must have been something else." She had turned and now was looking at me. It was the look she used to have when she was a child and she needed reassurance, the way she did when she was two and the noise of the vacuum cleaner had frightened her. "I don't like to think of Grandma in a home."

"What did you want me to do?" I asked. I did not like to think of myself as the kind of person who put her mother in a home.

"Couldn't she have stayed with you? You could have had full time help. It wouldn't have been for long. She's getting old. How long could it be?"

"It could be years, that's how long. Years." She did not understand; she did not want to understand. She was just like my mother, I thought bitterly, wanting it done her way but wanting me to do it. No wonder they hit it off so well.

"I know it's been hard, Ma." Julie had come to stand before me. Now she took my hand and held it. "I know it hasn't been easy. But I feel bad when I look at Grandma. I feel bad to think my grandmother had to end up in a home."

"How do you think I feel? Do you think I want my mother in a home? I remember when they put my grandmother in a home." I pulled my hand away from her grasp and began fluffing the pillows on the sofa. I did not want to get into an argument. To her I was "mother", the person who fixed things, the one who took care of things. She didn't see me, the person I was, the person I wanted to be.

I stopped fluffing the pillows. Why should Julie be different? I had felt the same way about my mother. I wanted her to fix things, to make them right. I had not been able to see the person she was. I saw her only in terms of me, what she did or didn't do.

"I did the best I could," I said. There was nothing more I could say. That's the way it was between mothers and daughters. We were mothers as long as we lived, and daughters even longer, our mothers living on in us. "I did the best I could," I said again.

"I know, Ma," said Julie. She came over, put her arms around me and held me close. "I know, Ma," she said as she stroked my back.

Life is a word that passes and is no more. There are no second chances.

Mine was not the first mistake. My mother made them, and her mother before that.

Everything is relative: rich and poor, true and false, good and bad. It depends on who you are, what you carry with you, what you remember.

The sins of the mothers, the mistakes of the daughters.

A blow passes, a slap heals, a word lingers.

My mother said we were the same. Was she right?

My mother doesn't love my father. It is nothing new. Love has nothing to do with marriage, she says. Love is for the books or in the movies or when you're young before you get married. Marriage is for making a living, having a home. Marriage is the way men and women live, the way they take care of each other. Marriage is for having children. Sometimes it's easy, and sometimes it's hard. My mother's marriage is hard.

My father lost his mind, my mother says. He doesn't get dressed or go to work. He doesn't leave the house. He sits and cries, sits and talks foolishness, gets up in the middle of the night, forgets where he is going, tells stories about his life, tells lies, embarrasses my mother. My mother has put away his razor and hidden his nail scissors. She has put the sharp knives in special drawers. She says we must not leave my father alone even for a minute: he might harm himself, God forbid. He might jump off the roof.

"You'll end up in Kings County," she yells at him. "You'll end up in the crazy house," she says, but not too loud. She doesn't want anyone to hear. She doesn't want the neighbors to know about our shame.

My father doesn't look crazy; he looks the way he always has except he needs a shave. His face and neck are covered with grey stubble. It looks like chicken feathers before they're singed. In the morning, my mother sees that he gets dressed. He wears pants with suspenders over his union suit, black high button shoes, white socks. He does not wear a shirt.

"What does he need a shirt for?" my mother says. "He's not going any place."

My father sits on his bed and stares; he sits at the kitchen table and cries. "He's like a baby," my mother tells Uncle Arthur. "A baby. Oh, what has become of me? What has become of my life?"

On Saturdays, my mother and brother work in the store; my sister visits a friend; I stay home to keep an eye on my father.

"Eat your soup," I tell him. I talk to my father the way I hear my mother talk: cold and angry. I think this is how you talk to a crazy person.

My father begins to cry. Tears roll down his cheeks and on his neck; his nose begins to run. He wipes his face with the back of his hand.

"Have mercy," he says in Yiddish. I am startled. My father never speaks Yiddish. For years my mother has criticized him for being like a *goy*. My father did not study in Yeshiva the way my grandfather did. He wasn't raised in Yiddishkeit like my uncles. He came to America when he was a little boy, an orphan, a boarder in other people's houses. He lived with *goyim* and learned their ways.

"Have pity," he says again. Then in English, "What good is it? Who knew how it would all turn out? Oh, Malkele, Malkele! Who knew?" He wrings his hands, his chest heaves up and down. "My head hurts. My head hurts," he says.

I put my hand out, touch his shoulder. I am afraid he will bang his head against the wall. "Eat your soup," I say harshly. I want to carry out my duties as my mother's daughter. I don't know what else to do, what to say. I am already in high school, almost a woman. He is my father—I'm not supposed to take care of him. He is not supposed to cry.

"Oh, what a mistake." He rocks back and forth as if he is in Shul praying. "I shouldn't have married her. She was no good, a *furbissene*. She made me break the Sabbath. Now God is punishing me. All she thinks about is money, all she thinks about is respect."how it looks

He's right, I think. My mother is not afraid of God or what He will do, only of people and what they might say. My chronic anger at my mother is always ready to be aroused.

"Why did you marry her?" I ask. I want to stop his crying but I am also curious. Did he love her? Didn't he know what could happen? He could have married someone else, he could have had a different life.

"Why?" I ask again as I hold the spoon up to his lips. "Nobody made you."

He sits up straight. For a moment he looks like he used to, like he did when he went to work.

"She made me," he says. "You don't know." He takes a sip from the spoon. "I was a boarder in their house, with Bubbe and Zayde. I wanted to marry Bertha." Tears roll down his cheeks. The soup dribbles out of his mouth. I give him a dish towel so he can wipe his face. He wanted to marry Aunt Bertha! Is this one of his lies, one of his crazy stories?

"Bertha. I wanted to marry Bertha. Then she told me... she told me... Bertha was damaged... Bertha was used." He opens his mouth as if waiting for me to put the spoon in. I don't want to feed him. I want to hear the rest of the story. I want to hear about my mother.

"She told me I should marry her... she was the oldest... the best... she went to her father... the Zayde... she told him I had to marry her... I used her, she said. He made me." My father stops talking. He stares straight ahead. Then he laughs. "She lied."

I put the spoon in the bowl. He is crazy. I don't want to hear his crazy stories. I don't want to know my mother married my father because of me. I want to run away. I have seen something ugly, something I don't want to see.

I put the bowl in the sink and take my father into the bedroom. He sits on the edge of the bed staring at the walls. He cries.

Uncle Arthur comes upstairs. He tells my father it's no good staying in the house all the time, he should be with people. He tells my father he's going to take him downtown. My father goes in the car with Uncle Arthur. Uncle Arthur takes him to the crazy house.

My father is not allowed visitors; he is having shock treatments. They will jolt his brain back the way it's supposed to be. They will burn out his bad thoughts.

I try to imagine my father in the crazy house, behind barred windows. He is not like them, the crazy people I see in the movies, the crazy people my mother took me to see in Kings County. I remember the way he gave me a lollipop, the way he pinched my cheek. I am afraid for my father, and for me.

"Don't worry," my mother tells me. "It's a fancy place. It's for rich people, on the East Side, right near the mayor's house. It's nothing, a nervous breakdown. He was always nervous."

As soon as my father can have visitors, I decide to go alone. I want to see for myself. I tell my mother I have to stay late in school, that we're rehearsing a play. I tell my friends I have to go to the doctor. I don't want anyone to know about my father.

My father sits in the recreation room with the other men. Even though the chairs are filled with patients, the room is very quiet. No one is talking. I have never seen my father in pajamas and a bathrobe before.

My father doesn't recognize me. I tell him who I am. I tell him again. He smiles. "Oh!" he says. "You were a beautiful baby. Such a beautiful baby." I remember again how he used to pinch my cheek. "I tried," he says. "I tried. I told her not to hit you. I told her. You were such a beautiful baby."

I have forgotten my mother's beatings, that my father did not help me. My father remembers things from long ago, but he can't remember things from now.

The other men sit and stare. The shock treatments are working; the men are quiet.

"Come," I say. "Let's go for a walk. Show me your room." I do not want anyone to hear what we say.

171

We walk up and down, my father holding my arm. His feet drag, his slippers slide. I can look into his face. I am as big as he and stronger.

He sits down on the bed in his room. He looks tired, the life blood drained from his face. I think: This is how he will look when he's dead.

"Pa. Pa," I say. "It's me." I want to bring him back to life; I want him to know it's me.

His face breaks into a smile. He knows who I am. "Millie," he says. "I must tell somebody... I must tell you... the women... in the store... in the back... a sin... on the Sabbath... they let me... she made me do it... she wouldn't sleep in the same bed... it's her fault... Malkele, Malkele." He rolls from side to side as if trying to stand up. He reaches out to take my hand, as if to hold on. I stand just out of reach. This is what it means to be crazy. "Malkele, Malkele," my father cries. "I did wrong... I went with other women... I went in the back with the colored."

The tears well down his face, getting caught in the stubble, dropping off his chin. People cry when they're unhappy and when they're sad. They cry when they hurt. My father hurts, the pain so deep, it touches the wound inside me.

Just as suddenly as it began, it is over. His face becomes still, his eyes close, he puts his head down on the pillow. I lift his feet onto the bed. He is asleep.

I look around to see if anyone heard. I am alone with my father. No one heard.

I leave the room, hurry through the hospital. I don't want to hear crazy stories. I can't believe what my father said. Lies. All lies. My father wanted to marry Aunt Bertha and now he's in the crazy house. My mother says my father talks foolishness; my father says my mother told lies. My mother blames my father; my father blames my mother. Who is right? What is true? How will it end? It's not like a book where you can see how it began, where you can figure out the end because you know the beginning.

One thing I know: this will not happen to me. No one will make me crazy.

12

It's strange how time passes and we remain the same. How we live as if nothing will change, how we see but do not notice.

The attendant said it had been a good day. My mother had cooperated in getting dressed, she had gone down to lunch, she had not complained.

I stood in the hallway near my mother's room waiting for her return. A tall man with a walleye shuffled over. "Are you a doctor?" he asked. "No," I answered, surprised he would think so. "Do I look like a doctor?"

He considered my question. "Well, you can't tell by looks," he said. "Look at me. I have two degrees. I used to be a lawyer. Don't think because I'm here that I'm nobody. I was a captain in the fire department. I'm a Yankee. My family goes back three hundred years. I'm not riff raff like these people. I didn't get off the boat."

He looked healthy enough, this tall man with blue eyes the color of my mother's. But he had to be sick or crazy or he wouldn't be here. Since he looked healthy, it must be his mind that was sick, sick enough to require a place where there was always a registered nurse available and where a doctor came every day, even on weekends.

My mother had ended up with crazy people.

"They stole my teeth," she said as soon as she saw me. The attendant shook her head, adjusted the brakes on the wheel chair, helped my mother into bed and left.

"They stole my teeth." My mother pointed to the empty space where the top half of her dentures should have been. Good, I thought, she can still complain. Anger was good; it got the circulation up. Anger could keep her going, keep her alive.

I went out to the desk to speak to the nurse in charge. "Why would anyone steal her teeth?" she asked. "These old people. She probably threw it down the toilet, or dropped it someplace. They forget."

"My mother wouldn't do that," I said. "Her mind is clear. It's only her body that's weak." I was angry at the nurse. How could she think all old people were the same? How could she think my mother was crazy?

I went back to my mother's room. I told her not to worry, I would call the dentist and have new teeth made.

"What good will it do?" she asked. "I can't eat anyway."

I asked her if she was warm enough. She didn't answer. I put the shawl around her shoulders. She did not push it away.

I began to unpack my shopping bag. First the hard candies she liked. She took one and put the rest on her lap.

I took out a package of old letters I had found under the towels in the linen closet. They were were written in Yiddish and Russian. Some of the envelopes were postmarked Brookline, Massachusetts. They had been written in 1926, 1927, before she was married, before she met my father. I thought she'd like to see them. We could talk about how her life was then; I'd find out about my roots. I thought of it as if it were an oral history project.

She pushed the letters away. "Forget them," she said. "What's gone is gone."

I put the letters aside and took out a cardboard box full of costume jewelry I had found at the bottom of my father's old chifferobe.

"They're not real," my mother said sifting through earrings and necklaces. "Except the pearls. Your father gave them to me as an engagement present. They're opera length."

I dropped the pearls over her shoulders. "They're beautiful," I said. I could not imagine my father giving my mother pearls.

"Take them home," she said. "They'll steal them here." Her fingers curled around the beads so tenderly, I thought she ought to have them.

I began to pin a circle pin to her shawl. "Too much," she said. "The pearls are enough." She still knew when enough was enough.

I put the box into her top dresser drawer, on the side near her bed, the side that held the flowers Julie sent. Julie sent something evey week, flowers, a card, knick knacks.

"The jewelry is in the box," I told my mother. "Here in the drawer." I wanted her to have her own things, to feel at home.

I took out the picture album I'd brought. We had worked on it one evening when my mother was still in her apartment. My friend Laura had come with me. My mother had played hostess, making tea, serving it in the carnival glass cups she'd gotten at the movies. She had berated me for not bringing cake. "I have nothing in the house," she said to Laura.

Still it had been a pleasant visit. I thought working on the album had made it pleasant. Now I thought we could recapture the spirit of that afternoon by putting the album in order while she told me the story behind the faces. She could tell me the names of the people and their relationship to her and I would write them down.

She pushed the album away. "There's plenty of time," she said. "I'm not dying yet."

I put the album back in the shopping bag. I pulled a chair up to the wheel chair. We sat, I looking out the window, she looking toward the door.

After a while, I stood up to leave.

"Help me," my mother said. "I have to pee."

"I'll call the attendant," I said.

"No," my mother protested. "She won't come. She's no good. They're all no good. Rotten. They're all rotten. They let me stay all night in a wet bed. All night I lay in pee."

I pulled the covers back. My mother's legs, still shapely, once her pride and joy, were useless now. She wore socks on her feet, the kind I used to wear as a child. My mother had never worn socks even in the winter when it was cold. She'd always worn stockings fastened to her corset, or rolled below the knee.

I helped her sit up. The toilet was at the other end of the room. Could I get her there? What if she fell? What if she hurt herself?

"Let's use the chair commode," I suggested the way a nurse might.

My mother hooked her hands around my neck, her arms resting on my shoulders. I lifted her just high enough to slide her over to the chair. For a moment my mother's face rested against mine, her breath near my ear.

"I'm finished," my mother said after a while.

I took my place facing her. She hooked her hands around my neck, her arms resting on my shoulders. I lifted her just enough to get her back to bed. She did not weigh much.

I arranged the pillow to support her back, and pulled the covers up. She looked so small. I turned to look out the window at the brick wall of the apartment house across the yard. I could not bear to look at her.

Three days later the manager of the Nursing Home called. My mother was showing signs of distress: her lower extremities were swollen, her kidneys not functioning. She had been taken to the hospital. He said he did not believe in extreme measures especially with old people, but her heart was strong so he had taken steps.

"A real fighter, that woman," the charge nurse said admiringly. "We had to tie her down. It's nothing," she assured me. "It happens that way sometimes, but she'll come around. It's for her own good. We can't have her climbing out of bed. She might fall and break her hip. Then where would we be?"

She motioned me down the hall toward my mother's room. "Her heart is strong. Like a woman of sixty. I can't believe she's almost ninety. Stubborn, these old ones. They really hang on."

Suddenly I had a vision of my mother as she had been when I was a child, sitting at the kitchen table patiently unknotting a tangled ball of wool. "It's still good," she said. "Why should I let it go to waste?"

I walked down to my mother's room. Sounds of coughing, fragments of words filled the hallway. I came to my mother's room. "Help me," I heard her say. "People save me! God, help me."

Two beds lined the farther wall, a curtain stretched between them, the bars raised. A lump filled the middle of each bed. Each lump was an old woman. The lump in the bed on my left was connected to tubes and bottles and machines. The lump that was my mother had her arms tied to the bars with gauze strips. Tied like an animal. The way her own mother had been tied. Even my father was never tied, even when he was institutionalized and had to have shock treatments, he was never tied. She looked straight up, her eyes fixed on the ceiling. Her cheeks were sunken, her mouth hung open, she had no teeth. "Aah! Aah!" she moaned.

I made my body into a shell: I needed to protect my heart

"Untie her," I told the nurse. Together we helped my mother out of bed and into an easy chair.

"I will be responsible," I told the nurse.

"I'm sorry," I told my mother. "I'm sorry."

I spent the day with my mother. I fed her lunch. I arranged for private nurses to watch her so she would not need to be tied. I pushed her wheel chair up and down the hall.

I remembered how she had cooked for the Germans during World War I. I remembered how she and Aunt Bertha had hidden in the barn, how a Polack had found them, how my mother had scared him off with the gun she took from the Germans. I remembered how she was before she was my mother.

I remembered how she managed when my father died, she arranged for the funeral, kept the house, rented the apartments. She did it all alone, never asking for help. She had been a landlady, a grandmother, a widow, playing each role as if she were an actress on stage before an audience.

I remembered how she used to look when I was a little girl, her apron over her house dress, standing in the kitchen making carrot cookies, sitting at the table restringing a broken necklace, patiently knotting the thread between each bead.

Back and forth I walked, caught in the rhythm of the turning wheels, clocks tickimg, hearts beating. I remembered how I used to sit in a carriage and how she pushed me, and how her umbrella made a circle around her head.

All afternoon I pushed my mother up and down the hallway, remembering.

That night I had a dream. In the dream my mother cried and held her arms out to me. Her face was smooth, uncreased by life. I wiped the tears from her unblinking eyes. I used a diaper soft as breath. Still I left smudge marks on her slippery face. I looked again. The face was mine.

Marilyn and I are friends again, the way we used to be. So when she gives a party, I'm invited.

We play "Spin the Bottle." I get Shecky. Shecky is supposed to be a big kisser.

We go into the bathroom and close the door. It's dark. I wait. "Well," he says. He sounds reluctant, scared.

He pushes me up to the wall, his lips against mine. I feel the pressure of his teeth. "Okay," he says. "You've been kissed."

We return to the living room and Shecky changes his seat. Those are the rules: the boys change seats so they can get to kiss different girls. Shecky gets Dorothy next. They stay in the bathroom a long time.

The girls giggle, the boys raise their eyebrows, poke each other with their elbows and say, "Wow." Marilyn smiles but she looks as if she is going to cry. She's putting up a front the way my mother does. She doesn't want anyone else kissing Shecky. She thinks kissing means love. I know kissing is just a game.

The next morning my mother asks me questions. She wants to know about the house and what kind of clothes the girls wore. She wants to know about the food and how we spent the time.

I tell her about the dancing, about the clothes, about "Spin the Bottle."

"What kind of game is that?" she asks.

I describe the game. She slaps my face. "Don't talk about such things," she says with clear distaste. "I don't want to hear what you do."

Wednesday is Current Events Day in history class. We tell the teacher the news of the world: The work on the East River Drive is proceeding on schedule... The Battle of Stalingrad goes on... The Nisei on the West Coast have been interned, their homes and lands confiscated... German spies are report-ed to have landed off the coast of Long Island...

The teacher cautions us against spreading rumors.

"Loose lips sink ships," says Jack Hazelnuss. The class laughs.

"What is an American?" the teacher asks.

"Anyone born in America," says Marilyn.

"Anyone who becomes a citizen," says Butch.

"An American fights for freedom and justice," says Lily Jablonsky.

"It's how you feel, your attitude," says Don Schaffer.

"You have to be loyal. You have to have allegiance," says Murray Weiss.

"The Nisei were loyal," I say in a whisper loud enough to fill the room. "They didn't do anything wrong."

"They attacked Pearl Harbor," says Butch.

The teacher makes believe he didn't hear what I said. He announces a contest, "I Am An American." Everyone in the class has to write a composition. The best three will be read in the auditorium. The winner will get a medal.

I't's quiet in the classroom. Everyone is thinking, thinking about being an American. I am thinking about the Nisei. Aren't they American? I am thinking about the Germans and how they put Jews in concentrations camps. I want the war to last long enough for me to grow up and join the WACs. Can I be Jewish and American? My mother says you're born a Jew but anyone can become an American. I want to go to Palestine and build a Jewish National Homeland. Is that disloyal?

I think about being American. I want to be the best American, to make my country proud. I press foil from cigarette packages into a ball... I make sure we observe the dimout... I collect newspapers. I check the pail of sand on the roof in case of fire... I knit helmets for Bundles for Britain...I wish I could give blood. I wish we could plant a victory garden... I was born in America... I am an American,

My mother is not an American. My father became a citizen a long time ago, before he married my mother. My mother is an alien.

Uncle Arthur makes fun of her. "Such a fancy lady, so refined," he says, "and she's not an American."

My mother curls her lips together and sticks out her chin. "I'm a better American than you are," she says. "At least I'm not getting rich from the war."

Uncle Arthur is selling black market. He sells chickens above the fixed price, he sells to the highest bidder. He takes payoffs.

"Why not?" he says. "This is America. Anyone can get rich. All you need is brains. Besides," he always adds, "who am I hurting? It's not like I'm hurting anybody."

I make believe I don't hear my uncle's words, that I don't know what he's doing. In my heart I know he's wrong. He should be punished—he's breaking the law. He is not American. I am ashamed of him.

My mother studies every day, preparing for the citizenship test. She does not want to be sent back to Europe. More than that, my mother doesn't want anyone to know she's not a citizen. She has her pride.

She goes to citizenship class in the school in the next neighborhood. That way, she thinks no one will know what she's doing. No one will know if her English isn't good enough, or if she fails.

I go on paper drives. Door to door I ask for aluminum pots and pans. In the movies I see *In Which We Serve*. I listen to *One Man's Family* and feel sad when Jack Barbour goes off to war. I babysit. I save my money for a cashmere sweater and saddle shoes and pearls. I want to be a real American.

The history teacher has chosen the entries for the contest. He calls the students one by one to read their compositions. He starts with the third place winner and goes on to the best.

He calls Marilyn. "I, too, regret I have but one life to give for my country."

He call Don Schaeffer. "We are a nation of immigrants," Don reads. "The melting pot is a forge out of which comes a new man: American."

I wait for the teacher to call me. I am the best writer in the class. The teacher calls Murray Weiss. "I am an American," Murray reads. "I believe in freedom and justice for all."

"I'm proud of you," the teacher says, "all of you, those who won and those who didn't. You are all Americans."

I want to ask about my compostion, why I didn't win. I begin to raise my hand. He looks at me, then looks away. I put my hand down. He did not like what I wrote, what I said about the Nisei, what I said about America behaving like the Germans. He does not think I am a good American.

"I'm sorry you didn't win," Lily says when class is over.

I put my lips together and clench my teeth. I don't want to cry. I don't want the teacher to see, I don't want Lily to feel sorry for me. I have my pride.

I help my mother for her citizenship test.

"Who wrote the Declaration of Independence?" I ask.

"Name the governor of New York," I demand.

We practice the pledge of allegiance.

On the day of the test when I come home from school, I ask my mother what happened.

"I didn't go," she says, pointing to a bandage wrapped around her ankle. "I hurt my foot. I couldn't walk." She sounds angry as if someone hurt her. "I'll go next time," she says. "You can always try again."

I change my clothes and go sit on the porch. This time I know not to talk. I wish we could choose our mothers the way we can choose to be American.

I think about what people say and what they really mean, about words and the ideas that go with them, about words and the feelings behind them. I must be careful. People don't like to hear the truth.

The subway train is crowded. I stand in the center of the car near the door. "Attention! Attention!" I call. Beginning is the hardest part. "Help build a Jewish National Homeland. Plant a tree so the desert will bloom." I shake my blue and white Jewish National Fund box. My speech is finished. I walk up and down the aisle thrusting the can in front of each face. "Give," I demand. "Even a penny counts. Help our people so they will have a home when the war ends." At Nevins Street I change for the train going back to East New York. I wear the blue workshirt and green tie that shows I am a member of Hashomer Hatzair.

I am no longer Millie or even Malke. We choose new names when we become *Shomrim*, names to reflect a new conscious-ness, a Zionist consciousness. I chose Judith. "Praise Judith," says the Bible, "because she saved her people." I want to be a modern Judith, a pioneer just like the ones who settled the west, except my frontier will be Palestine in the east. I imag-ine an army of Jews crossing the ocean to build a homeland, marching up to Jerusalem, planting the flag of Zion atop the Wailing Wall. We will make the desert bloom, and then, once again, the Jews will be a nation among nations.

I imagine myself on a kibbutz, gun in hand, guarding my comrades. I dream of going to New Jersey for training. I dream of making my dreams come true. I dream that my mother will allow me to go to New Jersey for a weekend even though she does not allow me to stay out overnight.

"So now you're a Zionist," My mother says with a sneer as I get ready to go to a meeting. "Jews! They're always trying to make the world better. In Europe we had the Bund. They were going to change Russia. *Ah zuch oon vey.* Where are they now, the Bundists? Dead, lying in the ground with the other Jews."

I comb my hair and adjust my neckerchief. I pretend I don't hear. She thinks I'm like her; she thinks I think the way she does.

"At least you're fighting for Jews," she says. "At least you're not a Communistke. Better a Zionist than a Communist. Better a Zionist than to be like the *goyim*. But better nothing. Better to look out for yourself. It's not too early to think of the future. It's not too early to think about a husband."

I put my coat on and walk to the door. It's better to keep quiet than to get drawn into an argument. "Free love. Free love. That's what they believe. Like animals. The girls are whores. Be careful you don't become a whore," she yells after me as I go out the door into the hallway.

What does she know? I think as I hurry down the street. I'm proud to have a cause, proud to believe in something. I don't want my life to be an accident, without meaning.

Marilyn, Lily and I are the only girls in Latin class. Marilyn is taking Latin because she wants to be a nurse. I'm taking Latin because I want to go to college, and Lily is taking Latin because she wants to understand the mass when she goes to church.

I like Lily. She is an intellectual. She goes to the city, to dance recitals and chamber music concerts, to Greenwich Village. She and Marilyn go together.

Lily invites Marilyn and me to go to a Gilbert and Sullivan concert. I'm embarrassed to say I don't know who Gilbert and Sullivan are. But I accept the invitation.

Lily says I can sleep at her house, so I won't have to walk home alone late at night.

"So now you go to concerts," my mother says. "Tell me what kind of a concert is it? What kind of music is it, that's too good to hear on the radio?"

"It's for school," I say. "The whole class is going," I lie. Mixing the truth with a lie makes it less a lie.

"I'm sleeping at Marilyn's house," I say from the doorway. I've waited until it was time to leave before telling the real lie.

"What kind of business is that, not sleeping in your own bed?" my mother asks. "Whoever heard of such a thing?"

"Everybody does it," I say adding to my lies. "Marilyn's mother said it's better if we go home together." Lying is easier with practice.

My mother likes Marilyn; she says Marilyn knows how to bend the world to her breeze.

We meet at the train station. We talk.

Marilyn asks me who my favorite composer is. "Tchaikowsky," I say.

"Pedestrian," she says. "A romantic." She says my taste needs to be refined.

Marilyn talks about art. She's been to the exhibit at the Museum of Modern Art. I tell her I have a copy of "Starry Night" I cut out of a magazine.

"Impressionism is out," she says. "Art has gone beyond subjectivity."

Lily talks about Leadbelly, a folk singer who was once a member of a chain gang. She sings unions songs, songs from The Mikado.

Lily has her own room. There is a cross on the wall over her bed. She has her own dresser, her clothes organized, her sweaters neatly rolled, arranged by color. She has two cashmere sweater sets. She has a drawer for gloves and scarves, berets and handkerchiefs. On the top of the dresser is a jewelry box where she keeps her necklaces and earrings. She is very neat. She has a pull out bed for me. I'm too excited to fall asleep right away, too excited thinking about the life I'm going to have.

In my sleep I hear knocking. It's not a dream: I can see it's beginning to get light outside. The knocking gets louder.

I hear Lily's mother go into the kitchen. A door opens, I hear voices.

"Where is she? I want to see where she is." It's my mother's voice.

I get out of bed. My mother is standing in the doorway.

"So! Here you are. Sleeping with *goyim!* Liar! *Meshumed!"*

My mother looks wild, like a crazy woman.

Shame covers me. I feel myself shrink into nothing.

"I'm sorry," I say to Lily. "I'm sorry," I say to Lily's mother and father.

I want to cry but I close my throat. The tears make a lump in my chest. I wish I could disappear.

I put on my clothes and follow my mother home. She talks all the way, about how she went to Marilyn's house, how ashamed she is, how worried about what will become of me. "Liar! Liar!" she says over and over again.

I think about dying. I see myself standing on a platform waiting for a train. There are two beams of light, then it's too late to get out of the way. I jump. Everybody will know she made me do it. They'll cry and say, "What a shame. So young. Her whole life before her."

She'll be sorry then. But it will be too late.

13

The last time I saw my mother she was in the nursing home in her room with the shades drawn and her bed curtained off.

She wore a short cotton nightgown. Her face was full, unwrinkled, rosy, peaceful. She did not look sick. I pulled the sheet over her bare legs. She kicked it off. I pulled the sheet higher, up to her waist. She kicked it off.

"Ma," I said.

She opened her eyes.

"Millie?" she asked.

For a moment, our eyes held. For a moment, she knew me. Then she closed her eyes. I tried to give her water, to cover her legs. I tried to smooth her hair.

The manager said she was not eating. Her feet were swollen. It was a bad sign.

I had seen dead people; I had seen people moments after death, but I did not know how a person dies, how it happens.

"There's plenty of time," my mother had said when I brought her the photo album. I believed her.

I went back to her room. I gave her some water. I tried to give her juice. She closed her lips. Even now her will was unbroken. As weak as she was, only half conscious, she could still close her lips.

She lay in bed, small, like a child, so little, my big mother. Seeing her so often, I had not noticed the changes taking place. Spending so much time together had pushed us even further apart. We were like long lost relatives whose only connection was an accident of birth.

Her eyes opened, stared, the same penetrating look she had when she said she could see into my head. What did she see? Her eyes were dark, the dark where all things have their beginning and their end.

The manager said they would wait another day or two and then force feed if I insisted. I remembered the scene in the hospital, I remembered how she was tied.

Sam was reassuring. "She'll pull through," he said. "She's had close calls before."

I called my brother. He agreed there was nothing to be done. We did not want our mother tortured. I called my sister, she cried because there was nothing she could do.

I did not hear the phone in the middle of the night. I had taken a sleeping pill so I could get a good rest. I was sound asleep, dreaming. In my dream my mother looked the way she did when I was a child. She wore an apron over her house dress. She walked back and forth busy with her work. I reached out to her. I did not speak. She did not see me. I reached out again. My hand touched air.

The phone rang again at five. It was over.

I am sixteen. My mother says it's time I started going out. She says all I do is hang around the school yard playing ball, sit around the house reading a book, walk the steets with a bunch of girls who have no future, no future at all. It's time, my mother says, to take things in hand. How else will I ever get a husband?

"What is love?" she says. "Can you eat love? Love is for the movies. Marriage is for living." She means the word in all its shadings. Life is a war without an end, marriage the major battle.

"It's like buying potatoes," she says of men. "Sometimes you get a rotten one, but mostly, they're all the same." I think I know exactly what she means. She is worried about the future and who will provide for it. It's a man's world, she says, and a woman is known by the man who keeps her. What matters is money. A doctor is best; there will always be sick people. An accountant is good; in America money talks.

I think she is wrong. Love is what counts. Marriage is a trap from which there's no escape. Love can set me free.

On Saturday I wear my new black dress. The vee neck is cut low, the velvet belt emphasizing my bust and hips. I wear high heeled sling back T strap shoes; I carry white gloves and a black velvet clutch. "Get the whole outfit," my mother said. "It's the look that counts."

She thinks the way you dress is what you are. If you look like a lady, men will treat you like one. I take comfort from my dress, from the words inside my head, I want to grow up; I want to find love.

I have curled my eyelashes, patted Max Factor foundation beige on my nose, and outlined my lips in Tangee red. My hair ripples from a center part, one wave falling alluringly near my right eye. I am waiting for my date.

"You'll like him," my mother says.

I don't answer.

"What is there to like or not to like?" my mother continues. "A good boy. A certified accountant. Aunt Gussie's cousin Rosie knows his mother."

She means his family met with her approval, she means he makes a good living; she thinks a rare opportunity has come my way. I wait for her clinching words: "He'll show you a good time and all for free."

There is nothing to say, it has all been arranged. I am up for auction, on sale to the highest bidder, a collaborator in my mother's plans for my future.

"Take a look at Millie," says my sister. "Who do you think you are, the Queen of Sheba?"

"If you don't want to get your feet wet, you'd better wear galoshes," giggles my brother.

"You look nice," says my father from the corner in the kitchen where he sits. He is better now but he does not go to work.

I ignore them. I stand in the kitchen, waiting for my date. I can't sit down. I don't want to crease my dress, or take a chance of getting a run in my stockings; I don't want the boned girdle poking in my ribs.

My date arrives. He is as tall as I, short for a man. A man is supposed to be taller than a woman, my mother says, as if that's a reason she and my father are always fighting. My father is short, like my date.

I have gone on dates before, to neighborhood movies, parties, the beach. But I have never gone to dinner first, and then to Radio City Music Hall. I have never had a date arranged, never dated a man. Perry Rosenberg is twenty three.

"A good age," my mother says. "A CPA. He is ready to settle down."

He has brought a corsage. Gardenias. I pin them on. He shakes hands with my father, compliments my mother on her house, talks to my brother about the Dodgers, pats my sister's head. He takes my elbow and we leave.

We take the subway to the city. I wait, casual and nonchalant, for him to get the change and drop it in the turnstile. There is a seat for me. He stands over me hanging onto the straps. Tall and short, fat and thin, rich and poor, the female sits, the man stands over her. It is Saturday night and I am out on a date.

"T-bone steak and baked potatoes?" he says as if asking my permission. I nod. We are in a restaurant with linen cloths on the table, linen napkins for our laps. Rolls sit in a basket, pats of butter ride on cakes of ice. The steak is thick, the potatoes slathered in cream. I calculate the cost. He is a big spender. I have ice cream for dessert. He has coffee, black. I have not yet acquired the coffee habit—milk is still my drink.

I watch him from the corner of my eyes. He blots his lips with every bite. He smiles. I ask about his job; he talks about psychological attraction. "I've been watching you," he says. "I've analyzed your type. You're a mesomorph. You'll go for ectomorphs, for someone tall and skinny. But you'd be better off with someone like me, an endomorph. Those are the types you'll choose."

He smiles. I know he means more than he says. But I don't know what exactly. "Have you read *War and Peace*?" I ask. "I'm halfway through."

He laughs. "Someone like me will be best," he says.

He pays the check and leaves a tip. He takes my arm; it's clear he's been around.

We sit in the second row of the first tier of the balcony. I, centered in my seat, my arms well within the armrests, look straight ahead. I don't want to offer provocation. I sense his arm come to rest behind me. As if observing someone else, I watch his arm slide around the seat, the scent of Old Spice brushing past my nose. One hand closes on my shoulder just as the other closes on my knee. I don't move. I don't want to lead him on; I don't want it thought I asked for it. "Men want whatever they can get," my mother said. "They can want but you don't have to give. They'll try to take, but hold on. Otherwise you'll never get a husband."

All around us, on the crowded subway, couples are returning from their dates. Perry and I stand together in the center of the car, holding on to the pole. He smiles. I smile back. Playfully he pokes my fingers. He pulls them up, one by one. I don't resist. It's his move.

We walk the streets to my house. I feel myself begin to tense, my breath shallow, my heartbeat fast. He puts his arm around my waist. His fingers squeeze. I am stuck among my different feelings: embarrassed that he knows I wear a girdle, glad that all he felt was bone and rubber, excited at having a grownup evening, worried at what is yet to come.

Inch by inch, his hand creeps up. He cups my breast, squeezes. I pretend to stumble; I clutch his arm as if in need of help. "These shoes," I mumble. "The heels are really high."

He takes the hand I freely give. He locks his own around it, like a vise. I am a captive.

We walk up the stoop to the porch. I begin to say goodnight. "It was a lovely evening. Thank you so much."

He opens the door to the vestibule. One more door and I am home free.

"Thanks for the flowers, too," I say. "Gardenias are my favorites." He does not seem to move, but I find myself maneuvered up against the wall.

"Is that how you thank me for a lovely evening?" he asks.

My heart begins to pound. He has gone all the way this evening—flowers, dinner and Radio City Music Hall. You have to pay for what you get, nothing's free. A kiss can't hurt, I think. He presses up against me, his mouth on mine. I keep my lips sealed tight.

"Don't you know how to kiss?" he asks with feigned disdain. "I'll show you." He pushes hard against my lips, my body pinned against the wall. My lips part. His tongue intrudes. Mechanically it roots around. I feel my throat begin to close. I hope I don't throw up.

While one hand pins my shoulder to the wall, the other zeroes in for a breast. He rubs. Round and round. He presses his knee between my legs. Push. Push. My legs open. He moves and thrusts, gyrates and thrusts. I feel his thing sticking against my dress. I wonder if his fly is open. I wonder when he took the time. I'm glad I wore a girdle.

This isn't the way I thought it would be. It's not the way it is in the books or what they show in the movies.

I know the way to safety. I move my arm. I hope he doesn't notice. I reach my hand across the wall and press.

"Who's there?" my mother's voice asks. "Who's ringing the bell at this hour?"

He is startled by the voice.

"Goodbye," I say and run into the hall. "Thanks again."

I smile as I run up the stairs. I've won the fight. He'll call again, I know. He has not gotten what he paid for.

I am not afraid. I'll find a way to save myself. Someday I'll fall in love, get married. But I will choose. Not my mother. My life will be the one I make, not the one my mother plans.

I kept the casket closed. That's what she would have wanted, I told myself. Didn't she keep my father's casket closed? I had reminded her how she had stood looking at her mother lying in the plain pine box, how she had stood, silent, staring, before they closed the lid. Didn't I have the same right, the same need? I wanted to see my father one last time. I was still living in Chicago then, and she had made the arrangements before I could get back to New York. There was nothing I could do.

Now she lay in a closed pine coffin covered with a black flag embossed with a white star of David. I sat in in the first pew as a bereaved daughter should. My brother sat on the aisle, my sister Tibby, between us, a handkerchief to her eyes, a sigh on her lips. The grandchildren, in-laws, sat behind us. There are procedures to a funeral, customs and ceremonies for all the rites of life. It is only the dying we each do our own way, only dying we do alone.

My daughter Julie had come from Chicago. Doug was with her. "It's hard, Ma," she said as she hugged me. "It's hard to lose a mother." Then she hugged me again. "I love you," she said.

Matthew and his wife Robin had come from California. Matthew told me Robin was pregnant. He told me if they had a girl they would name her Sarah for my mother. "I always liked Grandma," he said. I knew he was trying to please me. I did not remember that he liked her. I did not remember anything good that had to do with my mother.

My brother Alvin's three boys had come to the funeral. Not boys, men. And Tibby's son Fred, named after our grandmother. There was no name for my father who had died after all the grandchildren had been born.

All my cousins came: Toby and Jerry and Leo and Sidney and Bea. Bea cried. "She was a wonderful woman," she said.

"She was always kind to me." Bea hugged me again and again as if to bring us back to what we were, as if the years between had never been.

"Do you remember the cookies she used to bake, with colored sprinkles on them and powdered sugar? And the shapes! She had a special food for every holiday. She always invited me. She always made me feel at home, as if I belonged." Bea hugged me again. "You were lucky," she said, "to have a mother like that. There were times I was jealous." She looked embarrassed, then gave me still another hug.

My mother always wanted a Sunday funeral, a day when people had time to go to the cemetery, when they had time to visit afterward. She did not like Friday funerals, when people had to hurry home for the Sabbath. Still it was a big crowd. Even the manager from the nursing home was there.

"Sarah Abramowitz of Blessed Memory." The Rabbi began his eulogy. "We are here this morning to escort her body and her soul to her eternal resting place."

She had not been left alone. A member of the Burial Committee had sat with her from the beginning, from the moment her soul began to rise up to God. But she had died alone. No one had held her hand. She had died alone. I had slept through her dying and I did not view the body. I did not wash her, or comb her hair. I did not clean her nails or look upon her face. I kept the casket closed.

"We can control many things," the Rabbi said. "Even to some extent our bodies. If we don't want to see, we close our eyes. If we don't want to hear, we tune out. We can even learn to lower our blood pressure. But there is one thing that goes its own way. Life. We have no control over our lives."

No, I wanted to say, that's not true. Maybe we can't control our dying, but we can control our lives! It was not all in God's hands, not all an inevitable consequence of that first throw of the dice. What about free will? What about choice?

I would not have left home if I had not believed in choice. I had not wanted to be like my father who gave up control of his life to my mother or like my brother and sister who had never taken control of their lives. I wanted to be like my mother. At least in this. My mother had made her own life, or so I thought, even though she blamed others for how it turned out—my father, Uncle Arthur, the Polacks, me. But all I blamed was her.

"Naturally, when you say the name Sarah Abramowitz, the Fineman family comes to mind," the Rabbi continued. "Sarah Abramowitz was born a Fineman and she never forgot that."

I felt a pain enter my heart, like a pinch or a squeeze. Even now at her funeral, my mother was still a Fineman. Even now at her death, my father was pushed aside.

My father. I had not said goodbye to him either. He had never been quite the same after his hospital stay, still gentle, kindly but quieter, more withdrawn. We never discussed the stories he had told. He died of a heart attack one summer on vacation in the Catskills. He came from Shul on a Saturday, stepped into the bungalow, said, "Good Shabbos," and dropped dead. He had a Sunday funeral, and even though there was barely time to put an ad in the paper, hundreds came. My mother was proud of the funeral she made. My mother kept the coffin closed. "Jews don't view the body," she said. The soul was what mattered. As soon as the mourning period was over my mother gave his clothes away. She burned his papers in the furnace. She gave his *tefillin* to a Yeshiva. She obliterated all traces of his life. Except his name and his children. Except me and my memories.

I remembered how my mother told me stories about my father, how he used to be rich, how he and his brother owned Pelham Bay, how he lost his money in the crash, how his partner jumped out the window, how my father was no good. He was too American, she'd said, rich but common, a man without refinement.

She told me how she could have married many times, how she could have had Max but Bubbe would not allow her to marry a cousin. She told me my father was a liar, that he had been married before, that she had to get married again to make sure it was all right. My mother cried as she sat at the kitchen table and told me these stories. I remembered feeling sorry for her, my mother who always knew what was right and wrong, who was not afraid even of God, my mother who always said, "Hold your head up and never show the world you are beaten," my mother was crying.

I felt Sam's hand on my shoulder. I touched it with mine. Steadfast Sam. I had bound myself in a marriage as if it were a wall against the outside world, a refuge, a shelter, the place where I was safe. Was that so different from what my mother had wanted? She thought marriage would give her a place in life, keep her safe. It did not turn out the way she had expected. I had not wanted to be like my mother. I wanted life to be a straight line, not a circle in which I went round and round.

"The parents, Faygel and Jacob Fineman," the Rabbi continued. "I remember Faygel quite well. How many parties, how many affairs she made! Mama Fineman, they called her. Mama Fineman. And her daughter, Sarah, Sorke, blessed be her name, was just like her mother. She never lost contact with the old neighborhood, with her old friends, with her *Yiddishkeit*. She was a *Yiddishe froi*. Her *Yiddishkeit* was a merit, a source of inspiration during her lifetime, and she transplanted it to members of her family. Surely now her spirit will remain with her loved ones here, as she herself goes to rest in the bosom of her family."

"Your daughter is coming, Bubbe," I said to the air. "Your daughter is coming."

My grandmother. She always had a blue and white box for charity in the kitchen. She always gave me a quarter. She always told me to be good. She hugged me. My grandmother. Strong. A survivor. She took the bedding my mother wanted.

Like mother, like daughter? The acorn does not fall far from the tree. Soon my mother would be in her grave. Now I could tell her my troubles the way she used to tell her mother. Now I could ask her what I never did.

"I could go on and on," the Rabbi said. "About all the wonderful things Mrs. Abramowitz did, the many acts of charity

she performed, but if we had to pick one point, one quality..."
his voice trailed off. I could not imagine what one quality
could sum up my mother.

"Not long ago," the Rabbi said. "there was a song circu-
lating. Wherever you went, you heard this song. The song
stayed with me because of the text of some of the words:
'Honesty is such a lonely word'. If I had to use one word to
sum up the life of Mrs. Abramowitz, that would have to be the
word."

I sat up straight, my attention caught in the net of words.
Honesty. The word to sum up my mother.

The Rabbi continued. "The song tells us that honesty is
such a lonely word because there's so much fake going on, so
much not true. People aren't true to themselves, and they're
not true to one another. So for those people, honesty is a lonely word. For Mrs.Abramowitz, honesty was the key. She never
let on if she was lonely or not. If she had something to say,
she said it. If she had something to do, she did it. She meant
what she said and she said what she meant. She was an
emesse mensch."

Honesty. And pride. And show. And refinement. And
righteousness. Her own beliefs. Her own needs. They were
enough for her. She did not need me.

I cleared my throat, spat in a tissue. I felt a wave of sympathy flow toward me. They thought I was crying. I had not
cried. My friend Laura cried, but I, who cried in the movies,
and when a parade passed with the flag flying and the band
playing, I had not shed a single tear. I had my own kind of
honesty.

Without warning, completely unexpected, the hard knot
inside my heart began to open, expand, fill. I was sorry for her.
I felt sorry for my mother. Things had not turned out the way
she'd planned.

I had not seen it before. I had seen only what I remembered. How she had hit me. How hard she had made growing
up. How I had to leave home. How she didn't care. How she
didn't love me. I had never seen her: the girl who cooked for

the Germans, the young woman who could not marry the man she loved, the immigrant who had to cope with a new culture, the old maid who had to get married, the wife whose husband had betrayed her, the old woman who had only her kind of honesty to keep her company.

"The word 'mother' is one of the most beautiful words in the dictionary," the Rabbi said. "Sarah Abramowitz was a mother, a grandmother, a wife. She was good. She was respected. She left her mark."

The eulogy was over.

The sun shines through the side of the window where the shade does not reach. I can hear the twitter of the birds, smell the lilacs that grow in the yard. Tibby is still asleep in the next bed, the moment is all mine. It's spring and I feel happy.

I plan my day. First I will get the urine specimen I need for chemistry class, then I'll wash and dress, my green skirt and white blouse over my gym suit so I'll be ready to set up for volleyball. Today's the day I work in the Dean's office instead of lunch. After school, I'll meet Marilyn.

School shapes my life. When I graduate, I will go to college, the ticket to the life I want.

There is a half glass of fresh squeezed orange juice on the kitchen sink. My mother has left a half glass of orange juice for me every morning since I first started kindergarten. She says orange juice will keep me from getting sick. She thinks leaving orange juice is what a mother does. She gets up every morning and squeezes oranges so everyone can have a half glass of fresh squeezed orange juice. She does not strain the juice, so there are always pits to pick out.

I don't usually see my mother in the morning. She always has something to do after she squeezes the juice. Always busy, she likes to get a good start on the day.

I drink the juice and put the glass in the sink. It's 7:15 and I'm eager to get to school.

I put the urine filled jar in a paper bag, pick up my books, and turn toward the door. My mother is standing in the doorway. I did not hear her come in.

"What are you carrying?" she asks. My mother is not one for saying hello or goodbye.

"A jar," I say. The less she knows the better things are.

"Do you think I'm stupid that I don't know it's a jar," my mother says. She puts her lips together in the way that makes her jaw stick out. She moves her feet apart and puts her hands on her hips. She means business. I will have to tell her something.

"It's for school," I say. "For an experiment." How can the truth hurt?

"Experiment! What kind of experiment?" she demands.

Can I tell her about the PH factor? Can I explain acid and alkaline? I close my lips just the way my mother does. Two can play at this game.

"So. What's in the jar? What can you find in the house for an experiment?"

"It's for school," I repeat. "For chemistry. It's urine. My own urine." I don't want her to think I've taken something that isn't mine.

"I knew it. I knew it," my mother shouts. She takes a step in my direction. She's not as big as I thought she was. I can push her away if I have to. Still I'm afraid of her, and what she can do.

"Tell me the truth!" she demands. "Tell me who the boy is." I stare at her open mouthed. Is she crazy? Is she going crazy like my father did?

"Tell me," she screams. "Tell me. Was it Rosenberg? What's his name? I want to know who did this to you."

It's a mistake, I tell myself. She doesn't understand about chemistry and school. She thinks I'm pregnant, she thinks I'll end up the way she did. I take a deep breath. I'm getting ready to explain.

"You think I was born yesterday? You think I don't know what it means when a girl takes urine in a jar? Who is he? Tell me who he is, and I'll make him pay. He'll pay, I tell you. He'll pay," my mother screams in my face.

Her eyes look ready to pop out, her hands wave in the air. She's crazy, I think, crazy. "It's for school," I whisper. "For school." I stand still. I don't want to push her anger. I go deep inside myself, where she can't hurt me.

My mother walks toward the kitchen. I see my chance, I run for the door.

When I get to the Dean's office at the beginning of the fifth period, Mr. Mulvane is standing in the doorway. He ushers me into his inner office ignoring the boys already crowding the reception room, closes the door, puts a hand on my shoulder and quickly removes it. My heart begins to beat faster. Something is wrong. Things are not the way they should be.

"Your mother," Mr. Mulvane begins. "Your mother was here in school."

My mouth opens, the breath escapes. "Nothing's wrong," he says reassuringly. "Everyone's all right." He turns his back as if he is looking for something in the file cabinet. My mind races with possibilities—my father, my brother, my sister. "Your mother came to see Mr. Lieberman."

I gasp. My mother has gone to the principal! Like God, he appears only at special occasions, sitting on the stage in the auditorium, handing out diplomas at the graduation, someone seen only from a distance, never spoken to unless he speaks first.

"She wanted to know... she wanted to know...," Mr. Mulvane stammers, his face red. "She wanted to know if there really was a chemistry experiment, if you really needed that," he hesitates as if searching for just the right word, "jar."

In the silence, a roar inside my head, shame fills the room. Invisible, still it clings. Slime I can not wash off.

"She didn't understand," Mr. Mulvane says. "It's nothing. It happens sometimes. Mr. Lieberman called me, and I said I'd talk to you."

There are worms on my skin, crawling things trying to get inside. I lower my head, I don't want Mr. Mulvane to see.

"I thought you'd want to know," he says. "Sometimes parents don't understand about school."

I nod. "She's an immigrant," I say in explanation or apology, for her or for me. My vision blurs, I feel myself begin to shrink. Soon I will disappear. There are two Millies now, one inside and one who stands before the Dean.

Mr. Mulvane excuses me from work for this period. I walk away, out through the outer office, past the boys waiting with their probation cards, through the empty halls.

In the girls' room, I head for the farthest stall and stand with my face against the door, my books in my arms. The shame that covered me has disappeared. Hate takes its place. Odorless, colorless, deadly as poison, it seeps into my pores. I hate her. I wish her dead.

For a long time, I stand, face pressed to the door. I know my mother will not die, and neither will I. I am afraid of some horrible collapse in myself, some defeat undermining my will. I am bound up with my mother, but I can escape. I can leave, start again. There is still time. I imagine myself riding in the back of an open truck, up and down hills like a roller coaster, alone, free. Free of my mother.

For a moment, at the cemetery, I felt confused. I was still caught up in winter, with its browns and greys, and here it was almost summer with its greens and yellows. My mother had died on Shavuot, the holiday of the first fruits, the holiday where you read the Book of Ruth, Ruth who said to Naomi, "Wherever you go, I will go." It was the beginning of summer and I thought it ought to be winter. People ought to die in winter. They ought to be born in the spring and die in the winter. I wanted life in harmony with nature.

It seemed only yesterday I had been here, standing at these same graves waiting, waiting so I could leave. Why had I been so impatient? Why couldn't I have waited for the Yiddle she wanted? Would it have made a difference? Would she be alive now?

I watched as the coffin was lowered between my father's grave on one side and Uncle Arthur's on the other.

I stepped forward and said the Kaddish when my brother did. It was my right even though women were not required to pray.

I asked the Rabbi to say a prayer for my father, Hymie Abramowitz, for Uncle Arthur and Aunt Bertha. I asked him to pray for my mother, to pray that she was safe with her mother.

I stepped back from the open grave, turned to walk away, my head down. I felt someone's arm around my shoulder, strong, firm. Even before I looked up, I knew. Sam. He was always there when I needed him. I could count on him, he was not like my father. I was not the kind of wife my mother had been.

"Thank you," I whispered. He smiled. I did not need to explain. He understood. He kept his arm on my shoulder as we walked toward the car.

Tibby took Charlie's arm, Alvin moved closer to Gail. My mother was the one who held us together. What would happen to us now? Would we visit, speak, touch? Or would we drift apart, family in name only?

Julie kissed my cheek. Matthew hugged me. It was over, but I did not feel free. There was none of the sense of release I had expected. Something was still missing. The Rabbi had spoken about many things: honesty, Jewishness, respect, family. He had said nothing about love.

Words are a convenant between us and God, a contract we make with the past, a hedge against chaos.

To pronounce a word is to invoke its essence.

Yisgidal v'yisgadash...
Magnified and sanctified, your name is great.
Mother.

Sarah, the mother; Mother, the matriarch.

Hated, feared, admired, loved.
In her there is always 'other'.
Vain, proud, powerful, angry. Always angry.
I rejected her as I thought she rejected me.

"I will teach you to disobey," she said. Did I misinterpret?
Did she mean what she said?
I did not want to disappoint her.

Forgive me, Mother, I was angry.
Forgive me, Mother, I was hurt.
Forgive me, Mother, I forgot you, too, were a daughter.

I see now you were weak and vulnerable; you made
mistakes. People make mistakes.
I was a child; I thought like a child.
I am grown now.
It's what we learn that counts, the way we live that makes
a difference.

A mother is a daughter's tradition.
A daughter is a mother's immortality.
You did not get what you bargained for.
You said, "If you don't know where you came from, you
don't know who you are."

How alike we are, after all!

The sky is dark now, you must be cold.
The wind blows and the air moans.
Oh Mother! If only I had comforted you, held you against
me, rocked you into sleep.
If only I had held your hand.
Tenderness is learned early in one's life... I could not give
what I didn't get.

Oh Mother! Now we can talk, I can tell you my troubles

the way you used to tell your mother. Now I can ask what I never did.

Did you love me?

Were you glad I was born?

14

I am free now. She is dead and buried.

Restless, ill at ease, I walk the rooms where she lived. Almost, I have forgotten what hurt so much.

I should have loved her more, I tell myself. She should have loved me better.

She was deprived. Should I have had so little?

I should have held her hand. She did not say goodbye.

The life I made was even and unbroken, like a stone worn smooth by currents. I was content to let the swirls and eddies pass me by, content to sit unmoving and unmoved. And all the time, a piece of me was missing, and all the time, like salmon to the season and ocean to the tides, she pulled me. Nothing warmed the solid core of ice. I was hers, Millie Abramowitz, never me, Millie Kaits, the woman I became.

I touch the things her hands have touched. I pack the clothes that graced her skin. I drown in camphor, spice and sweat. It's left to me to close the place, to sort and pack, to order things, and end them up.

I roll her corsets tight. I count the gloves—twenty-three. I slip one on, blue with white dots. It fits.

In a closet like the one in which I used to hide, hang her dresses. The velvet jade green gown she wore to Alvin's wedding, the sequined blue, the flowered prints—one in lilac, one in red, one black and white, each in a plastic sheath. Not quite a rainbow, not the smell of roses, more like mothballs mixed with talcum. On the floor and on the shelf, boxes, some still new, some yellowed, some already crumbling into dust.

My mother was a saver. She saved as she had lived. Things she used every day were worn through, things that showed a person's worth, things she valued, were put away and carefully preserved, interred against a rainy day that never came, embalmed in tissue paper, shrouded in sheets, preserved, emblems of her life, badges of what she was, like medals advertising valor.

On the floor a pillow case is stuffed with rags, bits of fabric saved from sewing, a piece from a dress I wore to school, a scrap from a curtain, a length from a quilt cover that even now lies across her bed. A picture book of what we wore and how we used to look.

Memory is a form of imagination, I know that now. I can never know the whole story, what really happened. Even what I used to feel is hard to know, mixed as it is with who I was and who I am. I see things now I never saw before; I miss things now I never knew I had.

In the box, stacks of hats nest one in the other. Nearby a coffee can is filled with buttons. Who knows now what dresses they came from? Here's a chain of brightly colored rings, a belt made from matchbook covers. Why would she save these things? They were not mine. They must be Tibby's. She was always good at making things. Tibby. I feel sorry for her now, the war between us gone. We are not alike, but sisters still. Who else can remember the way things used to be? Who else knows me as I was?

Here is a fox neckpiece, beady eyes still intact, two legs gone for good... a tablecloth embroidered in red and green, the hem unfinished... a silken gown and pegnoir set, too good to wear, too good to give away... a book of etiquette written in Yiddish, printed in Poland... a book on child care written in Yiddish, printed in New York... reminders of who she was, who she thought she ought to be.

We are all actors in plays we think we write ourselves. We forget we come into existence on a stage already set.

In a metal storage box, I find my father's pen and pencil set, a gift commemorating the time when he was rich. I remember how we used to go to the ocean so that he could throw his sins away, how he turned his pockets inside out and said his prayers, how the water looked, like fish, grey and black and silver where the sunlight hit it.

The world goes by unnoticed while in the darkened closet. I string together memories, hoping for a thread to lead me through the maze. Was there a reason for my pain? Is there something I don't know?

Here is my mother's citizenship paper. I remember when she passed the test, how we couldn't tell the neighbors. Everyone thought she'd been a citizen for years. "Honor is dearer than money," she said.

I always knew my mother by her words. The things she said still play inside my head, an endless tape.

Anger is like a thorn in the heart.

The smoothest way is full of stones.

Better to bear curses than to be pitied.

Better a crooked foot than a crooked mind.

Life is the biggest bargain, we get it for nothing.

I knew my mother by her words, but who knows me? Who knows enough to know me now?

I turn back to the things that hold me, the key to what I think there used to be. I want to remember. I think of memory as a capillary leading to a larger source, a vein perhaps, or even an artery. I want to remember it all. I know it will be twisted and true; I know I will forget, but still, I hope, something will reveal the truth beyond mere fact.

I struggle with some of the boxes on the shelf. How did she get them up? I can barely take them down.

Here wrapped in a napkin, my brother's baby bracelet, his honor roll certificate from fourth grade, his high school diploma. His achievements. My brother. He tried. Perhaps he suffered even more than I. Such pressure to achieve and be a man. I always thought he didn't feel. Perhaps he felt and learned early how to shield himself from pain. Perhaps he felt and couldn't show it.

One box is different from the rest. Plastic swaddles it from the elements, a cord holds the plastic in place. Another gift ungiven is what I think, bought then reconsidered as too good or too expensive, kept intact, ready for the day it might be needed. Beneath the plastic, the box is tied with ribbon, red, thin, dime store stuff. Inside the ribbon, an envelope is stuck, the handwriting familiar, the return address Chicago. Mine. Even before I open it, I know what it will say. It's the letter I wrote three months after I left home, the letter I wrote saying I wasn't coming back.

I remember now how I left home. I graduated from high school and I told my mother I had a summer job. I said only what was necessary, not one word more. I wanted to avoid a scene.

"Chambermaid," she said. "Cleaning other people's dirt." I let her talk, I didn't even try to explain.

I got up early the next morning. I waited for Tibby to go to school. I packed my clothes in a shopping bag, my books and shoes in cardboard carton tied with rope. I made the bed, straightened the rug. I wanted to leave things neat.

I planned to leave the house before my mother woke. I didn't want her questions or her answers. "What good is school?" she'd asked. "Can you eat books? You think learning will make you different. You'll end up the same. Maybe worse." She wanted me to live the way she did, to be like her. I wanted something else.

In the bathroom I take my nightgown off and hang it on a hook. I look at myself in the mirror of the medicine cabinet. Who am I? Who am I going to be? I back up against the wall until I can see down to my belly button. I wish for those trick mirrors that make you smaller, small enough so I can see all of me.

My neck is short, my shoulders strong and broad, my breasts round and firm. My waist was small, my hips wide. It means, my mother said, childbirth will be easy for me. I look down at my legs, strong, straight and smooth. I shaved them the day before. I touched the bush between my legs, the secret place I need to guard.

I close my eyes. In the mirror of my mind I see a door. Behind it, another. Behind that, another still. I stand at the threshhold. I want adventure, excitement, love. I am not afraid.

I dress in clothes I like the best, a polo shirt and pedal pushers. They are old and worn and fit me like a glove. I have to leave before I'm stopped; I have to go before my mother catches me. I'm off to start my life.

When I open the bedroom door, my mother stands there like a spy. "Where are you going?" she demands as if she knows nothing of my plans.

I tell her as I have before that Marilyn is waiting for me, that we have to catch a bus.

""Let her wait, the trouble maker. She looks like a prostitute. All that make up. She's a bad influence. I never liked her." She shakes her head and takes a step toward me.

"Where will you sleep? How will you live? A girl seventeen, in the mountains. How will it look?"

That's all she cares about, I think, how things look. She doesn't care about me, what I want.

She seems to see something on my face. Perhaps she does have the power to see inside my head, the way she says she can, because she turns and marches down the hall to the door. She snaps the lock, slides the chain in the bolt, and stations herself, arms outstretched, between the posts, a living bar to my escape. "Shame! Shame!" she says. "You won't leave."

·   ·   ·

I remember how I clenched my teeth. Something inside me came together, curled up in a ball, became a pit, a stone, a rock, a fist. I had to get away, or I'd be caught forever.

"You can't stop me," I said. "If I don't go now, I'll go some other time. In the middle of the night. You can't watch me every minute. You have to eat. You have to go to the bathroom. I'll find a way."

She stared at me as if she hadn't heard a word. For a moment things hung in balance. A kind word was all I need-ed. One word could have turned the tide.

I watched as she lowered her arms; her shoulders sagging. She clutched her chest. "Oh! That it has come to this! What good is a life that it should come to this?" She began to cry. She lifted her apron, held it in front of her face and sobbed.

She was playing on my sympathy, I thought, acting as if she hurt. I tightened my grip on my packages. I would stand there forever if I had to. I could be as stubborn as she.

Slowly then, she took a step. Then another, moving toward me, her feet shuffling in her worn slippers.

"God will punish you," she said. "You'll see. God will pun-ish you."

Then she turned, away from the door, away from me, to sit in the kitchen, her forearms on the table, one hand clasp-ing the other as if she needed to hold on.

I've won, I thought as my fingers fumbled with the chain. It was easier than I had imagined.

"Goodbye," I said as I went out the door. "I'll write."

"Goodbye," I said silently as I walked down the stairs and out on the street. Goodbye, I said and thought I meant just what I said.

But something pulled me, held me, nagged inside my head. I was never good at letting go. I always needed things complete: the picture hung, the table set.

She was my mother. She must have held me in her arms once. She fed me, cared for me when I was sick. I was born of her flesh. She must have loved me.

We lived together, mother, daughter, never touching, never reaching, even when we tried, even when we meant to. Once again I wonder if I've been fair. Had she, too, felt like an orphan? What of the man she loved and couldn't marry? Was there sorrow lurking in the shadows of her life, pain I never saw? She wanted, she needed. She, too, hurt. She was admired, respected, feared, but who had loved her? Even I, her daughter, never said I loved her.

I turn back to the box that held the letter. I lift the cover, fold the tissue paper back. There, folded as if the body it contained had just this moment flown away, is my Heidi dress, the handkerchief I carried on that day slipped in trailing folds inside the bodice edge. I catch my breath, afraid to stir the time that holds it all, afraid the light of day might wipe it all away as objects in long lost tombs are said to crumble at the touch when snatched by thieves.

Yet even as I stand and look, something inside me moves. "She saved my dress," I say out loud. "She saved my dress."

A slow return of warmth creeps through my bones. A rush of air, an echo of a sound passes through my lips. "She saved my dress," I say once more.

I put the box away, back upon the shelf where it belongs. I close the closet door. I walk the rooms she used to know, following my thoughts. The sun still shines, dimly though, through the dusty glass.

I stand still... I listen... I think I hear her calling, here among the things she saved. "Millie, Millie, daughter mine." I think I see her sitting on a throne, high up. She spreads her knees, makes a cradle with her dress. I climb her legs and sit inside her lap. She holds me. She pats my back. She nuzzles my cheek. She whispers, "I'm glad you were born."

Then I remember how it all began:

Light cuts the air, the white light of summer noon. The clop clop of footsteps fills the empty street. In the distance a black blur appears. It grows larger and larger. There are legs beneath it. A pocketbook swings from one side. A shopping bag hangs from the other. The blur comes closer. Only when she is upon me as I sit strapped in my carriage do I see it is a person.. My mother bends to look at me. She pats my cheek. Her big black umbrella. a canopy above us, shields us from the sun.

Life in my inner city parish in Liverpool is full of tensions and demands. Alongside the disorder and struggle sit moments of joy and hope in a place where need is very evident. Within the busyness that we can all get caught up in, I know that I can be in danger of being swept along in the activity, not pausing to reflect and most of all forgetting the essential act of listening. Sometimes we need help to do that, and within this book, as it moves from reflection on Scripture to the affirming stories from varied and different places, I have found this. In some places I have been reminded of things I knew but too often have forgotten, and in other places challenged to risk more in the knowledge that we are loved and called to share and live out that love.

I am grateful that Paul and Angus have written this book because they are both able to draw upon rich experience and connections with people who give insight and understanding. Most of all, this book has stirred me to think and reflect further on love which is at the heart of the gospel and, as Lesslie Newbigin said, 'The gospel is not just the illustration (even the best illustration) of an idea. It is the story of actions by which the human situation is irreversibly changed.'*

Canon Roger Driver, Team Rector of Bootle Team Ministry, Area Dean of Bootle, Liverpool Diocese

---

* Lesslie Newbigin, *The Gospel in a Pluralist Society*, 1989.

Just Love

Personal and social transformation in Christ

Angus Ritchie and Paul Hackwood

To the people of
St Peter's, Bethnal Green
St Oswald's, Chapel Green
All Saints, Horton
The Parish of the Divine Compassion,
Plaistow & North Canning Town and
St Margaret's, Thornbury

First published in Great Britain in 2014

Instant Apostle
The Hub
3-5 Rickmansworth Road
Watford
Herts
WD18 OGX

The views and opinions expressed in this work are those of the author and do not necessarily reflect the views and opinions of the publisher.

British Library Cataloguing-in-Publication Data

A catalogue record for this book is available from the British Library

This book and all other Instant Apostle books are available from Instant Apostle:

Website: www.instantapostle.com

E-mail: info@instantapostle.com

ISBN 978-1-909728-13-4

Printed in Great Britain

Instant Apostle is a new way of getting ideas flowing, between followers of Jesus, and between those who would like to know more about His Kingdom.

It's not just about books and it's not about a one-way information flow. It's about building a community where ideas are exchanged. Ideas will be expressed at an appropriate length. Some will take the form of books. But in many cases ideas can be expressed more briefly than in a book. Short books, or pamphlets, will be an important part of what we provide. As with pamphlets of old, these are likely to be opinionated, and produced quickly so that the community can discuss them.

Well-known authors are welcome, but we also welcome new writers. We are looking for prophetic voices, authentic and original ideas, produced at any length; quick and relevant, insightful and opinionated. And as the name implies, these will be released very quickly, either as Kindle books or printed texts or both.

Join the community. Get reading, get writing and get discussing!

Acknowledgments

This book has benefitted from years of relationships and conversations, and it would be impossible to provide a comprehensive list of those who have contributed to it. Our decision to dedicate the book to the inner-city parishes where we have ministered reflects our debt to these and many other witnesses to the transforming power of Jesus Christ.

We are grateful to Caitlin Burbridge and Andy Walton for their help in compiling the stories in the book, and to David Barclay, Dominic Black, Tim Clapton, Jess Foster, Bill Holiday, Miko Giedroic, Brunel James and Tim Thorlby for their feedback on earlier drafts of the book.

Much of this book began life as addresses and lectures given by Angus to ordinands in the Dioceses of Worcester and Wakefield, and to supporters of The Children's Society. We want to thank them for their helpful comments and questions.

Most of all, we are deeply grateful for the support of Jennifer and Rowena, and all our families, friends and colleagues – both in the writing of this book and in our wider ministries.

Angus Ritchie and Paul Hackwood
Feast of St John of the Cross, 2013

Contents

Introduction

This book is about *love*. No other word creates so many opportunities for confusion and misunderstanding. We say that we love our spouse, our house, our best friend, our favourite meal... or our local football team. It is hard to think of another word that has such a variety of meanings!

Even when we know the context, the word can generate false expectations and lead to pain and disappointment. As we grow up, we learn to our cost that 'I love you' means very different things to different people.

Take a look at this week's Top 40, or at the films that your local cinema is screening. It's a fair bet that many of them will have 'love' in the title. On the surface, the dominant culture and the Christian faith speak with a single voice. They agree that love is a treasure beyond price; that it is the one thing for which we would – and should – give up everything else:

> Love is strong as death, passion fierce as the grave. Its flashes are flashes of fire, a raging flame. Many waters cannot quench love, neither can floods drown it. If one offered for love all the wealth of one's house, it would be utterly scorned.
> *Song of Solomon 8:6-7 (New Revised Standard Version)*

> Love never fails. But where there are prophecies, they will cease; where there are tongues, they will be stilled; where there is knowledge, it will pass away. For we know in part and we prophesy in part, but when completeness comes, what is in part disappears ... And now these three remain: faith, hope and love. But the greatest of these is love.
> *1 Corinthians 13:8-10,13*

Who could disagree with that?

Love and the cross

But what do these words actually mean? What kind of love does the Bible have in mind?

In Christianity, the central image of love is not a romantic embrace, or the bonds of marriage, family or friendship. It is something altogether more disturbing: a man executed upon a cross by an occupying regime. As Jesus tells his disciples:

> If anyone comes to me and does not hate father and mother, wife and children, brothers and sisters – yes, even their own life – such a person cannot be my disciple. And whoever does not carry their cross and follow me cannot be my disciple.
> *Luke 14:26-27*

These are difficult words. They go to the heart of His mission and His message. They are meant to disturb and provoke us, to shake us out of the complacent assumption that we know what it is to love.

One of the ways our culture seeks to domesticate Jesus is to say He is simply 'a good man who taught us the importance of love and compassion'. To say that is to tame Him, to make *Him* conform to *our* ethical consensus. His sayings are designed to shock and to disturb. His central invitation is to 'follow me' – for it is only by walking the way of the cross that we find out what 'love' and 'compassion' really mean.

Structure of this book

Each chapter of this book considers a different aspect of love. Christlike love is in some ways tremendously simple, and yet it involves holding a number of surprising things together: it is both merciful *and* just; it is universal *and* yet deeply personal; it involves vulnerability *and* yet it is the most powerful force in the universe. In every chapter, one of these paradoxes will be explored. The chapters each fall into four sections:

Introduction: an initial discussion of one aspect of love.

Gospel: reflection on a passage which speaks about that same theme.

Stories: one or two stories of modern discipleship which cast light on this aspect of love and how we might embody it today.

Action: a final drawing together of the discussion, moving on to a small, practical suggestion for action in the week ahead.

Lent: walking the way of love

From the earliest days of the faith, Lent has been a season when Christians seek to renew their walk in the way of the cross.

The Gospel passages used in *Just Love* are the ones that are read in many churches on the Sundays of Lent. But the book can be used at any time – whether or not you go to church, and whether or not your local church keeps the different seasons of the Christian year – for these Gospel readings, and the questions they raise, are of value in every situation and season. They help us to understand the meaning of the cross and, in doing so, they help us to understand what it *really* means to love.

And in the end – as the Bible and our culture agree – that is the one thing that really matters.

Chapter 1
Spiritual *and* Embodied

Introduction

Love is the most spiritual of experiences, but it cannot be separated from its physical expression. If a couple were to say that their love for one another had become so 'spiritual' that they never even touched each other, we would know that something was seriously wrong. The love we have for our friends – our mutual concern and affection – is revealed in gestures as well as words. But there is more to both kinds of love than these gestures. For our affection to count as genuine love, it needs to be shown in our ongoing care for one another – in ways that have a real and lasting cost. When I say, 'I love you,' what makes it true (or false) is not just my feelings at that moment, but also my behaviour in the months and years ahead.

The Bible describes love with great beauty and intensity, most notably in the Song of Solomon. This is not a book that spares its readers' blushes! There is usually embarrassment in church when its vivid descriptions of romantic desire and love are read at Sunday services. Nonetheless, we *do* read it in church because it is part of Holy Scripture, part of God's self-revelation. Because such a love poem has been placed in the Bible, we learn that our physical desires and loves are deeply spiritual matters. According to the Song of Solomon, they offer us an image of the love God has for us. For Christianity, as for Judaism, 'spirituality' is not about running away from our bodies and our desires. It is about learning to embody God's love ever more faithfully.

The Bible takes our material nature seriously. In its teaching on both personal and economic relationships, the central

17

question is how our physical interactions are going to embody faithfulness, generosity and love. We can exploit one another's bodies – viewing other people simply as instruments of our own pleasure and power – or our physical interactions can help us grow into the image of God. It is through the practical love we show to our fellow human beings that we grow beyond ourselves. Love of God and love of neighbour are absolutely inseparable – and love of neighbour has a material, as well as a spiritual, dimension.

As Archbishop Justin Welby explains:

> When Christians speak in public about community flourishing or about justice, there's always someone who will pop up and ask why we're sticking our noses in, as if these things were miles away from the proper concerns of Christianity.
>
> Recently there have been the issues of money and credit unions and power costs of which the church has spoken. Stick to God, we are told. So we do, and we find ... Jesus saying: Love God, love neighbour.
>
> The common good of the community and justice are absolutely central to what it means to be a Christian. They flow from the love of Jesus on the Cross, offering salvation, enabling justice and human freedom.[1]

This combination of the physical and the spiritual runs through the teachings of the Law and the Prophets, but Christians believe it reaches its completion in Jesus. In the incarnation, God's Word of love becomes flesh. In Christ, God does not give us a set of commands or ideals, but becomes a human person, offering us a wholly different level of

---

[1] Address to the Church Urban Fund *Tackling Poverty Together* conference, 13 November 2013.

relationship. Shane Claiborne – a leading figure in the 'New Monasticism' movement – writes that:

> Jesus shows us what God is like with skin on – in a way we can touch, feel and follow. My Latino friends have taught me the word *incarnation* shares the same root as *en carne* or *con carne*, which means 'with meat'. We can see God in other places and at work throughout history, but the climax of all history is Jesus.[2]

In Christ we see not only that God *loves,* but that God *is love* – for He reveals to us that God is Father, Son and Holy Spirit. As the priest and community theologian Kenneth Leech puts it, 'in God there is social life, community, sharing. To share in God is to share in that life.'[3] So when we love, we do not simply *imitate* God. We participate in His very life. This is what the First Letter of Peter means by calling us 'partakers of the divine nature.'

Union with God sounds a very spiritual thing. But the Bible tells us that this *spiritual* union involves some very practical actions. Through our practical compassion and our action for justice, we share the very life of God:

> No one has ever seen God; but if we love one another, God lives in us and his love is made complete in us.
> *1 John 4:12*

The theologian Stephen Long gives us a set of questions to ask of all our interactions with other people:

[2] In Shane Claiborne and Tony Campolo, *Red Letter Revolution: What if Jesus really meant what he said?* Thomas Nelson, 2012, p.7.
[3] *True Prayer*, Morehouse Publishing, 1995, p.8.

Is charity furthered? Do our exchanges point us to our true source? Do [they] fit the mission Christ has entrusted to us? Do [they] allow us to participate in God's holiness and God's perfections? All Christian churches, orders and vocations cannot be faithful if they fail to ask and answer this question: How do our daily exchanges promote that charity which is a participation in the life of God?[4]

This last sentence captures a question at the heart of the Gospel: how do we embody God's love, faithfully and generously? For the Christian, our daily interactions in the workplace and the home, the shop and the factory, the community centre and the boardroom should be forming us more and more into human beings who can love. Through these exchanges, we are either sharing God's love or rejecting it.

Gospel

The story of Jesus' transfiguration offers us a vision of the physical world shining with God's light and God's glory. The timing of the story is significant, both in the Gospel of Matthew and in the church's pattern of readings.

Matthew places the story just before Jesus speaks to the disciples about His forthcoming death. Before Jesus walks the way of the cross, He gives His closest followers this 'mountain top' experience: a vision of the ultimate destination.

In the Church of England, the passage is read on the Sunday before Lent. In Roman Catholic churches it is a couple of weeks later. In each case, as we begin Lent, we are given a vision of where the journey ends. The Transfiguration expresses in *story* what this chapter has been describing in *concepts*. As we see

---

[4] *Divine Economy: Theology and the Market*, Routledge, 2012, p.269.

Jesus glorified, we see the destination God has planned for those who love Him:

> After six days Jesus took with him Peter, James and John the brother of James, and led them up a high mountain by themselves. There he was transfigured before them. His face shone like the sun, and his clothes became as white as the light. Just then there appeared before them Moses and Elijah, talking with Jesus.
>
> Peter said to Jesus, 'Lord, it is good for us to be here. If you wish, I will put up three shelters – one for you, one for Moses and one for Elijah.'
>
> While he was still speaking, a bright cloud covered them, and a voice from the cloud said, 'This is my Son, whom I love; with him I am well pleased. Listen to him!'
>
> When the disciples heard this, they fell face down to the ground, terrified. But Jesus came and touched them. 'Get up,' he said. 'Don't be afraid.' When they looked up, they saw no one except Jesus.
>
> As they were coming down the mountain, Jesus instructed them, 'Don't tell anyone what you have seen, until the Son of Man has been raised from the dead.'
>
> *Matthew 17:1-9*

This passage presents us with a vision of a creation transformed and renewed in Christ, a physical world which shines with the divine glory. While it speaks of a universal promise, it is rooted in a very particular story.

The presence of Elijah and Moses – representing both the Prophets and the Law – reminds us that Jesus is rooted in the community of Israel, a people formed by God's calling and His promise.

Stories are the essence of the Bible. The medium is part of the message. All too often we want to rush past these specifics, the unpronounceable names and often perplexing narratives. We want to tidy the Bible up and make it simpler – boiling down its complexity and variety to find a 'spiritual essence'. But the untidiness of Scripture, and the specificity of its stories, is part of the revelation. We need to face it, not evade it. Richard Chartres, the Bishop of London, has expressed this powerfully:

> *We* want neat orderly systems which our minds can comprehend and *God* gives us Himself in the answer he gave to Moses – simply 'I am'. *We* want absolute truth nailed down in propositional form and we are given a huge drama, a symphony of the many ways in which *God* has related to human kind. *We* want bottom lines for life and *God* gives us those and then moves beyond them to the law of love ... The Bible reveals truth, tragic and glorious; bloody and violent; nurturing and inspiring by breaking in upon our understanding from another realm and taking us by surprise.[5]

Stories

If stories are the essence of the Bible, they must also be the essence of theology. To speak of God's love, we need lived examples as well as abstract ideas. That's why each chapter of this book includes a story of modern discipleship, set alongside the Gospel passage.

In this chapter, we have chosen the story of two Church of England parishes in the poorest neighbourhoods of Bradford

---

[5] Sermon at launch of St Mellitus College, London, 2 July 2008.

and of London. As we read these stories, we see at once how the spiritual and the physical are intimately connected. Transfiguration has a social and a personal dimension.

St Peter's, Bethnal Green

In 2012, a project called *Leaves on the Line* mapped life expectancy in the areas around each of London's Tube stations. In the journey between two adjacent stops – Liverpool Street in the City of London and Bethnal Green in the East End – life expectancy drops by seven years. According to the Church Urban Fund, the parish of St Peter's Bethnal Green is in the top one per cent in terms of the prevalence of child poverty. As Adam and Heather Atkinson tell their church's story, we see at once how the spiritual and the physical are intimately connected. Transfiguration has a social and a personal dimension.

When Adam and Heather Atkinson led a 'restart' of this inner-city parish – as part of a church planting process instigated by Holy Trinity Brompton – their first task was to *listen*. Adam explains, 'This was our way of expressing the centrality of face-to-face relationships, and the building of genuine mutuality. The idea was that we wanted to really *know* what the concerns of the local community were, rather than simply presuming – and to work with the community to achieve real and lasting change.'

The process of listening to congregation members and to the wider parish was itself understood as an attempt to discern what God was already doing in Bethnal Green, and what He had laid on its people's hearts. A range of other activities have helped to deepen the church's life of corporate prayer and discernment – both setting up 'Life Groups' (cell groups with Bible study and sharing of experience at their heart) and holding events in which the riches of both the catholic and charismatic traditions could be shared across the church.

Two key issues that emerged from this process of listening were a concern about the safety of local streets and a growing amount of food poverty – individuals and families who could not afford to eat.

Because St Peter's is committed to acting *with* the poorest and not simply *for* them, the church joined London Citizens (the capital's community organising alliance – see text box). This brought it into relationship with other institutions in the area, including schools and colleges. Soon, it became clear that school pupils also had fears about safety. Young people were asked to pinpoint on a map areas where they felt especially threatened. The results showed that they were particularly worried about crossing one of the main roads in the area – Hackney Road. It emerged that some pupils would take several buses to avoid walking across the road, which was a gang boundary. For a short period of time, one of the local schools worked with local police, and the shift pattern of officers was changed. This led to a striking reduction in crime.

Introducing Community Organising

London Citizens is the capital's community organising movement – part of the national Citizens UK alliance. Community organising involves building an alliance of religious congregations, schools and civic associations to work together on issues of common concern. It seeks to build a 'relational culture': encouraging people to share their stories, through one-to-one conversations (see Chapter Two) and then to come together and identify the ways in which their areas can be changed for the better. When people with common concerns are in relationship, they are in a position to challenge those with the power to deliver change (be that environmental improvements, better pay for workers, or improved public services).

While the campaigns are on specific, winnable issues, the wider goal is to build a local and national alliance with an ongoing set of relationships of trust and commitment – where each successful campaign not only brings a tangible result (such as improved social housing or higher wages) but develops grassroots leadership and the power of people in Britain's poorest neighbourhoods to work together for the common good.

St Peter's has tried to tackle the issue of food poverty in three different ways – supporting local Foodbanks, campaigning through London Citizens for a Living Wage and against exploitative lending, and by setting up a monthly community meal after Sunday worship. The congregation are asked to bring enough food with them to share. The intention is to provide so much that there is food left over for people to box up and use during the week.

As Adam says, the Community Lunch is 'by no means the answer to every food-related problem, but it's a start at making things easier. This has also been a great way of integrating new members into the church, getting younger and older people to interact over some food and conversation. We think Foodbanks are valuable but we want to do more than simply make a one-way donation. We want to build relationships, and see what we can do together.'

He goes on to explain that practical care and action to tackle injustice 'help people to experience something of the Kingdom of God. But we also want people to know the King for themselves.' It is not that social action occurs *in order to* convert people. Rather, social action and sharing the faith are both practical expressions of the church's faith and love. Three years in, the evidence is that this approach is bearing fruit. The Sunday congregation has more than doubled, with growth across ages, races and social classes – and many more people (of all faiths and none) work in partnership with the church.

St Stephen's, West Bowling

West Bowling is an area just to the south-east of Bradford. This diverse and deprived neighbourhood is perhaps one of the most challenging places in the country in which to minister. The early 2000s saw a significant change in the way St Stephen's saw its ministry to the local community.

Up until the end of the 1990s St Stephen's was a 'traditional Anglican church' with a good teaching ministry which called for a faithful response. The problem was that fewer and fewer people were responding. There was a gradually dwindling congregation and therefore a smaller and smaller capacity to reach out to the wider parish with practical love. The connection between this spirituality and the reality of the context became increasingly strained as the years went on. The congregation became older and less able to maintain both the building and a lively community of faith. It slowly edged towards crisis.

In 2004 when Jimmy Hinton took over as vicar, the church was in a perilous state. The Diocese of Bradford had indicated that this was 'make or break' for St Stephen's. Jimmy worked in ministry closely with his wife Sarah, and the Hintons were given three years to turn things round.

The first thing the Hintons did was to open the church doors and welcome everyone into the building. They focussed their work on developing a presence in the community: they started children's work, opened their own home and even installed a snooker table in the church to encourage people inside. They set themselves the task of building relationships with local people and offering hospitality and welcome. Gradually people started to come to church because of the ethos of welcome that had been generated.

Out of this developed a more grounded spirituality that took seriously the brokenness and the pain of the context. It was an incarnate spirituality which sought the presence of God in the relationships that had been built with local people. This is a spirituality that is meaningful to those who live in the area. People there are keen to belong to a community based on principles of loving acceptance, and this has enabled many to begin to experience joy and mutually supportive friendships.

The church is now at the centre of local community life and provides a hub around which much of the life and vitality of the neighbourhood revolves. It expresses a spirituality which is embodied in the reality of people's lives. In doing so, it speaks the truth of Christian faith in ways that are actively engaged with the complexity and diversity of the context.

Action

What does this story mean for us? How do we live out this vision – of physical and spiritual 'transfiguration' – in our local context?

Stephen Long's question supplies our starting point: *how do our daily exchanges promote that charity which is a participation in the life of God?* It invites us to begin, not with *action*, but with *observation*. Before we seek to do anything new, we need to look for the signs of God's life in our 'daily exchanges' – in the encounters we have in our homes, our workplaces, our neighbourhoods and our church. Only when we have discerned where God is at work will we know how and where to follow as disciples.

A discipline you could take up during Lent (or indeed at any time of year) is the use of the Examen. This simple process is described in the text box below. It provides a structure for reviewing the events and encounters of each day, to discern where God has been at work. It also helps us to identify the points at which we have frustrated that work so that we can repent and learn from our mistakes, asking God not only for forgiveness, but also for a change of habits and of heart. The Examen weaves together the physical and the spiritual, the holy and the day-to-day. It can help us to put the ideas contained within this chapter into practice in our own lives, in a simple, concrete way.

Each chapter of the book ends with a suggestion for practical action, and whether you are using *Just Love* for individual devotion or reading it in a group, we suggest that you use the Examen as this chapter's practical exercise. It is, of course, primarily about *personal* change. The stories of St Peter's and St Stephen's remind us that transfiguration also has a corporate dimension. How do we discern and respond to God in our work for social transformation?

The Examen: A spiritual exercise for the end of each day[6]

Developed by St Ignatius, The Examination of Consciousness (Examen) is intended as a short period of reflection, used for 10-15 minutes at the end of each day. It is a simple, practical way to seek and find God in all things and to gain the freedom to let God's will be done on earth. The Examen has five steps:

1. Recall that you are in the presence of God. No matter where you are, you are a creature in the midst of creation and the Creator who called you forth is concerned for you.

2. Give thanks to God for favours received. Pause and spend a moment looking at this day's gifts. Take stock of what you received and gave.

---

[6] Based on a guide to the Examen by St Ignatius' Church, Boston (USA).

3. Ask for awareness of the Holy Spirit's aid. Before you explore the mystery of the human heart, ask to receive the Holy Spirit so that you can look upon your actions and motives with honesty and patience. The Spirit gives a freedom to look upon yourself without condemnation and complacency and thus to be open to growth.

4. Now examine how you have lived this day. Recalling the events of your day, explore the context of your actions. Review the day, hour by hour, searching for the internal events of your life. Look through the hours to see your interaction with what was before you. Ask what you were involved in and who you were with, and review your hopes and hesitations. What moved you to act the way you did?

5. Pray words of reconciliation and resolve. Having reviewed this day of your life, look upon yourself with compassion and see your need for God and try to realise God's manifestations of concern for you. Express sorrow for sin, give thanks for grace, and praise God for the times you responded in ways that allowed you to better see God's life.

The Atkinsons' ministry at St Peter's began with a *listening* exercise. At the heart of this process was face-to-face engagement – both one-to-one conversations and discussions in small groups. The aim of this process was not just to discern people's needs, but also to develop the capacity of church members and others in Bethnal Green to act together for change. Surrounded by prayer and reflection, this process functioned as a kind of corporate Examen.

In the final chapter, we describe a simple tool which helps churches to listen to their neighbours and to take action with them for the common good. This chapter has cast some light on why these practical issues are of such spiritual significance. The struggle for a more just society is an essential part of the church's calling – part of what it means to be co-workers with God, making the whole of creation radiant with His glory and His love. But that corporate struggle must begin with a personal commitment, and personal devotion. The Atkinsons and the Hintons, and the many others with whom they built these powerful community ministries, were first of all people of prayer: people who looked and listened to discern where God was at work in their everyday encounters. The personal and the communal aspects of ministry must go together. Practices such as the Examen enable us to root our work for social justice in a prayerful and personal walk with Jesus Christ.

Chapter 2
Urgent *and* Patient

Introduction

The Bible tells us that love is patient and kind, and takes no account of wrongs (1 Corinthians 13:4-5). But it also talks of love as an inextinguishable, fiercely blazing fire (Song of Solomon 8:6). There is a tension here; it is sometimes hard for us to hold together the *patience* and the *urgent action* to which love sometimes calls us. How can we be calm and patient when someone we love is suffering?

'Immediately' is one of the most common words in Mark's Gospel. The opening chapters are incredibly fast paced. Jesus' ministry is shown to have a focus on those the world ignores or condemns. He reminds the religious leaders of the purpose of the Law: not to be another burden on the vulnerable, but a means of protecting them from injustice (Mark 2:23-3.6). He compares Himself to a thief, whose purpose is to tie up the strong man and plunder his property (3:22-27). Of course, Jesus' purpose is not to turn the world upside down, or to steal someone's rightful goods, but to turn an *upside-down* world *the right way up*, restoring just stewardship to a creation which is being pillaged and misused. Where there is injustice and oppression, any genuine love for our neighbours leads inevitably to this sense of urgency. The lives and stories of those in greatest need, and the violence and wastage of potential in our communities, cry out for immediate action.

Pastor and civil rights activist Martin Luther King wrote these words from his cell in Birmingham City Jail:

More and more I feel that the people of ill will have used time much more effectively than have the people of good will. We will have to repent in this generation not merely for the hateful words and actions of the bad people but for the appalling silence of the good people. Human progress never rolls in on wheels of inevitability; it comes through the tireless efforts of men willing to be co-workers with God ... We must use time creatively, in the knowledge that the time is always ripe to do right.[7]

As we shall see later in the chapter, King's sense of urgency went along with an extraordinary patience. This is a combination that we see even more clearly in Jesus' ministry and mission.

Jesus' earthly ministry begins with 30 years of waiting; immersing Himself in the life and experience of a carpenter in Nazareth. This is surely the last thing we would expect! When God becomes human, in a world filled with such pressing need, He spends around 90 per cent of His earthly life *being with* people – present among some of the poorest and most marginalised people upon earth. As the priest and theologian Sam Wells puts it:

> Jesus spent a week in Jerusalem working for us, doing what we can't do, achieving our salvation ... He spent three years in Galilee working with us, calling us to follow him and work alongside him ... But before he ever got into working with and working for, he spent thirty years in Nazareth being with us, setting aside his plans and strategies, and experiencing in his own body not just the exile and oppression of the children

[7] Letter from Birmingham Jail, 16 April 1963.

of Israel, but also the joy and sorrow of family and community life.[8]

Gospel

After all this waiting, the first event in Jesus' public ministry is His baptism, at which a voice from heaven confirms that Jesus is God's Son and instructs its hearers to 'listen to Him'. As we read the Gospels it is reasonable to think, 'Surely now, after all the waiting, we are going to see some action!' In fact, we have to be patient once again. For after His baptism the first thing Jesus does is to go into the wilderness, for 40 days and 40 nights of struggle and discernment. The story of those 40 days is our Gospel reading for the first Sunday of Lent – linking this experience of Jesus to this season, and its 40 days of self-denial and prayer:

> Then Jesus was led by the Spirit into the wilderness to be tempted by the devil. After fasting forty days and forty nights, he was hungry. The tempter came to him and said, 'If you are the Son of God, tell these stones to become bread.'
>
> Jesus answered, 'It is written: "Man shall not live on bread alone, but on every word that comes from the mouth of God."'
>
> Then the devil took him to the holy city and had him stand on the highest point of the temple. 'If you are the Son of God,' he said, 'throw yourself down. For it is written, "He will command his angels concerning you, and they will lift you up in their hands, so that you will not strike your foot against a stone."'

---

[8] The Nazareth Manifesto, online at https://web.duke.edu/kenanethics/NazarethManifesto_SamWells.pdf (accessed 1 December 2013).

Jesus answered him, 'It is also written: "Do not put the Lord your God to the test."'

Again, the devil took him to a very high mountain and showed him all the kingdoms of the world and their splendor. 'All this I will give you,' he said, 'if you will bow down and worship me.'

Jesus said to him, 'Away from me, Satan! For it is written: "Worship the Lord your God, and serve him only."' Then the devil left him, and angels came and attended him.

Matthew 4:1-11

The temptations Jesus faces are deeply revealing. Indeed, it is only in the final temptation that the underlying issue is unmasked. Initially, the temptations have a superficial plausibility. Why *shouldn't* Jesus use His power to become some kind of wonder-worker? After all, He has just had his divine status confirmed dramatically in the presence of the crowds who were following John the Baptist. Producing miracles on demand would surely secure Him a quick following. In a world of hunger and need, and of injustice and oppression, why not build a mass movement by turning stones into bread?

The third temptation reveals the underlying issue. Such wonder-working would in the end be *idolatry*. In all the temptations, the devil has been trying to appeal to the human ego. Although superficially attractive, all three temptations are in fact inviting Jesus to transfer His loyalty away from His heavenly Father, to allow His mission to be driven off course by a desire for status and for quick success.

The story of Jesus' temptation helps us to understand why, in the early stages of His ministry, He is so reluctant to let anyone know He is the Messiah. The word 'Messiah' conjured up images of power and kingship which were at odds with His ministry and mission. The people were looking for a powerful king who would sort things out quickly and dramatically –

whereas Jesus was engaged in a much more patient and fundamental process of transformation.

Jesus knew that no amount of *words* would correct the people's expectations. This may explain why He was wary of being hailed as the Messiah. It would only be His deeds – the pouring out of His life upon the cross, and the vindication and completion of that offering on Easter Day – that would enable the people around Him to understand the true nature of the Messiah. And, as the events of the Gospels unfold, we see how right Jesus was. Even after teaching His disciples clearly and repeatedly on the issue, and entering Jerusalem on a donkey (in a parody of earthly pomp), both the crowds and the disciples still misunderstood the kind of Messiah Jesus was going to be, and so they abandoned Him, some in anger and others in fear and disappointment.

The crowds were looking for a dramatic exercise of earthly power to overthrow the Roman regime. But Jesus' mission was – and is – about a deeper, more fundamental change than the replacement of one violent regime by another. Jesus' mission was to proclaim, and indeed to bring into being, a very different kingdom, one in which the whole cycle of violence and hatred is to be overcome with love. The cross, and not the sword, is the weapon needed for *this* battle.

If Jesus had to spend time wrestling with false directions and temptations, His followers surely need to do the same. For we, too, face temptations. One temptation we face is that of egoism – the temptation (seen in this Gospel passage) to act in ways that keep us busy, and feed our self-importance, but do little or nothing for the Kingdom of God. As Martin Luther King's letter reminds us, there is an equal and opposite temptation – to confuse patience with procrastination, and in the name of 'spirituality' to avoid the tough choices and uncomfortable actions that the Gospel calls us to. The way of the cross involves patience, but it also involves courage – a sense of the sheer *urgency* of Christlike love.

The English word 'anger' comes from the Norse word *angr*, meaning 'grief'. Anger is a sign that something is not right. So it is right to be angry at injustice, at wasted potential and at blighted lives. Indeed, it is an utterly biblical emotion. The Gospels record a number of occasions when Jesus is angry. In Mark 1, He is 'indignant' when He meets a leper, and sees his plight (verse 41). Two chapters later, when the religious leaders criticise Him for healing someone on the Sabbath, we read that He 'looked around at them in anger ... deeply distressed at their stubborn hearts' (verse 5).

Christians often find it hard to deal with the idea of Jesus being anything other than calm and placid. Perhaps this is why the most significant occasion of His anger, the cleansing of the Temple, is so rarely depicted in stained glass or other forms of Christian art.

When we look in detail at the story of Jesus' cleansing of the Temple, we see how His actions hold together the urgency and patience we have been discussing. The cleansing of the Temple was not the result of a spasm of rage, or a loss of self-control. Jesus was certainly angry. However, His anger remained firmly at the service of His mission. It was not allowed to distort that mission. The sequence of events in Mark 11 is very striking: Jesus entered Jerusalem on a donkey and then 'went into the temple courts [and] looked around at everything, but since it was already late, he went out to Bethany with the Twelve' (verse 11). The next day He returned and

> entered the temple courts and began driving out those who were buying and selling there. He overturned the tables of the money-changers and the benches of those selling doves.
> *Mark 11:15*

The cleansing of the Temple was planned and no doubt prayed over, as Jesus was all too aware that it was part of a series of actions that would lead Him to the cross.

We have already mentioned three stories in the Gospels where Jesus' anger leads Him to speak out or to take action (the healing of the leper, the healing on the Sabbath and the cleansing of the Temple). But on many other occasions, Jesus walks away from conflict or provocation (e.g. Mark 12:13-17).

For anger to be Christlike, it requires us to cultivate *urgent patience*. It requires our anger to be disciplined by love, humility and prudence. In the rest of this chapter, we will consider how each of us can make that happen – beginning with two stories of modern discipleship, and then considering their application to our lives.

Stories

Rosa Parks and Martin Luther King

Most people remember Rosa Parks for a single, iconic act. On the bus home from work, she sat down as usual in the area reserved for black people. As the front (which was reserved for whites) filled up, the bus driver moved the 'Colored' sign behind Parks, and told her to move to the back to accommodate the extra white passengers.

Her refusal to move, and her subsequent arrest and dismissal from work, led to the Montgomery Bus Boycott – a 381-day protest which ended with the Supreme Court ruling that segregation on buses was illegal. The boycott campaign was coordinated by a previously little-known Baptist pastor, the Revd Martin Luther King, Jr.

In a society that values the individual above all else, the stories of Rosa Parks and Martin Luther King have been distorted in predictable ways.

The way the story is told, Rosa Parks is seen as an accidental heroine – an ordinary woman who simply had a flash of anger, or tiredness. Nothing could be further from the truth. Like the cleansing of the Temple, her act of defiance was calculated. Moreover, Parks was not acting alone. She had been active in the civil rights movement for more than a decade, and in the summer of the bus incident she had attended a school in Tennessee for civil rights training.

As she said later:

> People always say that I didn't give up my seat because I was tired, but that isn't true. I was not tired physically, or no more tired than I usually was at the end of a working day. I was not old, although some people have an image of me as being old then. I was forty-two. No, the only tired I was, was tired of giving in.[9]

As the story of Parks and King is told, their Christianity is often downplayed. In a new biography of Rosa Parks, Jeanne Theoharis seeks to correct this. She reminds us that Parks was a lifelong member of the African Methodist Episcopal Church and was never without her Bible.[10]

In his blog on 'faith, transformation and social justice,' Jon Kuhrt makes the same point about King. In doing so, he draws our attention to the simple one-page pledge which King's campaigners had to sign:

> I hereby pledge myself – my person and body – to the Nonviolent Movement. Therefore I will keep the following Ten Commandments:

---

[9] *USA Today*, 3 February 2013.
[10] Jeanne Theoharris, *The Rebellious Life of Mrs. Rosa Parks*, Beacon Press, 2013.

1. Meditate on the life and teachings of Jesus.

2. Remember the nonviolent movement seeks justice and reconciliation – not victory.

3. Walk and talk in the manner of love; for God is love.

4. Pray daily to be used by God that all men and women might be free.

5. Sacrifice personal wishes that all might be free.

6. Observe with friend and foes the ordinary rules of courtesy.

7. Perform regular service for others and the world.

8. Refrain from violence of fist, tongue and heart.

9. Strive to be in good spiritual and bodily health.

10. Follow the directions of the movement leaders on demonstrations.[11]

The pledge shows what it means for faith to be both spiritual and embodied, and for action to show both the patience and the urgency of love. Our all-too-impatient culture could learn a great deal more from the examples of both Parks and King if it recognised that their courageous actions and fiery oratory were the fruit of patient prayer, study and organising. Our culture loves heroes, but Christianity invites us to instead be *saints*: people for whom Christ, and not self, is at the centre of the story. Parks and King have precisely that quality, a genuine Christian sanctity that the retelling of their stories so often obscures.

---

[11] Jon Kuhrt, 'The Secularisation of Martin Luther King' at http://resistanceandrenewal.net (accessed 1 December 2013).

Hull Youth for Christ

Hull Youth for Christ has existed in the city since the 1950s. Its original vision was to support and resource the city's churches by developing youth work in local congregations, and from time to time organising larger events and rallies. Over the years, it has become a vital institution in the city's life. However, the 1990s were a 'crunch time' for the organisation: it found itself in crisis as many local churches lacked the capacity to engage in youth work in the way they had done in the previous decades. Hull Youth for Christ found itself looking for a new identity.

In the early 1990s, after a review of the work, the organisation decided to focus its energy and resources on one of the poorest areas of the city. A team of four workers was established with a team leader to share a house together in the Boulevard area of Hull – an 'incarnational' presence, committed to living and listening to the local community.

At the time, this was a radical response, and one required by the changes in the context. However, it caused a considerable amount of tension. The local community did not fully understand what the team was trying to do. Churches across the city felt they had lost a resource, and the residents of the Boulevard were puzzled by these strangers who had taken up residence in their midst.

There are now six members of the team living in three houses in the same street in the Boulevard area of the city. Chris and Anna (the couple who lead the team) and their colleagues are well aware of the costs of living in this struggling community. But they are deeply committed to sharing the lives of their neighbours: building real relationships and entering into the experience of local life at real depth, so that the problems the wider community faces (such as the quality of local schools, and access to adequate healthcare) are also their problems. This is a different model of community engagement from that of many government agencies or even charities whose staff 'dip in and out' of local life through targeted short-term interventions.

The relationships on which Chris and Anna's work depends – and which enable it to have a real impact – only exist because of their many years of patient and careful presence and engagement in local life, and the ways in which they have engaged with many individual neighbours. None of this has been easy. Like others in their team, Chris and Anna continually have to wrestle with the choices that are thrown up by life in the neighbourhood. These choices are very raw and real, and demand a response: 'Do we move out for the sake of our kids' schooling?' 'How far do we shape ourselves and our work to match the requirements of potential funding bodies or produce the "results" they are looking to see?'

It is their deep personal faith, and their relationships on the Boulevard estate, which enable Chris and Anna to live with these questions and tensions – to live with integrity, and to live sacrificially – in a way that is bearing fruit for God's Kingdom and showing Christlike love to young people living with deep poverty and alienation.

Action

What might help us to follow these examples? Obviously, the very season of Lent is given to us so that we might follow Jesus more and more closely – echoing His 40 days of fasting and prayer in the wilderness. But, whatever the season, there are two important gifts which God offers us to get this balance right, holding together urgency and patience.

Firstly, of course, He has given us *Himself*. A little later in the chapter we will consider how the practice of silence can help us attend to God's presence and to grow in patience and discernment. But God has also given us *one another*. The institution of the church is itself a gift, and one that both demands and cultivates our patience. It is to this unfashionable gift that we now turn.

Patience and the church

For nearly everyone, 'spirituality' is a more attractive term than 'institutional religion'. It is common to contrast the (dynamic) 'spiritual message of Jesus' with the (stagnant) 'institutional church'.

Yet, the stories of this chapter – from 1960s America and contemporary England – illustrate the vital role local churches have in acting with compassion and working for social justice. Churches are a vital force for engaging people in practical action – both works of mercy and action for justice. It is through these institutions that we see the intentional nurturing of relationships, local leadership and vision. Their rules, procedures and commitments may seem old-fashioned, but some such framework turns are essential if our 'spiritual' aspirations are to be made flesh.

We see the same struggles in the early church in Corinth. St Paul is not a legalist: he urges the Corinthians to live Spirit-filled lives, and warns that without love, their faith and virtue are as nothing. And yet he makes equally clear that love involves discipline, humility and commitment. They – we – are called into the church, called to be one body in Jesus Christ. That involves one of the most fundamental and difficult of spiritual challenges: living alongside a bunch of people who you haven't been allowed to choose.

Institutions are imperfect because humans are imperfect. We need to be patient with one another, and it takes patience to live within the church. But that is our calling,

It is one thing to note that the institutional church is full of sinners and to bemoan its structural and individual failings. That's all true. It's quite another thing to imagine that we are less vulnerable to sin, less open to delusion, when we seek a spiritual path in isolation from our neighbour. It is together that we grow into Christ. The very things that we often chafe against in institutions – the way they restrict our freedom to act spontaneously, without engaging with and consulting those around us – are a necessary part of doing anything together. Jesus recognises this, which is why his attitude to institutional religion is more nuanced than we might initially think.

Jesus' teaching and actions expose the dark side of institutional religion – the ways it can abuse power, creating self-serving and self-important hierarchies. But He does not propose an individualistic 'spiritual' response, detached from the life of a wider community of faith. Far from it: Jesus is an observant Jew, attending, praying and teaching in the synagogue, and He establishes the church as an ongoing expression of His mission of love.

Patience and silence

While God has given us each other, His greatest gift to every person is of course *Himself*. The heart of our spiritual life is our one-to-one relationship with God in Jesus Christ.

When we talk of 'silence' and 'contemplation', many Christians tune out, assuming the subject isn't for them, that it's all too difficult and is better left to a contemplative elite. Sometimes those who write books on prayer collude with this: it is made to seem very complicated and technical. The best writing on prayer, like Jesus' own teaching, is in fact very simple and practical. It is accessible to all. The challenge is not whether we *can* follow it, but whether we are willing to go through the discomfort – and sometimes the sheer boredom – it involves.

There can be no doubt that Jesus was a 'contemplative'. On His fast of 40 days – and again and again throughout the Gospels – He leaves the noise and confusion of the crowds to be alone with His heavenly Father. He is sceptical about the excessive use of words in prayer, whether they are liturgical formulae or free-form intercessions. Jesus tells us to be still, to pray simply and honestly – and to listen to what God has to say to us. From the way He teaches against wordy prayer, and the sheer length of time He spends in prayer, it is clear that much of Jesus' time was indeed spent in silent communion with His heavenly Father.

Silence is not an evasion of the world around us. To be silent before God is a profoundly countercultural act. It is to prioritise communion above output and achievements, and to recognise that mission is first and foremost God's activity; that before we act we must first discern how and where He is at work. Jesus' communion with His Father enables Him to know when to act and when to refrain from action, to see into the hearts of those He meets, and to recognise the Father speaking through them.

One of the reasons we run away from silence is that it brings us face to face with *ourselves*. That is not a comfortable thing. When we sit still, we become aware of the cacophony of thoughts and feelings rattling around inside us. We need to be encouraged by the testimony of those who have persevered in such prayer for years: it remains a struggle, with distractions and with boredom.

Often we become dispirited in prayer because we imagine the next person is having a much richer, better spiritual life. In fact, part of the challenge of silent prayer is that we can't 'do it well'. We have to try and set aside the idea of achieving something, or worrying about whether our prayers are going better or worse than those of the next person. Prayer is not a competition, nor a pious form of entertainment in which we train ourselves to receive wonderful, ecstatic experiences. Silent prayer is exactly what it 'says on the tin': a matter of stopping, being still and seeing what happens when we seek to spend time consciously and quietly in the presence of the One in whom 'we live and move and have our being' (Acts 17:28).

It is easy to extol the virtues of silence in a rather pious-sounding, abstract way. It is much harder to work it out in the messiness of our personal life, and the life of a local church. The text box below suggests some very practical, mundane first steps: simple things we can do to help our minds and hearts remain in focus. No technique will stop us being distracted when we pray – and the key thing is simply to refocus when we realise our mind has wandered off. It happens to everyone. The challenge is simply to persevere rather than distracting ourselves further by becoming frustrated by the way our mind wanders. We find it hard to do this because it is so humbling – none of us does it *well*, and so it is a great equaliser. (Archbishop Michael Ramsey once said that in half an hour of silence, he probably only actually prayed for five minutes.)

Silence calls us away from frenetic activism. But it is not 'other worldly'. One of the fruits of silence – something we do not feel in the times of silent prayer, but which we begin to notice in the rest of our daily life if we regularly set aside times for silent prayer – is that we become more attentive to what is going on in ourselves and in the lives of the people around us. Tim Clapton is an Anglican priest who has spent many years working in deprived communities in different parts of England. He reflects:

There is a stillness to be practiced in Christian spirituality, through which we hear the heart-beat of God in the world. But trying to walk with God is often more about being unsettled, uneasy and restless.

Where do our silence, meditation and stillness lead us? I believe silence is prayer only when we are changed by it, and it propels us to a closer communion with our neighbours, and indeed with all creation. We cannot separate the spirituality of silence, meditation and contemplation from engagement with the community. It drives us to a greater engagement – a greater attention to the created order.[12]

Silence is unsettling, because the moment we are still, we realise how broken we are: how distracted and distractable, how full of uncomfortable feelings and emotions. It's tempting to keep ourselves busy precisely so we *don't* have to face this hard reality! If we are willing to spend time in silence, our action becomes less and less driven by anxiety, guilt and ambition. Instead, it becomes a more authentic response to the love poured out for us in Christ.

The motivation for Christlike love is a very simple one: we love because God first loved us (1 John 4:19). In one of his books, Nicky Gumbel (Vicar of Holy Trinity Brompton in London) reminds us that it is meditating on what God has done for us that is the fountain of authentic Christian action:

> As we look on the cross we understand God's love for us. When the spirit of God comes to live in us we experience that love. As we do so we receive a new love for God and for other people. We are set free to live a life of love – a life centred around loving and serving Jesus and loving and serving other people rather than a life centred around ourselves.[13]

That's why meditation on the life of Jesus was the very first of Luther King's 'Ten Commandments'. Spending time in communion with God – praying as Christ Himself prayed – is vital if our actions are to flow from this, the only source of peace and healing. When our actions flow from that sense of

---

[12] Unpublished correspondence.
[13] Nicky Gumbel, *Why Jesus?* p.12.

being loved, they can be truly grace filled, and so be truly transformational.

Two actions

What actions might each of us take in the week ahead to respond to these reflections? We want to suggest two answers, one of which is 'contemplative' and the other more 'active'. It is in holding these two together that we cultivate a truly Christlike capacity for love.

The first suggestion is that we spend time each day in silence. The first text box below gives some practical suggestions as to how we might still our minds and our bodies to be more deeply aware of God's presence. The second suggestion is that we spend time listening to other people: that we make time to get to know someone in our own congregation or community. It is from such patient, intentional encounters that the ministry of Chris and Anna has grown – and through which the church becomes a more faithful embodiment of the patient yet urgent love of Jesus Christ.

Beginning to pray silently

Anthony de Mello suggests the following practice to prepare us for silent prayer:

1. Take up a comfortable and relaxing position. Your eyes may be gently closed or fixed on an object nearby, more or less three feet away.

2. Feel your clothes touching your shoulders.

3. Feel your back gently against the chair.

4. Feel your neck, gently moving your head forward and back, right and left.

---

5. Feel your chest expanding as you inhale, and relaxing as you exhale.

6. Become aware of the feelings on your right arm ... in your left arm ... in your right hand and in your left hand. Keep your hands open in a receptive and relaxed manner on your legs. Also feel your hands, lightly moving each finger.

7. Feel the soles of your feet touching your shoes.

He goes on to say, 'Simply getting in contact with oneself and feeling the reactions of the body are helpful for entering into dialogue with God, but the greatest obstacle to interior silence is nervous tension.'[14] At this point, you may wish to either focus on a simple phrase such as 'Jesus Christ, Son of God, have mercy on me, a sinner', or focus on the sensation of your breath entering and leaving your body. The aim of having such a focus is to give your mind something to *do* so that it does not wander and distract us from resting in the presence of God. The aim is not to *think* about God but to simply rest in the One in whom 'we live and move and have our being.' Whenever you sense your mind wandering, simply return to the phrase or the sensation of breathing.

Initially, we suggest that it is advisable to set aside 10-15 minutes for this practice, and to consider lengthening the period as time goes by.

[14] Online at http://www.catholicireland.net/praying-body-and-soul-methods-and-practices-of-anthony-de-mello (accessed 1 December 2013).

Engaging with our neighbours

The 'one-to-one' is at the heart of the community organising work discussed in Chapters One and Two. Very simply, this is a conversation where we seek to find out more about the story and interests of another person in our congregation or neighbourhood whom we don't yet know well. What do they care about? What are their hopes and concerns, for themselves and for the neighbourhood in which they live? It is a remarkably simple idea, but this kind of respectful listening to those around us tends to be squeezed out in busy lives, and in a world where people increasingly engage with the socially similar and the like-minded.

In the week ahead, try and set aside time for at least one 'one-to-one' conversation with someone you wouldn't otherwise get to know – and see how it goes. You may decide you want to make a habit of it!

Chapter 3
Merciful *and* Just

Introduction

One of the earliest Christian heresies was Marcionism, which claimed that there were two distinct and competing deities – an 'Old Testament God' of vengeance and the 'New Testament God' of love. We can still find echoes of that view today. It is a common misconception that the New Testament speaks of a merciful deity whereas the 'Old Testament God' is vengeful and legalistic.

In fact, the two Testaments speak with a much more united and nuanced voice. *Both* speak of God's infinite mercy *and* of His righteous judgment. The New Testament includes some of the most fiery and blood-curdling passages in the Bible (most of them are in the Book of Revelation), and the Old Testament includes many of the verses that speak most powerfully of God's mercy.

Jonah famously flees from his mission to preach repentance to Nineveh and ends up in the belly of the whale, precisely because he knows God is merciful. The reluctant prophet foresees that God will not in the end wreak destruction. When God forgives Nineveh, we are told that:

> to Jonah this seemed very wrong, and he became angry. He prayed to the Lord, 'Isn't this what I said, Lord, when I was still at home? That is what I tried to forestall by fleeing to Tarshish. I knew that you are a gracious and compassionate God, slow to anger and abounding in love, a God who relents from sending calamity.'
> *Jonah 4:1b,2*

The Bible ascribes to God the traits of mercy and of righteous judgment, often in the very same passage. Don't these two qualities pull in different directions?

We certainly *experience* some kind of balancing act, some kind of trade-off, between being too merciful and sticking too much to principles and rules. But the Bible suggests that, at a deeper level, mercy and justice pull in the same direction:

> Mercy and truth have met each other: justice and peace have kissed.
> Truth is sprung out of the earth: and justice hath looked down from heaven.
> *Psalm 84:10-11 (Douay-Rheims Bible)*

> Here is my servant, whom I uphold, my chosen one in whom I delight;
> I will put my Spirit on him, and he will bring justice to the nations.
> He will not shout or cry out, or raise his voice in the streets.
> A bruised reed he will not break, and a smoldering wick he will not snuff out.
> In faithfulness he will bring forth justice; he will not falter or be discouraged
> till he establishes justice on earth.
> In his teaching the islands will put their hope.
> *Isaiah 42:1-4*

Isaiah is saying that it is precisely *through* His mercy that God will bring about justice. The two go together. Indeed, the Book of Proverbs suggests that God's just dealings with us are an expression of His love:

> My son, do not despise the Lord's discipline, and do not resent his rebuke, because the Lord disciplines those he loves, as a father the son he delights in.
> *Proverbs 3:11-12*

51

This passage will strike a particular chord with parents. It says something they know to be true in the bringing up of children. Discipline and the setting of boundaries are not opposed to love and mercy. Indeed, discipline is part of a parent's love for a child, for it cultivates in the child the habits that are needed if he or she is to flourish alongside other human beings.

At the heart of the Gospel is the conviction that we find 'life in all its fullness' (John 10:10, Good News Bible), not by pandering to every immediate desire or by placing our own ego in the driving seat, but by opening our hearts to the needs of those around us. Martin Luther defined sin as *cor cervatus in se* ('the heart closed in upon itself'). It is through our fellow human beings that we hear God's summons to grow beyond the prison of the solitary, self-absorbed ego. It is through them that we learn the art of generous self-offering, of learning, exchange and journeying together. It is a painful process, for even though we recognise its value, our sinful, selfish nature resists it (cf. Romans 7 – discussed further in Chapter Five). The discipline God metes out to us, and that parents are called to show to children, is the discipline of love – opening our hearts both to the *demand* and the *gift* of other people.

The process of bringing up a child is one of mutual growth and enrichment: the care of a child, in all its vulnerability and need, is part of how adults continue that process of spiritual growth. Children help adults to grow up, for they present a demand and a gift which is more insistent and persistent than almost any other. In that process, both discover the need for justice (clear rules and boundaries, and taking responsibility for actions) and for mercy (forgiveness and compassion that goes beyond rules and entitlements). Love requires both; they are complementary and not in competition.

Gospel

The Gospel reading set for the Second Sunday of Lent includes the most famous verse in the Bible – John 3:16 – which sums up God's mercy in just 26 words. The wider passage gives the context for this great affirmation:

Now there was a Pharisee, a man named Nicodemus who was a member of the Jewish ruling council. He came to Jesus at night and said, 'Rabbi, we know that you are a teacher who has come from God. For no one could perform the signs you are doing if God were not with him.'

Jesus replied, 'Very truly I tell you, no one can see the kingdom of God unless they are born again.'

'How can someone be born when they are old?' Nicodemus asked. 'Surely they cannot enter a second time into their mother's womb to be born!'

Jesus answered, 'Very truly I tell you, no one can enter the kingdom of God unless they are born of water and the Spirit. Flesh gives birth to flesh, but the Spirit gives birth to spirit. You should not be surprised at my saying, "You must be born again." The wind blows wherever it pleases. You hear its sound, but you cannot tell where it comes from or where it is going. So it is with everyone born of the Spirit.'

'How can this be?' Nicodemus asked.

'You are Israel's teacher,' said Jesus, 'and do you not understand these things? Very truly I tell you, we speak of what we know, and we testify to what we have seen, but still you people do not accept our testimony. I have spoken to you of earthly things and you do not believe; how then will you believe if I speak of heavenly things? No one has ever gone into heaven except the one who came from heaven – the Son of Man. Just as Moses lifted up the snake in the

wilderness, so the Son of Man must be lifted up, that everyone who believes may have eternal life in him.'
For God so loved the world that he gave his one and only Son, that whoever believes in him shall not perish but have eternal life. For God did not send his Son into the world to condemn the world, but to save the world through him.
John 3:1-17

God's desire, we are told, is for all to be saved. His purpose in Jesus Christ is wholly merciful. Nicodemus stands on the threshold of faith, drawn by Jesus but unwilling to bear the cost and the conflict of discipleship. Jesus presents the invitation to be 'born again' – to walk the way of the cross, to die to self and enter the fullness of 'eternal life'.

Dietrich Bonhoeffer, the Lutheran pastor and theologian who was martyred in Nazi Germany, talked of God's grace being 'free' but not 'cheap'.[15] This passage helps us to see what Bonhoeffer meant. Jesus speaks of a grace that is completely free. God's response to the sin of the world is not condemnation or vengeance, but the offering of His very self. That is the meaning and mystery of the incarnation: the one who dies on the cross is not simply a holy man, or even just the 'son of God'. Jesus is also *God the Son*. Every time Christians recite the Nicene Creed in church, they reaffirm that the one who hung upon the cross is

> God of God, Light of light
> very God of very God
> begotten, not made
> of one being with the Father
> through whom all things were made.

---

[15] Dietrich Bonhoeffer, *The Cost of Discipleship*, SCM Classics, Chapter One.

The cross reveals God's heart of compassion and mercy. While the crowds were crucifying Him, Jesus was praying, 'Father, forgive them, for they do not know what they are doing' (Luke 23:34). We cannot doubt that such a prayer reflects the mind and heart of God, for (in Michael Ramsey's words) 'God is Christlike, and in him there is no unChristlikeness at all.'[16]

God's grace is *free*. Indeed it is infinite. But that does not make it *cheap*. Mercy tempers judgment, but it does not evade the reality of sin and of our guilt. The lengths God goes to on the cross to redeem us from our sins shows us quite how seriously He takes sin – and therefore how seriously we need to take it. When Bonhoeffer attacks 'cheap grace', he is warning us not to take issues of sin, justice and forgiveness too lightly.

In saying this, Bonhoeffer is simply echoing the message of St Paul. In his epistles, St Paul is urging his readers to avoid these same distortions of the Gospel. The first mistake – which remains a constant temptation for all Christians – is to behave as if grace is *not free*, as if it is earned by our good deeds. St Paul reminds his readers that their salvation comes 'not from yourselves, it is the gift of God' (Ephesians 2:8). The second mistake is to think that if salvation is a gift, we can now do whatever we like (that's what Bonhoeffer meant by 'cheap grace'). St Paul rejects this equally forcefully (1 Corinthians 6:12f). As followers of Jesus Christ, we are called to take up our cross, not to win our salvation, but in response to God's great love for us. We love because God first loved us.

In first-century Palestine, and in our own age, the world rejects and crucifies God's love. Therefore, if we follow Jesus Christ this will inevitably involve tension with the wider culture. We won't have to go looking for it – but we need to be aware it always accompanies Christian faithfulness. The reason for this is simple. The Gospel demands a personal and social

16 Mike Higton, *Christian Doctrine*, SCM Press, 2008.

transformation which each of us, at some deep level, resists (cf. Romans 7:15), *even though* it is through that transformation that we grow into 'life in all its fullness'.

If we truly love our neighbours, then, we will not always be liked by them. There is no doubt that the Gospel calls us to works of mercy: to feed the hungry, clothe the naked and visit those in prison (Matthew 25). But to stop there is to hear only one part of its transforming message. The Gospel speaks to us of *justice*; it calls to *repentance*. Jesus' mercy never colludes with our sinfulness. It calls us on to a change of direction in both our personal and common life.

For this reason, we are called to share our faith (cf. the Great Commission in Matthew 28) and to challenge injustice (cf. Mary's song in Luke 1 and Jesus' description of His mission in Luke 4). These two activities call our world to personal and corporate conversion. It is tempting for Christians to restrict their witness to works of practical compassion, for it is a less controversial ministry. But evangelism and action for social justice are not optional extras. If we truly love our broken world, we need to challenge as well as to serve it.

We must be suspicious of collusion with injustice, and heed Jeremiah's warning against proclaiming 'peace ... when there is no peace' (Jeremiah 6:14). Christians are instead called to be a sign of that true peace which was won for all people on the cross, and which will be made complete when our hearts and communities have been transformed by His justice *and* His love. The story of discipleship which is given below – of one east London Christian and her involvement in the Living Wage Campaign – offers us a striking example of what that looks like in practice.

Story

In 2000, a number of organisations in London Citizens undertook a 'listening exercise' – the kind of process we described in Chapter One. They sought to identify the matters of concern to people of different faiths and cultures, to identify some issues on which common action could be taken. An issue which came up with great frequency was the fact that many east Londoners lived on poverty wages. Those who were parents and carers had to make the agonising choice between having enough *time* for their children and having enough *money*. Research by UNICEF and the Children's Society shows this is an issue across the United Kingdom (see text box).

Sister Una McCreesh was very involved in this listening exercise, and deeply concerned by these parents' testimonies. As the head teacher of a local Catholic school, Sister Una knew the impact of poverty on educational opportunity. If parents did not have time for their children, and if they could not afford to feed them well, and to rent housing that gave them space to study, it was that much harder for children to flourish.

Out of this research came the demand for a 'London Living Wage' – a rate of hourly pay sufficient for families in the capital to participate fully in society and also to enable parents and carers to devote sufficient time to the children in their care.

The east London skyline is dominated by the towers of Canary Wharf. As the listening campaign was going on, a new tower was emerging – HSBC's global headquarters. The appearance of yet another glittering building reinforced local anger about the Wharf. While a great deal of money had been invested in the development to 'regenerate' one of London's poorest neighbourhoods, most of the east Londoners who worked in the development were missing out on its benefits. They were cleaners, caterers and security staff on poverty wages. As Sister Una and her colleagues argued, if employers on the Wharf were to pay a Living Wage, the development would at last be living up to its promises to east London.

Low pay and family life

In an essay for The Children's Society, Professor Tess Ridge describes child poverty from the perspective of young people themselves. It's a point of view we don't often hear in public debate – and Ridge's article shows why we need to listen. In it, we hear the voices of Kim and Martin talking about the way poverty places them on the edge of their social groups:

> I'm worried about what people will think of me, like they think I am sad or something.

> [My classmates] go into town and go swimming and that, and they play football and they go to other places and I can't go ... because some of them cost money.

In stark contrast to the narrative of feckless scrounging, her essay shows that children are forced to take far *more* responsibility than they ought. Here is Courtney explaining how she tries to shield her parents from the impact poverty is having:

> Well I don't like asking Mum for money that much so I try not to ... I just don't really ask about it ... It's not that I'm scared it's just that I feel bad for wanting it. I don't know, sounds stupid, but, like sometimes I save up my school dinner money and I don't eat at school and then I can save it up and have more money. Don't tell her that!

Child and family poverty has an impact on relationships. Ridge's essay shows how poverty alienates children from their peers, and research by UNICEF shows that it also affects relationships within the family.[17]

Although Britain remains one of Europe's wealthier countries, the UNICEF report shows us to be the country in which the average child has the least amount of undivided attention from a parent or carer. Churches have played a central role in the Living Wage Campaign precisely because they understand the link between low pay and this lack of adult care and attention.

Along with other London Citizens leaders, Sister Una signed a letter to Sir John Bond (the Chairman of HSBC) asking for a meeting. When the letter went unanswered, Sister Una's community had an idea. Their Catholic parish had a congregation of 1,500 which generated, among other things, vast quantities of 'candle money' which they banked each week at their local branch of HSBC. They decided to take a break from this weekly banking process – and just before Christmas, in full view of the media, they took a vanload of coins to central London, with banners demanding a meeting with the Chairman, and paid them into the Oxford Street branch. The results were immediate: 20 minutes into the action, a meeting with a senior manager was arranged. It took two more years of tenacious campaigning to secure a meeting with Sir John, in which he was brought face to face with the people who cleaned his office after he went home from work, and with the stories of their struggle to bring up their children. He and his bank agreed to move from simply *making charitable donations* towards

---

[17] See Tess Ridge, 'Children's experience of poverty' in Angus Ritchie (ed), *The Heart of the Kingdom,* The Children's Society, 2013 and UNICEF, *An overview of child well-being in rich countries,* 2007.

just employment practices. HSBC became Canary Wharf's first Living Wage employer.

For Sister Una, as for all the Christians involved in this campaign, acting for justice had a spiritual dimension. The call for a just wage, and the flourishing of family life, are at the heart of Catholic social teaching.

In 1981, Pope John Paul II wrote of

> the right to exist and progress as a family, that is to say, the right of every human being, even if he or she is poor, to found a family and to have adequate means to support it; the right, especially of the poor and the sick, to obtain physical, social, political and economic security [and] the right to housing suitable for living family life in a proper way.[18]

Likewise, in his encyclical on social justice, Pope Benedict XVI wrote of the right to 'decent' work. He said this meant

> work that expresses the essential dignity of every man and woman in the context of their particular society: work that is freely chosen, effectively associating workers, both men and women, with the development of their community; work that enables the worker to be respected and free from any form of discrimination; work that makes it possible for families to meet their needs and provide schooling for their children, without the children themselves being forced into labour; work that permits the workers to organize themselves freely, and to make their voices heard; work that leaves enough room for rediscovering one's roots at a personal, familial and spiritual level; work

---

[18] *Familiaris Consortio*, 46.

that guarantees those who have retired a decent standard of living.[19]

As these passages indicate, the church's understanding of *mercy* leads on to action for *justice*. Treating people with genuine dignity and respect involves creating an economic system in which the poorest can do more than rely on the charity of the powerful. The challenge Sister Una and her colleagues presented to HSBC was to go beyond paternalism, and to invest in and respect their workers as people with equal worth and dignity. It is to Sir John's credit that he and his bank responded to that challenge.

The Living Wage Campaign has borne rich fruit. Through the vision of leaders like Sister Una, and the courage of thousands of low-paid workers who have been willing to speak and act together, the campaign alone has lifted more than 15,000 people out of poverty in London alone, putting an extra £100 million into their pockets. It has now turned into a wider movement, with Archbishop John Sentamu agreeing to chair a national Living Wage Commission. Initially dismissed as 'impractical', 'it now has the support of all the main party leaders. Employers in Canary Wharf now speak of a 'business case' for the Living Wage – because the cost of a just wage is balanced by improved productivity, reduced sickness and increased staff retention, which cuts recruitment and induction costs.

Action

Not all of us are in a position to start a national campaign. So how, in *our* daily lives, can we act in ways that are both

---

[19] Caritas in Veritate, 63.

merciful and just? How can our Christian witness be challenging and prophetic – not shying away from the hard questions about personal and social transformation?

When we try to follow the example of people like Sister Una, we discover that there are numerous pitfalls and temptations. One temptation is to become judgmental and 'preachy'.

Jesus tells stories which are about learning from the outsider, and being willing to be blessed by the person who is different from us. He is aware that, without constantly remembering their own sinfulness, His disciples will become arrogant and self-satisfied.

The actions already suggested in this book can help us ward off these temptations.

The Examen (described in Chapter One) is invaluable in guarding against the temptation to arrogance. Each day we need to ask not just how we have blessed those around us, but how God has been blessing us *through* other people. The Examen invites us to:

> Give thanks to God for favours received. Pause and spend a moment looking at this day's gifts. Take stock of what you received and gave.

It also invites us to acknowledge when pride and self-justification have got in the way of genuine Christian ministry:

> Ask to receive the Holy Spirit so that you can look upon your actions and motives with honesty and patience. The Spirit gives a freedom to look upon yourself without condemnation and complacency and thus to be open to growth.

While we need to avoid being 'preachy', this fear should not paralyse us. We can't make it an excuse for inaction. The text box below suggests some very practical actions we can take to support the churches' campaign for a Living Wage. They are things which any reader can do in the week ahead. It is from such small beginnings – little steps taken by thousands of people of faith – that the Living Wage Campaign has come to have such an extraordinary impact in east London, and now across both capital and country.

Four actions you can take to support the Living Wage

1. Say 'thank you' to a Living Wage employer on a postcard. *There is a list of accredited employers at http://livingwage.org.uk*

2. Use their services. Show practical and financial support whenever you can.

3. Ask the question. Speak to your favourite shop or business – ask if they pay the Living Wage; ask them whether they have thought about it and explain why it's a good idea.

4. Use your pension fund to persuade businesses to pay the Living Wage. Campaigning charity ShareAction wants to change businesses for the better by working with the pension fund investors who own them. Pension funds can use the power of their shares to challenge the companies they invest in to pay the Living Wage. *More information at http://fairpensions.org.uk/justpay.*[20]

---

[20] Accessed 13 January 2014.

Chapter 4
Personal *and* Universal

Introduction

The Bible is full of names, obscure names that are hard to pronounce and impossible to place. Every reader in church dreads the genealogies in the Books of Chronicles and Kings, or at the start of Matthew and Luke's Gospels. It is very tempting to wish them away as arcane or irrelevant – to think we can peel off the layers of history in Scripture to get to some kernel, some essence of the Gospel.

But these names are part of the essence. There's a reason God's Word comes to us in stories which tell *of* and are addressed *to* particular communities. The Bible deals with specifics, not abstractions. God's love is personal *and* universal.

That's difficult for us to grasp. If we have brothers or sisters, we will know this all too well. In families there is almost always at least *some* sibling rivalry. It is hard for children to accept *both* that their parents love them very deeply *and* that there is another person who is loved with just the same intensity.

The same is true within the family of God. It is hard for us to hold together the knowledge that God has made us, chosen us and loves us infinitely and personally, with the knowledge that He *also* made, chose and loves every other human being with that same depth and intensity.

While it's a struggle to hold those two insights together, they are both at the heart of the biblical message. The Bible tells us that the people of Israel are chosen and loved, but the God who saved and delivered them also cares for others:

'I have loved you with an everlasting love;
I have drawn you with unfailing kindness.
I will build you up again, and you, Virgin Israel, will
be rebuilt.'
Jeremiah 31:3-4a

'Are not you Israelites the same to me as the
Cushites?' declares the Lord.
'Did I not bring Israel up from Egypt,
the Philistines from Caphtor and the Arameans from
Kir?'
Amos 9:7

The New Testament begins by making this very same point, albeit in a rather more oblique way:

This is the genealogy of Jesus the Messiah the son of
David, the son of Abraham:
    Abraham was the father of Isaac, Isaac the father of
Jacob, Jacob the father of Judah and his brothers.
Matthew 1:1-2

Matthew, the most Jewish of the Gospel writers, begins with this genealogy. It is much dreaded by those who have to do readings in church, and can seem very dull to the congregation, but it is of great theological significance. What Matthew is doing is establishing Jesus' Hebrew lineage. He traces the generations from Adam through to Joseph, and on just four occasions a mother is mentioned alongside the father. Their inclusion is unusual, as women did not usually feature in the genealogies of the Old Testament.

For Matthew, it is significant that at least three of the women featured were Gentiles. Two of them (Tamar and Rahab) have some association with prostitution. Bathsheba (who may or may not have been a Gentile, but is simply identified here as the woman 'who had been Uriah's wife') commits adultery with King David, who then ensures the death of her Hittite husband so that he can marry her. Matthew's choice of these particular women makes a significant point: that the grace of God does not come through purity either of blood or of action. The genealogy reminds us that the people of Israel have a unique place in the story of salvation. God's love is particular and personal – but the inclusion of these four women reminds us that His love is also universal. From the start, people of many different races and cultures have been drawn into that story, and in Christ, salvation now dawns for the whole of the human race.

Gospel

These same themes – the themes of purity and impurity and of the personal and universal nature of God's love – are found in the Gospel reading for the Third Sunday of Lent:

So [Jesus] came to a town in Samaria called Sychar, near the plot of ground Jacob had given to his son Joseph. Jacob's well was there, and Jesus, tired as he was from the journey, sat down by the well. It was about noon.

When a Samaritan woman came to draw water, Jesus said to her, 'Will you give me a drink?' (His disciples had gone into the town to buy food.)

The Samaritan woman said to him, 'You are a Jew and I am a Samaritan woman. How can you ask me for a drink?' (For Jews do not associate with Samaritans.)

Jesus answered her, 'If you knew the gift of God and who it is that asks you for a drink, you would have asked him and he would have given you living water.'

'Sir,' the woman said, 'you have nothing to draw with and the well is deep. Where can you get this living water? Are you greater than our father Jacob, who gave us the well and drank from it himself, as did also his sons and his livestock?'

Jesus answered, 'Everyone who drinks this water will be thirsty again, but whoever drinks the water I give them will never thirst. Indeed, the water I give them will become in them a spring of water welling up to eternal life.'

The woman said to him, 'Sir, give me this water so that I won't get thirsty and have to keep coming here to draw water.'

He told her, 'Go, call your husband and come back.'

'I have no husband,' she replied.

Jesus said to her, 'You are right when you say you have no husband. The fact is, you have had five husbands, and the man you now have is not your husband. What you have just said is quite true.'

'Sir,' the woman said, 'I can see that you are a prophet. Our ancestors worshipped on this mountain, but you Jews claim that the place where we must worship is in Jerusalem.'

'Woman,' Jesus replied, 'believe me, a time is coming when you will worship the Father neither on this mountain nor in Jerusalem. You Samaritans worship what you do not know; we worship what we do know, for salvation is from the Jews. Yet a time is coming and has now come when the true worshipers will worship the Father in the Spirit and in truth, for they are the kind of worshipers the Father seeks. God is spirit, and his worshipers must worship in the Spirit and in truth.'

The woman said, 'I know that Messiah' (called Christ) 'is coming. When he comes, he will explain everything to us.'

Then Jesus declared, 'I, the one speaking to you – I am he.'

Just then his disciples returned and were surprised to find him talking with a woman. But no one asked, 'What do you want?' or 'Why are you talking with her?'

Then, leaving her water jar, the woman went back to the town and said to the people, 'Come, see a man who told me everything I ever did. Could this be the Messiah?' They came out of the town and made their way toward him.

Meanwhile his disciples urged him, 'Rabbi, eat something.'

But he said to them, 'I have food to eat that you know nothing about.'

Then his disciples said to each other, 'Could someone have brought him food?'

'My food,' said Jesus, 'is to do the will of him who sent me and to finish his work. Don't you have a saying, "It's still four months until harvest"? I tell you, open your eyes and look at the fields! They are ripe for harvest. Even now the one who reaps draws a wage and harvests a crop for eternal life, so that the sower and the reaper may be glad together. Thus the saying "One sows and another reaps" is true. I sent you to reap what you have not worked for. Others have done the hard work, and you have reaped the benefits of their labour.'

Many of the Samaritans from that town believed in him because of the woman's testimony, 'He told me everything I ever did.' So when the Samaritans came to him, they urged him to stay with them, and he stayed two days. And because of his words many more became believers.

They said to the woman, 'We no longer believe just because of what you said; now we have heard for ourselves, and we know that this man really is the Saviour of the world.'
John 4:5-42

This must be one of the longest passages set for any Sunday in the Christian year! It encompasses the themes we have already discussed: that God's love is deeply personal and yet is universal in its reach. As the woman's response indicates, it was extremely unusual for a Jew (let alone a leading rabbi) to speak to a Samaritan; still more unusual to accept their hospitality. In this simple interaction, Jesus reveals to us the *universality* of God's love and also teaches us the importance of mutuality – of being willing to receive from others as well as of being willing to serve them. Jesus' first approach is a humble one. He has a need, and He asks the woman to meet it.

The encounter between Jesus and the Samaritan woman is also a very *personal* one. God's love in Christ may be universal, but it is also very particular and concrete. He knows and attends to the detailed circumstances of our lives. The universal nature of God's love doesn't gloss over the difficult details (in this case, the woman's five previous husbands and her current cohabitation) and it sees through our evasions and distractions.

This woman has much in common with the four women who were part of Jesus' family tree. Like them, she is a Gentile. Like them, her personal life is complex. She probably received much self-righteous condemnation from those who thought themselves more 'pure'. Yet she becomes one of the first evangelists, bringing her neighbours to a personal encounter with Jesus as their Saviour.

Just Love is written in a multi-faith society. Christians often talk as if 'multi-faith issues' are something new. In fact, the

New Testament is full of inter-faith encounters. From the 'Wise Men' who kneel before Christ (cf. Matthew 2) to the Samaritan woman in this passage; from the polytheistic Greeks with whom St Paul debates (in Acts 17) to the Jewish faith in which Jesus Himself was formed, the New Testament shows the early Christians seeking to live peacefully and faithfully in the midst of religious diversity.

How does their example help us to live faithfully and generously in our multi-faith society? How are Christians to bear witness to the love of God – His love of each particular individual, and His love for the whole human race – in their relationships with neighbours of other faiths and of none?

Jesus' encounter with this woman provides us with an excellent starting point. He meets her where she is and begins by recognising what *she* can give *Him*. It is all too easy for Christians to address non-Christians from a position of smug superiority, as if our role is only to *give* and the role of others is only to *receive*. From the beginning, Jesus' encounter with the woman stresses mutuality, a feature we see repeated in the story of Kerry and Nick Coke (told later in this chapter).

We can also learn from the way the Samaritan woman shares her faith with her neighbours. She doesn't get in the way: she tells them what Jesus has meant to her, and then lets them get on with a face-to-face encounter. Her neighbours say, 'We no longer believe just because of what you said; now we have heard for ourselves.' This is surely the ideal outcome of all Christian witness. As St Paul says to the Corinthians, 'What we preach is not ourselves, but Jesus Christ as Lord' (2 Corinthians 4:5).

There is a great temptation, especially when Christians live alongside neighbours of different cultures and classes, to confuse the invitation to *meet Jesus Christ* with the invitation to *become like us*. That is a dangerous mistake. Perhaps it is what St Paul means by 'proclaiming ourselves'. The invitation of the Gospel is not to join a club of like-minded people from a particular culture or a particular social class. It is to encounter Jesus Christ, and to allow God to make each of us into the unique disciple God wants us to be. Each new member changes the church and makes it something richer and broader.

In the village where Angus grew up, the church sent a monthly newsletter to every home. On the front of each issue was a simple message: *The family of God is never complete without you*. That church recognised each new Christian as a gift to the existing body – someone from whom the 'old hands' in the congregation had something to learn, as well as something to share.

Of course, evangelism is only one aspect of the church's relationship with those outside its walls. *Generous Love* (a report by the worldwide Anglican Communion on inter-faith dialogue) reminds us how much the church has to learn from others:

> It is not for us to set limits to the work of God, for the energy of the Holy Spirit cannot be confined. 'The tree is known by its fruits' (Matthew 12.33) and 'the fruit of the Spirit is love, joy, peace, patience, kindness, generosity, faithfulness, gentleness and self-control.' (Galatians 5.22f) When we meet these qualities in our encounter with people of other faiths, we must engage joyfully with the Spirit's work in their lives and in their communities.[21]

The foundation of our relationship with our neighbours, whatever their faith or worldview, must be love – a love which recognises them as children of God, which seeks to learn from them and to be blessed by them, as well as to bless and to teach them.

---

[21] Anglican Consultative Council, *Generous Love: The truth of the Gospel and the call to dialogue*, p.2.

Without love, all our attempts to witness to Christ will count as nothing. For without love, we are merely salesmen and women of a particular philosophy or worldview. If our love is truly Christlike, it cannot be manipulative or possessive. We cannot simply love our neighbour in order to convert them. Rather, our love must have that same unconditional, personal and universal quality we see in Jesus.

This point was made well by Pope Benedict XVI:

> Charity ... cannot be used as a means of engaging in what is nowadays considered proselytism. Love is free; it is not practised as a way of achieving other ends. But this does not mean that charitable activity must somehow leave God and Christ aside. For it is always concerned with the whole man. Often the deepest cause of suffering is the very absence of God. Those who practise charity in the Church's name will never seek to impose the Church's faith upon others. They realize that a pure and generous love is the best witness to the God in whom we believe and by whom we are driven to love. A Christian knows when it is time to speak of God and when it is better to say nothing and to let love alone speak. He knows that God is love and that God's presence is felt at the very time when the only thing we do is to love.[22]

Mercy, justice and evangelism are all aspects of Christian witness. They are truly Christlike when they are each carried out with humility, integrity and, above all, love. The stories below show us what that can look like – and how it can change lives.

---

22 *Deus Caritas Est*, 31c.

Stories

Stepney Salvation Army

When Kerry and Nick Coke were posted to start a Salvation Army church in Stepney, they had no idea what to expect. They knew little about East London and had no experience of working in a predominantly Muslim community. They decided to spend the whole of their first year in the community just finding out what it meant to live there. They attended as many local groups and activities as they could, and they talked with people and listened to their experiences.

Kerry and Nick had a son by this point so attending parent groups was a great way to get to know others in the community. They were keen to work out how God might want to use them there. They felt it would be important to blur the boundaries between church and community, asking themselves how people could belong without naming themselves a Christian, and yet ensuring that they kept Jesus Christ at the centre of everything the community did.

The group who attend church on a Sunday are diverse in ethnicity and socio-economic background. The Sunday gathering is relatively small (and growing), but the number of people the Stepney Salvation Army connects with each week is nearer 200. Kerry explains:

> We like to think of ourselves as the corner shop church, not the supermarket. We have an essential function, but we're not glamorous. We can be with people where they are.

All activities that the church is involved with have grown out of connections with individuals, and this is reflected in the ability of the church to grow its impact despite not having a building. 'People show up because we've met them, not because they want to see what we do.'

One of the things that really struck Kerry about the neighbourhood was the lack of integration between different sections of its diverse community. Each parent and toddler group would gather people from a specific ethnic or socio-economic bracket of the community. Kerry decided to set up a low-key parent–toddler group where people from different communities in the area could bring their children together. Before they knew it there were 50-60 parents (mainly mothers) bringing their toddlers together each week. Out of this group has grown 'BabySong' – a form of musical therapy to help parents and children bond – which has helped the group to grow even further. Tom Daggett, an intern from the Contextual Theology Centre, helped Kerry to develop this musical programme, and it is now being replicated by churches in other parts of east London.

Intent on bringing together men as well as women of different backgrounds, the church also began a football group. The football sessions are open to the community and bring together unemployed young people, those who are homeless and those with high-paid jobs in the City of London. All those involved love playing together, and through that process they have begun to form friendships and find out about each other's lives. It's a very simple process, and it has been highly effective. For many members of this community, football is 'the only thing that provides a structure to their otherwise empty week.

Having developed deep friendships with many in the community, the church was keen to address the root causes as well as the symptoms of the challenges they faced – low incomes, long-term unemployment and inadequate housing provision. Therefore, in 2007, the church joined London Citizens. A significant proportion of the church's members are now actively involved in community organising. Through the same processes of listening described at St Peter's, Stepney Salvation Army have taken action on a series of issues. These include affordable housing, street safety and the Living Wage.

The willingness to love unconditionally – to extend hospitality and yet also to receive help and blessing from their Muslim neighbours – is a key to the extraordinary impact of Kerry and Nick's ministry. When Angus asked one of their closest Muslim friends why the Cokes had such an impact in the local community, he answered as follows: 'I knew Nick and Kerry really trusted us when they asked us to babysit their children. No white person had ever asked my family to do that before.' Because they were willing to trust their neighbours – to share their lives and receive their help – they have been able to be powerful channels for God's work of personal and social transformation.

The Ark

The Ark is based in two adjoining ex-council houses on the Preston Road Estate in Hull. It is a welcome refuge and resource for women in need who have found the courage and confidence to begin to change their lives, and also offers shelter and support to their families.

As so often is the case, this vital piece of work started in the back of a local church. It initially offered support to women caught up in prostitution or drug addiction – or, very often, both. The congregation donated good-quality second-hand clothes and goods to the project. With these, and a kettle and some biscuits, the Ark was launched!

By September 2001, it was able to open for three mornings a week and a more formalised management structure began to emerge. From this small beginning, the Ark is now based in two adjoining houses which have been remodelled and refurbished to a high standard. They provide a welcoming space for the young women and their children to come for the good-quality second-hand shop, for coffee, cookery lessons, and to use the small upstairs rooms for counselling and family access. Most important of all, they find friendship and support from Lindsay Sutherland (the church worker who heads up the project) and from her team of volunteers.

From the early days the vision of the work was clear and already well formed. In the words of its early literature, Ark is 'Inspired by Christ to offer a place of love, hope and encouragement to local women'. The outworking of this vision is to provide a place of sanctuary – 'a place of hope, safety and encouragement and where there is the potential for change. A place where the love of Jesus is shared and nothing is expected in return'.

The project embodies a very powerful statement about God's unconditional and universal love. The practical welcome and hospitality of the Ark has frequently elicited a very personal response. Lindsay's belief and experience was that people generally already feel dissatisfied with, or 'bad' about, their lives and seek change when they see other ways of being lived out before them. This very practical and personal embodiment of the Gospel, and of its universal call to love, encourages them to change. For Lindsay, *this* is the way love bears witness and transforms lives. It's not a matter of attaching strings to the love we offer as Christians.

Equally importantly, the Ark has sought to avoid creating dependency. It seeks to move those it helps beyond the apathy and the fatalism of being a 'victim' into a greater sense of autonomy, self-determination and self-worth. It is through the friendships which are formed at the Ark – friendships that express mutuality and interdependence – that such a transformation becomes possible. For Lindsay, the foundation of all this work is the unconditional love of God in Jesus Christ – a love which is universal and yet deeply personal.

Action

Works of mercy, action for justice and our sharing of the Christian faith each have intrinsic value – for each is an expression of the unconditional love which flows from the heart of God. When our relationships with people of other faiths and worldviews begin to deepen, it is a natural part of that process for all parties to share that which is of deepest significance with the other.

Generous Love describes this process well:

> As ambassadors of Christ, our mission is to meet, to greet, and to acknowledge our dependence on other people and on God: 'We do not proclaim ourselves; we proclaim Jesus Christ as Lord and ourselves as your servants for Jesus' sake'... True hospitality is not about concealing our convictions, but about expressing them in a practical way. We ourselves can in turn receive in friendship the hospitality of others, which may speak powerfully to us of the welcoming generosity that lies at the heart of God. Through sharing hospitality we are pointed again to a central theme of the Gospel which we can easily forget; we are re-evangelised through a gracious encounter with other people.[23]

The willingness to be 're-evangelised' through our encounters with neighbours of other faiths has been a vital part of Christian witness in the East End of London. The story of Nick and Kerry Coke is one that reveals a generous desire to bless their neighbours *and* a humble desire to be blessed by them. This reflects the practice of Jesus – a Jewish rabbi who is willing to be challenged by a Syro-Phoenician woman (Mark

---

[23] Anglican Consultative Council, *Generous Love*, p.13.

7:24-31) and to have as one of His first evangelists a Samaritan woman with a very complex private life.

Christians who live in multi-religious contexts often find that their neighbours teach them to be more faithful to Jesus Christ. For example, those of us who live alongside Muslims find that their discipline in prayer, their strong sense of the *Ummah* (that is, the community of believers) and the seriousness with which they take Qu'ranic teaching on economics all invite us to re-examine *our* Christian discipleship. We begin to ask: How disciplined am I in my life of prayer? How faithful is my sense of the unity of the body of Christ to the words of the Gospels and of St Paul? How often do I explain away and 'spiritualise' the teaching of the Bible on possessions and in particular on lending and borrowing? *This* is what it means for our Muslim neighbours to 're-evangelise' us. In these and other ways they call us to a deeper faithfulness to Jesus Christ.

As the story of Stepney Salvation Army shows, common action does not imply the elimination of theological disagreements. It does not require Christians to dilute their commitment to the distinctive truths of the Gospel. Indeed, as Christians and Muslims work together, we come to see more clearly where understandings diverge. For example, we share with our Muslim friends the conviction that God is 'compassionate and merciful', but our engagement with them makes us even more aware of the distinctiveness of the Christian belief that God's love is *vulnerable* as well as powerful (a subject we shall return to in Chapter Six). As we come to know another faith more deeply, we are made more aware of the extraordinary nature of the claims of Christianity: the combination of 'meekness and majesty' which we confess in our crucified and risen Lord, and the way Christianity holds together an understanding of God as 'Wholly Other' with the belief that He has become flesh in Jesus of Nazareth, in whom we become 'partakers of the divine nature' (2 Peter 1:4, Authorised Version).

The text box below suggests a simple exercise you can do to find out more about your neighbourhood and your neighbours – what cultures and faiths they are from, and what social issues you and they face. How do you and your church seek to build relationships with your neighbours – both to act together on issues of common concern and to give witness to the love of Jesus Christ in both word and deed?

Making sense of your context

What different religions and cultures are present in your local context? How does the church respond faithfully and effectively to the Gospel calls to works of mercy, action for justice and the sharing of the faith?

Go to http://theology-centre.org/my-context to find out more about the context you live in (using the statistics on religion and ethnicity from the 2011 Census, and statistics on poverty from the Church Urban Fund). The site also has some Bible study materials – exploring the Gospel call to mercy (Matthew 25), justice (Luke 1) and making new disciples (Matthew 28).

Chapter 5
Generous *and* Disruptive

Introduction

Human beings are creatures of habit. That's not always a bad thing. As one psychologist puts it:

> Habits are indispensable because they allow us to create predictability, to act automatically, and to accomplish things efficiently. Habits are goal-directed and functional – they have an objective and they serve a purpose. Habits can serve us well when they help maintain and enhance how well we perform, and they can serve us badly when they undermine and harm how adequately we function.[24]

All too often, we stick to established patterns of behaviour, even when we know that they are destructive. As Pickhardt observes, 'people are so deeply invested in their own status quo – in how they are used to operating, which is familiar, predictable, and comfortable.' We are scared of change, even when we know our existing behaviour is damaging us. 'Better the devil you know,' we say to ourselves, 'than the devil you don't.'

---

[24] Good habits are harder to start than to put off; bad habits are easier to start than to shut down. (Carl Pickhardt, 'Adolescence and the development of habits' at http://www.psychologytoday.com/blog/surviving-your-childs-adolescence/201201/adolescence-and-the-development-habits, (accessed 1 December 2013)).

Pickhardt sometimes works alongside Alcoholics Anonymous groups, and these provide further examples of the ways in which we humans remain attached to the things we are used to – even when we are trying to shake them off.

When we seek to cast off destructive habits, it can feel as if we are at war with ourselves. Part of us knows that change is needed, but another part of us is deeply resistant. Willpower alone does not seem to be enough. Indeed, it is significant that Alcoholics Anonymous build reliance on a 'Higher Power' which is built into the 'twelve-step' recovery process. Human beings need to recognise our need of help.

Because of our ambivalence about the changes we need, we experience God's love as disruptive as well as generous. We need His transforming power, and yet we find that transformation deeply painful.

In Romans 7, St Paul gives a powerful account of the way in which we humans feel at war with ourselves – and the role of God's grace in this struggle to shake off our destructive patterns of life:

> I do not understand what I do. For what I want to do I do not do, but what I hate I do ... I have the desire to do what is good, but I cannot carry it out. For I do not do the good I want to do, but the evil I do not want to do – this I keep on doing...
>
> So I find this law at work: Although I want to do good, evil is right there with me. For in my inner being I delight in God's law; but I see another law at work in me, waging war against the law of my mind and making me a prisoner of the law of sin at work within me. What a wretched man I am! Who will rescue me from this body that is subject to death? Thanks be to God, who delivers me through Jesus Christ our Lord!
> *Romans 7:15, 18b-19, 21-25a*

Here, St Paul is going even deeper than psychology. He is suggesting that, behind our individual *habits* of destruction, there is a destructive *worldview*. The 'law at work in me' is the worship of something other than God. It is sin – the idolatry which places something or someone else at the centre of our lives.

Different people may have very different 'idols'. They include money, success, popularity and immediate gratification. Or they may be more subtle, and less obviously destructive.

It is even possible to make morality into an idol. I can become so worried about 'doing the right thing', so focussed on my own righteousness and virtue that I turn in upon myself. I become joyless and less capable of genuinely mutual love. This is what some have called the 'hardening of the oughteries'. It is dramatised most famously by Charles Dickens in his novel *Bleak House*, through the character of Mrs Jellyby.

We see her through the eyes of Esther Summerson, the heroine of the novel. Esther is visiting Mrs Jellyby at home with her companion Ada:

> Mrs Jellyby, sitting in quite a nest of waste paper, drank coffee all the evening and dictated at intervals to her eldest daughter. She also held a discussion with Mr Quale [another visitor]; of which the subject seemed to be — if I understood it — the brotherhood of humanity; and gave utterance to some beautiful sentiments. I was not so attentive an audience as I might have wished to be, however, for Peepy and [Mrs Jellyby's] other children came flocking about Ada and me in a corner of the drawing-room to ask for another story; so we sat down among them, and told them in whispers Puss in Boots and I don't know what else, until Mrs Jellyby, accidentally remembering them, sent them to bed. As Peepy cried for me to take him to bed, I carried him upstairs; where the young

woman with the flannel bandage charged into the midst of the little family like a dragoon, and overturned them into cribs.

After that, I occupied myself in making our room a little tidy, and in coaxing a very cross fire that had been lighted, to burn; which at last it did, quite brightly. On my return downstairs, I felt that Mrs Jellyby looked down upon me rather, for being so frivolous; and I was sorry for it; though at the same time I knew that I had no higher pretensions.[25]

Mrs Jellyby is consumed by her so-called 'charity' for those in need abroad. She can sermonise at great length about the 'brotherhood of humanity' and yet neglects to care for those who are right in front of her. Indeed, she is rather suspicious of those who show such care and regards their concern for the needs of the Jellyby children as mere 'frivolity'.

For Mrs Jellyby, the objects of her charity are just that: they are *objects*. They allow her to project an image of generosity, whilst in fact mistreating those in her immediate care. Mrs Jellyby speaks endlessly about duty, but knows nothing about love.

The Bible teaches that the cultivation of genuine love is a work of grace. It isn't something we achieve on our own. The tragedy of Mrs Jellyby is that her so-called 'concern' for people on the other side of the world, and her need to preserve a self-image of charity and righteousness, prevent any *truly* compassionate encounters with *actual* human beings.

The Orthodox writer Jim Forest warns us that Mrs Jellyby's mistake is one that people make in every generation:

> Many saints of the last hundred years would readily recognise Mrs Jellyby and could identify her real-life counterparts. In Russia, for example, in the mid- and

---

[25] Charles Dickens, *Bleak House*, Bradbury & Evans, 1853, p.29.

late-19th century there was an explosion of radical movements which, while dedicated to various social reforms, abandoned care of neighbour and relative as a bourgeois waste of time.

Forest goes on to show that the two antidotes to this temptation are found in 'a deep, disciplined spiritual life' – an openness to God's forgiveness, grace and presence – and a cultivation of love that is concrete and not merely abstract:

> God is love. We move toward God through no other path than love itself. It is not a love expressed in slogans or ideologies, but actual love; love experienced in God, love that binds us to those around us, love that lets us know others not through ideas and fears but through God's love for them: a way of seeing that transfigures social relationships.[26]

We need to take to heart the message of St Paul's letters – that righteousness is not something we earn but is a gift from God. Only then can we truly transform and expand our hearts. And when our hearts are thus transformed, our actions will flow from a genuine love of other people, and not the (self-centred) desire to prove ourselves worthy. Without that grace, we become like Mrs Jellyby. Our lives are like 'a resounding gong' or 'a clanging symbol', bringing all too little of God's love and peace to those around us (cf. 1 Corinthians 13).

God has to shatter our idols and to break our destructive habits if we are to grow into 'life in all its fullness'. That is a painful process. As *Bleak House* reminds us, human beings are capable of making the very best of things – even morality itself

---

[26] Jim Forest, *Mrs Jellyby and the Domination of Causes*, The Orthodox Peace Fellowship – online at http://www.incommunion.org/2006/02/19/mrs-jellyby-and-the-domination-of-causes (accessed 5 June 2013).

– into idols. We cling to our idols tenaciously, even when we know that they are bad news. That's one reason why these two aspects of God's love – its infinite generosity and its painful disruption of our lives – always go together.

There's another reason why God's love causes disruption in our lives. When we follow Him, and we begin to change, others will resist that change. That's no great surprise, and it doesn't mean we're better or more holy than those around us. *They* resist the change for the same reasons *we* resist it! But it makes the journey of personal transformation in Christ a lot more challenging. In seeking to change, we have to contend not only with our own idols and destructive habits, but also with those of the culture around us.

That's why the Gospels warn us that following Christ is therefore both liberating and costly. Jesus promises us true freedom, in these inviting words:

> Come to me, all you who are weary and burdened, and I will give you rest.
> *Matthew 11:28*

But a few chapters later, He warns us that this 'freedom' has its cost:

> Whoever wants to be my disciple must deny themselves and take up their cross and follow me. For whoever wants to save their life will lose it, but whoever loses their life for me will find it.
> *Matthew 16:24-25*

Gospel

These two sides of Jesus' invitation – the generosity *and* the disruption, the freedom *and* the cost – are brought home to us in the Gospel reading for the Fourth Sunday of Lent.

If you are reading this book alone, you should read the passage below a number of times, each time from the point of view of a different character (the man born blind, his parents, the neighbours and the Pharisees). If you are reading this in a group, you might divide these tasks among you and share your reflections afterwards.

As he went along, he saw a man blind from birth. His disciples asked him, 'Rabbi, who sinned, this man or his parents, that he was born blind?'

'Neither this man nor his parents sinned,' said Jesus, 'but this happened so that the works of God might be displayed in him. As long as it is day, we must do the works of him who sent me. Night is coming, when no one can work. While I am in the world, I am the light of the world.'

After saying this, he spit on the ground, made some mud with the saliva, and put it on the man's eyes. 'Go,' he told him, 'wash in the Pool of Siloam' (this word means 'Sent'). So the man went and washed, and came home seeing.

His neighbors and those who had formerly seen him begging asked, 'Isn't this the same man who used to sit and beg?' Some claimed that he was.

Others said, 'No, he only looks like him.'

But he himself insisted, 'I am the man.'

'How then were your eyes opened?' they asked.

He replied, 'The man they call Jesus made some mud and put it on my eyes. He told me to go to Siloam and wash. So I went and washed, and then I could see.'

'Where is this man?' they asked him.

'I don't know,' he said.

They brought to the Pharisees the man who had been blind. Now the day on which Jesus had made the mud and opened the man's eyes was a Sabbath.

Therefore the Pharisees also asked him how he had received his sight. 'He put mud on my eyes,' the man replied, 'and I washed, and now I see.'

Some of the Pharisees said, 'This man is not from God, for he does not keep the Sabbath.'

But others asked, 'How can a sinner perform such signs?' So they were divided.

Then they turned again to the blind man, 'What have you to say about him? It was your eyes he opened.'

The man replied, 'He is a prophet.'

They still did not believe that he had been blind and had received his sight until they sent for the man's parents. 'Is this your son?' they asked. 'Is this the one you say was born blind? How is it that now he can see?'

'We know he is our son,' the parents answered, 'and we know he was born blind. But how he can see now, or who opened his eyes, we don't know. Ask him. He is of age; he will speak for himself.' His parents said this because they were afraid of the Jewish leaders, who already had decided that anyone who acknowledged that Jesus was the Messiah would be put out of the synagogue. That was why his parents said, 'He is of age; ask him.'

A second time they summoned the man who had been blind. 'Give glory to God by telling the truth,' they said. 'We know this man is a sinner.'

He replied, 'Whether he is a sinner or not, I don't know. One thing I do know. I was blind but now I see!'

Then they asked him, 'What did he do to you? How did he open your eyes?'

He answered, 'I have told you already and you did not listen. Why do you want to hear it again? Do you want to become his disciples too?'

Then they hurled insults at him and said, 'You are this fellow's disciple! We are disciples of Moses! We know that God spoke to Moses, but as for this fellow, we don't even know where he comes from.'

The man answered, 'Now that is remarkable! You don't know where he comes from, yet he opened my eyes. We know that God does not listen to sinners. He listens to the godly person who does his will. Nobody has ever heard of opening the eyes of a man born blind. If this man were not from God, he could do nothing.'

To this they replied, 'You were steeped in sin at birth; how dare you lecture us!' And they threw him out.

Jesus heard that they had thrown him out, and when he found him, he said, 'Do you believe in the Son of Man?'

'Who is he, sir?' the man asked. 'Tell me so that I may believe in him.'

Jesus said, 'You have now seen him; in fact, he is the one speaking with you.'

Then the man said, 'Lord, I believe,' and he worshiped him.

Jesus said, 'For judgment I have come into this world, so that the blind will see and those who see will become blind.'

Some Pharisees who were with him heard him say this and asked, 'What? Are we blind too?'

Jesus said, 'If you were blind, you would not be guilty of sin; but now that you claim you can see, your guilt remains.'
John 9:1-41

Reading this story from the viewpoints of these different characters highlights their very different responses to Jesus.

The generous, healing love of Christ enables the blind man to see. Ironically, it is the man who has spent most of his life blind who sees most clearly. Precisely because he has had the most immediate and liberating encounter with Jesus' love, he is willing to accept the cost of discipleship. He cannot but bear witness to what he has experienced. By contrast, the man's parents and the Pharisees are unwilling to accept the disruption that following Christ would involve. The parents are fearful of the consequences of answering the religious leaders' questions, and so leave their son to his fate: 'Ask him. He is of age; he will speak for himself.' The religious leaders have vested interests to protect – and so, as Jesus indicates, their rejection has a greater culpability. Although they claim that they can see, they turn a blind eye to the signs of the Kingdom.

We are not told what happened to the man's neighbours, or what they decided to do. Like us, they have a choice. Do they respond to the signs of the Kingdom? Or do they hold back, because the price is too great? So many of Jesus' parables pose that same question to us: do we recognise the Kingdom as the 'pearl of great price' and pursue it with all that we have and all that we are? Or do we find its cost too great and allow 'the worries of this life' to choke off our initial enthusiasm (cf. Matthew 13)?

In this book, we have focussed a great deal on the social dimensions of the Gospel, and of the transformation that is wrought in Jesus Christ. This has been deliberate: all too often our individualistic culture plays down the corporate dimension of the Christian faith.

But the Gospel also presents us with a direct and personal invitation. It demands of us a direct and personal decision. We have to decide whether to say 'yes' to Jesus Christ in the very depths of our own hearts.

As Pope Francis reminds us, it is only when *we* say 'yes' to Jesus Christ that we can help others make that same liberating and yet costly choice:

We need Christians who make God's mercy and tenderness for every creature visible to the men and women of our day ... [We must] have the courage to swim against the tide and to be converted from idols to the true God ...

The Church says as she stands amid humanity today: Come to Jesus, all you who labour and are heavy laden, and you will find rest for your souls. Come to Jesus. He alone has the words of eternal life.

Every baptized Christian is a 'Christopher', namely a Christ-bearer, as the Church Fathers used to say. Whoever has encountered Christ ... cannot keep this experience to himself but feels the need to share it and to lead others to Jesus. We all need to ask ourselves if those who encounter us perceive the warmth of faith in our lives, if they see in our faces the joy of having encountered Christ![27]

Story

Growing up in the east end of London, in a neighbourhood where street violence was common, Peter Nembhard learnt his own set of destructive habits. His anger at injustices and slights, real and perceived, led him into a series of violent fights – and eventually into prison.

Peter was converted after narrowly avoiding death. He had gone to a party with one of his best friends and had very nearly been drawn into a fight when someone deliberately pushed and jostled him. 'Something in me said, "Don't respond. Just leave it this time."'

[27] Pope Francis, *Address to Plenary of the Pontifical Council for Promoting the New Evangelisation*, 14 October 2013.

Sadly, when his friend received the same provocation from the same person, he chose not to turn the other cheek. In the fight that followed, he received a fatal stab wound. 'That was a wake-up call,' explains Peter. 'I realised that could so easily have been me – and that I needed to change my way of life. That same evening, I gave my life to Jesus Christ, and from then on I have been trying to draw others away from these same destructive habits.'

Peter's conversion led to a profound disruption in his life, as he sought to leave the destructive habits of his past behind, in ways that challenged and confused those around him. As he grew in faith, Peter was deeply influenced by the story of Moses – a man who began his adult life by murdering an Egyptian who was oppressing a Hebrew slave and who was taught by God to discipline and channel his anger, and to lead his people to freedom. Called to be a pastor in the Pentecostal church, the story of Moses provided Peter with the model for his own ministry – learning to channel his anger at injustice in constructive directions rather than letting it be an idol which controlled him.

Peter's own experience of saying 'yes' to Jesus led on to a desire to share his faith with others – to help them to discover their true freedom in Christ, and to shake off the same destructive habits. He is now the Senior Pastor of ARC, a Pentecostal church in Forest Gate, which is changing the lives of young people caught up in violence and gangs.

The congregation now numbers more than 250, with young people making up at least a fifth of the congregation. Many of them come to church independently of their parents. A significant number come from deprived and challenging backgrounds: some have been involved in prostitution, drug addiction and gang violence, and others have experienced domestic violence. Considerable thought and prayer is given to ensuring these individuals feel welcomed into the church family.

Pastor Peter's 'yes' to Jesus Christ has made him a compelling evangelist. In the same way, those whom God is drawing to faith through ARC are becoming bearers of the good news. Young people in the church have developed the *Stop Da Violence* campaign, which seeks to educate and inform young people about the serious dangers of gang culture as well as to encourage them to find positive ways to use their energy and gifts.

The programme began with an annual event which brought together young people to share their message against violence through rap, dance, spoken word, drama and other talents. More than 500 young people have attended each year, and now a recording studio is owned and used in partnership with other local organisations as a place where mentoring is provided for young people.

Action

Pastor Peter's story tells us what it means to be 'evangelists' – people whose lives bear witness to the transformation which is brought through Jesus Christ. As Pope Francis' words remind us, evangelisation involves deeds as well as words. It requires the transformation of *our* hearts, so that they are no longer in the grip of idols and destructive habits. Pastor Peter's powerful ministry, which has saved and changed so many lives in east London, began with his own 'yes' to Christ.

In Chapter Two, we were reminded of the 'Ten Commandments of Nonviolence' which were kept by the Christians who worked with Martin Luther King in the struggle for racial justice. These 'Commandments' were spiritual disciplines which developed a deeper openness to God's grace, and weaned people off destructive habits and attitudes.

We have already suggested that regular use of the Examen can help us to do just that: it opens our eyes both to God's transforming action in our lives and to the points of sin and resistance in our hearts and therefore in our habits. From time to time, however, it is useful to stand back a little further – to take stock not just of the day that has just passed, but also of the wider state of our relationship with God.

This is not the kind of process where we can award ourselves 'marks out of ten'. Instead of worrying about where we *now stand*, we can focus instead on how to *move forward*.

That's what the exercise in the text box below is designed to help us do. Using the framework of King's 'Ten Commandments', it suggests some questions we might ask to help us walk more faithfully and effectively with Jesus Christ. Some of them will take a lifetime to answer! And we don't need to answer them alone – many of the issues raised below are things we need to discuss with our closest Christian 'soul friends' and those who pastor us.

Taking stock: allowing God's grace to transform the habits of our hearts

1. Meditate on the life and teachings of Jesus.

How do I allow the stories of the Gospels to reshape my attitudes? Are there fresh ways I could engage with Jesus' life and teachings? Helpful practices for reading Scripture, which are particularly useful for the stories of Jesus' life, include Lectio Divina *and Ignatian meditation. The Bible Society has produced a guide to reading Scripture more meditatively,[28] and Fr Gerard Hughes' book* God of Surprises[29] *is a classic on Ignatian spirituality, teaching us how to read the Bible while engaging our imagination.*

---

[28] *See* http://www.biblesociety.org.uk/about-bible-society/our-work/lectio-divina/ (accessed 10 January 2014).

[29] Darton, Longman and Todd, 2008.

2. Remember the nonviolent movement seeks justice and reconciliation – not victory.

How do I combine courageous confrontation of injustice and wrongdoing with a genuine love of my (temporary) opponents? Do I pray for them? If I am in a situation of conflict, what would 'justice and reconciliation' mean, as opposed to 'victory'?

3. Walk and talk in the manner of love; for God is love.

What habits prevent me from walking and talking 'in the manner of love'? Who or what do I find helpful in overcoming them?

4. Pray daily to be used by God that all men and women might be free.

Is this one of my daily prayers? Given the routines and demands of my life, how might I best spend time in prayer each morning dedicating the day to God?

5. Sacrifice personal wishes that all might be free.

What wishes do I have that get in the way of this journey to freedom – whether habits that keep me enslaved in ways I want to escape, or desires that restrict the freedom of others? What might I do this Lent to break one such habit or lay down one such desire?

6. Observe with friend and foes the ordinary rules of courtesy.

How have I interacted with friends and foes this week? When have I broken the 'ordinary rules of courtesy'? What might I do to put that right?

7. Perform regular service for others and the world.

What act of service might I take up in the days ahead as positive habits which bless my neighbours and enlarge my heart?

For some practical Lenten ideas, look at the daily suggestions at http://www.40acts.org.uk/[30] — you won't be able to do them all, but you could pick one or two! Tear Fund has a website, targeted particularly at younger adults, with ideas for practical action — see http://rhythms.org[31]

8. Refrain from violence of fist, tongue and heart.

When have I been violent in my words and attitudes to others, even if not in my physical actions? What are the triggers of that violence? What does it indicate is unresolved or unhealthy within me? How can I address this?

9. Strive to be in good spiritual and bodily health.

How do my physical habits affect my spiritual well-being? (This may relate back to my last answer.) Do I take care of my body as a 'temple of the Holy Spirit'? What might I do to be a better steward of it, as a gift from God?

10. Follow the directions of the movement leaders on demonstrations.

What place does obedience have within my life as a Christian? How is my obedience to God expressed in a willingness to learn from those around me, and to be a reliable and constructive member of the wider body of Christ? How do I discern when authority needs to be challenged, and when it needs to be respected?

---

[30] Accessed 10 January 2014.
[31] Accessed 10 January 2014.

Chapter 6
Vulnerable *and* Powerful

Introduction

Christianity has a complex relationship with power. At one level, any faith that confesses God, to be 'creator of heaven and earth' – and that holds God to be infinitely powerful and infinitely loving – *must* have a positive attitude to power. Like Judaism and Islam, Christianity maintains that all power ultimately comes from God and that God's loving-purposes will in the end triumph throughout the universe.

Where Christianity breaks new and controversial ground is its claim that this one God is revealed most completely through Jesus Christ: that the love and power of God became flesh in the vulnerability of a child born in a stable, and the agony of a man crucified as a common criminal. As St Paul writes:

> Jews demand signs and Greeks look for wisdom, but we preach Christ crucified: a stumbling block to Jews and foolishness to Gentiles, but to those whom God has called, both Jews and Greeks, Christ the power of God and the wisdom of God. For the foolishness of God is wiser than human wisdom, and the weakness of God is stronger than human strength.
> *1 Corinthians 1:22-25*

We need to be careful here not to misrepresent St Paul. He is not suggesting we should run away from power, or that power is somehow an inherently bad thing. From Paul's earliest writings to the later Pauline epistles, 'power' is used as a positive term:

[Our] gospel came to you not simply with words but also with power, with the Holy Spirit and deep conviction.
1 Thessalonians 1.5a

I pray that the eyes of your heart may be enlightened in order that you may know the hope to which he has called you, the riches of his glorious inheritance in his holy people, and his incomparably great power for us who believe. That power is the same as the mighty strength he exerted when he raised Christ from the dead and seated him at his right hand in the heavenly realms, far above all rule and authority, power and dominion, and every name that is invoked, not only in the present age but also in the one to come.
Ephesians 1:18-21

We cannot, therefore, read his words in 1 Corinthians as a *rejection* of power. Rather, Paul is saying that our understanding of God's power needs to be reshaped by the cross. The cross shows us a love that is vulnerable *and* victorious; weak *and* powerful.

St Paul's message is that in Christ, the worldly hierarchies of status and of power are reversed. As he points out to the Christians in Corinth:

Brothers and sisters, think of what you were when you were called. Not many of you were wise by human standards; not many were influential; not many were of noble birth. But God chose the foolish things of the world to shame the wise; God chose the weak things of the world to shame the strong.
1 Corinthians 1:26-27

What implications does this have for our lives as disciples? How would our church need to change if it were to take this message more deeply to heart?

These are crucial questions to be asking as we come to the end of this book. In the last five chapters we have explored many different aspects of personal and social transformation in Christ. The challenge of this final chapter is to put this vision into practice. If we are going to be co-workers with Christ, if we are going to be part of his transforming work, we need to understand the nature of His power – and how He seeks to share that power with us.

Every community has its own idea of what things and which people are at the *centre*, and who and what are at the *margins*. That was as true of Jesus' society as of any other. There were two overlapping centres of power: the Empire (with Rome standing at the centre of political and military power, and the palace of King Herod being the outpost of that power in occupied Palestine) and the Temple (the heart of religious power, held by the 'lawyers and teachers of the law'). In Jesus, God becomes flesh at the very margins of this social order. As Kenneth Leech writes:

> [Jesus] was born into a double system of exploitation in Palestine. While the Roman empire imposed economic control through taxes, and political control through its officials, the Palestinian state operated through the Temple which demanded contributions in the form of tithes and other funds ...
>
> He was born in the specific circumstances of a census which had been set up in order to implement the poll tax. Ninety per cent of the population of Galilee were peasants. These oppressed peasants were 'the people' who, according to the gospels, heard Jesus gladly. The burden of taxation was the central economic fact of life, and led to conflict with the

priestly aristocracies, so much so that in AD 66 rebels burnt the record of debts in the Temple.

There was high unemployment, with many looking for work, and the violence went far beyond Herod's slaughter of innocent children. It was out of this deeply disturbed climate of alienation, upheaval and resistance that the 'marginal Jew' called Jesus came. The climate of colonial rule, oppressive taxation, accumulating debt and bankruptcy, forced migration and revolutionary uprisings, formed the background to Jesus' proclamation of the Kingdom of God.[32]

Too often in theology we focus entirely on what Jesus and His disciples taught, without noticing this extraordinary fact about who and where they actually were. How the world looks depends on where you are standing, and Jesus stood with, among – not merely for – the poorest of His age. Where He stood is part of what He reveals.

No other books of the time are written in such popular, common Greek as the Gospels. None are so focussed on the 'multitude' (*ochlos*). The Gospels are written from a unique social perspective, precisely because the world looks different from the perspective of the poorest and most vulnerable.

Jesus' own teaching emphasises the importance of this perspective. In His words and in His deeds, He places the youngest and the poorest at the heart of the Kingdom. He tells His disciples that when they welcome children and when they care for those who lack food or shelter, they are welcoming and caring for Him (Matthew 18:5, 25:34-40). But He goes further than this. He suggests that if we are to speak of God – to do theology, as it were – we must adopt their perspective. In Matthew 11:25, he prays:

---

[32] Kenneth Leech, *We Preach Christ Crucified,* Darton, Longman & Todd, 2006, p.39.

> I praise you, Father, Lord of heaven and earth,
> because you have hidden these things from the wise
> and learned, and revealed them to little children.

This is why Christian theology must pay particular attention to the perspective of the margins and not simply issue well-meaning pronouncements from the centre of power and security. Time and time again, the Bible tells us that the God of power and love is to be found on the margins rather than in the centre.

Both of the organisations promoting this book exist to ensure that the experience of the poorest and most marginalised is heard in the wider life of the church – and that it is placed at the heart of theological reflection. The Church Urban Fund was founded in 1988, as part of the Church of England's response to the *Faith in the City* report, published three years earlier.

Faith in the City was written in a time that has real echoes of our own – where England's poorest communities were on the sharp end of an economic downturn and cuts in public services. In the words of one Anglican leader, it 'began a movement which was partly political (with a small p), partly theological and partly spiritual'.[33] It was 'political' not in a partisan sense, but in that it spoke of the realities of where power and wealth were located – and it sought to bring both the teachings of the Bible and the voices of England's poorest neighbourhoods into the conversation about society's values and priorities.

One of the messages of *Faith in the City*, borne out by 25 years of work by the Church Urban Fund, is that churches in the poorest and most marginalised communities are not simply a *burden* on the wider body of Christ. They are a *gift* to that wider body, as they have a particular insight into the nature of the Kingdom, and the ministry of Christ the King. For as we

---

[33] Graham Smith, sermon at civic service in Norwich Cathedral, 5 June 2005.

have seen, Jesus knew insecurity, poverty and indeed exile as a refugee.

The work of the Contextual Theology Centre is inspired by that same conviction: that theology must begin with Scripture and the living tradition of the church, but also with the experience of those who stand on the margins in our own day. The Centre's work grows out of churches on the margins who are involved in community organising – working in the midst of weakness and vulnerability to build a powerful movement for social justice.

We will return to these themes later in the chapter, as we look at a story of modern discipleship; a story from the inner-city which speaks of both God's vulnerability and His power. But, as in all the chapters of this book, we will first explore a passage from the Gospels which casts light on these same themes.

Gospel

The Gospel reading set for the Fifth Sunday of Lent is John 11:1-45. At this point in Lent, we turn our hearts and minds more clearly to Jesus' death and resurrection – as we prepare to make the journey from Palm Sunday (which is just one week away) through Maundy Thursday and Good Friday to the silence of Easter Eve, and the glorious new dawn of Easter Day itself.

John 11 tells the story of Lazarus' death, and of Jesus raising him to new life. It contains the shortest – and one of the most famous – verses in the whole Bible: 'Jesus wept' (verse 35). In just two words, this verse captures the vulnerable love of Jesus. Christians believe this love is at the very heart of God. The story of Lazarus speaks both of God's solidarity with our pain and of His power to bring new hope and life.

On his arrival, Jesus found that Lazarus had already been in the tomb for four days. Now Bethany was less than two miles from Jerusalem, and many Jews had come to Martha and Mary to comfort them in the loss of their brother. When Martha heard that Jesus was coming, she went out to meet him, but Mary stayed at home.

'Lord,' Martha said to Jesus, 'if you had been here, my brother would not have died. But I know that even now God will give you whatever you ask.'

Jesus said to her, 'Your brother will rise again.'

Martha answered, 'I know he will rise again in the resurrection at the last day.'

Jesus said to her, 'I am the resurrection and the life. The one who believes in me will live, even though they die; and whoever lives by believing in me will never die. Do you believe this?'

'Yes, Lord,' she replied, 'I believe that you are the Messiah, the Son of God, who is to come into the world.'

After she had said this, she went back and called her sister Mary aside. 'The Teacher is here,' she said, 'and is asking for you.' When Mary heard this, she got up quickly and went to him. Now Jesus had not yet entered the village, but was still at the place where Martha had met him. When the Jews who had been with Mary in the house, comforting her, noticed how quickly she got up and went out, they followed her, supposing she was going to the tomb to mourn there.

When Mary reached the place where Jesus was and saw him, she fell at his feet and said, 'Lord, if you had been here, my brother would not have died.'

When Jesus saw her weeping, and the Jews who had come along with her also weeping, he was deeply moved in spirit and troubled. 'Where have you laid him?' he asked.

'Come and see, Lord,' they replied.

Jesus wept.

Then the Jews said, 'See how he loved him!'

But some of them said, 'Could not he who opened the eyes of the blind man have kept this man from dying?'

Jesus, once more deeply moved, came to the tomb. It was a cave with a stone laid across the entrance. 'Take away the stone,' he said.

'But, Lord,' said Martha, the sister of the dead man, 'by this time there is a bad odor, for he has been there four days.'

Then Jesus said, 'Did I not tell you that if you believe, you will see the glory of God?'

So they took away the stone. Then Jesus looked up and said, 'Father, I thank you that you have heard me. I knew that you always hear me, but I said this for the benefit of the people standing here, that they may believe that you sent me.'

When he had said this, Jesus called in a loud voice, 'Lazarus, come out!' The dead man came out, his hands and feet wrapped with strips of linen, and a cloth round his face.

Jesus said to them, 'Take off the grave clothes and let him go.'

Therefore many of the Jews who had come to visit Mary, and had seen what Jesus did, believed in him.

John 11:17-45

In one sense, we can understand the raising of Lazarus as a foretaste – a paler shadow – of the events of Holy Week and Easter. Jesus enters into the sorrow of the family and friends of Lazarus. He weeps because He is 'deeply moved in spirit and troubled'. And yet He demonstrates God's power over death as He raises His friend from the dead.

103

The story seems like a 'pale shadow' because Lazarus is only raised to continue his mortal life. He continues to have a body that will one day die again. In the raising of Lazarus, death has only been postponed, whereas the resurrection of Jesus defeats death forever. As Jesus declares to the grieving Martha, 'whoever lives by believing in me will never die.'

But if that was *all* there was to the story of Lazarus, there would be no need to read it any longer. After all, why read the 'pale shadow' when (at the end of each of the four Gospels) we have the real thing?

We still read the story of Lazarus because his situation mirrors our own. Jesus *is* indeed the resurrection and the life, and as Christians we believe that death has been defeated. But people still die, and the power of sin and death is still very active in our broken world. The words of this reading are very familiar because part of it is read at many funeral services. Most people who are reading this book will have heard vicars reading these words of Jesus to a grieving congregation. On the surface, it a jarring passage. How can we proclaim that 'whoever lives by believing in me will never die' when we have, right in front of us, the coffin of someone who has done just that?

The answer is that Jesus' words were spoken in exactly that context: in the midst of grief and death, the raising of Lazarus is just one of many glimpses in the Gospel of the dawning of God's life-giving Kingdom. Each of those little, temporary victories of life is a sign of that final victory of life – a down payment, if you like, on God's eternal promise.

We read the story of Lazarus because we are like Lazarus, Martha and Mary: people who catch a glimpse of new life dawning in a world where sin and death still have a hold. Just as Jesus' ultimate victory is won through human weakness, so we participate in His victory and come to know His power when we are willing to be vulnerable.

The novelist Helen Waddell depicts the medieval theologian Peter Abelard and his friend Thibault discussing the suffering of Christ. Thibault points to a fallen tree that has been sawn right through the middle:

> That dark ring there, it goes up and down the whole length of the tree. But you only see it where it is cut across. That is what Christ's life was: the bit of God that we saw.[34]

The cross of Christ reveals the very character of God. It is foreshadowed in the prophets of Israel. For they show us how deeply God has engaged with His world. They show us how much our disobedience and suffering causes Him distress. The Servant Songs of Isaiah 53 show us God's response: that it is in His nature to bear the pain of this broken world, and that this divine self-offering will bring to the world healing and new life.

As we have seen in previous chapters, there are two truths that all Christians need to hold in tension. On the one hand, Jesus' death and resurrection is a once-and-for-all victory. It is complete in itself; we do not need to do anything to win our salvation: we are saved by Christ's sacrifice, not by our own self-offering. But, on the other hand, we must never forget that we are commanded to follow in His footsteps. He tells us to 'take up [your] cross and follow me' (Matthew 16:24). The vulnerable love of Jesus, shown forth upon the cross is *both* the all-sufficient act that has won our salvation *and* the pattern for every Christian life.

This is why Jesus gives us the sacrament of Holy Communion. Different traditions and denominations call it by different names. Even within the Church of England (to which both authors belong), different congregations call it the 'Mass', the 'Eucharist', the 'Lord's Supper' or 'Holy Communion'.

---

[34] Helen Waddell, *Peter Abelard*, Literary Guild, 1933, p.269.

These names reflect different understandings of what *precisely* Jesus meant when He first said 'This is my body' and 'This is my blood' (Matthew 26:26, 28).

This much is surely clear, and common to us all: Jesus was giving to the church an ongoing material token of His love – of His sacrifice and of the new life that flows from it. In the Eucharist, we are given both a sign of Jesus' self-offering and an invitation to share in that sacrifice – to 'drink from [His] cup' of suffering (Matthew 20:23). In it, we both *receive* and *become* the body of Christ. We are drawn into His self-offering – and find in it the power which can alone bring new life.

That is why Christian worship must never be escapist. The Eucharist calls us to engage with the reality beyond the church's walls. Indeed, it calls us to love that demands everything we have and all that we are. And it feeds us with the One in whom alone such love is possible.

As Ken Leech has put it, sacraments are not 'freak events in a world that runs according to different rules.'[35] The Eucharist shows us the purpose and the destiny of the whole world. Like the raising of Lazarus, it provides us with a foretaste of the new creation; a glimpse of resurrection life. And it reminds us of the price that Christ has paid to make it so. In doing so, it calls us to become His hands and feet today so that God's Word of love continues to become flesh, not only on the altar but in the life of each communicant. Alongside the Eucharist, then, go 'Eucharistic lives'. What we celebrate in our liturgies, and confess in our creeds, needs to be shown forth in our lives. In our last two stories of modern discipleship, we have chosen testimonies which show the power of God in the midst of human weakness and vulnerability.

---

[35] Kenneth Leech, *Prayer and Prophecy: The Essential Kenneth Leech*, Darton, Longman & Todd, 2007, p.238.

Stories

Charlotte Wood and Gracechurch Nottingham

For all the ways in which we think our society is 'open' and 'lets it all hang out', mental health remains a very real taboo. We struggle to be honest about it – even though the best research suggests that 25% of people will experience mental health problems at some point in their lives.

Charlotte Wood developed depression and anxiety as a teenager, and subsequently had very serious problems walking. Successive doctors assumed these were side effects of her depression, when in reality Charlotte was also suffering with muscular dystrophy. It was only when she left home and went to university in Nottingham that her new GP recognised that Charlotte had both mental *and* physical illnesses.

Two years ago, Charlotte's health deteriorated to the point where she needed to move into residential care. At that point, she got to know Debbie, another resident who was being treated for spina bifida. What her carers failed to recognise was that Debbie also had a mental illness: as well as spina bifida, she was suffering from acute depression. She felt like she wanted to die and, as a consequence, stopped eating. Tragically, despite many visits from professionals in physical healthcare, her mental illness was not diagnosed until too late, and she died in hospital from malnutrition.

By this time, Charlotte was worshipping at Gracechurch Nottingham, a congregation deeply committed to both the personal *and* the social dimensions of the transformation which Christ brings. Gracechurch was a founder member of Nottingham Citizens – part of the same community organising movement as London Citizens (see page 24). As we have explained, the ethos of community organising is to build the power of the most vulnerable and marginalised communities to achieve social change.

Charlotte's church undertook a 'listening campaign' within Gracechurch – the same process we described in Chapter One in Bethnal Green. A more modest version of this process – with a particular focus on financial issues – is outlined in the text box at the end of this chapter. The issue of health and social care came out as a top priority – and, in particular, the ways in which people's physical healthcare needs to be considered at the same time as their mental well-being. As Charlotte and Debbie's stories show, when the two are kept in separate 'silos', serious mental and physical conditions go untreated, with sometimes tragic consequences.

This listening campaign has led (as in the Living Wage Campaign described in Chapter Three) to action, in which Charlotte has played a leading role. Patients admitted to hospital in Nottingham with physical conditions will now have a fuller screening for mental health issues that may be occurring at the same time. Other structural changes are taking place in Clinical Commissioning Groups which will ensure the NHS has a more 'joined up' approach to physical and mental care.

One of the mottos of community organising is that it doesn't do for others what they can do for themselves. This campaign is a good example: it has not been carried out *for* those who were previously marginalised, but *by* them. Charlotte testifies to the powerful impact the campaign has had on her confidence. 'Being part of Nottingham Citizens has given me a really good opportunity to do something useful on a flexible basis. I'd never done anything like this before. It has been really good – and has opened my eyes to a lot of things. Without work, I had been lacking a sense of purpose. This has given me confidence.' And she sees this campaign as a central part of her ministry as a Christian: 'The Bible is quite clear that Christians should be concerned for people's welfare – challenging injustice as well as offering relief.' Her work in Nottingham Citizens has enabled

Charlotte to live out this Gospel command – and shows the power of God at work in the midst of human vulnerability.

The Cantignorus Chorus at St Paul's, West Hackney

Like many church buildings up and down the land, an extraordinary variety of groups meet at St Paul's, West Hackney. As well as the Sunday Eucharist and weekday worship, the church has a range of groups meeting in its halls, many catering for vulnerable adults.

In the autumn of 2013, its vicar, Fr Niall Weir, decided to explore ways in which these diverse groups might be brought together. Working with Tom Daggett (the Community Music Coordinator at the Contextual Theology Centre), he founded the 'Cantignorus Chorus'.

Tom – who worked previously as an Organ Scholar in Oxford University – takes up the story, as he describes their first rehearsal:

> An astonishing 55 people showed up for the first rehearsal of the 'Cantignorus Chorus'. They were clients and staff from groups based at St Paul's – North London Action for the Homeless, Narcotics Anonymous, Open Doors (a charity for vulnerable women), 4Sight lunch club (for local West Indians with mental health issues), an over-50s dance group, Family Mosaic Housing Association, Growing Communities grassroots gardening project – not to mention members of the church congregation and the wider local community.
>
> The choir is a celebration of Hackney's diversity; it recognises the fact that life can be difficult for all of us – regardless of our circumstance. This theme is strongly reflected in the song we're seeking to learn

and record, 'Holding out a helping hand to you', written by Fr Niall himself.[36]

The choir is supported by 'Near Neighbours' – an initiative funded by the Government and administered by the Church Urban Fund and CTC, which seeks to deepen the relationships between different groups in our increasingly atomised society, using the relationships and networks of the Church of England to bring together people of very different cultures and faiths.

Tom continues the story of the first rehearsal:

> Gradually, the room filled with more and more interesting people, from every walk of life, who approached with a nervous excitement. At 7 o'clock, a warm introduction was given, highlighting the diversity in the room, why we were here, and what I was expecting of them! There was a buzz about the room. Within the first 5 minutes, the church was filled with glorious 3-part harmony, which blew me (and the singers) away. Thus commenced the best rehearsal I've ever been part of. Many things surprised me about it: the wonderful range of people and of life scenarios in the room; the pure joy which came through singing together; the utter dedication from everyone to try their best; the respect the group had for me as well as for each other; and their willingness to come back next week and give it their all once more.[37]

Since that first night, the Chorus has gone from strength to strength. With two backing tracks – recorded by local schoolchildren and by the Choristers of St Paul's Cathedral –

---

[36] http://www.theology-centre.org.uk/introducing-the-cantignorus-chorus/ (accessed 11 January 2014).
[37] Ibid.

'Holding out a helping hand to you' was released as a single in advance of Christmas. It has brought joy to many homes and provides another powerful example of what happens when those who are so often pushed to the margins find their voice.

Action

The Cantignorus Chorus provides a wonderful *finale* to our collection of stories of modern discipleship. In this book, we have considered many different aspects of love: its urgency and its patience, its mercy and its justice, its universality and its particularity. But we must never forget its sheer *delight*.

As we have sought to stress throughout this book, the personal and social transformation that is given to us in Christ is not a human achievement – not the product of our best efforts, but of lives which begin with delight and gratitude for what God has done for us.

Christianity is a matter of contagious *joy*. This is not a naive joy, which pretends suffering does not exist, but the joy which has truly walked the way of the cross and found in it the light and life of Christ. It is from such a journey – of vulnerability and of solidarity – that the music of the Cantignorus Chorus is born.

There is another lesson we can draw from the stories of Charlotte and of the singers of west Hackney. In a society with a yawning gap between rich and poor, it is tempting to talk of 'just love' in terms of what the poor and marginalised need from the rich and privileged. But the Gospel makes a far more radical claim. It reveals that we are *all* impoverished by these injustices, and that we grow into God's love *together*. From the perspective of the Gospel, the rich need the poor even more than the poor need the rich.

Bishop Michael Ipgrave reminds us of the tradition, from its earliest centuries, of the 'lordship of the poor' within the church:

> The first reference to the poor as 'lords and masters' is in the life of St John the Almsgiver, Patriarch of Alexandria (c. 560–619 CE). John had a strong sense that in the heavenly court – in stark contrast to the corrupt imperial regime of his day – it was the dispossessed who were influential as courtiers and patrons:
>
> 'Those whom you call poor and beggars, these I proclaim my masters and helpers. For they and they only, are really able to help us and bestow upon us the kingdom of heaven.'[38]

How can those who are rich experience the poor 'bestow[ing] upon [them] the kingdom of heaven'? And how can the church ensure that those in greatest need experience the 'Good News for the poor' that Jesus promises at the very start of his public ministry?

The message of this book is that the place to start is not with *action* but with *listening*. Each of the actions suggested in its different chapters have suggested ways that individual readers might listen more intently to God and to neighbour. But the stories in this book have shown that individual action is not enough: as we explained in Chapter Two, following Jesus Christ involves being an active part of His body.

That's why the final action suggested in this book is a *corporate* action – one which a growing number of churches are taking. The 'Money Talks' described in the text box below offer a simple, practical way to get local people talking about money,

---

[38] Michael Ipgrave, 'The Gospel, poverty and the "lordship of the poor,"' in Angus Ritchie (ed.), *The heart of the kingdom: Christian theology and children who live in poverty,* The Children's Society, 2013.

poverty and social injustice – to listen, and to build the capacity to act.

If you are reading this book as a group, this might be something you could organise together. If you are reading it as an individual, you could talk to your church leader about how, and with whom, to make it happen. And if you are not yet part of a church, we hope the stories and reflections in this book have encouraged you to take that first step across the threshold.

We cannot transform our lives, let alone our broken and unjust world, on our own. We need the love poured out in Jesus Christ, and (however frustrating they may sometimes be) we need our brothers and sisters in His church. These words of the Second Vatican Council – brought to life in such a fresh and vivid way by Pope Francis' engagement with his brothers and sisters of other faiths – capture the distinctiveness and yet the universal nature of the Christian hope:

> By holding faithfully to the Gospel and benefiting from its resources, by joining with everyone who loves and practices justice, Christians have shouldered a gigantic task for fulfilment in this world, a task concerning which they must give a reckoning to Him who will judge everyone the last of days.
>
> The Father wills that in all [people] we recognize Christ our brother and love him effectively, in word and in deed. By thus giving witness to the truth, we will share with others the mystery of the heavenly Father's love. As a consequence, men [and women] throughout the world will be aroused to a lively hope – the gift of the Holy Spirit – that some day at last they will be caught up in peace and utter happiness in that fatherland radiant with the glory of the Lord.[39]

---

[39] *Gaudium et Spes*: The Pastoral Constitution on the Church in the Modern World, Second Vatican Council, 93.

'Money Talks' – listening to your neighbours, and taking action with them

A Money Talk is a simple tool to help your church listen to people's experiences of poverty, and identify some practical actions which can be taken *together* in response. Money Talks can be held in the church or in another meeting place in the neighbourhood, and should involve as many local people from different groups and backgrounds as possible.

After a brief introduction, attendees break up into small groups to discuss three questions:

1. *What impact is today's challenging economic situation having on:*
• *You, your friends and family?*
• *Young people and children that you know?*
• *Your neighbourhood?*

2. *What changes do you think would make a positive difference to these issues in our community?*

3. *The church is engaged with these issues:*
• *in its teaching and preaching*
• *in campaigning and organising for social justice*
• *in the practical care it offers to people in need*
• *in the way it invests its own assets and pension funds*

What do you think about the way your church handles these issues? What one thing would you like to see the church do differently – or do more?

Over the last year, around 50 churches in London have engaged in this process – and this has led them to practical action such as establishing Foodbanks, setting up links with local credit unions and campaigning against exploitative lending. Experience suggests that the process works best when the Money Talk is accompanied by:

- teaching in church (both through sermons and Bible study groups) on the spiritual significance of these economic issues

- a serious attempt to reach out to communities beyond the church's walls in advance of the event

- an ongoing process of local engagement and action (e.g. community organising)

The experience of churches that have organised Money Talks is that they are an excellent way of drawing worshippers and neighbours together across cultures and social classes – enabling the church to respond to social injustice in a way that gives those in greatest need an active voice in shaping their future.[40]

---

[40] Resources for holding a 'Money Talk' and for reflecting on these issues theologically have been produced by the Contextual Theology Centre for the Church Urban Fund. They can be downloaded at http://theology-centre.org/sharing/courses-and-resources.

...his book in a small group: a short guide

Whether in Lent or at another time in the year, this book is designed to be used by small groups as well as individuals. We suggest 60 to 90 minutes is the ideal time for such gatherings, and you may find the following structure helpful:

- Begin with a short prayer, including a few moments of silence, to enable people to remember they are in God's presence and to lay before Him any distractions or concerns that the events of the day have generated. Ask God's blessing on the discussion, and pray that it may lead to practical action.

- In week one, invite everyone to give their name, the neighbourhood in which they live (if all from one church) or a church or other organisation they are involved in, and one thing that makes them angry or sad about the state of their neighbourhood.

- Read aloud, slowly, the Gospel passage under discussion in the chapter, having asked each person to listen and identify one sentence that stands out for them in the passage, and to say why it stands out. (This is a simple, non-threatening way to encourage everybody to participate in the group right from the start.) After the passage is read, leave a short time of silence before asking people to start sharing.

- Move on to discuss that week's chapter of the book. Encourage people to read the chapter in advance, but don't assume everyone will! Make sure that someone in the group has been briefed to begin the discussion with a clear, well-structured presentation of the key points in chapter – (1) the aspect of love being discussed; (2) what the Introduction says about that aspect of love; (3) what light the Gospel reading casts on that aspect of love; (4) how the stories reveal that love being embodied in the lives of individuals and communities; and (5) what questions that raises for us today. (This should last no more than five minutes.)

- Some of the 'Actions' (e.g. the Examen in Chapter One, and the silence in Chapter Two) can be carried out within a small group. Others (e.g. the 'one to one' in Chapter Two) need to be carried out during the week. The final action (the Money Talk) would need to be planned as a separate event. Depending on the action, leave enough time to either do it during the session or to discuss how people will do it later on.

- Finish with a time of prayer (this might end with the Grace or the Lord's Prayer).

the